TREASURES *of the* NORTH

TREASURES *of the* NORTH

TRACIE PETERSON

BETHANY HOUSE
MINNEAPOLIS, MINNESOTA

Cover design by Andrea Gjeldum

Published by Bethany House Publishers
11400 Hampshire Avenue South
Bloomington, Minnesota 55438
www.bethanyhouse.com

Bethany House Publishers is a Division of
Baker Book House Company, Grand Rapids, Michigan.

Printed in the United States of America

Library of Congress Cataloging-in-Publication Data

Peterson, Tracie.
Treasures of the north / by Tracie Peterson.
p. cm. — (Yukon quest ; 1)
ISBN 0-7642-2378-X (pbk. : alk. paper)
1. Yukon River Valley (Yukon and Alaska)—Fiction. 2. Frontier and pioneer life—Fiction. 3. Women pioneers—Fiction. 4. Alaska—Fiction. I. Title.
PS3566.E7717 T74 2000
813'.54—dc21 00-011575

BOOKS *by* TRACIE PETERSON

www.traciepeterson.com

Controlling Interests
The Long-Awaited Child
Silent Star
A Slender Thread • *Tidings of Peace*

BELLS OF LOWELL*
Daughter of the Loom • *A Fragile Design*
These Tangled Threads

DESERT ROSES
Shadows of the Canyon • *Across the Years*
Beneath a Harvest Sky

WESTWARD CHRONICLES
A Shelter of Hope • *Hidden in a Whisper*
A Veiled Reflection

RIBBONS OF STEEL†
Distant Dreams • *A Hope Beyond*
A Promise for Tomorrow

RIBBONS WEST†
Westward the Dream • *Separate Roads*
Ties That Bind

SHANNON SAGA‡
City of Angels • *Angels Flight*
Angel of Mercy

YUKON QUEST
Treasures of the North • *Ashes and Ice*
Rivers of Gold

NONFICTION
The Eyes of the Heart

*with Judith Miller †with Judith Pella ‡with James Scott Bell

03C

TRACIE PETERSON is a popular speaker and bestselling author who has written over fifty books, both historical and contemporary fiction. Tracie and her family make their home in Montana.

Part One

JUNE-AUGUST 1897

In thee, O Lord, do I put my trust: let me never be put to confusion. Deliver me in thy righteousness, and cause me to escape: incline thine ear unto me, and save me.

PSALM 71:1–2

CHAPTER ONE

A GOSSAMER WRAP of glittering ivory danced across Grace Hawkins' shoulders and enveloped her in its folds like the kiss of a summer breeze. Huge brown eyes stared out from a china doll face, serving only to accentuate the delicacy of its owner. Her expression might have suggested serenity, but the mood in her heart suggested quite the opposite.

"My dear, you look radiant."

"Thank you, Mother," Grace replied, trying hard to smile. She had no heart for this evening or for the charade she was about to play. This should have been the happiest night of her life; instead, Grace dreaded it as she would have a dose of the cook's tonic. Neither she nor her governess, Karen Pierce, could abide the smelly concoction and usually found an unlikely place to dispose of it before being found out. Pity Grace couldn't dispose of her unwanted fiancé as easily.

Grace sighed. There were a great many things she and Karen had managed to avoid in life; however, engagement to Martin Paxton didn't appear to be one of them. Karen's quick thinking and understanding of the world would do little to free Grace from her father's demands.

And unlike Karen, who held animosity for any man's demands, Grace had worked hard for a genteel balance. She could be her father's obedient daughter, gentle in spirit and silent unless spoken to, but she could also be a reflection of her teacher. Unfortunately, as Grace grew older and began to see life for herself, the two natures warred against each other, causing her no end of frustration and confusion. Underlying Grace's seemingly serene personality a storm was brewing, and she couldn't help but wonder if this particularly unpleasant situation would be the missing element to unleash that storm.

"Your fiancé will be very impressed, I've no doubt," her mother chattered on. "A woman of quality and beauty is not easily found. You will make him proud."

But what will he make me? Grace wondered. She'd already met the formidable man, and while he was handsome enough, despite a thin jagged scar that marred his jawline on the right side of his face, his personality suggested an aloofness, a kind of cold shoulder that left Grace wondering if there could be any hope for love to grow.

Looking up, Grace caught sight of her own reflection in the mirror. *My, but I'm all grown-up.*

The gown, of ivory and rose, seemed to shimmer at her every move. Tiny summer roses fresh from the garden had been sewn into the neckline, sending a delectable fragrance—sweet and airy—wafting through the air. Their deep pink color appeared shaded and muted through the veil-like covering of Grace's wrap. The teasing effect hinted of something more—something pure and special. Grace thought it a symbolic statement of her own purity, veiled and delicately concealed, yet evident for the world and one man's picking.

Her mother had commissioned the gown in honor of her engagement, and Grace could tell by the pleased expression on her mother's face that the dress was exactly what she had hoped for. Status and appearance were of great importance to her mother. The society pages would be positively ringing with praises for the couple on the morrow, giving fuel to her mother's energies to plan the wedding of the century.

"Karen, put another pin in her hair," Mrs. Hawkins commanded. "Right here where the curl seems wont to slip away."

Karen, ever patient with her employer's demands, did as she was instructed, then stood back. Mrs. Hawkins nodded and lifted her chin as she drew a deep breath. "There will not be another young woman half so beautiful. I will go and attend to our guests. Karen will bring you to your father when the time is right." She looked back at Grace and nodded again. "Oh, I do hope the photographer has arrived!"

She opened the door, then paused again, her nervous excitement irritating Grace. "Whatever you do, Grace, don't sit down! We mustn't have you wrinkled. Karen, you remind her," she said, as if Grace were only five years old instead of twenty.

Both Grace and Karen nodded in agreement. Myrtle Hawkins seemed satisfied and turned to go.

Watching her mother leave, Grace felt her hopes and dreams dissipate. "How can they do this to me?" she whispered loud enough for only Karen to hear.

"I can't abide it," Karen agreed. "It's tantamount to slavery."

Grace lifted her sorrowful face to her governess, the term

revealing little of the depth of affection the two women shared. "That's exactly what it is. They are selling me to the highest bidder. Oh, Karen, what am I to do?"

Shaking her head, Karen moved to close the door between Grace's bedroom and her sitting room. "You could always run away. We've discussed this before."

"I know," Grace said, moving to sit, then remembering the warning. Her mother would never forgive her for showing up wrinkled to her own engagement party. She sighed. "They're all going to know the truth of it. All of society—all of Chicago." Her mournful words hung heavy on the air. "Everyone who is anyone knows I've not been courted by Mr. Paxton. He's nothing more than my father's business associate."

"Well, he certainly thinks of himself as something more," Karen replied. "I've never seen a man hold such influence over your father. Why, the man practically ordered your father into giving this party tonight. I heard him myself. So did the rest of the house staff."

"I know," Grace replied. "I don't understand the situation any more than you do. I want to be a good daughter and do what is expected of me, but frankly, Mr. Paxton frightens me."

"Did you tell your mother?" Karen questioned.

"I tried. She said it was a simple matter of virginal nerves," Grace stated, her cheeks warming. "She said all young girls fear the expectations of their husbands and that I should simply pray on the matter and trust God for the best."

"I agree we should pray, but I know better than to believe this is simply a case of prewedding jitters. You do not love the man and he clearly does not love you. In fact, he almost seems to resent you and everyone else in this house."

"I know," Grace moaned, "but what can I do? I've tried to talk to Father, but he'll not see reason." She paced nervously, the glimmering gown swirling around her heels. "I'm a mere woman of twenty. Father still sees me as a child, and children, in his estimation, should be seen and not heard."

"I believe that to be his estimation for women in general," Karen replied with a hint of resentment in her tone.

"Father treats Mother with respect," Grace countered. "He used to listen to her counsel all the time. It was only in this decision to marry me to his associate that he rejected any influence from her."

"Probably because he knew what she'd say. I believe your mother wants to see you happy, even while pleasing her social circle. I also believe she had planned for you to marry one of the Willmington boys."

Grace nodded. "Poor Mother. Father actually yelled at her."

"Well, don't take it on your shoulders," Karen encouraged. "Your mother has known well enough how to make a go at marriage. She's shared a silver wedding anniversary with him. That must account for something."

"Perhaps if my brother, Amon, had lived. Mother said that Father was so happy having his firstborn to be a son. When Amon died, Father was inconsolable. I must have been a poor substitute."

"One child is never a substitute for another," Karen chided. "Now listen. You cannot go downstairs looking all glum. Whatever choice you make in the future, whether to go through with this and get married or run away, you must at least give your mother and father a pretense of contentment. It would greatly shame your parents in the eyes of their peers should word get out that you do not desire this union."

Grace contemplated her governess's words. She was so grateful for the companionship she shared with Karen. They were more like sisters than anything. Karen had been her teacher and friend for over ten years, and Grace loved her more dearly than anyone else. Karen's wisdom had always been a gentle guide, directing Grace to acknowledge her position and duties.

A quick glance at her watch and Karen motioned to the door. It was time for Grace to make her appearance at the party. "Well, we cannot delay this another moment. Chin up."

Grace took a deep breath and lifted her face. With the slightest hint of a nod, she followed Karen. They passed from the bedroom into the sitting room and out into the long hall of the west wing. Grace tried not to feel unduly worried—in fact, she tried not to feel anything at all. Her fear for this evening was beyond anything she had ever known. She remembered her mother suggesting that with any luck they would persuade Mr. Paxton to have a long engagement, maybe as much as three or four years. Grace agreed that perhaps in sufficient time she could come to fear him less and care about him more. But while her mother had hopes for such delays, her father implied that quick action was of the utmost importance. His attitude and insistence were puzzling.

Myrtle Hawkins had told her husband that in no uncertain terms could the wedding take place before a period of one year had passed. She would not have society believing her daughter in need of marriage. The scandal would be hard-lived, and even if the couple were slow in producing heirs, Myrtle knew how tongues would wag if the proprieties were overlooked. But despite her mother's protests, her father was unwavering in his decision. Grace had been heartbroken over her father's firm resolve to see her quickly joined with Mr. Paxton.

"I wish you could stay with me," Grace said, breaking free

from the memories. "Mother has always been generous about allowing you to accompany me."

"But this is an occasion for grown-ups, not innocent maids with their nannies," Karen countered. "You are already such a delicate and petite thing, most people assume you to be years younger. My appearance would only enhance this."

"I cannot bear it," Grace said, fighting to hold back her tears. "I cannot have that man handling me."

"He won't be allowed to touch you," Karen replied. "Not in this ever-so-proper social gathering."

"But remember what he did last night after dinner?" Grace said, shuddering. "He thought nothing of touching me." She could still feel his warm hand upon her arm. He had stroked the smooth skin of her forearm in a most intimate manner before bringing her hand to his lips.

Karen reached out to dab the corners of Grace's eyes with her handkerchief. "Put those thoughts aside. The man was out of place, but no doubt he was simply overcome by his admiration for your beauty." She smiled. "Now, be brave and strong. The Lord will go before you."

Grace nodded. She could only pray it was true.

Karen's plans were for a quiet evening in Grace's private sitting room. Reading a fashionable ladies' magazine would help to wile away the hours and hopefully keep her from worrying too much about Grace. It was true that in the last couple of years—years in which Grace had not really needed a governess—the two women had grown very close. Karen enjoyed their relationship, perhaps partly because she had been raised in a big family with plenty of siblings. She had always known what it was to have company and someone to whisper silly secrets to. Grace was an only child who had often seemed lonely.

Karen had first come into the Hawkins home when Grace had been but ten years old. The child already commanded proof of impeccable manners and rigid social graces, but she bore evidence of something else as well. Grace seemed lost—almost shunned. Her mother, a wealthy socialite, and her father, a successful entrepreneur, seldom had time to share with their child. They appeared to love Grace, to hold genuine affection for her, but their busy lives seemed far more important. Grace had been left at the mercy of nurses and the house staff, despite the fact that she adored both her mother and father.

Private schooling had been considered prior to Karen's appearance in their lives. Myrtle Hawkins had heard of the social benefits of boarding schools abroad, but Grace had pleaded with her mother not to send her away. Myrtle Hawkins seemed to understand her daughter's fear of separation and finally gave up the idea. After that, Karen had been hired and a new kind of family was born.

Stretching, Karen glanced at the clock. The party had scarcely begun. And it would be the first of many to come. Over the next few weeks there would no doubt be a parade of events to honor the couple.

The thought of Grace marrying brought another realization into Karen's life. At thirty years old, she was hardly good for anything but serving as a governess or a maid. No man would want to marry her at such a late stage of life, and few women would want an attractive woman in their house, even to perform the duties of governess.

Karen tried to play down her appearance. She felt blessed to have been given thick hair the color of strawberries and honey, but given her position, she bound it tightly in a bun and covered it with a net. No sense in giving anyone a chance to accuse her of prideful behavior by wearing her hair lavishly pinned, as she might style Grace's hair.

Her figure, while less curvaceous than desired in society, was long and statuesque. She stood at least half a foot taller than her charge, but she was not unreasonable in her height. By wearing her corset fairly loose, Karen had been able to avoid displaying any accentuated womanly curves, and taking the advice of her aunt Doris, herself a spinster teacher, Karen chose to dress in dark, matronly fashions.

"Do not give yourself airs, child. The more simplified your appearance, the less threatening you will be," Aunt Doris had declared.

Thinking of her aunt caused Karen to automatically think of other concerns—of her father. Wilmont Pierce, Doris's brother, had gone north to the Alaskan Territory some five years earlier. He and Karen's mother had felt a calling to minister to the Tlingit Indians who lived in and around the southeast panhandle. Things had gone well at first. After trying several locations, the Pierces finally settled near the area of Skagway and Dyea. Other missionaries were already set up in the area, but the husband-and-wife team was well received by their brothers and sisters in Christ. Those already stationed in the wilds of this new land felt gratitude at seeing yet another American couple. Homesickness abounded and everyone desired news of home.

Karen's mother had written of great happiness in her new home. But as time went on, Alice Pierce found herself weakened by the elements. Months of sickness led to Alice becoming bedfast and weeks later she had succumbed to pneumonia. The news of her mother's death had devastated Karen.

Staring into the fireplace, Karen contemplated her position. She could now go north and help her father. In the absence of her mother, her father could probably use someone to assist him in his work. She was, after all, college educated and trained to teach. She could certainly make more of a difference there than she would in Chicago.

"Perhaps once we find out what the terms of Grace's engagement will be," Karen whispered, "then I will know what to do."

The idea of leaving Grace sorrowed Karen. Grace had been much like a little sister. Karen had been put in charge of Grace's education, teaching her all manner of basic learning in addition to foreign languages and etiquette. While Karen's family was hardly equal to the social standing of the Hawkins family, her own background had afforded her a complete and well-rounded education, including extended time spent at a rather refined women's college back East.

Karen could have married on at least four different occasions. The men had been well-heeled and respected in the community. Their growing importance in the city could have seen Karen as mistress of a considerable fortune by now.

She smiled, however, and shook her head as the flames in the hearth danced hypnotically. "But you would not release me to marry them," she murmured prayerfully. And indeed, that was exactly why she had remained single. God had called her to singleness, at least for a time. He had made it clear to her that her focus at this point in her life was to be Grace Hawkins.

"But that's changing now," she said aloud. Then a thought dawned on her. Perhaps Grace would want to keep Karen on as her personal attendant. Assuming the new responsibilities that would be expected of Grace, in addition to possibly moving to another city, would surely warrant the desire to have someone familiar at hand. Perhaps that was where God would lead her next. From there, maybe she would be allowed to stay on and help rear Grace's children. This thought, however, gave no real comfort.

Her father's lack of communication over the past few months was a growing concern. He should have written by now. *Unless something has also happened to him,* Karen rationalized. *He should have informed me that things were well or at least have noted his future plans.* The absence of a letter was giving Karen much reason to fear for her father's well-being. She even sensed that Aunt Doris was rather worried, although she would never admit it.

Bowing her head, Karen began to pray in earnest. "Show me the way, Lord. Show me what I am to do, because I fear I have two paths before me and neither one suggests itself over the other."

CHAPTER TWO

GRACE FELT A CHILL run up the length of her spine when her father presented her to Martin Paxton. It wasn't the first time they'd been introduced, by any means, but it was the most important.

"Mr. Paxton, may I present your future wife, my daughter, Grace."

Grace looked to her father, wondering momentarily if he could read the displeasure in her eyes. Quickly, she lowered her gaze to the ground and extended her gloved hand to Mr. Paxton.

"Miss Hawkins, may I say you are looking particularly lovely. Our engagement must certainly agree with you." Paxton's tone was edged with sarcasm.

The scoundrel! Grace thought, trying her best to refrain from giving any outward appearance of contempt.

"Mr. Paxton," she murmured, waiting while he kissed the top of her hand.

Involuntarily, she began to tremble. There was something about this man that exuded distrust and . . . evil. He smelled of it—if that were possible.

Grace attempted to pull her hand away, but he held it fast. The action caused her to meet his gaze, and she discovered an inkling of evidence for the power he held over her father. As he narrowed his emerald eyes, Grace couldn't help but feel drawn into his spell. He was handsome in a rather ruthless fashion, and his confidence made clear that his affections were seldom rejected.

Grace wanted to run away from this man as quickly as her gown would allow, but of course, she could not. To put up any kind of protest would signal to the guests, just now assembling in the drawing room to their right, that all was not as it seemed.

As if reading her apprehension, Paxton smiled. He knew how he was making her feel, yet he continued to do everything in his power to keep her feeling as she was. He was, she believed, reveling in her discomfort.

Grace looked to her father for help, then realized he was a poor source. Her father was already wiping great beads of sweat from his brow. The poor man looked terrified of Martin Paxton.

"I believe we should attend to our guests, Father," Grace said in as calm a tone as she could muster.

"Yes. Ah . . . yes. Of course . . . ah . . . you are right," her father fairly stammered, looking to Paxton as if for permission to move.

"Yes, we wouldn't want to delay in announcing our engagement, now, would we?" he questioned, leaning close to reach Grace's ears alone.

He spoke in such a way that his very words seemed almost threatening. Grace was beginning to weary of his manhandling of her father and of herself. Pulling away with great dignity, Grace tilted her chin enough to give the sensation of looking down her nose at Paxton.

"I believe, Mr. Paxton, it would be unseemly for you to escort me prior to the announcement of our engagement. In my father's house, he alone would have the right to escort his unmarried daughter."

Paxton straightened and gave her a rather cruel smile. "But of course, we wouldn't want to displace the rules of society."

Grace gave him a curt nod and turned to her father. His face had reddened considerably at her suggestion, but seeing that Paxton was unwilling for a scene, Hawkins quickly took hold of his daughter's arm.

"Shall we join our guests?" he asked.

Grace gave his arm a gentle pat. She wanted to reassure him that she could make peace with his decision, but in truth, she wasn't at all sure that it was possible. She knew the Bible commanded her to honor her father, but this wish—this command to marry Martin Paxton—was almost more than she could consider.

"Yes, let us join Mother and the others," she finally replied, entwining her arm around his.

They entered her mother's favorite drawing room, with Paxton close behind them. Grace allowed her father to circulate her through their many guests, while Paxton remained near the door. She prayed he might think better of the evening and escape before making her the object of his intentions.

"Why, Grace, you are positively glowing. Love will do that for a woman," a jovial Mrs. Bryant announced. Mrs. Bryant had been her mother's best and worst friend for some thirty years. Best—because the two had known each other since childhood and had endured many of life's trials and joys together. Worst—because the two women seemed to constantly be in battle to rival the other.

"Mrs. Bryant, it is good of you to come," Grace replied formally.

She completed the remaining introductions with the same patience one might need to endure a physical examination. It was a necessary yet troublesome event. One to be tolerated but certainly not enjoyed.

Grace remained at her mother's side after the introductions while her father stood nervously twisting his pocket watch chain. He was working up his nerve to announce the engagement, and had Grace not been angry with him for his lack of consideration, she might have felt sorry for him. But one glance across the room at Martin Paxton, and Grace felt anything but sorry. How could her father do this? How could he simply give her over to a stranger she did not love?

"My dear ladies and gentleman," Frederick Hawkins began, "we have—that is, Mrs. Hawkins and I—have invited you here this evening to share in a very important occasion."

He held the attention of every person in the room. Every person, with exception to Martin Paxton and Grace. Paxton had fixed his gaze on Grace and his piercing green eyes bore into her own. She felt undressed by his cool appraisal and reached up to tightly clench the wrap to her neck. He gave her a tight-lipped smile from beneath his pencil-thin mustache. He appeared amused and quite pleased with the knowledge that he'd unnerved her.

"And so we happily announce," her father continued, "the engagement of our daughter, Grace Hawkins, to Mr. Martin Paxton of Erie, Pennsylvania."

The looks of the assemblage passed from Frederick Hawkins to Martin Paxton, almost completely excluding Grace. She felt rather insignificant for the moment, though she hadn't long to suffer in that state.

Paxton gave a stiff, formal bow to the guests before crossing the room to join Grace. "I am quite honored to make the acquaintance of this dear family's friends. I have long sought the hand of my bride and will know great pleasure in your attendance at our wedding."

"When is that day to be?" Mrs. Bryant questioned, her exuberance extending beyond the proprieties.

On an occasion such as this, Grace knew it was an acceptable faux pas. She could have predicted such a question. What she could not possibly have anticipated, however, was Martin Paxton's response.

"Because there has long existed an informal agreement between families, I am certain we will marry without delay."

It took every ounce of willpower to keep Grace from pushing Paxton away. She held her tongue, controlled her expression, and refrained from balling her hand into a fist and putting it aside Paxton's Romanesque nose.

"Surely you do not mean to marry before the end of the summer?" Mrs. Bryant questioned, rather aghast.

Grace's mother laughed nervously. "Of course not."

Paxton threw her a glance that might have completely wilted a woman of more delicate constitution. Myrtle Hawkins, however, stood her ground.

"We've not arranged for dates and places," she said, smiling. "We want to enjoy the moment of this intimate announcement among friends. Come, enjoy some refreshments and perhaps we can convince Grace to perform for us."

"Oh yes, do," several women said in unison.

Grace felt Paxton tighten his hold on her arm. He probably knew nothing of her singing or playing of the piano and harp. He probably had no idea of her education or fluency in French and German. Looking up at the man who was to be her husband, Grace realized with great apprehension that this man knew nothing at all about her.

Grace sat down to the piano and began a rather melancholy sonata. Always one of her favorites, Beethoven's "Moonlight Sonata" stirred her in a way that she could scarce put into words. The progression of the chords, the melodic appeal of the haunting tune . . . it was something that reached deep into her soul.

Looking up only once, Grace found Paxton watching her with an unveiled expression. She could only equate the look to one of hatred, and yet he had no reason to hate her. She had not forced herself upon him.

As the last notes died down and the audience applauded her efforts, Grace got to her feet and gave a brief curtsy. Paxton was immediately at her side, offering his arm, along with a look that suggested she make no move to refuse him. Smiling in a rather fixed manner, Grace placed her gloved hand atop his and allowed him to lead her from the piano. Mrs. Bryant's youngest daughter, Hazel, quickly took her place at the bench and soon a rapid-paced Mozart tune sprang from the keys.

"I would have a private word with you," Paxton told Grace in a commanding way.

"It would hardly be fitting for us to be seen leaving the party," Grace replied, unwilling to look at him.

"I really care very little for the rules of society."

"So I had gathered from your comment of hurrying our wedding."

"I take it you disapprove," he said in a low, sarcastic tone.

"How astute of you to notice."

He pulled her arm against his side. "I pride myself in keeping track of the details, Miss Hawkins." He pushed her toward the open French doors and out into the garden. Swinging her around rather abruptly, he pulled Grace into a strong-armed embrace, then assaulted her mouth with his lips.

Pushing against the man, Grace struggled to end his liberties. Paxton would have no part of it, however. He was much stronger than she had anticipated and much more determined to explore her feminine charms than even Grace would have believed. When he dared to trail his fingers down her bare neck to the swell of her breasts, Grace brought her tiny heeled slipper down on his foot. The action surprised Paxton enough that he momentarily loosened his hold. This allowed Grace enough room to maneuver. With all the strength she could muster, Grace slapped Paxton's face.

"How dare you!"

Within a heartbeat, he slapped her back. Open and barehanded, he struck her with enough force to knock her back against the garden gate, the blow causing her to see stars.

Scarcely able to draw a breath, Grace struggled, unaided, to right herself. Protecting her throbbing cheek with her gloved hand, she looked up hesitantly as Paxton advanced. The look of hatred had returned to clearly mark his otherwise handsome features. Grace couldn't imagine why he should be so brutal with her. She had gone along—or at least pretended to go along—with the engagement. She hadn't caused him any embarrassment or reason to so abuse her.

Dragging Grace even farther into the garden, Paxton twisted her arm painfully and finally deposited her on an iron bench.

"Do not ever presume to put your hand to me," he said, his tone edged in a quiet rage. "No wife of mine will ever put me in line."

She looked up at him, still stunned by the sudden turn of events. In all her twenty years, Grace had known nothing but protection and security. Suddenly it was clear that this was all behind her now.

"You have no right . . ." she began.

His eyes narrowed, and in the moonlight Grace could see his leering expression as he sat down beside her and pulled her back into his arms.

"I have all the right I need. I will take what I want, when I want it," he said, his mouth beside her neck. He placed kisses down her shoulder, pushing aside the gossamer wrap. While holding her in place with one hand, he allowed the other to freely explore.

Grace knew she had only to scream. The open doors of the house were not but ten yards away. Someone would hear her and come to her rescue. She drew a deep breath.

He stopped kissing her momentarily and looked hard into her eyes. "Don't even think about it."

Her heart raced wildly. "What are you talking about? Unhand me!"

"Don't think to escape me or call someone to your side. Your father will lose everything if you refuse me."

Grace studied him carefully. "What are you saying?"

He reached up to draw his finger along her still-throbbing cheek. "I'm saying I can cause you far greater pain than a mere slap." He grabbed her chin and held it firm. "I'm saying that unless you cooperate with me and do exactly as you are told, I will ruin you and your entire family."

Fear as she had never known descended over Grace. She looked into the harsh face of her captor and couldn't so much as pray. The man clearly had plans for her family and those plans included their marriage. But for what purpose?

"Why are you doing this?" she finally found the courage to ask. "I've done nothing to you. I'm a proper lady, pure and innocent, yet you treat me as a harlot. Why should you take offense that I would defend my honor? Engagement or none, there are still proper behaviors to be expected."

He brushed his thumb against her lips. "I will brook no nonsense from any woman. You will do as you are told and never will I allow you to question me. You are property and nothing more."

"Nothing more?"

"Nothing more. This is obviously no love match. This is business—long, overdue business. You may have no understanding of such matters, but your father's very existence teeters precariously on the edge of your actions."

"My actions?"

"Of course," Martin Paxton replied. "No decent clergy will marry us unless you are willing, and no doubt your mother already has the church picked out. You will cooperate and willingly consent to this marriage or I will see your father destroyed."

"But why?" Grace questioned, her own fear now replaced with concern for her father and mother. "How has he so offended you?"

This question actually caused Paxton to release her. Standing up, he eyed her with a look of pure contempt. "It is a matter between men." He turned away from her as if contemplating further consideration.

Grace felt too shaken to stand, but her instincts told her that if she was to escape without further harm, she would have to make her way now. Without a sound, she got to her feet and hurried for one of the closer entrances into the house used by the house staff when collecting flowers for dinner arrangements and such.

She barely reached the door when Paxton seemed to realized her escape. She heard the heavy footsteps upon the garden path just as she closed the door behind her and slid the lock into place.

Paxton began pounding on the wood, threatening to shake the very foundations of the house into rubble. "Let me in, you fool!" he declared in a voice hardly louder than a whisper.

"Go back to the party," Grace called. "Go back and give my regrets. Tell them I've grown ill and my governess has seen me to bed."

"Open this door now!"

"No," Grace said, knowing there would be a heavy price to pay for her defiance.

CHAPTER THREE

"I CAN'T BELIEVE he did this," Karen said angrily as she pressed ice against Grace's swollen cheek. A reddish purple discoloration was already starting to mar the pale white skin.

"I can't believe it either. I honestly have no idea what is to be done."

"Well, it's obvious," Karen replied. "You must break off this engagement and tell your father why it is impossible to go forward with marriage to such a monster. I'm certain that if he knew how you were treated, he'd never consent to see you wed to Mr. Paxton."

Grace shook her head. "Mr. Paxton said he could ruin Father. Something has apparently happened between them, and Mr. Paxton has great power over Father."

"Perhaps your mother would know what it's all about."

"I don't know if she would or not. All I know is that I

cannot marry this man, and yet there seems to be no other way to help Father in his need."

"But, Grace, you don't even know what that need is. Perhaps Paxton is doing nothing more than bullying you. He probably knows of your apprehension and maybe has even heard rumors of your disinterest in marrying him. He probably hoped to frighten you into the union."

"Well, he did a good job."

Just then Grace's mother came into the room in a rush. "I heard that Grace was ill. Whatever is wrong?" She looked to Grace and then Karen. "Why has she an ice bag?"

Grace slowly removed the bag and could tell by her mother's reaction that the cheek was no better.

"Who did this?" Myrtle Hawkins demanded.

"Mr. Paxton." Grace's words were flat and unemotional. She had no way of knowing what her mother's reaction to the news might be. She hoped she might be sympathetic, but her parents were both acting very strange as of late.

Her mother came forward and studied the damage more closely. "What happened to provoke this?"

"I slapped him for taking indecent liberties with me," Grace replied. "He slapped me in return and told me that I was never to strike him again or question his actions."

"The cad!" Her mother's reaction was clearly one of disgust. "I shall speak to your father on this matter."

Grace reached out and touched her mother's hand. "Please, Mother, sit with me for a moment. I need to ask you something."

The older woman seemed to understand the importance and nodded. "We have a house full of guests, you know. I can't possibly stay long."

"I understand," Grace replied. "I wouldn't ask you if it

weren't of the utmost concern."

"I'll go," Karen suggested.

"No!" Grace declared. "I want you to stay. You know all about this, and we might very well need your thoughts on the matter."

"Whatever are you talking about?" Myrtle questioned.

"Mother, something is wrong. I can't even pretend to know what it is, but Mr. Paxton apparently has some sort of control—some power over Father. I wondered if you knew what it might be."

"Power over your father? Why, that's nonsense. Frederick would never allow anyone to dictate his choices."

"Mr. Paxton told me that should I be less than cooperative in giving myself to him, apparently with the benefits of marriage or without, that he would ruin our family and Father would suffer greatly."

Myrtle stiffened. "He has no power to ruin the Hawkins family. How dare he imply such a thing merely to obtain liberties with you!"

"So there is nothing he can do to hurt Father?" Grace looked at her mother to ascertain her confidence in the matter. Unfortunately, the older woman looked away, but not before Grace detected uncertainty in her mother's eyes.

Grace took hold of her mother's hand. "What is it?"

Karen watched in silence, but Myrtle seemed more than aware of her presence. She looked to Karen and then back to Grace, as if hoping someone might instruct her as to what to say.

"Your father hasn't been himself in weeks. I haven't any idea what is wrong. He used to be quite willing to talk freely to me, but lately he refuses. He came home one day and announced that you were to marry Martin Paxton, and when I chided him for inappropriately suggesting such a thing without a period of courtship, he told me to keep such thoughts to myself. He told me you would marry Paxton and that was his final word."

Grace shook her head. "Mr. Paxton must have some influence over Father that we are unaware of. But, Mother . . ." She paused and looked to Karen for reassurance. "Despite my love for you and Father, I cannot marry Mr. Paxton. He is much too cruel, and I will not suffer a husband who beats me."

"Neither would I ask you to," Myrtle said, her expression softening as she reached up to touch her daughter's cheek. Tears came to her eyes. "No one has ever laid a hand to you before this. No one ever had to. You were always such a sweet child, good as gold and never a problem. That he should strike you so offends and wounds me that I must say something to him before the night is out."

"Don't," Grace replied. "He might very well do the same to you."

"Nonsense. He wouldn't dare," Myrtle said, raising her chin defiantly. She thrust her shoulders back and appeared to take on a new resolve. "I will speak to him and to your father as well."

"Please, Mother, do not speak to Mr. Paxton on any of this. Talk to Father if you like, but leave it at that. Perhaps Father will finally relent and tell you what has happened. We should know the truth of that prior to making any other decisions."

With the last of the party guests on their way home, Martin Paxton bid Mr. and Mrs. Hawkins good-night with the best of wishes on the speedy recovery of his fiancée's health.

"I hope Miss Hawkins will feel better in the morning," he said rather smugly.

"I'm certain she will," Frederick replied, then turning to the butler, he checked to make sure Mr. Paxton's carriage had been brought around.

Myrtle Hawkins could barely contain her emotions as she bid the man farewell. "Good night, Mr. Paxton."

"If you'll both excuse me," Frederick interrupted, "my man tells me there is something that requires my immediate attention."

"Of course," Paxton said with a slight nod.

Myrtle waited for Paxton to leave, but instead he seemed to study her for a moment before speaking his mind. "Your husband knows very well what I expect, and now I believe your daughter knows as well."

"How dare you?" she barely breathed the words. Gone was any hope of containing her anger. "That child has never been struck in her life until now."

"She'd do well to learn quickly or she'll find herself receiving worse," Paxton said, eyes narrowing. "I tell you this and something more." He paused to make certain he held her attention. "You would do well to heed your husband's wishes and leave Grace to me."

"You, sir, are out of line," Myrtle replied. "I will not see my child married to a man such as yourself. I will not see her cruelly treated, beaten, and tormented."

Martin's expression suggested he held the upper hand. "Better beaten than on the street—or worse."

Myrtle had no idea what the man meant by his words, but one thing she knew for certain. Her husband had some explaining to do. Slamming the door behind Paxton only to hear him laugh from the other side, Myrtle went in search of Frederick.

Finding him just on his way up the stairs, she called out, "I would have a word with you, Mr. Hawkins."

"It's late. Must we talk now?" he questioned.

"It is imperative," she insisted.

"Very well." He led the way to his upstairs study and opened the door with his key. "Now, tell me what this is all about."

Myrtle began without hesitation. "That brute has struck our child."

"What? What brute?" Frederick asked in confusion.

"Mr. Paxton."

Her husband paled and took a seat behind his desk. "I'm sure you are mistaken."

"I am not!" she declared. "Grace has the bruise on her face to prove it. He tried to force himself upon her, and when Grace defended her honor, he struck her."

"Well, there you have it—just a lover's quarrel. I'm sure it will right itself within a day or two."

Myrtle could scarcely believe her husband's tone. "I tell you this man took liberties with our daughter, struck her for defending herself, and you believe it will right itself in a day or two? How can you be so heartless and cruel? Surely you cannot want to move forward with Grace's marriage to such a brutal man?"

Frederick Hawkins looked at her rather guiltily before turning his attention to the papers on his desk. He gave a pretense of shuffling the papers into order, but Myrtle knew he was simply doing this to avoid answering her question.

"Well?" Myrtle pressed.

He looked up. "The arrangements have been made. I've given my word."

"Then take it back."

"I cannot."

She shook her head. "Why? Why can't you dissolve the engagement?"

"Well . . . it is . . . it's just that . . ." He stammered and stuttered, seeming desperate to find an answer that might explain his insistence. "I cannot."

Myrtle folded her arms against her breast. "Frederick Hawkins, do you mean to sit there and lie to me? I am your wife. You have always discussed things of importance with me, yet two weeks ago you came home to announce that you were pledging our daughter in marriage to a complete stranger. Now that stranger turns out to be a monster, and you suggest it will right itself and that we should simply overlook the matter. I want to know what is going on! Why have you suddenly taken to cowering to Martin Paxton?"

Her husband's expression turned angry. "I cower to no one, dear woman. I simply believe this to be more of a lover's misunderstanding."

"One which resulted in our sweet child hideously bruised," Myrtle retorted. "Come see for yourself if you doubt my word."

"I do not doubt your word, but apparently you doubt mine."

Myrtle Hawkins sat down on the chair in front of her husband's ornately carved desk. The desk had been a gift from her own father upon the celebration of their marriage. A matching, more feminine counterpart stood in her own private sitting room. It was there that she wrote her correspondence and instructions for the servants. She had addressed the invitations to Grace's engagement party from that same desk. The party had seemed the right thing to do, in spite of her misgivings. Now she wished fervently that she might have fought harder to impose her own thoughts on her husband's rash actions.

"I do not doubt that you feel you must cooperate with this man's wishes, but what I do not understand is why. Grace suggested that Mr. Paxton was threatening in regard to our well-being. The man himself spoke threateningly to me only moments ago."

Frederick's face reddened. "The scoundrel! How dare he talk of our business to my womenfolk?"

Myrtle realized her husband's anger was motivated by some unnamed fear. "What has he to do with you, Frederick? What has happened? Please tell me."

He looked at her with such a pained expression that for a moment Myrtle nearly took back her request. Perhaps there were some things a wife shouldn't know in regard to her husband's business arrangements.

"I owe Paxton money," he finally said with great resignation. "A great deal of money."

Myrtle considered the words for a moment. "How? Why?"

He shrugged. "Bad business dealings. Paxton came along and bailed me out, but the price was Grace, along with repayment of the debt at an exorbitant interest rate."

"But why Grace? Why should the man impose himself on a young woman he doesn't even know?"

"I don't know!" Frederick answered, running a hand through his hair in frustration. "I just know that I cannot back out of the arrangement for Grace to marry Paxton." He drew a deep breath. "This union will allow for us to continue in the fashion and society for which we've become accustomed."

"But at the price of our daughter's happiness?"

"Since when has that figured into our decisions?" Frederick asked his wife quite seriously. "You've had your heart set on being the social matron of Chicago. You've worked hard to position this family among the very cream of the crop."

"With the intentions that our daughter might marry well, yes," Myrtle said, beginning to feel a strange sensation of misgiving and guilt course through her heart.

"Our daughter will marry very well. Paxton is worth a fortune. He may treat her with a heavy hand, but he has the money to give her whatever she desires. That is what counts, after all. I know it has always meant a great deal to you, and perhaps Grace will now understand why all those sacrifices have been made. Perhaps now is the time she make a few sacrifices of her own."

Myrtle felt rather sickened by his suggestion. She didn't like the woman he portrayed her to be. A money-hungry, social-climbing, coldhearted fish who put her position above her child. The realization overwhelmed her.

"I see by your silence that you agree."

"I do not!" Myrtle said, shaking her head. "What I agree with is that I have been mistaken. I have been cruel in my own fashion. I have worried over issues of society instead of working to draw our family closer. I have been a poor mother, indeed."

"Nonsense. You have done your duty as I have done mine. There is no backing out now."

"This is absurd. Of course you can back out." She reached up to unfasten the multiple strands of pearls around her neck. The symbols of their wealth weighed heavy on her throat, almost as if a noose were tightening. "Start with these. We shall sell whatever we need to in order to pay back the debt, but

Grace need not be a part of the bargain."

"You pride yourself on your social standing in Chicago," Frederick began. He sounded quite weary, as if the words themselves were exacting a great toll upon him. "Word would get around quickly. Our name would be ruined."

"I don't care," Myrtle replied. For all her previous concerns about such things, she quickly realized that Grace's safety and well-being were all that mattered. "Possessions are wonderful, charming creatures, but certainly no more so than the love of a child. Our daughter needs our protection."

"I cannot give it," Hawkins replied sadly. He hung his head. "We cannot go back on our word in this matter. You must understand."

"I do *not* understand!" Myrtle said, getting to her feet. "Your child is in danger for her very life."

"Now, Mrs. Hawkins, you know very well that many men are given to slapping their wives. Granted, I do not approve the practice, but perhaps in time—"

"I cannot believe you would even suggest such a thing. I will not stand here and listen to another word. If you will not protect our child and speak to that brute, then I will."

Frederick jumped up from his desk and crossed the room rather quickly. His portly frame did nothing to keep him from beating Myrtle to the door. "I forbid it! Do not put yourself in the position of going against my wishes. You cannot speak to Paxton on this matter. Do you understand me? If you care one whit for our own vows, you must agree to obey me in this one thing."

Myrtle felt floored by his appeal. Nodding her agreement seemed her only recourse. She reached out to touch her husband's face.

"I know you are keeping something from me. I don't

know why. We used to be able to face anything together. You cared about my opinion at one time. I fail to understand why now you withhold your heart and instead interject your demands."

Frederick's expression softened. "I do not seek to wound you, my dearest wife. But this is a matter that I must see through for myself. Our welfare is at stake, just as you suggested, but it would be even more so should you go to this man and try to arrange your own terms."

Myrtle nodded. "Very well, then. I won't speak of it to Paxton. But what do you wish for me to tell Grace? I will have to tell her that I appealed to you for help in the matter. Short of leaving her to believe you without feeling or concern, what am I to say?"

Frederick shook his head. "Tell her nothing. Say only that her father knows best."

The finality of her husband's words whispered over and over in her head, but still Myrtle knew no peace with his decision. She thought to go back on her own promise and telephone immediately for Paxton to return to the house. But instead she wearily made her way down the long hall, past the staircase, and down the wing where her daughter's suite could be found.

She paused at the door when she heard voices coming from the sitting room.

"I know it's just a matter of time before you marry some man," the governess was saying. "I really must consider what I am to do with my life now."

"But I want you to stay with me. Couldn't you be my personal maid? Oh, not as a maid, but as a companion?" Grace questioned. "You are my best and dearest friend. I cannot stand the thought of losing you to the northern wilderness."

"I would not be lost," Karen replied with a laugh. "At least I hope I would not be lost. I would, hopefully, be allowed to live with my father and help with the missions work. My aunt Doris would probably want to go as well. She's retired from teaching school now, and I know she worries about my father. If I leave Chicago, there would be no further reason for her to remain here."

"But you're talking of such a great distance. Thousands and thousands of miles. I could never just come for a visit and spend time with you."

"Then why not come with me now?" Karen suggested. "I would never want to be one to encourage you to go against your parents' wishes, but if what Paxton said in regard to ruining your father is true, then perhaps your father's decisions will be less than soundly based. Perhaps we should take matters in our own hands—after all, you will not turn twenty-one until December. If we can but delay any true decision until that time, you will have more legal right to refuse such a marriage."

"I believe your idea to have merit," Myrtle Hawkins said, coming into the room.

Karen and Grace both revealed stunned expressions. They had no idea anyone was overhearing their discussion.

"I apologize if my words seem out of line," Karen said, meeting Myrtle's fixed gaze. "I didn't mean to overly influence Grace's thinking, but rather seek to protect her."

"I realize that, my dear. You are not to receive an upbraiding by me." Myrtle looked to her daughter. "Would you like to consider accompanying Karen north?"

Grace seemed even more shocked by this question. She was speechless for a moment, so Myrtle continued. "If your aunt would act as chaperone," she told Karen, "I would be willing to consider the matter. We, of course, cannot say anything to Mr. Hawkins. He has his reasons for being fixed in his opinions, but I will agree with you—his thinking is less than rational in regard to whatever debt he owes Mr. Paxton."

"I would like to go with Karen," Grace finally replied. "I would do anything to keep from marrying Martin Paxton . . . even risk Father's disassociation."

Myrtle nodded. "We may both have exactly that by the time this ordeal is completed."

CHAPTER FOUR

AFTER A WEEK of feigning ill in order to allow the bruising on her cheek to heal, Grace was surprised when her mother suggested they go en masse and visit with Karen's aunt Doris.

"I'm certain the woman can help us to figure out what should be done," Myrtle said rather conspiratorially.

"But, Mother," Grace said as she adjusted her walking-out bonnet, "what would Father say if he knew you were doing this? I don't wish to come between you two. If Karen and I arrange this on our own, you can honestly say that you had no knowledge of the circumstances."

Myrtle looked at her daughter with such sorrow that Grace nearly broke into tears. It wasn't like her mother to have fears and regrets. Until now her mother's only concerns had been their social status, and this sudden change in her left Grace confused.

"I've been dealing with my heart, Grace. I know how consumed I've been by things that are unimportant." She reached out and lovingly touched her grown daughter's face. "I suppose seeing the way Mr. Paxton hurt you opened my eyes—rather like having the scales fall off. I think I was like the blind man in the Bible. Remember when the pastor spoke about the man whom Jesus touched? At first he only saw people as trees. Oh, God forgive me, but I think that is how I have been these long years."

"No, Mother, you only did what you thought right. You wanted us to have good things."

Her mother nodded. "Yes, but I sacrificed a good relationship with you. We could have been great friends. Instead, Karen knows you better than I do." She glanced to the governess and smiled. "How grateful I am that God sent you into our lives, Karen. I know He realized exactly what Grace needed. A big sister and mother all rolled into one. I'm glad she loves you so."

Grace reached out and embraced her mother. The tears were no longer held back. "But I love you as well."

Her mother held her tightly for several moments. "I know," she whispered. "I love you too. I love you enough to take you away from this situation until I can find out what is causing your father such a lapse in good judgment."

Hours later Grace found herself seated between Karen and her mother, while Doris Pierce, a rather severe-looking spinster, considered their plight.

"I do agree it's well past time to do something about Wilmont. I cannot abide that he should be among the tribes of the frozen north and not know whether he lives or has gone on to glory."

"I suggest that we might go north to Skagway, Aunt Doris," Karen began. "The situation is most urgent, and I fear that my father might very well need me."

"He may need us both, child. There is much to be done among primitive peoples." She smiled, suddenly breaking the look of sternness, "And much to be done with the Indians as well." She laughed at this, but it puzzled Grace as to what she was talking about.

"I've heard tell that more and more folks are headed up that way. Fur trapping, outlaw dealings, gold . . . You know, it's enough to cause a man to kill." She sobered. "I suppose that would be my biggest concern. How can I possibly agree to take two young women into the unknown with nothing more than myself and my trusty Winchester for protection?"

"I'm hardly one to be worried over, Aunt," Karen replied. "And we'll be careful with Grace—we'll dress her in unattractive clothes, bind her hair, and keep her head covered. As you have always told me, there is much a woman can do to refrain from bringing herself undo attention."

"Oh goodness, yes," Doris Pierce replied. "Why, we could even dress in breeches if the notion took us." She laughed again and to Grace she seemed such a mixture of contrasting personalities. One minute she was stern and severe, relating nothing but the worst of agendas. The next, she was laughing and making humorous statements—downplaying the dangers.

"The situation is most grievous to me," Myrtle suddenly offered. "I worry that should Grace remain anywhere in close proximity, Mr. Paxton and her father would simply find her and bring her back to face a fate worse than death."

"Well," Doris answered, "death is very much a reality up

north. Alaska killed my sister-in-law. It could well do the same to your child."

Myrtle nodded and seemed to contemplate the words. Grace felt as if she weren't even in the room. They didn't need her in order to continue the conversation.

"Perhaps better to die at the hands of God's creation than at the hands of a cruel man," Myrtle finally replied. She reached out and squeezed Grace's hand. "I feel confident that despite the defiance of my husband's wishes, this is exactly the right thing to do. I cannot hope for you to understand, but I feel very much as if I am saving Grace's life."

Grace felt her pulse quicken. She'd never heard her mother speak in such a fashion. Did her mother know something more than what she'd revealed? True, Paxton had cruelly hit her, but Grace hardly saw that as a suggestion of deadly intent. Still, she knew a growing worry that Paxton would hurt her in many ways beyond just the physical. She didn't want to be wife to him, neither did she want to see her father ruined.

"What about Father?" she questioned.

All three women turned to look at her rather intently. Grace felt the need to explain. "What will Mr. Paxton do to him?"

"Your father owes Mr. Paxton money," Myrtle Hawkins replied. "I feel there is surely more to it than that, but if there is, he will not tell me. Part of my penance for this situation will be that I sell whatever is necessary for him to meet his debt to Paxton."

"No!" Grace exclaimed. "I won't allow you to suffer on my behalf."

"Grace, should I allow you to marry Mr. Paxton, I will suffer dearly on your behalf."

"Well, it sounds as if we have no choice," Doris interjected.

"We can make our way within a fortnight. We'll take the train to Seattle, where Karen's oldest sister lives with her husband and family. From there, we will secure passage on a steamer and go north to Skagway."

"You will need money," Myrtle declared. "I will provide enough to help with the journey for all three of you. I know it is the only way to keep Grace safe. Once Mr. Paxton and Frederick realize she has gone, I'm certain my husband will do whatever it takes to locate her. It could very well be possible that Mr. Paxton will initiate his own search."

"If he is as determined as you suggest, what is to keep him from hiring someone to follow you and Grace even now?" Doris questioned.

Myrtle looked to Grace and then to Karen. "After encountering Mr. Paxton's threats, it is very possible. I hadn't even considered it. We should take every precaution."

"Well, for all purposes, Mrs. Hawkins, this looks to be nothing more than a social visit. We have gone together to visit your friends on many occasions. This will look like nothing more than that," Karen suggested.

Grace nodded, seeing how pale her mother had become. "Yes, I agree. We need to concern ourselves more with how to escape when the time comes to leave for good."

"Perhaps we can work on ways to throw this Mr. Paxton off the trail," Doris said, strumming her fingers lightly on the armrest of her chair. "I do believe there are some rather capable theater students who live just two blocks down. They were once students of mine when I taught secondary classes. I just might enlist their help. Perhaps we could have them pose as Karen and Grace and send them in one direction, while the girls join me to head in the other."

"Do you think we stand a chance of making it work?" Myrtle asked quite seriously.

Doris smiled. "I have a reputation for making the impossible work. With God, all things are possible."

Karen laughed aloud at this. "And with Aunt Doris, God has extra help to see matters to completion."

"Then can we count on you to aid us in our hour of need?" Myrtle asked hopefully.

"Oh, absolutely. I've not had a great adventure since five years ago when I accompanied several maiden teachers to tour the falls of Niagara."

Karen smiled reassuringly at Grace. "She didn't lose anybody then. I'm certain she'll not lose anyone this time."

Myrtle sat quietly in Grace's sitting room. Grace sat near her on the sofa and together they whispered and plotted while Karen made notes.

"My heart is so heavy," Myrtle said, leaning back as if physically taxed. "I have wasted many good years on the insignificant."

"But, Mother, you were brought up to care about such things. Grandmother placed great importance on social standings. You mustn't blame yourself for what has happened."

"Oh, but I do," Myrtle replied. "When your brother died as a little one, I thought my heart might break within me. Then I had you and I feared letting the bonds be too close. I didn't want to endure that pain again. I put you from me and chose instead to care about things."

She looked into her daughter's face. Only the slightest hint of the bruise remained on Grace's cheek. The handprint had been a strong reminder to Myrtle that her priorities had suffered greatly over the last twenty years. The past week had been a time of deep prayer and regret. Regret that she could have been so blind. Regret that she could not take back the choices—that she could not turn back the hands of time.

"I shall miss you so dearly," Myrtle said in a whisper. Her voice broke despite her efforts to keep her emotions at bay. "I feel as though I'm just seeing you for the first time, only to send you away."

"No more trees?" Grace asked softly.

Myrtle shook her head and reached out to take hold of Grace's hand. "No more trees. No more wealth above people. No more concern over social matters at the detriment of my loved ones. Grace, you must listen to me. I have no idea what kind of power Martin Paxton has over our financial well-being, but I do not want you to concern yourself with it. If we should lose it all, then so be it. I cannot stand by and be the woman I once was." She bowed her head. "I'm so ashamed that it should take something like this to open my eyes. How blind I have been."

"Mother, I don't understand," Grace said, putting her free hand atop her mother's chilled fingers. "This matter is grave, no doubt. But the seriousness in which you see it alarms me. I don't understand."

Myrtle met her child's gaze. "I can't say that I totally understand it myself. I have never been given to questioning your father's authority, but something in me rises up to rebel. I fear for you. I do not like Martin Paxton, and that he should exercise such demands on your father only proves that he is ruthless and unfeeling. I simply fear the outcome might be far worse than any of us could even now suspect."

"Then I will go, and I will endeavor not to fret over you

and Father. You must promise to write me, however. You must write or I will go mad with worry."

"I will write," Myrtle promised. "When it seems safe to do so, I will write."

CHAPTER FIVE

DEVIL'S CREEK, COLORADO

BILL BARRINGER paced the small cabin in a determined manner. For all intents he looked to be a man with a purpose, but nothing could be further from the truth. If he did have a purpose, it was only to keep the fear he felt inside from finding an outward expression. He tried very hard, for the sake of his two children, not to look worried.

"Will Mama have the baby soon?" twelve-year-old Leah asked softly.

"I'm sure she will," Bill replied. He ruffled the dark curls of his youngest. "Pretty soon you won't be the baby of the family anymore."

"But I'll still be your princess, right, Papa?"

Bill smiled. Leah looked so much like her mother. Soft dark curls, big blue eyes. Why, even at this tender age she bore the clear markings of a beautiful young woman. Before he knew it she would be courting and then married, and forgotten would be the days when she was her papa's princess.

"You'll always be my princess," he promised. "No matter if this baby is a boy or a girl, you'll have that special place."

Leah smiled and went back to her sewing.

"Why can't Leah cook the supper?" Jacob grumbled from the hearth. At fourteen, he was absolutely convinced that cooking was woman's work.

"Leah's doing the mendin'," Bill answered. "Besides, you're perilously close to being a grown man. You need to know how to fend for yourself. Cookin' a meal ain't nothing to be ashamed of."

Jacob lifted the ladle to sample the stew. "I think it's just about done."

Bill nodded. "Better check on the biscuits."

With his son momentarily occupied, Bill cast a quick glance at the bedroom door. His wife, Patience, as good as her name, hadn't uttered a sound since taking to her bed. A midwife from nearby had come to tend to the delivery, but other than an occasional instruction murmured in a low, hushed voice, even the midwife was silent.

I should never have left Denver, Bill reasoned as he resumed his pacing. At least in Denver they had lived in a decent house and he had held a regular job that brought in steady pay. But Denver had represented failure to Bill. A dozen years earlier he had been on top of the world. Rich from a bonanza of silver, Bill had taken the world for a ride—a wild, exciting ride that had merited him a house of some means and a happy family. Patience had lived the life of privilege he had always promised, and Bill had actually felt proud of his accomplishments.

They weren't rich by Vanderbilt or Astor standards, by any

means. But they were happy and comfortable and well set. At least they had been until silver was devalued in 1893 and depression set in across the country. Bill had gone from a life of happiness to one of fear and worry practically overnight. But that fear and worry were nothing compared to what he felt now.

Patience had delivered Jacob with relative ease, but Leah had come in a more difficult fashion and the doctor had suggested that additional children would be a risk. Patience, a god-fearing woman, had told the doctor flatly that she would have as many children as God gave her to bear. Bill, on the other hand, had been far more practical about the situation. He had suggested they do their best to refrain from additional pregnancies, pleading with Patience to stay strong and remain at his side. And with some disappointment, she had agreed.

Bill had figured them pretty much out of the woods when no other children followed Leah's birth. After nearly twelve years, he figured Patience was strong enough to endure whatever God sent their way. Now he wasn't so convinced.

Her labor had started at dawn, and after fixing breakfast for the family, she had taken herself to bed and asked Bill to fetch the midwife. There was an air of excitement among the family. This new baby, although unexpected, was a blessing they were all anticipating with great joy. Patience had told them all that God had smiled down upon them for a reason and that this baby would be a great happiness to them. Bill could only hope that to be the case.

Life was hard in the mining camps of Colorado, and Devil's Creek camp was certainly no different. If anything, it was only worse. Bill had tried to find other accommodations closer to town, but this run-down cabin was the only thing he could afford. Patience had assured him it would be sufficient, but Bill wasn't convinced.

Supper passed in a tense silence. Usually Patience would ask the children about their friends and what they had spent the day doing. Then Bill would ask them about their chores and make certain the tasks of the household were complete. This time Bill had no interest in conversation, and he could see that the children felt likewise.

By the time the clock on the mantel struck nine, Bill was nearly beside himself. There was no sense in pretending ease and assurance. The children knew he was afraid.

"Mama says when you feel bad, you should pray," Leah offered.

"Yes. Your mama would say that." Bill smiled. "That's why we're going to do just that. Jacob, leave off with those dishes and come on over here." Bill knelt down beside his chair. Leah smoothed out the skirt of her dress and did likewise.

Jacob lumbered over and yawned as he got on his knees. They were usually retiring by this time, yet Bill didn't have the heart to send them to bed before the baby was born.

Joining hands, Bill drew a deep breath, hoping it might put a tone of confidence in his voice. "Lord, we thank you for our blessings," he began. "We thank you for watching over us, and we ask that you would go now to be with our dear Patience. Help her to have a safe delivery. Give health to the baby and to Patience. In Jesus' name, amen."

Leah and Jacob both looked to their father as if to question what they should do next. Bill knew they were tired. They'd all been up since four-thirty that morning. "You can go to bed if you want," he finally said, "or sit here with me."

"I want to wait," Leah replied. "I want to see Mama and the new baby."

Bill nodded. "How about you, son?"

Jacob shrugged. "Guess I'll wait too."

Just as they were getting up from the floor, the midwife came out from the bedroom. "I need a word with you, Bill."

Bill felt his chest tighten. "Leah, help your brother finish up the dishes."

"Yes, Papa." She watched him with wide eyes that betrayed her fear. "Is Mama all right?"

"I'm sure she is. You just let me talk to Mrs. Reinhart and then I can tell you more."

He followed the midwife outside. The ink-black night was illuminated by thousands of pinprick stars, and Bill knew there was no other place he'd ever been where God seemed so close.

"I'm sorry, Bill," Mrs. Reinhart began, "but Patience isn't doing well. I'm afraid we may lose her and the baby."

Bill felt as if she'd delivered a blow to his midsection. For a moment he found it impossible to breathe. *Lose her? Lose the baby?* Although he had known it a risk to bear another child, he couldn't believe that God would wait twelve years to rob Bill of both the baby and his wife.

"I don't understand."

"Baby's caught," the woman said. "Patience is just too small. The baby is caught up inside and there's no way to get him down. I've tried, Bill, but without a doctor to take the baby through surgery, I'm afraid we won't be able to save them."

"Where is the doctor?"

"I couldn't say. He was on the other side of the pass. I doubt we could bring him here in time, but if you want to give it a try, that will be our only hope."

"No, don't say that," Bill said, shaking his head. "She can't die."

Mrs. Reinhart gently touched Bill's shoulder. "You could send your boy for the doctor, but I don't think you'd want to leave her now. She's askin' for all of you. I think she knows she's not going to make it."

He heard the words, but they made no sense to him. How could this be happening? Why would God do this to him? He'd tried to live a good life. He hadn't complained, even when the silver had dropped in price and they'd lost everything. Patience had helped him to see that God was in the details and that even in losing all their worldly wealth, they still had one another. How could he go on if he didn't have Patience to encourage him?

"I'll send for the doctor," he said, struggling to find some point of hope. "There has to be a chance."

"You do what you think is best," she replied. "But right now I think you'd better go talk to her."

Bill nodded. "All right. But I don't know what I'll say. What can I say?"

They went back into the cabin only to find that the children were nowhere in sight. The bedroom door was open, and from the dimly lit room, Bill could hear Patience's weak voice.

"Sometimes things don't work out the way we want them to," she was saying.

Bill moved to the door and could see that she had gathered her children to her side, much like a mother hen would gather her chicks.

"Please don't go, Mama," Leah said, her tearful voice cutting Bill to the heart. They already knew. Patience was already preparing them.

Patience opened her arms to her darlings, and Leah snuggled down beside her, putting her teary face to her mother's breast. Bill knew she was probably comforted by the steady beat of her mother's heart. Even Jacob, who considered himself too old for hugs and kisses, had knelt beside his mother and had now leaned across the bed to put his head in the crook of her arm.

"Remember what Jesus said," Patience whispered. She looked directly at Bill, even as she stroked the heads of her children. "He said he had to go to prepare a place for us. Remember?"

The children nodded, but neither spoke. Bill could see they were trying hard not to cry. He was trying hard too, but his vision was already blurred.

"I'm going to go to the place Jesus prepared," Patience said, her loving gaze never leaving Bill's face. "I want you to remember that, just like Jesus wanted us to remember it. I want to see you again in heaven, and there's only one way to get there. You must give your heart to Jesus and continue to live by what the Bible tells you. Will you do that for me?"

Leah lifted her head. "I will, Mama. But why do you have to go now? I don't want you to go." Her voice broke into a sob as she buried her face against her mother's neck.

"Oh, sweet baby, I don't want to go away, but God knows best."

"I think God's bein' mean if He thinks it's best to take you away," Jacob said, wrapping his arm tightly across his mother's still-swollen abdomen.

"No, Jacob, God is not mean," Patience said, trying her best to soothe his anger. "You mustn't be mad at God. He loves you so. Please promise me, Jacob, that you'll love Him and keep His word."

Jacob raised up to meet his mother's eyes. His lower lip

quivered as he opened his mouth to speak. No words came. He bolted from the bed and flew across the room, knocking Bill backward as he fled the room.

Bill could no longer stand the pain of the moment. "I'm going to send Jacob for the doctor," he said, struggling to keep his voice steady.

"No," Patience said, shaking her head. "It wouldn't help. God is calling me and the baby home. You must let us go."

Bill crossed the room and knelt down on the floor beside Leah. "Don't leave me, Patience. Don't leave us."

She reached out her hand and Bill took hold of her. "I would stay if I could," she whispered, her voice sounding even weaker. "You must all surely know that I would love to stay here with you."

"Please, Mama," Leah cried, wrapping her arms around her mother's neck. "Please."

His daughter's pleading only mimicked the cry of Bill's own soul. *Please stay with me, Patience. If you die, I die as well.* The words went unspoken, but they were forever chiseled on his heart.

"Oh, my precious ones," Patience murmured, "Jesus is here—He won't . . . leave . . . you." Her blue eyes met Bill's gaze for only a moment. Even in death, they were filled with the hope she'd known in her Savior. Without a word, she closed her eyes and said nothing more.

Bill saw the life go out from her. Still clinging to her hand, he knew the very instant she left his side for her heavenly home. Leah, still holding tightly to her mother, didn't seem to notice for a moment. Then, raising her head, her expression became the very image of brokenness.

"No!" she cried. "No!"

Leah's mournful wailing brought Mrs. Reinhart into the

room. The older woman reached down to comfort the girl. "Oh, darlin', your mama wouldn't want you to fret so." She led the crying child back into the front room.

Only Bill remained.

Looking down at the angelic face of his wife, Bill let go of her hand and reached up to touch her face. The woman he had loved so dearly for over fifteen years had gone to her reward without him. Somehow he had always figured they'd die together. He knew it was silly, but it was born out of the reasoning that he surely couldn't remain alive if she were not at his side.

"I love you, my darlin'," he said, smoothing back the dark curls that framed her face. Leaning down, he placed one last kiss upon her lips. She had deserted him, taking with her their unborn child . . . and his heart.

CHAPTER SIX

THERE HAD BEEN no money for a stone marker, but because the Barringer family was so well thought of, the mining association put together a collection. Someone voluntarily carved a headstone, chiseling the words *PATIENCE BARRINGER, 1865–1897*, while someone else agreed to make the casket. The local ladies' sewing circle came and dressed the body for burial, and the little congregation of the Baptist church brought contributions of food to help the family during their time of loss.

Leah and Jacob Barringer were rather relieved to see the townsfolk rally around them. Their father had spent that first week after their mother's death in near total silence. He cried a lot at night, and it frightened Leah, who herself felt rather lost without benefit of father or mother. Jacob did his best to remain strong and supportive. He hadn't teased her at all that week, but instead had surprised her with his kindness. Perhaps the most startling example came when Leah had been fighting to brush her long dark ringlets. Finding her hair hopelessly tangled, she burst into tears, wishing fervently for her mother. Without a word, Jacob had come to her, taken the brush from her hand, and had carefully, lovingly, worked through the tangles until her hair was completely brushed and in order. She had thrown herself into his arms, crying softly against the cotton shirt she had mended only the day before. They'd always been close, but now their bond had strengthened.

"Pa says we're leaving in just a few more minutes," Jacob called from the side of the little church.

Leah stood beside her mother's grave. The dirt was still mounded up, and the rocky terrain surrounding the little cemetery looked rather bleak. Leah hated to leave her mother and baby brother there. She had decided for herself that the baby was a boy. Her mother had thought to have another son and call him Benjamin. Leah had figured her mother to know best.

Kneeling in the soft dirt, Leah put a fresh bunch of wild flowers atop the grave. "We're leaving now, Mama. Papa says gold has been found up north. He believes we'll make our fortune there. When we do, I'm coming back to see that you have a beautiful new stone—one that has brother's name on it as well."

She arranged the flowers carefully and ignored the droplets of rain that began to fall. It rained almost religiously every afternoon about this time. Leah had learned to take it in stride along with everything else related to their life in Devil's Creek.

"I don't know when I'm coming back, Mama. I don't know if you can see me in heaven or not, but you told me when I was afraid, I could come to you and tell you. And,

Mama, I'm afraid. I don't know where we're going. I don't like our new life without you." She tried hard to keep from crying. "I know you said that God is always with us and that when we're afraid, the psalms said we could trust in Him. I know that bein' a good Christian girl is what you want for me, but I'm still scared."

Leah glanced up at the sky and let the steadily building rain mingle with her tears. "I just know you can see me, Mama. Please ask God to help me 'cause Papa just isn't the same. He's talking about glory and gold again, but his heart is so sad. Sometimes he just sits there staring at the fireplace, and I don't know how to make him feel better, 'cause my heart hurts too."

"Leah! Come on!" Jacob called.

Leah got to her feet and bowed her head for a little prayer. "Dear God, please keep my mama and little Benjamin safe. Don't let nothin' hurt them no more. And, God, if it ain't too much trouble, could you please help us on our way? My pa doesn't always think clear. Mama said he's a dreamer, and I know you understand what that means. So now we're headin' off for another one of Papa's dreams, and I'm afraid."

"Leah, Pa says come right now or he's heading out without you!"

Leah smiled. She knew better, but the threat meant business nevertheless.

"Amen," she whispered, then with one last glance at her mother's resting-place, she hurried down the slippery path to where Jacob stood.

"I had to pray," she explained.

"I know," he replied. "We're going to need a lot of prayers before this adventure is through."

Leah nodded solemnly, and she could tell by the look in

Jacob's eyes that he meant every word.

"We'll stay in Denver long enough to put some money together," Bill explained to the children that night. "I've got a couple of folks who still owe me money, and who knows, maybe they've struck it rich while I've been away. Anyway, I know Granny Richards will put us up until we can get on our feet."

Granny Richards wasn't really their granny, but the kids knew her to be a kind old woman who had given them treats when they were young. Bill knew the old woman would be delighted to see them again. He could only hope that she was still alive.

There hadn't been much in the way of possessions to either bring with them or leave behind. Bill felt profound sorrow that in the end, his wife had no more than two dresses to her name and a wooden crate with a few odds and ends of memorabilia. Pots and pans, along with other kitchen goods, and the meager furnishings that had made the cabin a home were hardly a legacy to leave to her children. But, knowing Patience, she'd probably never considered it a problem. She'd left them the important things. She'd given them love and acceptance, hope and a basic understanding of God. Those were the legacies Patience Barringer would want to be known for.

The mining company had owned the property, and because of that, Bill couldn't even raise a traveling purse by selling off the cabin. Instead, he sold off his furniture and what household supplies he didn't deem as necessary to take with them north to the Yukon.

Yukon. Even the sound of it promised something exciting and different. With Patience gone, it left only Jacob and Leah to reason with him and keep him from making rash decisions, and neither one of them were in any mood to argue his choice. Not that it would have mattered. Bill knew he couldn't have remained in the same town where he'd buried Patience and their baby. The very thought would have driven him mad. No, by leaving he could almost pretend that she was still alive—that circumstances had sent her elsewhere. Elsewhere, but not into the grave.

When the trio finally managed to arrive in Denver, no one was prepared for the madhouse of activities. Denver had grown up considerably over the last few years and was now a rather impressive town. Sitting like a sentinel at the base of the Rockies, the town seemed to almost shimmer in the golden summer sun.

Bill wiped sweat from his brow and headed the horse in the direction of the poorer district. Granny Richards, if she still lived, would not have moved. Of that, Bill was certain. She always joked that they would have to take her out feet first, and Bill had no doubt of the old woman's stubborn determination to make that true.

"When will we get there, Pa?" Jacob asked. "I'm so empty my ribs are touching my backbone."

"We ought to be there in a short while. Traffic is pretty bad here. This city is a lot bigger than it used to be. More people and more activities."

"More money, too?" Leah asked hopefully.

Bill smiled. "You bet, princess. More people always means more money. People go where the money's to be had. You'll see. We'll be on our way before you know it."

They all sighed in relief when they finally found their way to Granny Richards'. The little run-down house wasn't much to look at, but it beckoned them nevertheless. Bill spotted

Granny first thing. She was working the rocky soil at the side of the house. She seemed to work in a rhythm. Hoe a patch, pick out the rocks. Hoe a patch, pick out the rocks.

"Granny!" Bill called, jumping off the rickety buckboard.

The old woman looked up and put her hand to her head to shield her eyes from the sun. Lacking the funds and not caring one whit about convention, Granny saved her only straw bonnet for Sundays and church. Because of this, her skin was leathery and brown from the harsh Colorado sun.

"Bill? Bill Barringer?" she questioned, limping forward in an awkward manner. No doubt her rheumatism was taking its toll, Bill surmised.

"It's me," he called and went forward to greet her.

The old woman hugged him with an impressive grip. "So you've come back down out of the clouds."

"I have, Granny, but only for the moment." He grinned. "I was wonderin' if you could put me and the kids up for a few days?"

Granny looked past him to the wagon. "Where's Patience?"

Bill looked to the ground. "Uh, Granny, she passed on."

The old woman looked up and nodded. "The mountains are hard on folks, and your little Patience wasn't much more than a mite. How'd it happen?"

"She was trying to deliver a baby. Midwife said she was too small."

Again Granny nodded. "Just a mite. Just a mite. Well, God rest her soul."

Bill fumbled for the words. "I'm . . . well . . . I mean, the children and me—"

"No nevermind about explaining. You just bring down your things and come inside. Old Granny will fix you up with something to eat, and then we can discuss your plans."

Two hours and a full belly later, Bill found Jacob and Leah stretched out asleep on Granny's bed. He closed the door so as not to disturb them, then went to join Granny for another cup of coffee.

"Heard about gold in the Yukon," he said, as if Granny had asked him where he was headed. "Nuggets as big as a man's head. Just lyin' around for the takin'."

"It always is, isn't it?" Granny asked in a knowing tone. She looked at him with steely blue eyes that seemed to bore right through him. "Have you heard tell yet of a gold rush where the nuggets weren't as big as your head? What would the attraction be otherwise?"

Bill shrugged. "I saw the newspaper. They had a picture and everything. Two boats, one in Seattle and one in San Francisco, and both of them loaded down with gold."

"Until you see it firsthand," Granny suggested, "it's still just a rumor."

"No, Granny, these aren't just rumors. The papers wouldn't have run the story otherwise."

She laughed. "Put a lot of stock in papers, do you, boy?"

"Not near as much as in pictures," Bill admitted. "I saw the pictures. I'm tellin' you, Granny, there's gold in the Yukon."

"Bah! Who needs it? Better to do a decent day's job and be paid a decent wage."

"Well, that's why I'm here," he said, finishing off the coffee. "I plan to get me enough for the trip north, anyhow."

"What about them young'uns?"

"They're coming with me. They'll enjoy the adventure."

"What about schoolin'? Their ma, as I recall, held a high opinion of schoolin'."

Bill nodded. "Yes, she did. I'm certain there are schools up north. We're not the only civilized folks in the world, after all."

Granny went to the cupboard and took out a big yellow bowl. She went to the counter and put a smaller, red bowl heaping with green beans inside the first bowl. Bringing both to the table, she sat down and began to snap beans. "So what kind of work you thinkin' to find here?"

"Whatever makes me fast money. I can still deal a pretty fair game of cards," Bill said with a smile. "You know how it goes, Granny."

"Indeed I do," she answered. "I remember you gettin' into a fair heap of trouble with them cards, too."

Bill shrugged. "I was just a boy then. Patience . . . well, she changed my mind about games of chance. Guess her death has changed my mind again. At least it's a way to lay my hands on some cash."

"Don't reckon I can talk you out of it. Hate to see you spending your nights in places better left unvisited. Laws have changed, don't you know. Some of them activities are more likely to see you in jail rather than the bank."

"I don't plan to put myself in too much danger," he told her. He thought of Patience and how she would have given him the devil for even considering what he was about to do. He had to have money, however, and he had to have it fast. Anyone who understood gold rushes knew that you had to act without hesitation. If not, the land got snapped up before you even had a chance to show your face in the territory.

"Well, the young'uns can stay here with me. The garden needs weedin' and waterin'. There's always something they can help with."

"Jacob's big enough to get a job of his own," Bill said rather thoughtfully. He'd not thought of putting his son to work until just that moment. "Maybe he could deliver groceries or shine shoes. He's good with horses. Maybe he could work at one of the liveries."

"Could be. Sounds a heap better than what you have in mind."

Bill yawned and rubbed his bearded chin. "A man has to do what a man has to do, Granny."

"Especially when he's got no woman to fuss over him and keep him on the straight and narrow path."

Bill felt his throat constrict, guilt washing over him. Patience had always talked about the straight and narrow path. She believed that God's way was far more narrow a path than most folks wanted to believe. Bill considered himself a rather religious man, but he knew God understood when he ventured off the path to one side or the other. In fact, he believed God looked the other way in some of those particularly messy points of life.

"I saw you had a stack of wood in the back," he said, suddenly unable to deal with his own discomfort. "I'll just mosey on back there and split some of it for you. I want to earn my keep, after all."

"You'd earn it a sight better doing that than gambling it away or dealing in some other underhanded fashion," Granny said, never looking up from her beans. "Suit yourself."

Jacob woke up in a pool of sweat. The heat of the Denver afternoon had joined together with a hideous nightmare of being thrown into the pits of hell. Trembling, Jacob eased off the bed so as not to disturb Leah. He wiped his forehead with the back of his hand and tried to steady his rapid breathing.

From the time he'd been little, Jacob had known that his

mother's fondest wish was for him to accept Jesus as his Savior. In all the days that had followed from that first introduction to the Gospel message, Jacob had known that someday he would be left with a choice between deciding for God—or against Him. But someday always seemed far away. At least it had back then.

Years ago, he had figured his folks to live forever. The reality of death made little impact on his world. He'd known of folks who'd passed on. Had even heard stories of his grandparents and how they had died, but death didn't seem anything so immediate that he needed to actually make a commitment to God. After all, his mother said, it would be the most important decision in his life.

"Don't promise God anything, Jacob, unless you intend to keep that promise," she had said. *"Even the Word says it's better to make no vow at all than to make one and then not keep it."*

So Jacob had made no vow. Much to his mother's disappointment.

Now in the dark, musty room, Jacob felt overwhelmed with grief. His knowing God was the one thing his mother had longed for, and he hadn't even been able to give it to her on her deathbed. He shivered in spite of the heat. He could still see her eyes fixed on his face.

"God knows your heart, Jacob Daniel," she had whispered. *"He knows your mind. Whatever it is that's troubling you about saying yes to Him—He already knows."*

Jacob had supposed she had told him this to make him feel better, but instead it only bothered him more. If God knew—truly knew his heart and mind—then He knew that Jacob was a coward.

Leaning against the wall for support, Jacob bit his lower lip to keep from crying. He'd failed his mother and he'd failed God. What hope could there be now?

CHAPTER SEVEN

CHICAGO, ILLINOIS

"BUT, FREDERICK," Myrtle Hawkins tried to reason with her husband, "it's impossible to give our daughter the wedding she deserves on such short notice. Why, July twenty-fourth is scarcely but days away."

"It's just under a week. Good grief, woman, God only needed a week to create the entire world. Do you mean to tell me a wedding takes more than that?"

Myrtle tried to soften her tone. "My dear, I am hardly divine. I can't possibly be called upon to perform miracles. A proper wedding takes months to plan, organize, and prepare."

"Well, you have five days. I suggest you get on with the arrangements."

Myrtle folded her hands and tried hard not to lose her temper. She had already told Grace that this would be her final effort to get Frederick to see reason. If he refused, then Grace would accompany Doris and Karen north to Alaska.

"Freddy," she said, using her old nickname for him, "our daughter has pleaded to be heard on this matter. Won't you reconsider?"

Frederick Hawkins looked up from his paper. "I should certainly reconsider the matter if it were in her best interest, but it is not. I've tried to explain this to you. . . ." His words trailed off as he looked suspiciously at the table maid. "Leave us!" he commanded, and the young woman scurried from the room as if her skirts were afire.

Leaning toward Myrtle's side of the table, Frederick lowered his voice. "This wedding is imperative. I can say no more. Our family will see ruin if we refuse Mr. Paxton."

"But surely what the man has in mind—this blackmail—" Myrtle protested, "it can't be legal. Can't we go to the police or the courts? We have good lawyers on retainer; can we not present the case to them and allow them to earn their money?"

"No!" Frederick said, pounding his fist down on the table. "Confound it, woman, if you do not hear anything else I say, then hear this. Our Grace will marry Martin Paxton on July twenty-fourth. You will plan out the wedding and provide what comforts you can. There will be no other discussion on the matter."

Myrtle realized in that moment that her husband had just set her plans into motion. *Forgive me, God, if this is wrong, but I can't help but feel that I'm saving Grace from complete destruction,* she silently prayed.

Getting to her feet, Myrtle swept the train of her gown aside. "Very well, Frederick. I will go forward with my plans." At least she wasn't lying.

"You'll see in the long run that it's all for the best," he assured.

"I hope you'll try to remember those words," Myrtle replied. "I hope when Grace is far from us and you are lying awake at night wondering if you made the right decision . . . I hope your words still ring true."

He said nothing, but the expression on his face spoke volumes. Myrtle wanted nothing more than to burst into tears, but she was no young maid to be given to moments of emotional waterworks. As a matron of society she had often had to stand her ground in stoic fashion. She would lend an illusion of wedding preparation to their home, but all the while she would be plotting with Grace for her escape.

"Aunt Doris said the actresses will come tomorrow at exactly seven o'clock," Karen confided to Myrtle and Grace. "They will be dressed as maids and appear for all purposes to have come from one of the local agencies in order to help with the wedding."

"Wonderful!" Myrtle declared. "I will ring up and have other girls sent over as well. That way they may all mingle together. No one will be the wiser."

"I thought you might see the benefit in such a ruse," Karen replied.

Grace noticed the worry lines around her mother's eyes. She looked so tired and so worn from the events of the last few days. "Mother, are you certain that when all is said and done, you and Father will be able to patch this up?"

Myrtle patted her daughter's hand. "I know my husband very well. I know him so well, in fact, that I know this Mr. Paxton has done more than cause him to build an indebtedness in monetary means. No, there is more to this than meets the eye, and once you are safely away, I intend to know what it is all about. Frederick will calm down and see the sense of it. Whatever the price, it will be worth knowing that you are protected."

"But I don't feel that way. I don't wish to be protected at all cost," Grace protested. "If it means that either you or Father are left to suffer, then I want no part of that."

"We won't suffer, my dear. Just remember that. I have the jewels and other trinkets that can be sold. And there is property and such that can also be arranged for. Do not worry about us."

Grace nodded, but her heart felt even more heavy. Her mother had already given them a great deal of money. Money that Grace wasn't entirely sure couldn't be better spent elsewhere. Perhaps even in buying off Mr. Paxton.

The next twenty-four hours passed in a flurry of activities for Grace. Her father presumed her to be resolved to the wedding, and at one point over breakfast he had even made a rather pleasant speech about how this choice would have a way of benefiting them all in the long run. He was certain Grace could come to care for Paxton, while Grace knew in her heart that she had no intention of ever caring for the man.

After lunch in the afternoon, Grace and Karen pretended to be busy fitting Myrtle's wedding dress to Grace's more slender frame. No one anticipated seeing the women for the rest of the afternoon, and when dinner came and Grace pleaded a headache, no one thought it amiss that she should take her meal upstairs in the privacy of her room.

By seven o'clock, the temporary maids arrived and with them two actresses who were rather eager for their parts. Slipping the two women upstairs, Myrtle Hawkins met with Karen and Grace to listen to the final plans.

"This is Mavis and Celia," Karen explained. "Mavis will pretend to be Grace and Celia will be me. They will leave in the morning for a day of shopping. Should anyone be watching them, they will see the ladies in the carriage, making arrangements for Grace's trousseau.

"Meanwhile, dressed in their clothes," Karen continued, "Grace and I will accompany several of the maids on various tasks that you have outlined."

Myrtle nodded. "I have a list already prepared."

"Good," Karen replied. "Have it designed so that at the appropriate time, Grace and I can slip away unnoticed. Perhaps at the market."

Myrtle smiled. "That would work perfectly. I can assign each of those who accompany you to different tasks. One can go to the baker and one to the florist."

"Exactly. If anyone is watching, which hopefully they won't be if they believe us to be nothing more than servants, they'll suspect nothing," Karen replied.

"I do so appreciate what all of you are doing to help my daughter," Myrtle said, looking first to Karen and then to the other women. "I know that in time this will right itself and Grace will be returned to us. But in the meanwhile, I also know she will be safely kept from the ugliness of this situation."

Grace frowned. That her mother expected this to develop into something ugly and distasteful worried her greatly. Certainly she expected Paxton to be angry, even threatening, but he was a businessman and as such, surely even he would recognize there to be more power in keeping her father on his feet than in defeating him. He might never recoup the full extent of his losses otherwise.

Sleep came fitfully to Grace that night. The biggest worry they had was how to arrange clothing and traveling needs for the two women. Karen had finally hit upon having a couple of the carriage servants deliver two crates marked *Oranges* to her aunt. Inside would be trunks of neatly folded clothes, shoes, and other personal articles. When Karen and Grace finally made it to Doris, they would simply change clothes and slip away to the railway station, hopefully unnoticed.

Hopefully. It wasn't a word that held the greatest reassurance for Grace. Sitting up, unable to sleep, Grace drew her knees to her chest and tried to pray. Oh, how hard it was to pray when her world seemed amiss and words refused to come. She rocked back and forth, laboring to voice her petition to God, but her mind refused the order she so longed for. Rational thought was not possible.

I hope God understands. Surely He does, she reasoned. *He is, after all, God. He knows all—sees all.*

Outside a summer storm raged over the city, flashing brilliant streaks of lightning. In those moments when her room was illuminated ever so briefly, Grace caught glimpses of her many beloved possessions—her vanity chest lined with all kinds of perfumes and accessories, her books and cherished trinkets from childhood. How could she leave them all?

They are so much a part of me, she thought. Her doll collection was extensive and had been started when she was born. There were eighteen very special dolls, one given each year of her life. After that, her father had chided her when she'd questioned why the dolls had stopped. Instead, very prim and proper gifts were received. A carriage of her own with matching bays. New bedroom furnishings. Those were the type of gifts a grown woman of means might receive. The dolls, like her childhood and innocence, were to be packed away and given to another.

"Oh, Father," she murmured, "why did this ever happen? What did you do to cause such grief to fall upon your shoulders—and my own?"

She loved her father and mother despite their distance during her younger years. She had watched them from afar. Though not as the stick figures her mother had mentioned in her own confessions, but rather as beings of importance. People to be revered and in awe of, but not to be close to or loved by.

Grace supposed she understood that her parents, in their own way, did love her, but their love was far more calculated than Grace desired it to be. She had seen her friends and other families from the church or social settings. She had watched mothers and daughters share amiable moments of what could only be described as true camaraderie. And she had longed for that type of friendship with her own mother.

"Now it seems I might have it, but for my escape," she thought aloud. "Mother is so changed. She feels so responsible for this, and yet I know she doesn't approve of Mr. Paxton any more than I do."

His very name caused her to shudder. Suddenly feeling chilled, in spite of summer's warmth, Grace slipped beneath her covers just as another flash of lightning illuminated the room. Pulling the sheet high, like she did as a child, Grace murmured a prayer for protection.

"See me here, O God," she whispered. "See me and guard me. Protect me from harm and deliver me from the hands of my enemy."

Morning came too soon, as far as Grace was concerned. She dressed as she'd been instructed, shared breakfast with her mother and father, then upon her mother's comment to see to assigning duties to the staff, Grace asked to be excused.

"My dear, if I might have a word with you first," Frederick Hawkins requested.

Myrtle and Grace looked at each other as if to question which woman it was he spoke to.

"I only wish to speak with Grace for a moment."

Myrtle nodded and went about her business, while Grace tarried behind her chair. Clinging to the high wooden back for support, Grace waited to hear what her father might have to say.

Looking genuinely sorry, he met her eyes. "I would not have caused you pain for all the world. I know you fear this arrangement, but believe me when I say, in the long run, it is for the best."

"I know you want the best for me, Father," Grace replied, barely able to keep her voice even. "I have prayed about this and will do what I must."

He nodded. "Good. So long as you understand. A father must do what seems best—even when all around him suggest it to be otherwise. I am only doing what I feel will benefit you. Becoming a wife is a wonderful event in a young woman's life. I feel confident that you will want for nothing. Paxton is quite wealthy and has assured me that you will live in grand style at his home in Erie."

Grace nodded. She wanted so badly to explain herself—to tell him everything and hope he might understand her decision to defy him. Doing the only thing she could, Grace left the security of the chair and went to embrace her father. Kneeling beside him, she threw her arms around him in an uncharacteristic display of affection.

"I love you, Father. I know you have only tried to do your best for me. I'm sorry I haven't been the obedient daughter you deserve."

"Nonsense," he said, his body rigid and unresponsive.

Grace straightened, looked into his eyes, and realized he had put a wall up between them. He appeared to be fighting with every ounce of his strength to reveal nothing more than manly resolve.

Standing, Grace bit her tongue to keep from confessing her plan. *Better to leave now,* she told herself. *Leave quickly and quietly, remembering that you did what you could and that you aren't going out of a spirit of willfulness, but rather desperation.*

She fled the room, narrowly missing the butler as he came in to make the announcement that the minister had arrived to discuss the wedding arrangements. The words caused Grace to flinch as if struck. She hated lying to her father, but how would she feel knowing she had lied to a man of God as well?

Their plans went through as anticipated, and it wasn't until after she and Karen exchanged places with the actresses and were dressed in servants' uniforms that Grace realized the finality of the moment. For reasons that were beyond her understanding, she suddenly feared that she might never again step foot in her childhood home. Looking beyond the kitchen entryway, Grace found herself wanting to memorize every detail she could set her sights on.

Myrtle came to bid her daughter farewell, and in spite of their resolve to be brave, both women broke into tears.

"Please know how much I love you," Grace whispered against her mother's ear.

"I do know," Myrtle replied. "I love you with all my life." She pressed something into Grace's hand.

Looking down, Grace found a velvet bag. "What is this?"

"Consider it additional insurance," Myrtle replied. "I sold more jewelry. This is the money I received, as well as a few other pieces that you could sell later. Nothing sentimental, I promise. I want you to take it and be safe. Sew the money into the lining of your dress or jacket. Hide it away so that scoundrels and ruthless men will not seek to harm you in order to take it from you. The world is not a kind place, Grace darling. You must look to God for protection and wisdom."

Grace nodded and kissed her mother's cheek. "Don't forget to write to me when it is safe to come home."

Myrtle nodded. "I will. You know I will."

Grace tucked the bag inside her uniform apron and turned to Karen. "I suppose I am ready," she told her companion.

"Then let us be on our way. The world awaits," Karen said with a smile before adding, "or at least the nine-fifteen train does."

Grace refused to look back. She boarded the carriage along with the other maids and didn't so much as wave. Her mother had told her to act no more attached to the place than would a servant and to give it no further thought than one who was about her chores, soon to return.

But I'm not returning, Grace realized. *At least not for a very long time.* Somehow she knew this would be the case. With each turn of the carriage wheel, Grace felt her serenity and security slip away. Defeat weighed heavy on her shoulders. Mr. Paxton had taken her home away from her, after all.

Martin Paxton paced the confines of his hotel room and studied the papers he'd been given. The businesses he'd acquired while on his trip to Chicago were a critical start to helping him in his shipping endeavors across the Great Lakes. A start, but certainly not a completion.

"Boss?" a scruffy-voiced man asked in the doorway of the suite.

"What is it?"

"Came to report in. Davis is on the job now."

"Very well," Martin said, lowering the papers and waving him forward.

"The two young ladies, your fiancée and that Miss Pierce, they left the house this morning. Davis and I followed them."

"And?" Paxton questioned, irritated by the man's slowness.

"And they went to the dressmaker. They looked to be settin' up for a long spell, and so I told Davis to sit tight while I came back here to report in."

"Good. Now get back out there and keep an eye on them," Paxton replied. "I won't have Hawkins backing out of our transaction. Not after all he's done to cause me grief. It would be just like him to let his womenfolk talk him into other arrangements."

The man nodded. "Yes, sir. I'll get right back like you said."

Paxton flipped the man a coin and went back to considering the figures on the papers. Soon his plan would be well underway. He had Hawkins right where he wanted him, and in time he would exact his revenge. The very thought caused Paxton to feel energized and alive. Casting the papers aside, he decided an early celebration was in order. He would find himself a willing companion and a case of good liquor. Then he'd spend the evening in company of both—until one or both were completely used up.

CHAPTER EIGHT

MARTIN PAXTON read the final paragraphs of the morning paper before casting it aside with a smile. The proclamation from nearly every page had to do with the new discovery of gold in the northern territories of Canada. Not that gold hadn't been a disputed commodity from that area of the world for years, but it appeared that this time things were different. There were stories declaring the authenticity of the find and warnings from the Canadian government regarding the laws and conditions of coming into their fair country, as well as a bevy of advertisements that spoke to the heart of the matter.

GET YOUR GOLD RUSH BOOTS HERE!
DON'T FREEZE WHILE GETTING RICH—
BUY BREMEN'S LONG UNDERWEAR.
Guaranteed to keep you warm or your money back!

MOTHER MADISON'S TONIC!
Guaranteed to ward off the cold and
keep your bones strong
as you journey north to fortune and fame.

Paxton would have laughed if it hadn't been so completely pathetic. So what if two ships had docked on the West Coast bearing more gold than people had seen in their lifetimes? Was the average man really so dense that he believed himself to be the one exception to the rule? Did those people not realize what slim chances were to be had in amassing a fortune in such an unconventional way?

They heard the stories of riches and glory and were blinded to the truth. Never mind that alongside the story of one miner's newly gained wealth, another told of the hardships endured by those who had been less fortunate. Was it truly so easy to look beyond the several-thousand-mile journey to the hope that gold awaited them?

But in truth, Paxton couldn't have cared less. The Yukon gold rush was rapidly making him a wealthy man. Or at least in time it would. Already in the last week he'd bought up six small businesses and one rather large freight company, all because their owners were set ablaze by gold fever.

"Ridiculous fools!" Paxton declared to no one but himself. They were exactly the kind of men he'd spent his life preying on. Men easily turned by the glitter of gold or the flash of a woman's smile. Men who would sell their souls, and had, in order to have their dream.

Paxton found the entire matter to be one of clear profit. The country had long been in a depressed state since the silver panic of 1893. Parts of the country suffered more than others, with the western coastal states perhaps hardest hit. The timber industry slowed to a crawl and with it, jobs were lost in great numbers. Canneries, vineyards, and farms were also to share in the struggles. The gold rush came at the perfect moment—offering the perfect hope.

Taking up his freshly brushed suit coat, Paxton finished dressing for the day. He would call on Frederick Hawkins and see what news could be had of his upcoming wedding. The twenty-fourth was but two days away, and as of yet, the details coming from the Hawkins house regarding the arrangements were few.

He smiled to himself. His plans were so close to being realized. After a lifetime of plotting and planning his own brand of revenge against Frederick Hawkins, Martin Paxton was soon to know the satisfaction of breaking his adversary. The thought was exhilarating—it fueled him—fed him in the darkest hours of his life.

"You'll know what it is to lose the things you love most, Mr. Hawkins," Paxton murmured.

He checked his appearance in the mirror and thought of Grace Hawkins. Such a delicate and petite flower. It would be easy to crush her—to break her of anything even remotely related to a spirit or free will. It hadn't been his original plan to insist on marriage to the girl, but seeing how beautiful she was and knowing that it couldn't help but add injury to insult once the truth was learned, Paxton knew he had to have her. Knowing she was her mother and father's pride and joy made it only that much more satisfying.

The real dilemma was Grace herself. He hadn't figured it would be a challenge to win her over. Women usually came quite willingly when he beckoned, but Grace had been different. Her naïveté in dealing with suitors made her fearful and cautious. Those qualities did not suit Paxton's plan very well.

He had figured on seduction, fooling the daughter right along with the father. But no matter what he had done to try to entice Grace, she steered clear of him, hardly giving him more than a second notice. It was enough to wreak havoc with his rather oversized ego.

"She'll pay soon enough," he said, grabbing a brush to adjust the ebony wave of his hair. Grace Hawkins would hardly be so high and mighty when he dumped her in a hovel in his hometown of Erie and left her to fend for herself. Oh, he'd visit just often enough to threaten her and see to it that she stayed put. He'd alternate his visits so that he never arrived at the same time of day. That would keep her guard up constantly and wear her down more rapidly. She'd always be watching and waiting, never knowing for sure when he might return. He'd use her and abuse her as he willed, and when he was completely finished with ruining Frederick Hawkins, he'd return her to her father—a broken woman, a mere shell of the beauty she'd once been.

Delighted by his own deviousness, Paxton went downstairs to breakfast. The day was young and promised great reward.

Cooling his heels in Frederick Hawkins' study, Martin Paxton was not happy when word came that Grace was ill and would not be receiving visitors.

"I find your daughter's lack of cooperation disturbing," Paxton told a rather ashen-faced Hawkins. "She's refused to attend parties with me, denied me the pleasure of her company for dinner or other outings, and now, not but two days until we are to be married, she is too ill with a headache to see me."

"I cannot force her to get up out of bed for a social call.

You want her well for the wedding, don't you?" Frederick replied rather angrily.

Paxton raised a brow. "Be careful how you address me, good sir. I might find myself forced to divulge information that you would rather see forever silenced."

The effect of his words was clearly noticeable as Hawkins took the seat behind his desk. "You're getting what you want, but still I have no guarantee that you won't deceive me and tell your tales anyway."

Paxton smiled in great satisfaction. "No. You don't have any guarantee. You are completely at my mercy, and the sooner you accept it, the better off you'll be." He got to his feet and narrowed his gaze. "I will be here tomorrow at precisely four o'clock. Tell Grace to be ready for a carriage ride in the park. Tell her I will not brook any nonsense."

Hawkins nodded, and without another word Martin Paxton turned and left the house. A slow, burning anger stirred memories that he would just as soon have left in the darker recesses of his mind. Clenching his fists as he reached his carriage, Paxton vowed that nothing would keep him from bringing this fine family to the ground. He would leave them completely demoralized and penniless. They would have nothing but the clothes on their backs and the shoes on their feet, and even that, in Martin Paxton's opinion, would be too much kindness.

Back at the hotel, Martin let the strain of the day leave him. He studied a bundle of letters that had arrived with the afternoon post. One in particular caught his eye. Opening it, he read,

Dear Martin,

It was our pleasure to hear from you once again. I cannot

say the times have been kind on this most westerly coast of America. Here in San Francisco, shipping has seen both increase and decrease, and with the rapid growth of the rail lines, I worry that it will somehow fade altogether and Colton Shipping will be no more. Many of our dear friends have suffered grave financial setbacks, and some have even fled California for more lucrative promises back East.

The family is well; thank you for asking. I think often of you and your dear mother. I was truly sorry to hear of her passing. Please know you are welcome anytime in our home and please let me know if there is anything that we might do to help you.

Your servant,
Ephraim Colton

Martin refolded the paper and smiled. Ephraim Colton had been the only truly selfless person he had ever known. The man had shown great kindness to his mother and her family. In fact, at one time the two families had been the best of friends. Long before Martin had been born, the Coltons and Paxtons had shared a common interest in shipping on the Great Lakes. When Ephraim had moved his wife west in order to take over a San Francisco shipping firm, Martin had genuinely mourned the loss.

With barely a dozen years between them, Martin had looked to Ephraim as a father figure and older brother. Martin's own father had died when Martin was just a few months old. His mother blamed it on typhoid, but it was rumored and later confirmed by Ephraim that there had been trouble of a different kind. Martin Paxton, Sr., had been given to great bouts of drinking. It was far more likely that alcohol had killed his father rather than typhoid.

Over the years, Martin had done his best to keep in touch

with Ephraim. But in this recent correspondence, he didn't like the tone and worried that perhaps his friend was suffering his own financial setback. Ephraim would never be one to ask for help, but Martin knew his mother would expect no less from her son.

He contemplated the situation for a moment. Never one to give handouts, Martin knew the situation with the Colton family was unique for him. He didn't really care if the Coltons succeeded or failed in business, but if he helped them, he just might help himself as well.

Thoughts of the gold rush once again came to his mind. *There shouldn't be a ship on the West Coast that isn't benefiting from this rush,* Martin thought. *Railroads can hardly take people north to the Alaskan shorelines. They need ships.*

He quickly penned some thoughts related to Colton Shipping and arranged for a runner to deliver a message to the telegraph operator. He would do what he had to in order to see the Coltons back on their feet. If it benefited him in the process, so much the better. After all, he was a businessman.

Martin glanced at his watch as soon as the message was on its way. He had agreed to meet with a Mr. Jones in regard to selling him a warehouse near the docks. When a knock sounded on the suite door, Martin nodded, glad to see that the man was punctual.

"Come in," he called in a loud, booming voice.

The man, a few years Paxton's senior, bounded into the room. "Have you heard it, Mr. Paxton?" he questioned enthusiastically. "Gold! Imagine gold nuggets as big as dogs."

"Are we talking poodles or wolfhounds, Mr. Jones?"

Jones stopped for a moment as if considering the question, then laughed. "Who cares, so long as it's real and worth a fortune!"

"So you've caught the fever, eh?" Martin leaned back in his chair, already knowing the answer.

The man nodded. "I'm selling everything and going north. I plan to make my fortune and live out life as a wealthy man."

"Do you know anything about gold mining in the Yukon?"

Mr. Jones could not contain his excitement. "It's really rather simple. The stuff is spread atop the ground for the taking. I've already heard tell that you just walk about picking up the gold until you've collected your fill. It's in the creek beds and the rivers, it's on the mountainsides and in the streets. Why, one man said the natives use the stuff to make fences and to line their wells."

Paxton would have burst out laughing had the man not been so pathetic. "So you've come to sell me your warehouse?"

"That's right. I want to have traveling money. I plan to go in grand style."

"And just what style would that be in this situation?"

"I'll take a ship all the way around Alaska. A man can pay a pretty penny for it, but there are steamers to be had out of St. Michael that will take you east along the Yukon River and eventually land you in Dawson City. None of that strenuous hiking for me. I'm no billy goat to be climbing over mountains." He laughed in a grating manner that set Martin's nerves on edge. "No, sir, I'll stay aboard the ship until I reach the land of milk and honey."

"I thought it was all made of gold," Martin chided.

"And so it is," Mr. Jones replied. "And I intend to see my name assigned to a good portion of it."

"Very well," Martin replied. "Then let us get down to business. I'd hate to delay you further."

"Well, ladies," Aunt Doris began, "it appears we have arrived."

"Do you suppose anyone will be here to meet us?" Karen questioned, stretching across Grace to look out to the depot platform. "I suppose what with this craziness to go north, we'll never get out of here."

"What did the paper say about the gold rush?" Doris questioned. "Is it happening near Skagway?"

"No, the gold is much farther north. However, Skagway is the stopping-off point for northbound ships. The paper said the two towns are hardly more than tent cities, but that they are sure to grow with the popularity of the routes they offer. I remember mother's letters saying there was little more than a trading post and a Tlingit Indian village in Dyea and nothing of value in Skagway."

"Your sister stated that the ship they've booked us on will dock in Skagway. Do you suppose there is transportation to Dyea?" Doris questioned.

"I'm sure there must be. Both towns afford a passageway over the mountains and north to the Yukon, but apparently the trail is shorter or better out of Dyea. The papers don't give much information on it, but my deduction from personal accounts would seem to suggest that one route is superior to the other," Karen replied.

"My, my," Doris said, shaking her head. "Such a fuss. Greed. That's all it is, pure and simple."

Karen knew it to be true, but her heart was heavy nevertheless. With so many people vying for positions on the northbound ships, there would be no hope of privacy. On the other hand, with such a crowd they would not be easily remembered. What bothered her most, however, was how they would find her father with thousands of people pouring into the territory on a weekly basis.

"It looks rather frightening," Grace said, turning her pale face to Karen.

Karen smiled and clutched her friend's gloved hand. "Think of it as an adventure," she said. "An adventure that is certainly better than the one planned out for you back in Chicago."

Grace nodded. "I didn't mean to sound ungrateful."

"You didn't," Karen reassured. "Just remember what awaits you back there, and the future can't seem half so frightening. In this case, the evil we know is far worse than any supposed trouble we might conjure to mind."

At least she hoped that was the case, because given her own vivid imagination, Karen could conjure quite a few unwelcome thoughts.

CHAPTER NINE

SAN FRANCISCO, CALIFORNIA

ABOARD HIS SHIP, *Merry Maid,* Peter Colton pulled off his bandana and wiped it over his sweat-soaked hair. The day had been nothing but trouble. First he'd had to deal with torn cargo nets and a broken hoist. Then there was a mix-up of invoices and lack of cargo to load once the nets were replaced. Nothing was going right. In fact, not much had gone right in months.

Retying the scarf around his neck, Peter snugged a blue cap over his damp hair and wondered what he was going to do about getting the hoist repaired. He gave the bill of his cap a quick solid yank to shield the sun from his eyes and squared his broad shoulders. He'd have to reason it through later. Surely an answer would come to him.

"Captain, this message came for you," a scrawny-looking teenager announced. He thrust a piece of paper into Peter's hands before heading back to his original task.

" 'Come home at once,' " Peter read aloud. The script was clearly his father's handwriting. Fearful that something worse than a broken net had befallen his family, Peter barked out orders to his men, then hurried in the direction of home.

At nearly twenty-seven years of age, some thought it rather strange that he should still live at home with his father, mother, and younger sister, Miranda. But in truth, with the shipping business he was so often away that he thought it completely unreasonable to consider marriage and a home of his own. Not that he didn't long for a wife at times. There were always quiet moments when Peter silently wished for a companion with whom to share his ambitions and dreams. There were even moments of longing for the passionate touch of someone he could love. But he always put such notions aside. The shipping business was failing. His father's lack of direction and interest had cost them dearly. Bringing a woman into his life at this point would only complicate matters.

Besides, women were of a queer state of mind these days. They were more outspoken and demanding—so unlike his demure little mother who lived to serve her husband and children. So unlike his sister who, at four years his junior, worshiped the ground he walked on and sought him without fail for advice. In fact, his entire family looked to him for advice and wisdom. Even his father recognized that Peter had a certain gift for working a matter through to a more positive benefit and often yielded his own authority to Peter. That kind of adoration was hard to find in anyone, much less a wife.

Hiking up the dock to the embarcadero, Peter hailed a ride with a passing freighter and jumped off several minutes later. He was still a good six blocks from his family's three-story home, but he crossed the distance in brisk strides. He tried not to worry. The note did not necessarily denote a problem. Knowing his family's high regard for his opinion, they might just as well need him to make the final choice in some purchase. He breathed a little easier, sure it was nothing worth fretting over.

His home came into view. Sandwiched between and connected side by side with other town houses, the Colton home was not anything to brag about. It was clean and well kept by the women who loved it, but Peter knew there were repairs that desperately needed to be made. A broken step, a cracked window, and a desperate need for paint and a new roof were all listed in a ledger Peter kept. These, along with a dozen other minor problems, were enough to keep Peter on the ship as much as possible. There was no money to see to the upkeep of their home, and he hated that his family should have to live in such disrepair. But like the problems of his ship, Peter buried his concern in order to focus on the matter at hand.

Bounding up the front steps two at a time, Peter pulled open the screen door and called out, "Father! I'm here!"

Ephraim Colton, a wiry and weathered fellow in his fifties, appeared at the end of the hall. "We've gathered in the music room, Peter. Miranda was keeping us entertained while we waited to share the news."

"Good news or bad?" Peter questioned, tossing his cap aside.

"Good. Come and hear for yourself," he said, beckoning Peter to come quickly.

Peter nodded. His father's spirits seemed considerably lifted since their earlier talk at breakfast. In fact, he looked as if he could break into a jig at any moment.

Glancing at his sister, Peter took up a straight-backed chair and sat. Miranda, ever prim and properly attired, grinned and nodded at Peter as if to suggest he was in for a treat. Easing against the chair, he looked back to his father. "So tell me everything."

"Oh, Peter, it is the very best of news," his mother, Amelia, stated before her husband could take the letter from her hands. "Indeed it has made us all very happy."

"So tell me and let me share in your happiness."

"The letter is from our good friend Martin Paxton. He's been spending time in Chicago these past two months," Ephraim told his son. "While there, he's benefited from the news of the gold rush and wishes to help us benefit as well."

Now Peter's interest was captured. "In what way?"

"He wants to hire us to take freight to Skagway. With folks making their way north, Martin sees the profit of selling goods. He wants to give it a trial run and if the money is good, he will continue to invest with us. He's wired money to the bank here in San Francisco and told me to use it as I wish to get the ships up and running."

"Isn't Mr. Paxton generous to offer us such a commission?" his mother said with obvious adoration.

"What sort of interest is he charging us?" Peter asked quickly, as if to cast suspicion on the generosity of Mr. Paxton.

His father looked confused. "No interest. This isn't really a loan in full. The money is there for our use, true enough. But we will be purchasing supplies for Mr. Paxton's store and moving them north. We can take a reasonable shipping fee and take on passengers as well—if we choose."

"Sounds most agreeable," Peter replied, thinking of what it could mean for the family.

"Son, what are your views on this push to the north? Apparently there are more willing souls to head north than there are ships to crate them. Shall we join in this rush?"

"In truth, Father, I've considered this very thing," Peter admitted. "Seems like good money for minimal work, especially if we haul passengers without extending a lot of fancy services. Charge a fair price, but offer nothing more than two meals a day and shared quarters. Out of Seattle and with good weather, it would take no more than five days to reach Skagway."

"But I thought the most coveted route would go north around Nome and up the Yukon River," his father said.

Peter was surprised his father had become interested enough to remember these details. Even the excitement of easy gold had never been enough to turn his father's head.

"It's true," Peter began. "Many of the lines are offering service to the Yukon via an all-water route. But there are just as many who are dumping loads of passengers and goods off at the towns of Skagway and Dyea. I was talking to the captain of the *Florence Marie*, and he told me about the passageway and the harbors there. Neither town has much in the way of a dock, but that will soon change. They generally anchor offshore and use barges to take the goods and people to awaiting wagons. He assures me plans are already in the making for proper docks."

"And you think it would be better to bring folks into this Skagway rather than take the Yukon River route and deliver them to their destination of Dawson City?"

Peter nodded. "Much shorter time and less trouble; thus, we could charge customers less. I could make several trips a month and see immediate results. The Yukon route would take months, and frankly, without extensive repairs I doubt either *Merry Maid* or your *Summer Song* could withstand the harsh conditions."

"Aye, *Summer Song* would need work, that's to be sure. But

what of the trip to Skagway. She'll need work for that as well."

Peter considered the situation for a moment. "My suggestion is to take Mr. Paxton up on his offer, but to advise him that certain repairs and alterations will have to be made up front before we can proceed."

"But that might well result in him canceling his plans," Ephraim said. The worried look on his face spoke more than his words.

"If Mr. Paxton is the friend you claim him to be, he would not want you or me to risk our lives. In addition, he'd want to know his cargo was safe."

"Aye. I'll get a telegram off to him straightaway. But what of the alterations and repairs?"

"Yes, Peter, is there anything we can do to help?" Miranda asked.

Peter looked to the eager expressions of his sister and mother. "I can get Jim Goodson down to look over the accommodations on the *Merry Maid*. He can work miracles, and if there are funds to pay for them, Jim is the one I'd trust to do the work."

"Do you suppose he would have time to get right to it? Time is of the utmost importance," Ephraim replied.

"I'll clean up and go to see Jim. Meanwhile, Father, you must arrange for the goods Mr. Paxton wants shipped. I'm supposing he sent you a list?"

"Aye," Ephraim replied. "I can get to it after sending the post. We should make certain he wants us to continue despite the need for repair work."

"Very well. If his reply is positive, we will need to act fast. There is always the possibility that in the midst of this gold madness supplies will be unavailable. I would hate to disappoint such a generous man." Peter looked to his mother and sister. "As for you two, if you wish to be of the utmost help, assist me in planning for the sleeping arrangements. We'll need blankets and sheets, pillows and such."

"Of course," Amelia Colton replied, nodding. "We can see to all of that."

For the first time in months, Peter felt truly encouraged. "Good. Then let's get to work!"

Hours later after arranging with Jim Goodson for several alterations to the *Merry Maid*, Peter headed home. He'd decided it was in their best interest to get Jim right on the job. If Paxton wouldn't advance them the money, Jim was a good enough friend to wait until Peter could return. *One run,* Peter thought, *one run is all I need to make enough to pay off Jim.* Then he could see to their debts and get both ships properly fitted.

He hated that *Summer Song* and *Merry Maid* had suffered such wear over the years. It reflected poorly on him. He wanted nothing more than to show his father that he was fully capable of seeing to the needs of their family, and yet they were hopelessly in debt and perilously close to bankruptcy. Paxton's offer couldn't have come at a better time, and yet Peter had to fight back feelings of inadequacy.

"I should have figured a way out," he muttered to himself. He kicked an empty can out of the way and watched as the wind picked up the game and sent the object clattering down the road.

"If only Father would have—" He stopped himself in mid-sentence. He wouldn't bad-mouth his father. Ephraim Colton was simply not the best of businessmen. He'd made an adequate living for his family. Peter could not fault him for holding steady rather than pushing for great wealth. Neither could he fault his father for the depression that had robbed the shipping industry and everyone else of their well-being.

Merry Maid and *Summer Song* had been fairly new when his father had taken them on. They were small, classy new steamers with sail capabilities that made them both economical and efficient. The elder Colton had invested heavily, mortgaging everything he had and throwing in all his savings, which at that time had been considerable due to a family inheritance. But twenty years and a depression later, Peter could hardly find a way to keep their heads above the debt.

It was quite late by the time he reached the house, and Peter knew his family would already be asleep. Slipping quietly up the steps, he paused at the top and without thinking much about what he was doing, he sat down to contemplate their new situation.

The past months had weighed heavily on Peter, and he had worried over what they would do and how they would manage to keep in business. The gold rush news had brought a fury of activity to the bay area, but Peter had felt too cautious to simply jump in with both feet. It wasn't a lack of desire that had kept him homebound, but rather a measure of respect for his less-adventurous father. Ephraim Colton took things at a much slower speed these days. His father had suffered the past ten years, fretting and worrying about poor decisions. It had taken the spirit out of him. For as long as Peter could remember, he had known the business to be in trouble. Living in the west had seemed like Ephraim's dream come true, but the life here had been harder than he had anticipated, and his worries over his wife and children had caused him to change his thinking. He had once told Peter that nothing grieved him more than the thought of leaving a penniless widow behind to raise two children on her own. When a modest inheritance had come to Ephraim, he saw it as his ability to ensure his family's needs. His choices, however, hadn't been the wisest. The ships he'd purchased were costly and the resulting business transactions were not to the family's advantage.

With a sigh, Peter looked out past the streets and down over the hilly landscape to the bay. He could just barely make out the water—inky black but glistening in the moonlight. Yet he could see the ships' masts rising up like apparitions from a life forgotten. Sailing was not as popular as steam these days, and while *Merry Maid* and *Summer Song* were fitted for both, Peter still held a passion for a ship dressed in full sail.

He reflected once again on the day's events and realized that at just the moment they had needed it most, fate had intervened to give them an answer. Some might have said it was a divine intervention, but Peter found religious nonsense to be wearisome. There was no doubt a God in heaven, but Peter believed God must expect more of man than blind faith in a Savior. There had to be many people who walked the earth and did more than their share to aid and comfort the people around them. No doubt there were more ways to please God than merely accept faith in a solitary man who had walked the earth so many hundreds of years ago. Why would a God of infinite resources rely upon only one Savior for His world?

Smiling to himself, Peter felt a revival in his spirit. His family believed him to be fully capable of leading them into the next century. He wouldn't let them down now that he himself could see a way out.

Paxton's money was just the thing they needed. There had been no hope of taking out further loans against the ships or the house. Peter saw the mounting debt and lack of business and fretted that he'd never see Colton Shipping on solid ground. He worried that his family would see him as less than capable in ascertaining the proper business plan. The last thing Peter wanted to do was to disappoint his family.

The gold rush will be our deliverance, he now told himself. *There is more than one way to make a fortune from this adventure.*

Hearing the door open behind him, Peter turned. Miranda stood peering out. "I thought I saw you coming up the walk," she said softly.

Peter got to his feet. "I was just enjoying the evening air."

"May I join you for a moment? I have something to discuss."

"Wouldn't you be more comfortable inside?"

Miranda slipped out the door and pulled her shawl tight around her long, flowing nightgown. "No, I think the evening perfectly lovely, and since it is rather late, no one will see me here."

The breeze blew her long brown hair away from her face, and in the moonlight Peter could see the questioning look in her expression. "So you have something of great importance to discuss? Come sit with me."

Miranda joined him and together they sat down on the top step. "I wanted your opinion on a suitor. Well, a gentleman who would like very much to be my suitor."

"Who is this man?"

"Mr. Plimpton."

Peter thought for a moment. "The man who owns the grocery two blocks down?"

Miranda nodded. "Yes. He attends our church, and last week he asked me if I would consider walking out with him."

"And what did you tell him?"

Miranda smiled and reached for her brother's arm. Squeezing him gently, she replied, "I told him that my father and brother would have to be consulted."

"And how did he take this news?"

She frowned. "Well, not as I would have liked. He suggested that in this modern age it was hardly necessary for a woman to consult her family before giving her heart."

Peter bristled. "And your reply to that?"

"I was quite taken aback. I had heard other women talk thusly, but never a man."

"He doesn't sound like much of a man to me," Peter replied. "Not if he's suggesting an innocent young woman need not consult with her elders—her male elders—for proper direction."

"I felt certain you would see it that way," Miranda said, sounding a little disappointed.

Peter did not miss the tone in her voice. "Do you really wish to spend time with a man who would have so little regard and concern for your safety? A man who obviously would not find it necessary to take charge of your needs in a traditional manner, but rather would leave you to fend for yourself?"

She quickly shook her head and again squeezed his forearm. "Oh, Peter, it's not that. It's just that I'm nearly twenty-three. And I've already been engaged once and that turned out so poorly that I do not even wish to remember it."

"That is because you failed to bring it to me prior to agreeing to marry that cad. It's to your benefit that we found him out before you were legally bound. A divorced man would never be an acceptable mate. Much less a man twice divorced." Peter had offered to pay the man in order to send him packing and leave the naïve eighteen-year-old Miranda behind. It took less than half of what Peter had been willing to spend, and the scoundrel had disappeared without so much as a letter of explanation.

"I know," Miranda said wistfully, "but I long to marry and have a family of my own. I know there are good men out there—somewhere." She gazed off across the valley and out to the harbor. "I used to pretend when I was little that one day a man would come to me from the sea. He would have to be a sailor, of course, because Papa was a sailor. I used to sit and imagine that he would be a great ship's captain and that he would be tall and handsome like Papa." She paused and shook her head. "Such silly dreams."

Peter felt sorry for her, recognizing the longing in her voice that was so evident. He hoped a suitable match could be made soon; otherwise she might very well sink into a mire of sadness and regret.

"Not silly at all," Peter said encouragingly. "I promise that when this gold rush nonsense is settled, I shall pursue the matter of finding a suitor for you. There are indeed good men out there, both on the sea and off. I will prove it to you when time permits."

Miranda nodded. "I trust you to do right by me. You are so wise, Peter. You always see a thing for exactly what it is."

"I try to keep informed so that my family might not be caught unaware. You mean the world to me, little sister. You and Mother and Father. I will not see harm come to any of you."

"We are fortunate to have you, Peter. I know there are perils in making the wrong choices. I have friends who are so miserably matched that their hearts will forever be broken. I do not wish to be one of their number."

He smiled, feeling completely assured that he was doing the right thing. "You have put your trust in the right place," he told her. "I will never let you down."

CHAPTER TEN

AFTER THREE WEEKS in the cramped quarters of her sister's home, Karen was more than ready to negotiate with anyone who had a boat in order to get out of Seattle. The town itself was an absolute madhouse, but sharing space with five rowdy nieces and nephews, as well as a disgruntled sister and brother-in-law, made for an even more unsettling scene.

Willamina, nearly ten years Karen's senior, was not at all pleased to learn of her baby sister's desire to go north. Especially in light of the current run for gold.

"Father would never want to see you subjected to such people as you will find on your trip to Skagway. Such hoodlums and scalawags are not to be equaled. Why, just trying to go to the general store down the street here is like being thrust into a war zone," Willamina had declared. She had droned on for hours, suggesting that the sensible thing to do was for

Karen and Aunt Doris to take Grace and go back to their home.

But Karen couldn't go back. Even if Grace relented to her father's wishes and Aunt Doris grew too weary, Karen couldn't go back. With each passing day she longed for her father's company—longed, too, for a place she'd never before set eyes on. She had reread the letters that had been sent to her prior to her mother's death. How she missed her mother! Each letter was like a precious gem, rich with a wealth of information and tender affirmations.

Now, as Karen waited with Grace and Doris in the outer suite of some sea captain's room, she longed only for a quiet fire and solitude in which to read her letters once again. Instead, she found herself fashionably dressed in her navy walking suit with a straw and cloth bonnet she had never cared for, waiting on a man who seemed to have no idea of the time. Reaching up her hand, she wondered if she looked as misplaced as she felt.

The door to the adjoining room opened to reveal a girl with dark hair and eyes. Her dress was of a well-worn red gingham that came about four inches higher than fashion dictated. No doubt the child had grown some in height, but given their look of poverty, they probably couldn't afford to remedy the situation.

Behind her stood a boy probably somewhere in his middle teen years. With a wild tousle of golden brown hair, he stared at Karen with eyes that seemed hollow and lost. His dirty white cambric shirt was tucked into equally dirty jeans, and his boots sported a hole from leather so dried and marred that Karen wondered that he could even walk in them.

The girl stumbled as she reached the door, and Karen watched as the boy gently took hold of her to keep her from falling. The girl looked up at him with a gaze of adoration and appreciation. He patted her shoulder as if to set her back on her way but said nothing. They didn't look much alike, but the obvious protective nature of the boy for the girl led Karen to believe them to be siblings.

Turning back, Karen watched as two men shook hands. The bearded, dark-headed man, dressed little better than the boy, quickly joined his children.

"Let's go. We'll have to hurry to get everything we need for the trip," he told them.

Karen only realized she was staring when the man turned to her and nodded in a brief, almost matter-of-fact manner. She returned the nod, then dismissing any further contact, quickly turned her attention to the other man. He stood at least six feet in height, with broad shoulders and a lean waist. He had attired himself rather casually for a man of business. Truth be told, he was nearly underdressed for any occasion, yet where the other man and his children had been shoddy, he could be better described as careless in his fashion. His simple white shirt, sporting the newly popular turned-down collar, was unbuttoned at the neck to reveal just a hint of tawny gold chest hair. It was positively scandalous. His navy slacks were tucked into black knee boots and an unbuttoned vest of matching navy serge hung open as if to suggest the man had been disrupted in his morning toiletries.

"I'm Captain Peter Colton," the man boomed out the words authoritatively. "And you are?" He spoke particularly to Doris, much to Karen's relief. She had no desire to focus any more attention on this man than absolutely necessary.

"I'm Miss Pierce. My nephew by marriage arranged passage for us several weeks ago. I believe he told you we'd be coming by."

Colton nodded. "Come and join me." He looked past Doris to Karen and then to Grace. His attention lingered on Grace. "Are these your daughters?"

"Mercy, no," the woman replied. "I told you I am *Miss* Pierce. I am unmarried. This is my niece Miss Karen Pierce and her friend Miss Hawkins."

The captain frowned. "Where are your menfolk? Why are they not here? I thought you were to be accompanied by the gentleman who arranged this passage."

"No, my nephew merely booked passage for us in our absence. We had heard it was nearly impossible to arrange transportation to Skagway and wired ahead that he might secure us a position."

The captain sighed. "I'm not used to dealing with women and would prefer to talk to someone in authority over you."

Karen found his attitude unacceptable. "My father is already in Skagway, Captain, but at my age I'm quite used to fending for myself. My suggestion is that we find some middle ground on which we can deal respectably with one another. We are neither addlepated nor incapable of caring for our own affairs. My aunt and I have attended and graduated from one of the finest women's colleges in the country, and I feel confident we can fully understand and comprehend any contractual arrangements you wish to discuss."

Colton studied Karen for a moment, causing her to blush when his gaze traveled the full length of her and returned to settle on her face. "I can see you'll be nothing but trouble."

"How dare you!" Karen declared. "You are most insufferable."

"As are you," he countered under his breath.

Karen's eyes widened at this, but it was Doris who sought to intercede and smooth things over. "Captain, we are all a bit testy and tired. We have been traveling now for some time and at present do not have calming accommodations."

He smiled. "I seriously doubt there are calming accommodations in Seattle." Just as quickly as the smile had appeared, it disappeared and he continued. "I know there are many women joining the throngs headed north, but I'm not sure I'm comfortable with having you aboard my ship. You are unescorted and a danger."

Karen opened her mouth to protest, but Doris again moved to settle the situation. "I assure you, Captain, we are quite capable as God has made us so in the absence of reliable men. We will not be a bother or trouble you overmuch. We only ask for a room and meals, and we're willing to pay handsomely."

Karen watched as the sea captain rubbed a hand across his clean-shaven chin and cast another quick glance at the silent figure of Grace. "And what of you, miss? Have you a comment to make on your behalf?"

Grace smiled. "I am certain you are a reasonable man, Captain Colton. We are reasonable women. There must surely be a meeting of our minds somewhere within the confines of this predicament."

He smiled as if amused by her gentle spirit. Karen wanted to slap the smug expression off his face and demand that he give them passage. She was tired and grumpy, just as Aunt Doris had proposed, but the last thing she wanted to do was watch some seafaring oaf with a mean temper make moon eyes at her young friend. Feeling rather protective, Karen moved to position herself between Colton and Grace. She heard the captain's man arguing in the hallway with hopeful passengers. Realizing that she would have to soften her approach, Karen drew a deep breath and prayed for strength.

"So might we be allowed to continue our journey, Captain?" she forced herself to question in a calm and collected manner.

"I don't like the idea of taking unescorted women north, unless of course they are women who thrive on the arrangement of being unaccompanied for the purpose of their manner of employment. You aren't one of them, are you?" he questioned, giving Karen a look that provoked her spirit to anger.

Holding her temper, Karen replied, "You know very well we are not of that working class. We are only asking to take our place using the passage we have booked and paid for. We are not asking for you to be responsible for us."

"I am responsible for anything and anyone who boards and travels upon my ship," Colton replied. "And I do not like to take on unescorted women." He held up his hand as Karen opened her mouth to comment. "However," Colton continued, "since you are making your way to your father and will have the benefit of male protection once you have reached Skagway, I am more inclined to allow you to accompany us."

How very gracious of you, Karen thought sarcastically. She hated this man's condescending tone. Here it was, nearly the twentieth century, and he was acting as though they hadn't a brain or lick of sense among the three of them. She nearly smiled at the thought. Maybe they did lack sense. After all, here they were on the run from a powerful man who would no doubt strike out in some form of pursuit. Karen wasn't foolish enough to believe for a single moment that Martin Paxton would just leave off with his demands after finding out that Grace was gone. No, he'd follow them or at least break himself trying.

Then, too, there was the entire issue of having no idea

whether or not her father was still alive. And if Wilmont Pierce was still alive—where could he be found?

"I'll take you. I have a single cabin left," Captain Colton said, motioning the women to his table in the inner room.

All three followed, rather stunned by his announcement. Karen watched him closely. He was a very strange man indeed.

"You will have to share this cabin and do the best you can. There are two bunks with four beds available. Should I acquire another female passenger, I will be obliged to give her passage and the remaining bed. Take it or leave it." He looked at them hard as if to gauge their acceptance of this arrangement.

"We'll take it, of course, Captain Colton," Doris announced. "And should there be a need to share our cabin, we will do so quite willingly. I assure you, we'll be no trouble at all."

Peter Colton looked at all three women, then fixed his gaze on Karen. "I would not deem to call you a liar, miss, but in this case I will reserve judgment on the matter until time has proved the truth one way or the other."

Karen lifted her chin defiantly and narrowed her eyes. A thousand retorts ran through her mind, but she remained stiff and silent. There was no way this rogue was going to get the better of her.

Concluding his dealings with the three women, Peter announced that he would take no further appointments until after lunch. He closed the door of his suite and stretched out in utter exhaustion. What a day it had been!

He thought back to the trio of women and chuckled in spite of himself. There before him had been his complete summary of women. The younger dark-headed woman with her mild spirit and gentle manner. The older spinster with her no-nonsense approach and logical reasoning. No doubt she could take care of herself as well as any man could. Then there was the other woman. Miss Karen Pierce. Her spirit defied definition. Peter frowned. She was everything he had come to despise in women of the age. Self-assured, combative, and temperamental, Miss Pierce was the epitome of the modern women's movement. No doubt she had never married, and without explanation Peter was certain she had contentedly made that choice based on her own self-sufficiency and determination to prove herself. Not that he was generally so judgmental, but frankly, the woman screamed such declarations in her very mannerisms.

But he had to admit she was beautiful. What little he could see of her light reddish-gold hair struck him as appealing. Her eyes, blue as the sea on a clear day, blazed with a passion for life that promised some excitement for those who beheld them. They were so very different from the large brown eyes of Miss Hawkins. Those eyes reminded him of a frightened doe—so big with wonder and curiosity. She comported herself as a proper woman should. Her silent reverence and gentle manner were an attraction to Peter. He couldn't help but wonder at her age and her people. Why was she here? The Pierce women were heading north to family, but not so Miss Hawkins.

He pondered the matter for several minutes, then smiled. Perhaps he would have a moment to find out on their journey north. Perhaps he could get to know Miss Hawkins better and see whether her actions were genuine.

Peter picked up the log where he'd just registered his newest passengers. Pointing his finger to the place where Miss

Hawkins had signed, he found all the information he was looking for. Her name was Grace. A perfectly suitable name for such a lovely woman. And she was twenty years old. A perfectly suitable age for a twenty-six-year-old sea captain.

The thought rather startled Peter. He'd given no serious thought to women in some time. After all, the business had been in trouble and he had had nothing of his own to offer a wife. Grace's lovely image suddenly caused him to rethink his circumstances, and that was most frightening. Shaking off the thoughts, Peter was determined to think on the woman no more. At least that was his intention.

CHAPTER ELEVEN

MARTIN PAXTON cooled his heels in the Hawkinses' small front parlor. His patience at an end, Paxton tried to reason what his next step would be. If he pushed too hard, Frederick Hawkins would break and be of little use to him. However, if he didn't push hard enough, the man would simply string him along. The entire matter was quite irritating, but certainly no more so than the appearance of the parlor.

Fashioned to bear a flavor of the Orient, the walls had been papered in dark red with gold trim. Added to this, an artist had created a mural of silhouetted figures standing upon a curved bridge. The setting suggested a garden scene; the figures appeared to be lovers.

To accent the decorated walls, expensive oriental rugs were placed upon the dark wood floors. The wood trim along the doors and windows had been painted black and several large decorative chests had been placed amid dark walnut furniture to further set the mood. It all appeared quite fashionable—the smart sort of room a socially conscious family might promote. The kind of room Martin Paxton had no patience or appreciation for.

"We're sorry for having kept you waiting," Myrtle Hawkins announced as she slid back the double doors and entered the room. She refused to make eye contact and Frederick Hawkins cowered behind his wife, appearing ill at ease. Martin immediately sensed there to be trouble.

"Where is Miss Hawkins?" he asked, looking beyond the couple to the open hallway.

"I'm afraid Grace still has not returned," Myrtle explained.

Martin was livid. For over three weeks they had given him one excuse after another. First, Grace was to have been taken ill and quarantined as the doctor attempted to figure out what the problem might be. Next it was suggested that Grace needed to recuperate in the mountains where the drier climate might see her more rapidly healed.

"I've had all I'm going to stand for," Martin announced. "I warned you, Hawkins, what would happen if you failed to come through on this. You owe me a great deal of money, and I'm not a patient man."

Frederick Hawkins took out a large handkerchief and wiped his sweat-drenched forehead. "She has a mind of her own. I tried to tell you that when you insisted on Grace being a part of the arrangement."

"Grace is really rather young," Myrtle began.

"She's twenty years old. Most women are married by this age," Paxton retorted. He tried to keep his anger under control.

"Can't we all talk reasonably about this?" Myrtle suggested. "I'm sure we can come up with an acceptable alternative."

Martin wanted to slap the foolish woman. "And I am equally certain we cannot. I won't stand for being double-crossed."

At this, Myrtle crossed the room to a black lacquered cabinet. Opening the intricately designed doors, she reached inside and returned with a large black velvet case. "I assure you, Mr. Paxton, no one is trying to double-cross you. We apologize for our daughter's actions, but we can't very well force her to marry you when she's not even here." She placed the case on the table beside Paxton and opened it.

Gleaming up from a bed of velvet, Paxton found an elaborate diamond and emerald necklace, complete with bracelet and earrings to match.

"What do you think you're doing, Mrs. Hawkins?" Frederick asked his wife. "I've already told you Paxton isn't interested in your baubles."

Paxton studied the flawless gems for several moments before reaching over to snap the case shut. "Your husband is right. I'm not interested in your baubles."

"I assure you, Mr. Paxton, they are worth a great deal of money. I have more and you could easily sell them to meet whatever debt my husband owes."

"You're trying to back out of our arrangement. You are trying to dupe me," Paxton said sternly. His tone suggested he was reprimanding children. "I do not take kindly to being dealt with in this manner."

He casually reached inside his coat pocket and took out a cigar. Mindless of etiquette, he snipped the end and let the tip fall to the expensive carpet. Fishing a match from his pocket, Martin reached over to strike it on one of the artfully designed cases. Myrtle gasped as he lit his cigar. Taking several long draws of air to ensure the tip was lit, Paxton finally blew out the match and tossed it aside. Mrs. Hawkins' gaze followed the match all the way to the ground. "I warned you, Hawkins."

The older man began to pale. The reaction was not lost on Paxton. He leaned back casually against the doorway and eyed his adversary carefully. "You know what this means."

"I assure you that Grace simply needs time. Isn't that right, Mrs. Hawkins?" Frederick said, turning a pleading expression on his wife. "She needs time and consideration. She's led a very sheltered life."

"Regardless, she's still under your authority, not yet twenty-one. I fail to see why controlling her is such a difficult task. Then again, given the man I'm dealing with, perhaps it's not so difficult to understand."

Myrtle looked first to her husband and then to Paxton. "I fail to see why the jewels won't settle this between you." The expression of confusion lingered, even as she voiced her concern.

"The matter will not be settled because your husband fails to yield to my demands."

"Unreasonable demands," Myrtle Hawkins replied, squaring her shoulders.

Martin resented the woman's interference in the matter but knew Frederick Hawkins was perilously close to breaking. He had seen the man cower in fear as Martin's plan was laid out before him. He had watched the man slowly succumb to fear and anguish with every suggestion or requirement Martin had placed upon him. He was weak, and Paxton hated him for it.

"My dear madam, I fail to understand why you are even a

part of this conversation. I have conducted business with your husband and do not mean to begin a new term with you."

He drew leisurely on the cigar and blew out a great puff of smoke before flicking ashes onto the carpet. The look of horror in the eyes of his hostess only served to urge him on. Without warning, he tossed the cigar to the floor and ground it out beneath his boot. It was exactly as he wished to ground out the very memory of Frederick Hawkins—a complete eradication.

"Neither of you seem to understand the severity of this situation, so let me enlighten you. I mean to see our businesses joined through my marriage to your daughter. I mean to see your assets as my own. Your status in Chicago will be negated by my own higher, more influential position." He picked up the jewel case and flung it across the room, causing both Frederick and Myrtle to take a step back in fear. "I will not settle merely for baubles and trinkets. Grace is the price. I expect for you to have her delivered to me within the week."

He paused and eyed them both with a stare that drew upon all his hatred. "If you should either one believe me incapable of rendering your estate and circumstances to complete ruin, then by all means fail to meet this requirement."

Myrtle seemed to get her wind back. "I will never allow my daughter to marry you. You haven't the common decency of a true gentleman to respect a lady's lack of interest. Grace wants no part of you and I'm glad I helped her to escape!"

"Myrtle! Please be silent!" Frederick declared.

"Let her speak," Paxton said rather smugly. "This isn't anything I haven't already figured out. What I fail to understand is how you pulled the entire matter off right under my nose and the noses of my surveillance crew."

Frederick appeared stunned. "You had my daughter watched?"

"I have had you all watched," Paxton replied. "I will continue to have you watched. I will arrange for your mail to be gone through and I will study your every move, if necessary. I will find Grace, and you had better pray that when I do, I'm still of a mind to marry her."

"Never!" Myrtle cried. "I'll never agree to you marrying my child."

"Madam, marriage is the better alternative, believe me. I could do many things to discredit and disgrace this family. Just remember that and remember that I will find your daughter. You may count on it."

He walked to the front door where the butler stood stoically as if he'd not overheard the entire argument. "My hat!" Paxton demanded.

The man nodded and retrieved the black felt from the receiving table. Paxton turned only long enough to reiterate his demand. "One week. If she's not here in that time and standing with me to take her vows, I will bring you to the ground!"

Myrtle Hawkins felt the racing of her heart and actually feared she might collapse at any given moment. She could scarcely draw a breath after encountering Martin Paxton's rage. She looked to her ashen-faced husband and watched him as he clutched his chest.

"Frederick? Are you all right?"

"Leave me. I am well enough to know that if you do not rectify this situation immediately and bring Grace home, you will live to regret it. I, on the other hand, most likely will not."

"Please, Frederick," she pleaded. "Please tell me what this is all about. Tell me why you would rather give your daughter over to this man than face the loss of everything else."

He looked at her with such an expression of hopelessness that Myrtle worried he might indeed drop dead where he stood. "I cannot explain."

"Then I cannot contact Grace," Myrtle said sadly. "We may both be dead tomorrow, but I will not bring that child back to a life of brutal bondage with a man who so clearly holds no love for her. Had Martin Paxton voiced even a moderate amount of kindness and respect, I might well have gone along with you on this, but as it stands, I see him for the cruel monster he really is."

"Do not toy with him," Frederick pleaded. "He holds the ability to rob us of every happiness."

Myrtle shook her head. "He has already done that. He has driven our Grace away from us. We might never see her again, and we will have no one to blame but Martin Paxton and our own foolishness."

Paxton shook with fury as he threw his hat and coat across the room. Cursing, he poured himself a drink and tossed it back as if it could quench the fire that raged inside him.

How dare Frederick Hawkins stand up to him—knowing that Martin could and would crush him for his inability to meet the demands placed upon him? Pouring another drink, Martin paced the confines of his suite and tried to figure out what he would do next. Hawkins would suffer for this. So would his wife. They would feel the pinch as Martin began the systematic collection of all they held dear. By the time Chicago figured out what had happened, the Hawkins name would lay smoldering in ashes, just like part of the town had so many years ago after the great fire.

Then, when he finally had defeated them collectively as a family, he would destroy that bond between members by giving Myrtle the full knowledge of why he had come and why he held the power he did over her husband. With that, he would forever separate their close family, sending Myrtle one direction and Grace in another. Frederick would be left to perish in the mire of his own making. The thought left Martin with a smugly satisfying feeling.

"I will destroy your family as you did mine," he promised to the empty air.

Part Two

AUGUST-NOVEMBER 1897

But where shall wisdom be found?
And where is the place of understanding?
Man knoweth not the price thereof;
neither is it found
in the land of the living.
The depth saith, It is not in me:
and the sea saith, It is not with me.
It cannot be gotten for gold,
neither shall silver be weighed
for the price thereof.

JOB 28:12–15

CHAPTER TWELVE

"WE WILL BE UNDERWAY within the hour," Peter Colton explained to the three women. "I will lay out the rules for you so that there will be no question of them in the days to come. The first and most important rule is that I am in command of this vessel and you must heed my every demand."

Karen eyed the captain in irritation but said nothing. Grace was glad that her friend had taken the route of silence. It was frustrating enough to see that these two people clearly angered each other, but Grace's head was already hurting and she had no desire to listen to an argument.

"Number two," Colton continued, "you will remain inside your cabin with the door locked. The only exception to this is for the purpose of allowing your meals to be brought inside."

"And what are we to do about personal needs, Captain?"

Karen questioned sarcastically. "Surely we will be allowed access to a bathing room."

"There are pots under the beds for the obvious," he replied, "but there are no baths on this ship. The trip lasts but five days in good weather and the need for such luxury is quite unnecessary."

"I should have guessed. You smell as if you haven't had benefit of such a feature in some time."

Doris reached out and pulled Karen back a pace. "We understand, Captain, that these are your instructions. But might you humor us and explain why these regulations are necessary?"

Peter scowled and fixed his gaze on Karen. "This ship is loaded past maximum safety with men bound for the Klondike gold fields. They are bored and excited all at the same time. They are confined to a smaller space than even you have been privileged to manage. They will roam this ship at will and, short of causing trouble with my crew, will be allowed that free range for the duration of the trip. For your safety, these rules are put into place. I have no other choice."

"And what of the other women on board? Are you locking them up as well?" Karen asked snidely. "Are we all to be prisoners merely because we wear petticoats?"

Grace could see the captain had reached the end of his patience. "Perhaps we will feel better after some rest," she said, putting her hand on Karen's other arm. With Doris on one side and Grace on the other, it rather looked as if they were holding Karen back. Perhaps they were, for Grace could clearly sense her friend's desire for a verbal boxing match.

"I believe Miss Hawkins is right," Doris said, nodding enthusiastically. "A nap would be a proper thing for all of us."

Grace exchanged a look with Peter and gave him the tiniest smile. He seemed like a nice enough man. Pity that he and Karen had to be so constantly at odds.

To her surprise, the captain's expression softened, and he bowed before her and then nodded to Karen and Doris. "As I said, we will shortly be underway." He took his leave without so much as another word or look. Grace was almost relieved when he closed the door to their very plain cabin.

Releasing her hold on Karen, she wasn't at all surprised when Karen flew to the door and opened it as if to call out some further retort. Pausing, however, she seemed to realize how brazen she'd become. Slamming the door, Karen slid the lock in place.

"Have you ever known such an ill-mannered oaf? I cannot abide that man's company, even in moderation."

"So we've noticed," Doris said, smiling patiently. "He does seem to have an easy time of setting you off."

"It's his entire manner. He believes us to be subservient and incapable of tending to our own welfare. He thinks us scandalous for our unescorted travel—and he called us 'trouble'!"

"No, dear, I believe he called you, in particular, 'trouble,' " Doris replied.

"Exactly. He's hateful and mean-spirited." Karen pulled out her hat pin and jabbed it at the air. "That's what I'd like to give you, Captain Colton."

Grace couldn't help but smile. Her friend's rage at the man was a most uncommon reaction. Generally Karen held her tongue and her temper. She knew what was expected of a lady, and she had been schooled in genteel manners and acceptable decorum. Grace had never seen her overstep those bounds—until now.

"I believe the captain is merely trying to attend to our

safety," Grace said, smoothing down the windblown collar of her brown- and cream-colored afternoon dress.

"And we did not exactly endear ourselves to him with our additional luggage and goods," Doris reminded her.

"Everyone is shipping an exaggerated amount of goods. It's required of them," Karen replied. "Ours should be no different. Besides, I heard it said that one of those women of ill repute was even bringing a sewing machine. How necessary is that?"

"Well, perhaps she's in the process of changing occupations," Doris suggested with a pondering look that made Grace giggle. "Either way, it's not of any further concern. Dear me, five days from now you will never have to lay eyes on the man again."

"Thank the Lord for that," Karen stated, giving her hat a toss to the tiny wooden table.

"We should thank God for a great deal more," Grace interjected. "Did you see the thousands lining the docks, just pleading to be allowed passage? Why, I heard the captain say that some men even jumped off the docks and tried to swim out after the ship and sneak aboard."

"Gold fever will make a man do ridiculous things," Doris agreed. "And yes, we should thank God for our passage and our safety. I believe Captain Colton will work hard to ensure our welfare. He seems a most conscientious young man."

"Well, he gets no such kind word from me," Karen replied. "He's given us a cabin hardly bigger than a wash closet and insisted that it be our cell for the next five days. There is no privacy whatsoever here. A person cannot even tend to their needs without an audience."

"We'll make due," Doris replied. "Mercy, if we can't figure out how to afford ourselves that much consideration, we are not half the women I believe us to be."

"What do you suggest?" Karen questioned. "I mean, just look at this place."

Grace followed the sweep of Karen's arm with her own scrutinizing gaze. It was indeed a small cabin, probably only eight by eight. Two bunks had been built against the wall. One butted up against the other to make an *L* shape. Other than this, the only furnishing was a small crudely fashioned table and two chairs over which a lantern hung to provide their only light. The entire cabin, including the beds, table, and chairs had been whitewashed. Grace supposed it also helped to make the windowless room seem brighter.

At least it appears clean, Grace thought. *We could be stuck in a dirty steerage area where everyone lives atop everyone else.* Here the room might seem understated, but it was their own hiding place.

"There aren't even enough chairs for us to all sit around the table together."

"I suppose that will do away with any plans for a game of cards," Doris teased.

The things they had deemed necessary for the trip had been packed together into two steamer trunks and positioned against the wall. The sight of them gave Grace an idea. "We could use one of the trunks for a third seat. It's very nearly the same height as the chairs and that way we could all eat together."

"I suppose for five days we can endure most anything," Karen muttered. "And as long as we keep the door bolted, we won't have to endure Captain Colton's attention."

"He is a dashing young man," Doris said with a smile.

Grace felt her cheeks flush, for she'd already thought the

same thing. Turning toward the trunk, she hid her face for fear of being questioned.

"Too bad he doesn't have a decent personality to go along with those dashing looks," Karen remarked. "Perhaps God thought giving him both would rob a more deserving man of at least a positive personality."

Grace said nothing, but even hours later when the walls of the cabin began to close in on her, she was still considering Karen's words.

I think him to have a rather nice personality. He's stern, true enough, but there is something about him that appeals to me. Mr. Paxton is stern and demanding as well, but there is a cruelty in his actions that is lacking in Captain Colton's demeanor.

Thinking of Martin Paxton, Grace couldn't help but worry after her parents. Were they safe? Had he hurt them? She tried not to let the thoughts give way to fears, but inevitably images of Paxton had a way of tearing apart her confidence.

Tossing back and forth in the rock-hard berth, Grace finally gave up trying to sleep. Pushing back the covers, she slipped over the side of the berth and climbed down from the upper bunk. Fully clothed for fear of the ship springing a leak and requiring them to make some midnight escape, Grace tiptoed to the door. She had to have some fresh air. Even if she only opened the door for a moment.

Catching her toe against one of the chairs, Grace covered her mouth with her hand to keep from crying out. Pain shot up her leg for a moment, but she ignored it as best she could. She glanced over her shoulders to make certain she hadn't awakened Karen or Doris, but in the darkness, it was impossible to see.

Such blackness, she thought. It was rather like a tomb. The feeling caused the hairs on the back of her neck to prickle.

The stale salt air, combined with the moaning and shifting of the ship, left Grace in an alarming state of discomfort.

Just a little fresh air. That can't possibly hurt anyone. She slid back the lock and opened the door ever so slowly. Dim light flooded the room to her surprise. Outside in the narrow passage a wall fixture had been lit, much to Grace's delight. To her disappointment, however, the air inside the enclosed passageway was just as heavy as that of the cabin. Dare she go up to the deck?

She considered Captain Colton's words of warning—his orders were to be followed under penalty of expulsion. Surely he would understand. Beneath his gruff exterior, he seemed like a reasonable man.

Quietly, she pulled the cabin door closed behind her and decided to risk it. The feeling of being sealed in her own grave was much too great. It didn't help to have the snarling face of Martin Paxton haunting her sleep. The nightmares that concerned him were of no matter to anyone else, but Grace instinctively knew that this man would not give up without a fight. She felt certain inside her heart that he would seek to cause her family great harm.

Just thinking of the man caused Grace's pulse to race. What if he had already exacted his revenge? What if he had ruined her family and they were even now penniless and destitute? Her breathing quickened as she picked up her pace. As if Paxton himself were chasing her, Grace hurried up the steps and flung open the passageway door.

Cold damp air rushed over her face and body. It had a sort of calming effect that caused Grace to lean back against the frame, panting. Closing her eyes, Grace tried to settle her spirit. Prayer seemed difficult.

"Lord, I want to trust you. I want to believe I'm doing the right thing," she whispered.

"What are you doing out here?" Captain Colton's voice growled out, demanding an answer.

Opening her eyes slowly, Grace swallowed the lump of fear in her throat. She could see the displeasure in his face. His jaw was set firm and his eyes narrowed in a menacing way.

"I couldn't breathe," she said softly. "The air was so heavy and the room began to close in on me. I didn't seek to be disobedient. Please don't be angry."

He stepped forward and Grace cowered back, flinching as if he might hit her. Her action stopped him in midstep.

"I won't hurt you, if that's what you think." His expression softened. "I would never strike a woman. Let me escort you out on the deck." He extended his hand and Grace hesitated. "What is it?" he asked softly.

"I don't wish to cause you any trouble. You were so reluctant to take us on board, I won't have it said that I caused your disapproval," Grace replied. "I'll just go back to our cabin."

"Nonsense," he said, reaching for her. His grip was firm but gentle. "I promise not to say a single word about this to anyone. You will not bear any punishment from this on my part."

"I have your word?"

His lips curved into a smile and his eyes fairly sparkled. "You, Miss Hawkins, may have my word."

Grace allowed him to lead her to the deck rail. An invigorating breeze blew across her face and Grace breathed deeply and felt instantly refreshed.

"You are a puzzle to me, Miss Hawkins. I am usually a decent judge of character, but you have me completely stumped. You are nothing like your friend, Miss Pierce."

Grace smiled. "Karen has spent the last ten years as my governess. It's a wonder that I am not more like her. I always admired her spirit and tried to imitate her."

Peter shook his head. "Do not continue with that line of study. It would do you a grave injustice."

"You like her so little?"

"I find her annoying and troublesome."

Grace smiled, for her father had once said the same thing—or nearly so. "She is spirited and driven. Men seem to find that annoying in a woman."

Peter's brow raised. "So have you given yourself to the league of women who believe themselves to be poorly used by men?"

Grace could only think of Martin Paxton and the smile left her face. "Perhaps only by some men."

"Perhaps this is only true for some women," Peter countered.

Grace looked out at the black water, unable to discern much of anything. "I have myself been the victim of cruelty, Captain Colton. I did nothing to premeditate the action, but because I am a woman, I had no say in the matter."

"So you are running away?" he asked, then added, "I don't believe I would have thought you capable of such an action. No doubt your companions have influenced your choice."

"My companions have saved my life."

He turned and the collar of his shirt fluttered in the breeze, widening the opening at the neck. Grace watched in fascination as the wind toyed with his shirt and hair. In spite of the travelers who walked about the ship's deck, she suddenly felt very alone with this man.

"I should go," she said.

"No, stay a bit longer. I must know what you are running from."

Grace wondered if it could hurt to tell him the truth. Surely now that they were on their way to Alaska she could honestly explain her circumstance and not expect him to put her off at the next port. Her heart told her she could trust this man, and there rose up a longing inside of her to talk about her escape.

"I'm afraid you would simply find it unacceptable," she began. "A dishonoring of my father's wishes is where it all begins."

"Oh," he said, leaning casually against the rail. "How so?"

"My father arranged a marriage for me to one of his many business partners. The man was considerably older and I had never met him. When we did meet, I was still troubled by the arrangement but was willing to give it my best."

"I suppose he was ugly and fat?"

"Not at all," Grace replied, shuddering as she remembered the severely handsome face of Martin Paxton.

"Then what caused you to flee?"

A steel band seemed to tighten around Grace's chest, making breathing difficult. She hated even thinking about Paxton and his angry words to her the night of their engagement.

"He was unkind," she said softly, not wishing to go into the details of that event.

"Unkind?" Peter questioned.

He studied her for a moment, then reached out to touch her cheek. She flinched and moved away. He frowned, then a look of understanding came into his eyes. Grace flushed at his expression. He knew.

"He struck you." He said the words matter-of-factly, not expecting any admission on her part. "The brute. What was his supposed justification for hitting you?"

Grace licked her lips, tasting the salty air. She looked once again to the water. "He attempted liberties with me and I struck him first. This angered him and he hit me quite hard. It knocked me down and left a horrid bruise. Afterward, he gripped me tightly and shook me, promising worse if I refused him in any way or ever laid a hand to him again." Her voice broke. "I wanted to do what my father asked of me, but I could not. I could not marry that man."

"But why run away? Surely no one expected you to marry him after he revealed such a violent nature."

"My father apparently owed him. Perhaps in more ways than one. I don't pretend to understand or know why he made the arrangement in the first place, but once he knew how I was treated, I expected him to release me from further obligation."

"But he didn't."

Grace shook her head and reached up to wipe away a tear. She'd tried so hard to be brave about the entire matter. She loved her mother and father and missed them terribly. She could still see her mother's tear-stained face as Grace climbed into the carriage with Karen. She could still feel the panic that rose up inside her as the carriage passed through the back gate and took her away from the home she loved.

"So I have become a part of your little scheme," Peter said, almost good-naturedly.

Grace suddenly realized he could make life difficult for her. "Please, I beg of you. Please do not tell anyone of my passage north."

"I wouldn't," he assured. "I'm quite sorry for what you endured, Miss Hawkins. I would be the last one in the world to see you back in such a predicament. I have a younger sister, and should a man treat her in a similar fashion, I would probably break his neck."

Grace looked up at the captain, feeling he had become an immediate champion to her cause. "Thank you for your understanding. I do apologize again for breaking your rule about remaining in the cabin. It's just that it's so dark there, and with no light and little fresh air, I found myself quite overcome. I'll do my best to see that it doesn't happen again."

"I'm the one who is sorry. I'll do what I can to arrange better quarters for you on the morrow."

"Oh, please don't feel that you must go to any trouble," Grace replied. "I wouldn't wish to see anyone inconvenienced."

He reached out toward her again, this time more slowly. Hesitating before touching her arm, he seemed to ask permission with his eyes. When Grace didn't draw back, he placed his hand atop her forearm.

"I'll escort you back to your cabin. Tomorrow morning I would like to have all three of you as my special guests for breakfast. Do you suppose your companions would agree to this?"

Grace smiled, feeling almost giddy from the closeness of him. "I'm certain I can convince them. After all, it will get us out of that cabin."

He laughed softly. "Good. Then I will send someone to show you the way."

They walked back to the cabin and paused in the dim light of the hallway. Grace thought the captain even more appealing than she had before. His chin was covered with a light stubble and his wind-blown hair seemed hopelessly tousled. His lips were moving as he spoke of some matter, but Grace found herself unable to concentrate. Suddenly her mouth felt dry, and she had no idea what she should say or do.

"Until tomorrow," he said. "Sleep well."

Grace nodded and went quietly into the cabin. Sleep? How could she sleep after such a wonderful moment? Her heart felt lighter than it had in weeks.

"Where have you been?" Karen called out in a hushed voice as Grace climbed back into her bunk.

"Arranging breakfast with the captain," she replied rather coyly.

"What?"

Grace giggled and settled into her berth. "Go to sleep and I shall tell you all about it in the morning."

CHAPTER THIRTEEN

GRACE SLEPT THROUGH the night with nothing but pleasant dreams of her time with Peter Colton to mark the hours. She had surprised herself by realizing the awakening of her heart. Could this be what it was to fall in love? Smiling to herself, she stretched as best she could in the narrow berth and yawned.

"Are you going to tell me what happened last night?" Karen's voice questioned out of the silence.

Grace leaned up on an elbow as Karen managed to light the overhead lantern. With her golden red curls hanging limp to her waist, Karen looked years younger than her matronly thirty.

"I found the cabin closing in on me," Grace said, forcing herself to get up. She climbed down from her bunk and stretched. Aunt Doris moaned and rolled to her side from the bottom of the opposite berth.

"Oh, my dear girls, this is without a doubt the most uncomfortable bed in all of North America."

"I'm sure you are mistaken," Karen replied, "for I am certain my berth holds that honor." She grinned at her aunt's appearance, then laughed aloud. "We all look as though we'd experienced a tornado last night. Sleeping in our clothes, wrestling comfort from beds that refused us comfort." She turned to Grace. "Only Grace appears to have faired well through it all."

"That is because she is younger," Doris declared. "Youth has its advantages."

"I'm not that old," Karen replied.

A knock sounded on the cabin door, and Karen quickly pulled back her hair and tied it with a ribbon. "One moment," she called.

Aunt Doris got up out of the bed, holding a hand to the small of her back. "Oh my, there is no way to make ourselves presentable. Someone's at the door, and here we are looking a fright."

Karen unlocked the door and opened it only a fraction of an inch. "Yes?"

"Captain Colton says I'm to escort you three ladies to breakfast in his quarters."

Karen looked back at Grace before replying. "We'll need a few moments to freshen up."

"Aye. I've fresh water for you," the young man replied.

Karen opened the door a bit wider. Grace could see that the boy couldn't have been more than sixteen. "Here, I'll take it," she said, reaching out for the gray enamel pitcher and galvanized wash bowl. "Give us ten minutes, and we'll be able to join you." The boy nodded and Karen quickly closed the door.

"Well, what a pleasant surprise," Aunt Doris declared. "See there, Karen, our sea captain isn't quite so harsh as you would make him."

Karen placed the pitcher and bowl on the table and eyed Grace carefully. Grace felt her cheeks grow hot under the scrutiny. "What have you to say about this, Grace?"

Shrugging, Grace went to the pitcher and poured water into the bowl. "I say we have less than nine minutes left. You promised the boy we'd be ready."

Dipping her hands into the icy water, Grace splashed it against her face. It was only then that she realized she had no towel. "Oh, bother," she said, then without ceremony, she lifted the hem of her skirt to dab the water around her eyes.

"What are you doing?" Karen questioned. "One night on this ship and you've taken on the manners of a sailor?"

"I can't say that I've ever seen a sailor dry his face with his skirt," Grace said, laughing. "I'm merely doing what you've always taught me. I'm making do with the provisions at hand. I have a feeling we'll be doing a lot of that in the days to come."

Karen eyed her suspiciously. "You've taken on a new attitude. When we left, you were afraid—terrified, in fact. The world and everything around you was a threat to your well-being. What has changed?"

Grace hadn't realized her feelings were so transparent. She shrugged. "I guess the salt air agrees with me."

Aunt Doris took a comb from her bag. "A new attitude could suit us all. We've taken on a big challenge, and we'll need the heart of a lioness to fearlessly march into the days ahead." She combed out her long brown hair, then began braiding it. "I, for one, intend to be prepared for the change."

"As do I," Grace said, smiling. "Now, as for breakfast, I told you I had word from the captain last night that he would like to have us as his guests this morning."

"You spoke to the captain last night?" Doris questioned.

"Yes, she did," Karen answered for Grace. "I heard a noise and awoke to find Grace sneaking back into our room in the middle of the night."

Grace nodded when Doris looked at her in sheer horror. "I did leave the room, but I was not unescorted. I felt the walls closing in on me and the air was so heavy I could scarcely draw a breath. I went up the stairs at the end of the passage, planning only to get some fresh air, but Captain Colton found me there and offered to see me safely to the deck. We spoke on the matter of this cabin and he even said he would try to arrange better accommodations. Then he told me we were to be his guests this morning. Which, I suppose we must hurry to do or risk making him angry." She pulled down her own handbag and took out the key to her trunk.

"Well, I'm not convinced of his goodwill," Karen replied. "Suppose he just wants to have us to his cabin in order to announce that he's putting us off at the next port? You did break the rules, after all."

Grace unlocked her steamer and retrieved her brush. "I apologized for that."

"And he accepted?" Karen questioned. "That doesn't seem to fit the personality of the man who barked out commands to us just yesterday."

Grace thought Karen a very harsh judge. "I believe him to be concerned with our general well-being. Rather like you when you worry over a collection of children, wondering whether or not they are being schooled properly. You can't really control their destiny, but if you have anything to say about it—"

"Which I usually don't," Karen interjected.

"But if you did, you would voice your opinion and seek to aid them as you could. Captain Colton holds the responsibility for the crew and passengers on this ship. I'm certain he was only seeing after everyone's best interest." She finished combing out her hair, then twisted it into a lazy knot at the nape of her neck. "Now, will you help me pin my hair in place so that we aren't late?"

Karen said nothing more until they were marched to the captain's quarters and seated at his table. Grace felt suddenly shy and rather dowdy as Peter Colton joined them. He looked simply marvelous in his navy-colored coat and trousers. His white shirt was buttoned to the top, while the opened coat revealed a smartly cut waistcoat, complete with a gold watch fob, which he pulled from his pocket. Checking the time, he smiled.

"I hope I haven't kept you waiting too long." He snapped the watch case closed and returned the watch to his pocket.

"Not at all," Aunt Doris said, acting as spokeswoman for the group. "We were rather surprised at your invitation and prayed that we had not tarried too long in our morning routines for your sake."

Peter shook his head, and Grace noticed his clean-shaven chin. It was such a lovely chin, not too pointed or too square. There was just a hint of a cleft in the middle, and Grace found it rather attractively placed. Somehow, it added true character to the captain's face.

Peter motioned for them to take their seats but actually

came to assist Doris as she pulled her chair out from the table. Grace could not fault him for his deference to the older woman's status. Among the three women, Doris was certainly the one who should receive the most consideration.

The women couldn't contain their surprise when breakfast arrived. Brought to them by two of Peter's men, Grace found the service quite commendable and the menu most appealing. Scrambled eggs, fresh biscuits and gravy, and thick slices of bacon were the order for the day. This, accompanied by strong black coffee, left Grace no doubt how Peter managed to maintain his muscular frame.

"This looks fit for royalty," Doris announced.

"It does look good," Karen muttered.

Grace couldn't be sure, but she thought she heard her friend whisper something about being poisoned. She smiled to herself.

Peter started to dig into his food, but the three ladies remained motionless. He looked at them oddly for a moment.

"Might we ask a blessing?" Grace suggested.

Peter put down his fork and nodded. "If that is to your liking."

She felt a minor strain of disappointment that asking God's blessing was obviously not to his liking—or at least not to his routine. Bowing her head, Grace quickly asked God's guidance and safety for the trip and thanked Him for the food and Peter's generosity.

With the unison of amens from the women, Grace looked up to find Peter having already returned his attention to the food.

"Miss Hawkins mentioned the discomfort of the cabin," he said after several bites. "I have arranged new quarters for you. Even now your things are being moved. I hope you'll find the new cabin to be more to your liking."

Grace was deeply touched by Peter's generosity, but before she could comment, Karen jumped in. "You must have known it would be like a tomb," she said sarcastically. "Why your sudden change of heart?"

Captain Colton smiled rather stiffly as he addressed Karen. "I found your friend's manner and genteel expression to appeal to my sense of duty. She treated me with consideration, and in turn I find it quite natural to extend the same to her—to you all."

"I hope you will not be so unreasonable as to toy with her affections," Karen stated without warning. "As her guardian on this journey, I must say I would brook no nonsense in affairs of the heart, either real or imagined."

Grace felt her face flush with embarrassment. She wanted to melt into the rough wooden floor beneath her and never be seen again. She threw Karen a look that suggested it was uncalled for, but Karen would not be silenced.

"I suppose you are a worldly man, Captain, but my dear friend and charge has led a sheltered life. As a good Christian woman she believes the best of everyone around her, thinking that all people are honest with their intentions."

"Perhaps you would benefit by learning from her example," Peter suggested.

"Captain, you are an ill-mannered man!" Karen declared, pushing back her plate.

"And you are a self-centered woman who, seeing another, less sour-dispositioned woman receiving kindness, questions the motives of the giver without any real knowledge of the person or his desires."

"I know full well about the desires of men such as yourself," Karen answered angrily.

"That, Miss Pierce, truly surprises me, for I cannot imagine any man taking the time to express his feelings to you for any extended length of time."

Grace saw her friend's face redden and knew her temper to be clearly pricked by Peter's upbraiding. Looking to Doris for help, Grace prayed that the matter might be put behind them.

"Captain, I wonder if you might tell us of a reliable hotel in Skagway," Doris said as if nothing were at all amiss.

"No, ma'am, I am not at all familiar with anything being reliable in that town. Deviousness runs rampant and decent people are not without risk to their well-being."

"Sounds like life aboard your ship," Karen said, lifting a cup of coffee to her lips.

Grace could not understand why Karen had so completely taken a disliking to the captain. Certainly he had spoken his mind on the matter of women traveling unescorted, but that was his prerogative. She knew Karen to be outspoken on her views and to have a view on nearly every matter, but her response to Captain Colton was so intense and so evident that Grace couldn't help but wonder if her reactions were born of something else.

A sinking feeling came over Grace. Surely Karen couldn't find the man attractive and therefore be miffed to find her interest not returned. Or perhaps it was returned. Perhaps this was how people in love reacted to each other. There was a sarcastic playfulness to it. Neither one seemed completely disturbed by the other's actions, and the captain had positioned Karen at his left, while Grace had been appointed to sit directly opposite him at the small table.

The idea of her governess, who was so obviously closer to the captain's own age, falling in love with this fascinating man left Grace feeling rather under the weather. She pushed her food around the plate as if she were participating in the feast. But she never managed to eat more than a few morsels.

"Are you ill, Miss Hawkins?" the captain asked as one of his men returned to pour more coffee.

Grace looked up to find all eyes fixed on her. "I suppose I'm still trying to get used to sea travel. It is my first time."

He nodded sympathetically. "It sometimes takes a bit of an adjustment."

Grace nodded, then bowed her head and ignored Karen's look of concern. *Please don't love him,* her heart silently begged of her friend. *Don't be in love with Captain Colton, for I fear my heart has already taken up that occupation.*

Peter Colton knew his time would be better spent elsewhere, but nevertheless, he chose himself to deliver the trio of ladies to their new quarters. He was unexplainably drawn to Grace Hawkins, and even now had no desire to return to his duties. He wondered if she had slept well after her time with him on the deck. He wondered if she was still haunted by the painful memories of the fiancé she'd left behind. There was, of course, no opportunity to ask such personal questions, but that didn't stop Peter's mind from pondering the answers.

He stopped abruptly outside the door to the cabin and smiled. "Here we are," he announced. He hesitated, his gaze meeting that of Miss Hawkins. She smiled. Grateful for the excuse to further his stay, Peter spied the Barringers coming up behind the women and decided introductions were in order.

"Mr. Barringer, this is Miss Pierce, her niece Miss Pierce, and their friend Miss Hawkins. Ladies, this is Mr. William

Barringer and his two children, Leah and Jacob. They have the cabin next to yours."

Doris extended her hand. "Glad to meet a family man, Mr. Barringer. Is your wife traveling with you as well?"

Mr. Barringer looked to the deck. "My wife passed on some weeks back."

"Oh, I am sorry," Doris replied. "Life is such a precarious act. One minute we walk the wire with the greatest of ease and the next moment we find ourselves falling to the net below."

"And sometimes there's no net to catch us when we fall," Barringer countered with a sad sort of smile.

Peter thought the circus analogy rather amusing. The older woman was quite a character. Her trim little frame seemed more imposing than most. She could hardly have stood more than five foot two, certainly no taller than Grace Hawkins. She had been a schoolteacher, he'd been told, and given her prim and proper appearance he could well envision her in that position. No doubt she would have tolerated little nonsense from her charges. Still, he knew the woman to have a sense of humor. She'd entertained them with several stories over breakfast, and in spite of her independent nature, Peter found her to be enjoyable company.

Not so her niece, who seemed to take great delight in tormenting him. Her gold-red hair suggested trouble from the start, but even with his own superstitious tendencies, Peter had tried to give the younger Miss Pierce the benefit of a doubt. She had quickly proven his concerns on target, however.

Watching the women exchange pleasantries with the Barringer family, Peter found himself studying Grace. He had thought himself thorough in his assessment of her, but with each new opportunity to observe her, Peter found something new to consider. She wore her hair rather simply. Parted in the middle and pulled back into a casual loop at the base of her neck, the rich cocoa color beckoned his touch. The style seemed to suit her, but Peter couldn't help but wonder what her hair would look like, feel like, once Grace released it from the confines of the bun. Last night she'd been a bit disheveled, but nevertheless her hair remained in fair order and all the while he had envisioned it blowing in the wind.

As if realizing his consideration of her, Grace looked up and smiled. Peter felt his heart skip a beat. Her smile warmed him from head to toe. Chiding himself for feeling like a schoolboy, Peter couldn't help but enjoy the gift of her open friendship. He was glad she had defied her father and cruel fiancé to run away. If she'd remained in whatever place she called home, he might never have met her. And that, Peter decided, would have been a grave injustice to them both.

"So, Mr. Barringer, are you headed to the Yukon for gold?" Doris questioned.

"We are. We'll work a bit in Dyea or Skagway. I didn't have enough for supplies and passage north," Bill Barringer admitted, "but we'll manage it just fine. My children are hard workers and together we'll soon earn enough to send us north."

"Your children should be preparing for the school term," Doris said in a stern manner. "I spent my life teaching school, and I would not see a gold rush push aside the importance of education."

Barringer shrugged. "Folks have to do what they have to do. Jacob here is fourteen. He's had enough schooling to get him by. He can read and write better than I can. Leah is twelve, and I don't rightly figure a man is going to much care whether she has an education or not. She's as pretty as her ma was, and when she grows up she'll have suitors enough to keep her from having to worry about such things."

"Mr. Barringer, that is hardly a proper attitude to take," the younger Miss Pierce joined in. "We stand on the threshold of the twentieth century. Education is of the utmost importance for our children."

"I didn't realize you had any children," Peter couldn't help but comment.

Karen glared at him, her blue eyes narrowing. "I do not have children of my own, Captain, but like my aunt, I have dedicated myself to educating other people's children."

"Then perhaps you can start up a school in Dawson City or Skagway or help an existing one," Peter replied. "Either way, this man has the say over his family."

"I am fully aware Mr. Barringer is in charge of his family," Karen retorted.

"I wonder," Grace interjected, looking a bit tired, "if we might be allowed to go to our new quarters. I fear I'm feeling a bit overcome."

Peter wasted no time. "Mr. Barringer, please remember to keep your family contained to this end of the deck." Bill Barringer nodded as Peter turned. "Come, ladies, your cabin is just here on the other side of Mr. Barringer's."

He was grateful for Grace's interference, but at the same time he felt it necessary to put Karen Pierce in her rightful place. He had a low tolerance for arrogant women. Perhaps it was because they grated on his sense of propriety, but it was even possible they simply threatened Peter's own sense of power. He didn't like to think of it in that way—didn't like to imagine his own arrogance going toe to toe with someone else's, yet he knew very well that he could be a most prideful man.

She isn't going to usurp my authority on this ship, pride or no pride. I am in charge here. This is my domain, Peter thought quite seriously. He looked past Grace to Karen Pierce and decided then and there that he would do whatever it took to make her realize she had clearly met her match. He would stand his ground with her, and she would not get the better of him in any manner.

CHAPTER FOURTEEN

THE STEAMER *Merry Maid* sliced through the gray-green waters of Lynn Canal and slowly but persistently transported its passengers ever northward toward Skagway, Alaska. Skagway had become the start of the path to the Yukon, with its sister town of Dyea being the fork in the path. Both towns had their benefit for the gold stampeder, but neither were perfect.

Skagway had a better harbor, but Dyea was working on the possibility of extended wharfs. Dyea had the shorter Chilkoot Pass, but Skagway offered White Pass, a route that allowed for animals to pack supplies for a good portion of the distance. At least that was the theory. No matter the path, those who found themselves drawn north by the call of gold also found themselves face-to-face with a rugged, austere beauty that defied them at every turn. Some gave up to go home empty-handed and heavyhearted. Others pursued the dream and lost their lives, while a few fortunate souls managed to actually strike it rich.

Karen thought the stampeders rather amusing and sad at the same time. They were searching for something they'd never had, something they only dreamed of finding. They had risked life and limb to endure the difficult climate and conditions, and all for the remote possibility that they just might find gold.

Grown men—men who should, for all intents and purposes, be in their right minds—honestly believed the exaggerated stories of their predecessors. They talked of fortunes to be had for the taking—of a land where the biggest effort required of you was to bend over in order to pick the gold up from the ground.

Of course, Karen reasoned, they would probably think her decision for coming north to be just as crazed. But hers was a journey of purpose and need every bit as much as theirs. She, too, felt called to the desolate lands of Alaska, but the gold she sought came in human form.

She thought of her father momentarily. Wilmont Pierce was a hero of sorts to his youngest child. Karen knew him to be a wise and fair man, with both feet firmly planted on the ground. When he'd suggested the journey north, Karen had been surprised. It wasn't like him to go off on a whim. But somewhere along the way, he had read of missions being set up in the north. Missions that with the government's blessing were starting schools and changing the face of culture and purpose in the Alaskan wilderness. Her father had been appalled to hear that the natives were being stripped of their own ways and imposed with the manners, practices, and speech of the white American. He believed there had to be a way to blend both and still accomplish a positive result. And it was with that dream in mind that he took his wife and independently traveled north.

She admired her father for his decision. He was an opinionated man, but he was not unwilling to yield his philosophies if someone could make an argument for a better way. Unlike Captain Colton, Karen thought, who seemed only to find value in his own thoughts.

Still, he had managed to give them a lovely room with a window. Arranged at the bow of the ship, Peter had also quartered off a section of the deck that was to allow for private moments of refreshment for the little family and the trio of proper ladies.

Karen had figured the captain to be completely indifferent to their needs, but apparently he was not completely indifferent to Grace. The idea that he might well entice Grace with his charms, only to crush her spirits in the end, troubled Karen and made her quite anxious. Men like Colton and Paxton, men of power and knowledge, often believed the world and its people to be their playthings. How different they were from her beloved father.

Distancing herself from Grace and Doris, Karen spent a quiet morning moment to stand at the rail and study the landscape before her. The canal was not all that wide, but it was glorious. The day before, thick patchy fog had negated any possibility of studying the scenery around them. The captain had briefly shared of glacier ice and its pale blue beauty and dangers, but there was no hope of sight-seeing until the fog lifted. The weather had also slowed *Merry Maid* considerably, and at one point they barely crawled through the canal, the chugging rhythm of the engines bouncing off the fog to echo back at the passengers. It had been eerie, almost worrisome.

But that had been yesterday. Today the sun had already burned off the heavy cloud cover and the blue skies overhead promised a pleasing morning. The brisk breeze blew across Karen's face and body, chilling her thoroughly, but she didn't mind. It made her feel closer to her parents and the land they came to love.

It is a cold country, her mother had written. *Almost as if it played the part of the inhospitable neighbor.*

Karen had mused at her mother's poetic description. She called to mind other descriptions, however, that suggested the neighbor had softened enough to embrace and welcome her parents. They had made their home here, and her father had remained even after his beloved wife's death. That action spoke more than any words he could have written.

Calling upon her education and love of all things botanical, Karen studied the dark green carpeting of spruce and hemlock. Interspersed nearer the edge of various inlets, Karen made out black cottonwoods with their rough-ridged bark and droplet-shaped leaves. White-trunked aspen set amid lacy-leafed ferns seemed recklessly thrown out among the coastal setting, as if for variety.

With snow-capped mountains that jutted straight up out of the waters, the canal needed no man-made touch to maintain its course. Peter had told Grace that the waters were deep and cold—that a man overboard ran a bigger risk of freezing to death most times of the year than of drowning. No doubt freezing in this far north region was always a great concern.

There is a coldness to the interior lands beyond the pass that gives a person cause to wonder if ice would not better suit the tormenting regions of hell rather than fire, her mother had penned. *It chills the bones and leaves a body without hope of ever feeling warm again.*

The thought stimulated Karen's senses, however. She had known cold winters in Chicago. Days when the wind blew in off Lake Michigan and iced the air for weeks at a time. She had also known blazing hot summers that contrasted the winter in extreme opposition. She was ready for a change—ready to see this land her parents had so loved, to know the people her mother had given her life for.

What have you brought me to, Lord? Karen silently prayed as the glory of God's handiwork displayed its majesty before her. *What would you have of me? How can I best serve?*

Her thoughts went to Grace and her predicament. Karen didn't trust Martin Paxton and worried that, weakened by his threats, Grace's parents might well give in to his demands and tell him where their daughter had gone. If that happened, how could Karen hope to keep her young friend safe? She would not yet reach her majority for another four months, and besides that, Karen reasoned, as a woman her options were so limited. Grace was hardly trained to do anything but play hostess to a wealthy man. She could speak French and German fluently, sew beautiful pieces of fancywork, and sing and play the piano and harp as well as those talented souls they had often heard at the opera house.

But how could those skills possibly keep her alive and independent? Karen fretted, knowing that viable skills were absolutely necessary for survival in the icy north. Her mother had made that quite clear. She had written of chopping her own wood and piecing together fur-lined moccasins for herself and Karen's father. She had included entire stories in her letters that dealt with the harsh realities of life among such a hard and unyielding land. Alice Pierce had learned to hunt and fish as well as her husband, and in turn had spent a good deal of time smoking the meat to see them through the long winter months—months that could very well extend from September to May.

"What have I done?" Karen whispered to herself. *I should have required Grace to stay on with Willamina. At least in Seattle she might have been safe.* But even as Karen allowed the thought, she knew Grace would probably have become discouraged before long. And that in turn would have seen her heading home to Chicago and Martin Paxton's vicious cruelties.

Grace had developed into a much different woman than Karen had imagined. When she'd first taken the job as Grace's governess, Karen had seen the opportunity to mold and make Grace into an image of herself. Independent, intelligent, and completely self-sufficient. And while Grace was intelligent, she was far from independent and self-sufficient. *Perhaps my own strength overshadowed her development,* Karen thought.

Shaking her head, Karen tried not to allow her spirits to be overtaken by such thoughts. Surely God had a plan. He had seen them through this far, and with great success. He had given them a safe journey from Chicago to Seattle, and he had allowed for her brother-in-law to book them passage in such a way that they were not long delayed in heading north. Some folks who had booked passage after their arrival would not head north for months.

We've been blessed, she decided. *But where do we take ourselves from this point?* Her own plan was to find her father. No matter how long it took or how arduous the search, Karen would find him. His absence and lack of communication ate at her like a cancer. She felt with some certainty that he was still alive, but whether or not he was in peril or ill, she had no way of discerning.

What did worry Karen was that she had no idea how she

might go about finding her father once they arrived. Surely with the influx of gold rush hopefuls, the towns of Skagway and Dyea would be flooded with people. It would be rather like trying to find a needle in a haystack. Not only that, but even if she were able to locate locals who knew her father, they would probably only tell her that he'd gone over the mountains into the interior. Could she follow him? Would that be an option? She'd heard from her brother-in-law that already the Canadian government was tightening the reins on the rush into their Yukon. There were certain requirements to be met. *No doubt,* Karen thought, *women are discouraged altogether from the trek.*

"If Captain Colton had his way, there would be no women in the far north," Karen muttered, turning away from the railing. An image of Grace came to mind. There was one woman he would no doubt allow. Especially if she stayed within his reach. Somehow, Karen reassured herself, somehow there would be a way to keep Colton from hurting Grace. He would hopefully depart Skagway after depositing his passengers and their goods. She had heard him say that even though he was mostly working out of Seattle, his home was in San Francisco. Maybe he would return there and never pester Grace again. Maybe, but not likely.

Karen felt her irritation with the captain begin to mount. Surely he could see that Grace was special. That he needed to treat her with great care. At least he didn't stomp and snort at her like he did with his crew and Karen.

The entire matter made Karen feel very uncomfortable. Why did she feel so protective—so possessive of Grace? Was her anger at Peter Colton truly nothing more than a rivalry for Grace's affections?

"But she's like my own daughter in so many ways," Karen

murmured, shaking her head. Had she grown as overbearing as Grace's own parents? The thought brought about a resurgence of pride.

But I am like a parent to her—like a mother. I've been her companion since she was ten. I've been the one to calm her fears, to hear her prayers. I've been there when she's needed a friend, and I'm the one who taught her about the world and the kind of people who inhabit it.

And now he comes along thinking to . . . to what? Karen realized she had allowed her imagination to run wild. She had already determined that Peter Colton was up to no good. Had she falsely judged him? Had she assigned him a motive where there had been none?

The arrogance of her own heart weighed heavily on her mind. She had become a prideful woman, especially where Grace was concerned. Until that moment, Karen had never seen herself as anything more than the voice of reason and love for her young charge.

"But she's not so young anymore, and truly, she is not my charge. She ran away, and my own influence took her from those who were her authority. Oh, God, forgive me if I have erred," she prayed. "Help me to let go of this bond—to see Grace as the grown woman she is." She sighed and leaned back against the rail, adding, "And please help me to find my father, Lord. Finding him might well settle everything else, for if I can find contentment under his direction, perhaps the future will not seem so worrisome to me."

Upon their arrival in Skagway, Karen very nearly forgot her prayer, along with the hope and promise she felt for the future. Hundreds, maybe even thousands of people were in residence along the shores of Skagway. Not much to look at, the town seemed mostly to consist of tents and a very few clapboard buildings. All of these meager dwellings were outlined in muddy walkways and roads, if one could call a path still dotted with tree stumps a road.

"We've come to the end of the world," she muttered.

"That's certainly one way of putting it," Aunt Doris agreed. "My, but I thought for sure we'd find more civilization than this."

Even as the words were spoken, two parties of nearby stampeders broke into an argument that brought about the hurling of insults and more than a few threats. One man lifted a rifle and fired it into the air, but no one paid him any attention, except to push him backward into the shallow shore waters of Skagway Bay. This event seemed to signal a free-for-all that sent all parties into a full-blown war.

"I don't think civilization has yet arrived in Alaska," Karen replied with a sigh. "In fact, I seriously doubt they have even heard the word."

Peter found Skagway a little different with each new trip north. As more lumber was cut for buildings, the tent city was rapidly taking on a new shape. Docks were already being considered so that ships like *Merry Maid* might not have to put down their anchors in the harbor far from land while passengers and freight were ferried into the town. The current arrangement was most annoying to Peter, who had been spoiled by intricately designed harbor piers in his hometown of San Francisco.

Of course, Dyea had it worse still. The inlet was even more shallow as it approached that tiny town. Tidal flats stretched out far, making it risky and difficult to deliver passengers and their goods. In both places, the use of barges and scows took the people and products from the ships to the drier patches of tidal land where wagons would meet them. Then, for outrageous sums, these entrepreneurs offered to carry the crates to dry land. Early on, many people had protested the extortion and had decided to carry their own goods to shore piece by piece. They were to realize, however, that moving a ton of goods could be a lengthy process. This, coupled with the fact that tides came in with such ferocity and quickness, sometimes bringing thirty feet of water within eighteen to twenty minutes of time, left many a person minus their much-needed equipment. It didn't take long for word to get around and for most people to pay the money due the freighters.

All of these arrangements created a strange sense of community, to be sure. The gold rushers needed the shipping companies, the ferriers needed the passengers and goods, who in turn needed the freighters. It was like a society of mad dogs feeding off one another. And now Peter had joined their ranks.

It didn't bother him so much as annoy him. There was a good deal of money to be made in Skagway and Dyea. Perhaps in truth, the real gold could be found here rather than across the mountains and north. Passengers often waited months to recover lost supplies, meet up with loved ones, or make enough to equip themselves for the journey north. People like Bill Barringer who had come north with barely enough money for passage and who planned to work at whatever he could turn his hand to.

Peter thought them all fools. His steady income, although increasing from inflated rates, was a sure thing. After the rush died down, he would simply return to his home and continue the shipping business. So many of these people, however, would have nothing to return to—if they returned.

Mucking through the rain-soaked street, Peter made his way to a tent marked *Hardware and Stoves.* Seeing Martin Paxton profit from the loads brought north by his father, Peter had taken some of his own passenger profit and purchased a variety of items that he thought might suit the northern traveler. He'd tucked the goods amid the passenger supplies, telling no one of his plan. First he wanted to see if a profit could actually be made. Then he'd worry about where to go from there.

He'd made provision for the load of camp stoves, cots, and canvas tents to be brought ashore by one of the freighting companies. The goods came compliments of an arrangement he'd struck with Sears, Roebuck & Company, the entire package having cost him an investment of some twenty-two hundred dollars. He added in the inflated cost of the freighter, and still he could reap a handsome profit. If not, at least he could break even, and that would be the end of his private scheming.

"Welcome, friend," a man called from behind a makeshift counter as Peter made his way inside the tent store.

Peter eyed the man cautiously. The clerk wore an eye patch over his left eye and had a thick gray scar that started somewhere beneath the patch and ran down the side of his face to blend into his ragged-looking beard. When he smiled, he revealed that at least a half dozen teeth were missing.

"What can I do fer ya?" the man asked in a lazy drawl.

"I'm the captain of the ship *Merry Maid.* We've just put in this morning. I have a load of camp stoves, cots, and other equipment that would no doubt interest those heading north."

"Cheechakos!" the man declared and spit on the dirt floor.

Peter had never heard the word. "I beg your pardon?"

The man laughed. "Them wet-behind-the-ears stampeders. Cheechakos is what we old sourdoughs call 'em."

Peter nodded. "Sourdoughs, eh?" He smiled. No doubt those veteran souls of the north had plenty of other names to call each other as well as their newcomers. Peter decided against making a lengthy conversation. "So are you interested in my freight?"

"You betcha," the man replied. "I'll take it all. How much?"

Peter related the number of stoves and cots and proceeded to explain the size and style of canvas tents. "I have well-made tents, poles and pins included. All of the finest duck cloth—"

"You don't have ta sell me on 'em, Cap'n, just name your price," the man interjected.

Peter thought of his investment. "Four thousand dollars for the entire lot." He fixed his jaw, waiting for the man to protest.

"No problem. Wait here."

Peter nodded and quickly realized he should have been more careful in naming his price. The man hadn't even so much as raised a brow at his suggestion.

Glancing around as he waited for the man to retrieve his pay, Peter spied the price of a nearby cot made from duck cloth similar to those he'd brought with him. Five dollars! He'd paid only a dollar apiece for the ones he'd brought with him from San Francisco. With that kind of profit to be had, Peter could easily see the Colton Shipping firm on solid financial ground. They'd not be obliging in any way to Martin Paxton.

Thinking of Paxton caused Peter to think of his father. He'd have to help his father set prices for any freight not associated with the store Martin Paxton intended to build. Paxton would pay for shipping, but Peter knew his father would be a fool to let *Summer Song* be completely given over to Paxton's needs. Why, with this kind of money to be made, Colton Shipping could build their own store. The idea held great appeal to Peter. Diversifying their holdings could possibly prevent another run of bad luck. Perhaps building a store here while the rush was going strong, then selling it and reinvesting that money in yet another scheme later on, would see a continual flow of funds into the Colton coffers. Peter smiled. Financial independence suddenly seemed very possible.

"Here ya are," the man replied, bringing with him a canvas bag, along with a stack of paper bills. "There's coins and a few nuggets in the bag. Ya can have the nuggets double-checked at the assayers, but my scales are just as good."

Peter took up the bag. It was heavier than he'd expected. *What a strange way of doing business,* he thought.

Opening the bag, he had to see what was inside. He had to know what all the fuss was about. His eyes widened. Reaching inside, Peter drew out a nugget and held it up to the light. So this was what all the fuss was about.

His expression must have amused the store owner. Laughing, the older man muttered under his breath and slapped his knee. One word was all he said, but for Peter it said it all.

"Cheechako!"

CHAPTER FIFTEEN

KAREN WASN'T SURE what she'd expected of Skagway, but what she got wasn't exactly what she'd hoped for. Rough-looking buildings in various stages of construction were few and far between. Tents were the mainstay and were erected in a marginal semblance of order, some with signs declaring them to be hotels, restaurants, or shops. The streets themselves were in no better shape. It looked as if the people upon arriving in Skagway had literally had to hack their way through the forest. In many places, tree stumps were still standing in the middle of what appeared to be the planned roadway, and there was absolutely no consideration of a boardwalk for the pedestrians who crowded the streets.

The place was even more primitive than Karen had imagined. Somehow she had believed the place would have been settled by their arrival. She knew from her mother's letters that there was very little in the way of an established town, but given the stampede north and the modern innovations for settlement, Karen had honestly expected something more established.

Staring at the activity down the main street of Skagway, Karen felt like crying. Disappointment had washed over her from the moment the ferryman helped her to transfer to an awaiting path of tidal mud, and it was certainly no better now that the freighters had delivered their trunks and crates of supplies.

"Where do you want this stuff, ma'am?" a bearded man called down from his wagon.

"Goodness," Doris answered before Karen could think to reply, "where should we have it taken?"

The man shrugged. "Ain't a hotel room open in town, and I don't see a tent here amongst your goods. What'd you ladies think you were comin' to? A tea party?"

Karen resented the man's flippant attitude almost as much as her own disappointment. "We have come to be with my father, if you must know." She stood with her hands on her hips, hoping the stance looked intimidating.

"Well, he don't appear to be here. Probably already hiked over the pass," the man suggested.

"He's a missions worker with the Tlingit Indians," Karen informed him. "He was here long before the fuss over gold, and he'll be here long after the others have gone. Yourself included."

"Feisty thing, ain't she?" the man said, looking to Doris. "Feisty is good up here, but it still don't tell me where you need these things taken."

Doris nodded. "I'm sorry, young man. I'm not at all familiar with where my brother is staying. I believe he's often in

Dyea, but the ship wasn't headed to that harbor."

"Iffen you're headed Dyea way, you'd do best to have me take this to the flatboats on the river side of town. It's just down that road over yonder," the man said and pointed at a muddy path barely wide enough for the passage of a single wagon. "The best way to get this load to Dyea would be by having it floated over. You can ride as well." He tucked his thumbs into his suspenders and added, "And I've got a friend who runs some boats. He'll give you a fair price."

"That would be a first," Karen replied.

The man laughed, seeming unconcerned with her comment. "Take it or leave it, but iffen you want Dyea, that's my advice."

"Well, I trust you to know what's best," Doris said. "Should we walk or ride with you?"

"Ain't room but for one or two of you," he said. "'Course, that feisty redhead could probably put us all to shame. She's probably got more energy than these old nags."

Karen felt her cheeks redden. "I'd rather walk than ride with such an ill-mannered man."

"I'll walk with Karen," Grace suggested. "Why don't you go ahead and ride, Aunt Doris? You can arrange everything ahead of time, and when we arrive you can tell us all about it."

Doris nodded. "I believe that would be most advisable."

The teamster reached down to hoist the older woman up. Seeing this, Karen hurried to her aunt's aid and helped her from below. Together, they soon had Doris settled on the wood seat beside the driver.

"You gals just stick to the road. It goes straight away to where ya need to be. Just follow us."

Karen nodded, uncertain as to what they were getting

themselves into. For all she knew the man could be leading them off to their demise. Bill Barringer and his children, Jacob and Leah, came upon Karen and Grace just as the wagon pulled off. Each of the trio was heavily laden with backpacks and cases.

"You're the ladies from the boat," Leah said, smiling at Karen. "I remember you 'cause I liked your pretty hair."

Karen's anger eased a bit, but her fears mounted ever higher as the wagon moved off down the road. *Please help us, Lord,* she prayed before turning her smile on Leah Barringer.

"I remember you too. I wish I had time to chat, but we have to follow that wagon. We've a boat to catch that will take us to Dyea."

"That's where we're headed too," Bill replied. "Might we walk with you?"

Karen looked to Grace and nodded. "I think that would be very nice. In fact, I would call it answered prayer. I'm not sure either Miss Hawkins or myself expected to be quite so liberated upon our arrival to Alaska."

Mr. Barringer smiled from behind his beard and mustache. Karen thought him a sad sort of figure given his recent loss, but he always seemed to have a smile and warm word for his children. She had heard him one night when they had been gathered at the rail of the ship. He had promised them that God would make a way for their steps. That God knew what was best for their lives and that He honored a man who was willing to put his plans into action, counting on God for direction. Karen had thought it wise enough counsel, even while questioning the sanity of a man who would bring his children into such a chaotic environment.

"Mr. Barringer, isn't it?" she asked, not wanting to appear too forward.

"Yes," he replied. "But call me Bill. *Mister* hardly seems well-suited to this place."

"Perhaps that's all the more reason we should stand on formality," Karen replied.

"No, I like the idea of going by our first names," Grace interjected, surprising Karen. She smiled at Bill. "I'm Grace Hawkins, Bill. You feel free to call me by my given name."

"Grace is a pretty name," Leah remarked. Jacob, however, remained sullen and silent.

"Very well," Karen said, giving in. "My name is Karen."

"I like that name too," Leah said.

Karen couldn't help but be taken with the girl. She appeared so friendly and outward in her manner. She seemed needy for attention from other women. And why not? Karen thought. Her mother had just died and she was at a most precarious age.

"I think we'd better put our best foot forward," Karen said, watching the wagon disappear around the bend. "I wouldn't want my aunt to have to be alone for very long." Bill nodded and the group proceeded after the wagon.

Karen found the mud impossible to navigate. Her boots were hopelessly ruined and she only had two other pairs of shoes to use after these were spent. Perhaps her first purchase would have to be a sturdier pair of hiking boots.

We've been quite silly, she thought as they walked in silence. They'd purchased a variety of things—blankets, heavier clothing, gloves and such, prior to leaving Seattle, but there were so many things coming to mind that they were without. Good quantities of soap, for instance, and of course decent boots and heavy woolen hose.

"We used to live in Colorado," Leah said rather suddenly. "It kind of looked like this, only maybe not as much water."

"Definitely not as much water," Bill replied.

"We lived in Chicago," Karen told the little girl. "And we had plenty of water, but no trees like these and no mountains. My, but I really have enjoyed the sight of these mountains."

"Mama used to say mountains gave her hope for life's problems."

Karen smiled. "Why is that, Leah?"

"'Cause they have an uphill climb on one side and a downward slide on the other. No matter what kind of problem you have, Mama used to say you could always count on there being a downhill side eventually."

Karen saw Jacob's jaw clench tight at the mention of his mother. He looked away and acted disinterested, but Karen could tell he was hanging on his sister's every word. Bill Barringer, on the other hand, seemed to drift into a world of his own thought. From the way his eyes glazed over at the mere mention of his dead wife, Karen figured him to be pushing the thoughts of her aside. It was funny how everyone dealt with grief in their own way.

"So, Leah," Karen said, realizing that sharing conversation was much preferable to the silence, "tell me about Colorado."

"Oh, we were mining there. Pa used to have a lot of money in silver, but then it went bust."

Karen nodded. "I remember there were many problems with silver and a great many people lost their fortunes."

"Yup, our pa was one of them. So we stayed in Colorado and moved from our nice house and went to live in Devil's Creek. But there wasn't much there," she said rather sadly. "Our mama's buried there now, but someday we're going back to put a nice headstone on her grave. Pa said we could after we strike it rich."

Karen smiled, but inside she felt a deep sense of sorrow

for the child. To live on such hopes and dreams seemed almost cruel. But living with no hope would be even more cruel, and so she said nothing.

"What did you do in Chicago?" Leah asked. "Why'd you come to look for gold?"

Karen wondered how much they should share of their lives. After all, the fewer who knew of Grace's predicament, the better.

"I didn't come to look for gold," Karen replied. "I came to look for my father."

"Your father?"

"Yes. He's a missionary up here—somewhere. He works with the Indians."

"I didn't know there were Indians up here," Leah said, her eyes growing wide. "Are they the killing kind?"

Karen shook her head. "I don't think they'll mean us any harm. My father and mother lived here quite comfortably and never knew harm by the Tlingit."

"Klink-it?" Leah questioned, trying the word. "Is that what the tribe is called?"

"Very good," Karen answered with a smile. "I'll bet you were a top student in school."

"Used to be. I liked learning, but it's been a while since I got a chance to study."

Karen realized that the girl's father probably held little interest in his children's education. Conversations from the ship came back to remind her that he figured Leah to marry well and never need an education.

"I was Grace's teacher, so maybe when you're around in Dyea, you could come and study with me sometime."

Leah's entire face lit up. "I'd like that a whole lot. Do you think I could do that, Pa?" she asked, hurrying to keep step with her father. "Could I go and learn from Miss Karen?"

Bill and Jacob had remained silent as they plodded the trail in front of the women. At his daughter's question, however, Bill Barringer slowed a bit and looked down.

"Don't know where we'll be or what we'll be doing, princess. If we're around Dyea for a spell, you could sure enough go see Miss Karen from time to time."

"Oh, thank you, Pa!" Leah squealed in delight. She threw a look back at Karen that suggested she'd just been given a very precious gift.

They concluded their walk at the edge of a small boat dock. The teamster and Aunt Doris were already haggling prices for transportation, and Karen knew without a doubt her worldly wise aunt would never let anyone get the best of her if she had any say in the matter. Aunt Doris finally extended her arm and shook hands with a man they'd never before laid eyes on. Apparently he was the one who would take them to Dyea.

"Well, I arranged passage and transportation for our goods. The bad part is, it's going to take several hours before our turn comes up," Doris announced as she rejoined the group.

"I'd best go see what I can do about getting us passage," Bill mumbled before heading off in the direction Doris had just come from. Leah and Jacob seemed indifferent to the matter. Leah was already captivated by some strange tracks she'd found in the mud, and Jacob was staring off toward the mountains, as if to size up the challenge.

"I suppose if we must wait," Karen said, looking around her, "we should at least find some comfortable place in which to do so."

"Doesn't appear to be much available," Doris replied.

Grace surprised them all. "Why don't we just have them unload our things by the dock, and we can set up a little resting area."

Karen looked at the younger woman with a smile. "You're turning out to be more innovative than I would have given you credit for."

Grace laughed, appearing freer than Karen had ever known her to be. "I had a good teacher."

The change in Grace was startling. Karen couldn't help but wonder what had brought it about. There was that irritating matter of Peter Colton and his obvious interest, but it seemed that something more profound should account for this new side of Grace.

As the women went to work to arrange their trunks and crates in such a manner as to have a place to sit comfortably and rest, Karen couldn't help but tease Grace.

"You are different. I surmise that the mountain air has brought about a change in your personality."

Grace took off her jacket and tossed it aside. "No, I think it's the liberty this place suggests. What freedom! Have you ever seen the likes?"

Karen was enthralled. "What are you talking about?"

"This!" Grace exclaimed, waving her arms. "All of this. Look at the people here. Why, they come and go, dress in such a variety of fashion that no one pretends to know what is acceptable and what is not. You have men speaking to women and all go by a first-name basis. It seems that someone threw away the rules to proper society, and I'm surprised to say I like it." Her face took on an expression that suggested a pranksterish schoolgirl had replaced the prim and proper Chicago socialite.

"I would have never expected this," Karen replied. "Your

mother would be horrified." She laughed, but there was a certain amount of uneasiness that came with it. Had she unwittingly awakened a behavior in Grace that would have been better left at rest?

"Stop worrying," Grace said, sitting down atop her trunk. "I haven't lost my mind. I won't go off embarrassing you by frequenting the wrong places."

Karen sat down beside her while Doris busied herself with accounting for her latest crocheting project. "I'm not worried about having you embarrass me," Karen said, studying Grace very closely. "I just don't know what to think. When we left Chicago you were a frightened girl who was running away to put a nightmarish arrangement behind you. In Seattle, I found you ever the peacemaker, intervening when things were uncomfortable and certain to become unpleasant. On the ship . . . well, on the ship I saw you practically blossom overnight under Captain Colton's appreciative eye, and now here we are in Skagway and you are bold and radiant with joy, and I really don't know what to make of it."

Grace laughed and patted Karen's hand. "I was afraid. For a very long time I've been afraid. I don't even know that I can tell you why, but I felt that the only safe place for me was in the confines of four walls. Four very familiar walls. But spending time away from home, seeing new people, experiencing new lands . . . why, it's all enough to fuel my bravery and give me hope."

"And were you so very hopeless before?"

Grace sobered and nodded. "You know I was. I was so dependent upon you for hope and faith. I trusted God, but not enough. I prayed and pleaded my case, then cowered in the corner as if He'd never heard my words."

"I suppose I was also at fault in that," Karen replied,

knowing that she had never pushed Grace to be too independent for fear she might not need her governess-friend anymore.

"Not at all. You taught me all manner of things in which to find strength," Grace replied. "And God was at the very top of the list. I feel as if this trip has been my coming of age. I've opened my eyes to see the life around me and to realize for the first time that there is so much more than my own little world. I want to experience it all. I want to learn how to work with my hands and to cook and clean. I want to sew and see something take shape, something more important than a cloth for the table." Her words were spoken softly but with such great excitement that Karen couldn't help but get caught up.

"Good thing I came along, then," she told Grace with a grin.

"Why do you say that?" Grace asked, then quickly added, "Of course I'm glad you are here and know that none of this would have been possible had you not taken the first step in our escape."

"I say it because I've taught you many useless things throughout your childhood. Things your mother thought befitting a socialite's daughter. But now perhaps you would like to learn more beneficial skills. Between Aunt Doris and I we can surely teach you how to cook and sew. And maybe, once we find my father, you can learn a great deal more."

"I'd like that very much," Grace replied. Then holding up her feet she wrinkled her nose. "I'd like it even more if we could find some of those thick-soled boots like the men are wearing."

Karen laughed. "Me too. Who would have ever thought that the most enviable possession would be a pair of ugly old leather boots?"

"Hello, ladies."

Grace quickly put her feet down, and Karen knew without looking that Captain Colton had joined them.

"Why, Captain, how is it that you are here and your ship is out there?" Karen questioned, pointing toward the general area of the harbor. "We presumed you'd be gone by now."

"I had some things to arrange," he replied without the slightest hint of irritation in her manner. "What of you, ladies? Why do I find you here?"

"We were discussing boots and waiting for our turn to be taken to Dyea," Grace offered.

"Boots?"

Grace laughed and Karen watched as Colton's face lit up at the sight. "Yes, boots. Thick leather boots that do not fall apart in the mud," Grace proclaimed. "We were rather remiss in our preparations for Skagway." She lifted one foot and revealed her mud-soaked shoe.

"That will never do," Peter replied. "You must all give me your sizes and let me see what is to be done."

"Why would you spend your time in such a manner?" Karen questioned. She knew the answer but also knew Colton would never admit to it.

"Wet feet are a danger to survival. Being a schoolteacher, I would have presumed you to know such things," Peter said rather sarcastically. "But with Skagway given over to such rowdy dealings, I would much rather you allow me to go in search of proper footwear while you are safely awaiting your passage to Dyea."

"Hello, Captain," Doris said as she joined the party. Her crocheting was neatly tucked in the crook of her arm. "Are you bound for Dyea?"

Peter smiled and gave Doris a little bow. "No, Miss Pierce, I came for another purpose. But when I found your party here, I couldn't help but stop. I worried that perhaps something was wrong."

"Only in the sense of there being no hotels and that passage to our destination should take so long."

"No hotels?" Peter questioned. "But I thought you were joining up with the younger Miss Pierce's father."

"We will join up when we can find him," Doris replied. "He's a missionary in this area, but there's no telling exactly where he is. At times he lived beyond the mountains and north toward where everyone is fussing to be. Other times he lived near Dyea."

Peter frowned and Karen could see he was not at all pleased. "So you are to be three women alone?"

"It would appear that way," Doris replied. "But fret not, Captain. We will find some nook or cranny in which to stay."

"Have you a tent?"

"No, but perhaps we can buy one," Doris said, looking to Grace and Karen as if to ascertain their thoughts on the matter.

Before either could reply, Peter interjected, "I have a tent for you. I also have a proposition that until this moment seemed not at all reasonable. Now, however, I wonder if you might not find it to your liking."

"Tell us," Grace said enthusiastically.

Karen was more hesitant. "Remember, Grace, not all suggestions are necessarily beneficial ones." She watched Colton carefully, hoping he might betray some sign of his secret thoughts. Thoughts he might be unwilling to reveal. But to her amazement, he quite openly shared them.

"I believe this idea would benefit us both. I wonder if you ladies would have an interest in keeping a shop."

"A shop? What kind of shop?" Doris questioned.

"A dry goods—a supply store for miners and stampeders."

"And who would set up this shop?" Karen questioned.

"I would. I see the immense profitability in transporting goods as well as people to this region. With you ladies running the store, I would never fear being cheated."

"It wouldn't work," Karen replied without waiting for anyone else. "We have to find my father, and that will take time and effort."

"But a store, Miss Pierce, would allow you to meet many people without the need to frequent places maybe better left untraveled."

"But we will be in Dyea, not Skagway where the harbor is better."

"They are working on the harbor in Dyea, and while it isn't ideal, it's quite possible to put in and transfer the goods to barges. A store would give you an opportunity to make friendships and get to know the sourdoughs from the area."

"Sourdoughs?" Karen questioned.

Peter nodded. "Those more grizzled veterans who've been here more than a few months."

Grace reached out to touch Karen's arm. "I, for one, would like to consider this idea."

Karen felt a strange sense of being overruled. Especially when Doris nodded her enthusiasm. "Why, of course," she replied. "It would present a perfect solution. But wherever would you find a building for such an operation?"

"The tent," Peter replied. "I have a tent among my goods that's big enough to house a circus, or nearly so." He grinned and Karen turned away, feeling he was somehow mocking her.

"You could live in part of the tent," he continued, "and sell out of the other part. I could see to it that you have provisions for such a thing when I return on my next trip. I should be back here in a fortnight. In the meanwhile, you'd have no goods to sell. We could merely arrange for the tent to be put up on an acceptable site, and you could live there and even seek out Miss Pierce's father while awaiting my return."

"I think it sounds wonderful," Grace replied, getting to her feet. "Then if Karen and Doris wish to join up with Mr. Pierce, I might even choose to stay on and run the store on my own."

Karen turned around and looked hard at Grace. She was definitely not the same young woman. "Perhaps we're being hasty here."

"Well, you'll have a good two weeks to consider it," Peter replied. "For now, I'll arrange to have the tent put up and secured for your living. I can even supply you with a camp kit and three cots."

"Wonderful!" Doris exclaimed. "Ask and it shall be given."

"But you didn't ask me for a thing," Peter said, laughing.

"No, but I did ask God," Doris replied.

Grace laughed. "As did I."

Karen was the only one who said nothing. Somehow she just couldn't look at Peter Colton as a blessing. He seemed much more to be a thorn in the side. A handsome thorn, but a thorn nevertheless.

CHAPTER SIXTEEN

BILL BARRINGER checked his pockets one last time for any loose change he might have overlooked. Nothing! He had less than two bits to his name and no hope of getting north before the heavy snows unless he left soon.

The problem, as he saw it, was twofold. First, he didn't have the supplies necessary to go into the Yukon. The Canadians were rigid in their requirements to enter their country. They'd set up duty stations at the border and patrolled them with red-coated Mounties who would collect tax duties and enforce their demands. And those demands were even more impressive than they'd been rumored down in the lower states.

A ton of goods per person is what one person called it, but the real aim was to see that each traveler had the means of supporting himself for a year in the wilderness. Bill thought it all nonsense. There were surely game to kill and goods to purchase. It might be isolated on the other side of the mountain pass, but he'd heard of many a small town already being developed to accommodate the stampeders. And if that were the case, why should any man have to lug around four hundred pounds of flour or one hundred pounds of sugar? Not only this, but many of the requirements came in the form of tools, and why in the world couldn't a man just borrow what he needed from his neighbor?

The second obstacle and liability was the fact that he had children. Bill was quickly coming to understand that Leah and Jacob could never hope to pack their own provisions, and hiring packers from the local Indian tribes was clearly out of the question. Bill hadn't even figured out how to buy the provisions, much less pack them. The entire matter was enough to leave him completely discouraged. And while he'd never express himself in such a way as to let his children know the truth, Bill was beginning to think God held him a grudge.

After two weeks of working odd jobs, Bill's suspicions toward God were more firmly rooted. He could clearly see he was going to have to go this alone, if he was going to go at all. He had never for once imagined leaving the children behind, and even now as the solution became increasingly evident, he argued the point with himself.

Patience would never approve of leaving Leah and Jacob behind, he argued with himself. Standing over a stack of logs, Bill split the pieces into firewood and continued his internal conversation.

I could leave them with Karen Pierce and her aunt, he reasoned. *Leah adores them and is looking forward to getting some education from Karen. Those women would see to it that the kids were safe and sound. Jacob wouldn't like it, but he'd have no choice. He'd have to obey me.*

Bill brought the axe head down on the log. The dry wood split easily. *I could talk to the Pierce woman and see if she would allow me to leave Leah and Jacob. I could promise to send for them or return myself. I could promise her some of the gold I collect.* The entire matter seemed quite reasonable. Surely she would see the importance of keeping the children safe in Dyea while he went on into the Yukon.

Nagging doubts began to form in his mind, however. How would the children perceive this action? Coming so soon after the loss of their mother, they would certainly feel he was deserting them as well. Bill didn't want to give them that impression, but he also knew finding gold was their only chance to get back what they'd lost so many years earlier.

I'll just explain it that way, he reasoned. *They'll understand. They're good children.* He felt the sweat trickle down his back as he continued to chop the wood. He would still have to convince Karen Pierce, even if he could persuade Jacob and Leah. Then a thought came to him. Karen was looking for her father. As far as Bill knew, she hadn't found him, nor heard any word of him. *Perhaps I could offer to look for him.* The idea began to take root. *If I offered to look for him, the children could just naturally stay with her until my return.* The idea had great merit. Never mind that he'd be looking for Wilmont Pierce on the Chilkoot Trail north to the Yukon.

He finished his work and collected his pay before heading over to the Colton tent store. He tried to plot out how he might approach the subject without seeming desperate. Already the autumn had set in and time was getting away from them. Most folks told him he was a fool to even consider going on—that the police would close down the borders when the blizzards set in. But Bill didn't care. Even if he only made it as far as Sheep's Camp, some twelve miles away, he would be that much closer once the Mounties actually allowed folks to head north again. Besides, the bad storms might not even come and things would remain open and the travelers could just keep moving north. Either way, he didn't want to lose out on the chance of a lifetime.

Dusting wood chips off his jeans, Bill entered the store to find it stocked with goods. For the past two weeks there had been nothing but plank board stacked neatly in a pile at the side. Karen had informed him that these would be set atop barrels once Captain Colton arrived with the said barrels, the goods stored within them.

"Hello, ladies," Bill called out as he pushed through the already gathered crowd. "Looks like you're getting things set up for a day of selling."

"That we are, Mr. Barringer," Doris announced. "Have you come to purchase something, or were you looking for Leah?"

"Actually, I came to talk to Miss Karen, if she has a spare moment."

"Well," Karen said, looking at the growing crowd, "right now doesn't appear to be a good time for a talk."

"I understand," Bill replied. "Maybe later?"

Karen hurried to tuck the straw packing back inside the crate. Straw was just as valuable as most anything else. *She could probably sell it for a fortune,* Bill surmised.

"Look, Papa," Leah called from behind a stack of duck cloth tents, "I'm helping with the store."

Karen blushed slightly. "I hope you don't mind," she said, holding out a lantern for a potential customer to inspect. "We put her to work. We'll pay her, of course."

"I don't mind at all," Bill replied. "I was hoping both Leah and Jacob could find something decent to put their hands to." He wondered silently what Patience would have thought. Would she have been proud to have her able-bodied children working, or would she have been disappointed that he had taken them away from the safety they knew in Devil's Creek?

We were happy in Colorado, Bill thought. *We might have gone on being happy, even if we were poor, had Patience lived.* Even if she'd lost the baby they would have grieved, but together they would have made it through. Bill sighed and couldn't help but think of how it might have been.

Karen returned her attention to the customer. Within a moment she made the sale and stuffed the bills in her apron pocket. "I could meet you in a couple of hours," she suggested, seeing that Bill was still standing idle.

Bill hadn't realized how quickly he'd allowed his mind to wander. It took very little to find himself drifting back to Colorado and happier days. "Two hours would be just fine. How about we meet out back behind the tent?"

"Sounds good."

For the next two hours Bill attempted to think of various things he might say. He wanted to appeal to Karen's friendship with Leah. The two had formed a steady bond since Karen first offered to school Leah. They were often together, especially when Bill and Jacob headed off in the early morning hours to help with road improvements to Skagway. Leah liked Karen a great deal, and Bill couldn't help but wonder if she'd been seeking to fill the void left by Patience.

But while Leah was close to Karen, Jacob was close to no one. Not even to Bill. He rarely talked and was always moody. He wanted nothing more than to be left to himself. The boy was hurting, but certainly no more than Bill. It was impossible to help someone with their speck when the log in your own eye was blinding you to their need. Jacob had said very little since his mother's death. He'd been faithful to see to Leah's safety, but other than that, he was clearly not the same vibrant boy who'd pleasured their household some months earlier with tall tales of adolescent feats.

But then, Bill wasn't the same happy-go-lucky father, either. Patience's death had taken a big toll on all of them. The children mourned their loss of a mother, and Bill mourned the loss of his heart and soul. Patience had been his anchoring stone. She had kept him from being too headstrong or self-serving. Patience would never have approved the trip north, but then, if Patience had lived, they probably would never have thought to join in such chaos.

No, that wasn't true. Bill would have thought of it. The moment word came about two tons of gold shipping into Seattle's harbor, he would have been digging up maps and information to see what the easiest and quickest route north might be. He would have plotted and planned it out, and then he would have taken it to Patience, extolling for his wife all the virtues of such an adventure. Then after he had settled down, Patience would have explained the pitfalls. She would have no doubt talked to him about the children's needs and how such a plan would require far more investment than they could ever manage. She would have explained how supplies for just one person would have cost at least five hundred dollars and that they were lucky to have five dollars to their name on payday.

Bill smiled and he fixed her image in his mind. Soft, dark curls like Leah's and a face that must have been lent her by an angel. He could almost smell her sweet lavender soap. Almost touch her and . . .

"Pa? Are you all right?"

He hadn't realized that tears were streaming down his cheeks until he heard the voice of his daughter. Looking up, Bill wiped his face with a dusty handkerchief. "I'm fine, princess. Just fine." He looked at Leah and shook his head. She looked too old to be only twelve. What kind of trouble would that prove to be? Hadn't he already seen men eyeing her in a way that suggested they were considering how she might figure into their lives?

Studying her for a moment, Bill patted the crate beside him and motioned her to sit. She was the very image of her mother. How could he possibly leave her behind? How could he leave Jacob, whose spirit was still so wounded?

"Are you all right, Pa?" Leah asked again. She reached out her hand to take hold of his.

Bill closed his fingers over hers. "I'm fine. I was just thinkin' about your ma. I think she would have liked it up here. Don't you?"

Leah smiled. "I think she would have thought us plumb crazy."

Bill smiled and nodded. "I believe you're right." He gave her hand a little squeeze. "Fact is, I was just thinkin' that as well."

Leah shifted her weight and leaned against Bill. Her presence comforted him. How could he dare to venture north without them?

"Pa, are we always going to live in a tent?"

Bill put his arm around Leah's shoulders. "Of course not. Someday we're gonna have a fine house."

"Like when we lived in Denver?"

"You can't remember back that far," he said, reaching up to tousle her curls.

"I remember the way Mama talked about it, though," Leah replied. "She said it was so pretty. She had dainty cups and saucers to serve the church ladies tea."

Bill frowned. He was happy that Leah couldn't see his reaction. He remembered Patience boxing her collection of fine china and selling it to the secondhand store. It brought them just enough money to pay off one of their more pressing debts. He'd hated himself for letting her sell the collection, but hate soon turned to pity and misery. He could hardly even bear to look Patience in the eyes for weeks. She had told him it was all right, that they were only dishes. But he knew otherwise. He knew how much she'd loved her china.

"I promise you, Leah, one day you'll have a set of china just as pretty as your ma's," Bill declared. "As soon as we strike it rich up north, that'll be one of the first things we send off for."

Leah snuggled against him contentedly. Bill felt sheer gratitude that she didn't question him. She believed in him. Somehow that almost allowed him to believe in himself.

"I'm sorry it took so long, Bill," Karen said as she stepped around to the back of the tent. "Now, what can I do for you?"

Bill finished stacking some of the shipping crates and wiped the sweat from his neck and forehead. "I was just wondering if you'd had any word on your father."

Karen shook her head. She'd talked to so many people in the last couple weeks, and while some knew her father, none knew where he could be found. "I still have no idea where he is, if that's what you're wondering."

"I'm sorry. I was hoping maybe you'd found him and that I just hadn't heard."

"It's very kind of you to care," Karen replied, surprised by his concern.

"I wonder if you would mind," he began, "if I asked around and gave a bit of a look for him myself?"

Karen looked at the bearded man with surprise. "You? But why would you want to spend your time that way?"

"Because I know what it is to lose someone," he replied softly. "I can't go finding what I've lost, but you can."

Karen felt an overwhelming sensation of emotion. That this near stranger should care so much for her happiness and father's well-being was a pleasant surprise in this land of greed.

"I'm very touched that you would give of yourself in that way. My father is very precious to me," Karen said. She looked beyond Bill to the mountains. "I know he's out there somewhere. I feel it—down deep." She turned to Bill. "Do you know what I mean?"

He nodded and his expression suggested that he, too, had known what it was to be so closely bound to someone that he could tell whether they lived or died, even if they were far away.

"I have a photograph," she said. "I could give it to you and you could use it to ask questions. I've shown it around a few places, but of course there are places I cannot go—or maybe better said, I *should* not go." She grinned. "But I would go into the pits of hell itself if it meant finding him."

Bill nodded. "I understand."

His soft-spoken nature put her at ease. Looking at the man, Karen firmly believed he knew and understood her grief. Then it dawned on her that with Jacob and Leah, Bill would be rather tied down.

"Since you offer to do this for me, might I suggest something in return?"

"What?" Bill asked.

"Leah is a great help in the store. We've already sold most of the supplies Captain Colton brought this morning. However, we still have a few things and she could continue to help and I would also be happy to school her. Jacob too."

"Jacob has a full-time job. He just got it today. He's going to be helping to put in some of the dock piers. I'm not sure when they'll get started, but he shouldn't need you to fuss over him. It would be good to know that Leah is taken care of, however. I wouldn't want any of the menfolk getting the wrong idea about her."

"Absolutely not," Karen said, knowing full well the kind of ideas the gold-rushing fanatics might get. She'd already turned down eight proposals in fourteen days, most from men who were old enough to be her father, much less know him.

"If you would be willing to keep her here with you," Bill suggested, "I could put the tent up right here in back of the store. She and Jacob could sleep out here in case I was gone late into the night."

"Oh, Bill, you mustn't spend all your time searching for me," Karen chided. "You have to earn a living and see to those children. I wouldn't feel right if you sacrificed your own family for mine."

"I wouldn't be doin' that," he said. "I just figured your pa might well have taken himself up the trail a bit. It's only twelve miles or so up to Sheep Camp. I hear tell from the Tlingits here in Dyea that there are a lot of the Indian folk living in and around there, what with that being a good place to hire packers."

"Packers?"

"The Indians are packing goods over the Chilkoot Pass for the stampeders. Many of the Tlingits that were living down here have gone up the trail to earn money from the white stampeders. Since your pa is involved with teaching the Indians about God, I thought maybe he'd followed them to that place."

Karen felt a twinge of excitement. "You're sure it's the Tlingits? I mean, my father might have involved himself with other tribes, but those were the main people he felt called to minister to."

Bill nodded. "It's the Tlingits, all right. They used to have all the rights to the pass. I heard one old sourdough tellin' that they used to charge their own fees for crossing over the land. In fact, they wouldn't even allow traders in or out. They would buy the goods themselves and go over the pass and north to trade with the Yukon First Nations people."

"You've certainly learned quite a bit in your short time up here," Karen said, greatly impressed.

Bill nodded. "Pays to keep an open ear. Anyway, this fella told me that there were a great many Tlingits, men, women, and children, getting paid handsomely to pack the miners' goods up to the Scale and then up and over the summit."

"Is it a bad climb?" Karen questioned. "I've heard so many talking of the difficulties. I presume that this is the same pass."

"It is. It's the shortest route north and that's why so many folks are using it."

Karen realized that this might well be the answer to her long and arduous prayers. She would have a difficult time leaving Grace and Doris to go scouting about. Especially miles down unfamiliar trails, with little to protect herself and no one to help her.

"Well, is it a deal, then?" she asked. "I'll see to Leah and

Jacob. You can bring the tent here around back, but the children are welcome to stay inside our tent on nights when it looks like you might not return until late. I couldn't sleep knowing they were out there by themselves. I'll give them chores and they can earn their keep." She smiled and extended her hand. "Deal?"

Bill smiled and nodded. "Deal."

CHAPTER SEVENTEEN

KAREN STOOD OVER a pot of hot water playing referee to a washboard and her best Sunday blouse. It came as an amazing fact that she was so clumsy with such a simple task. She had once been responsible for washing all of her things, but after a time in the Hawkins household, she had been relieved of such duties. She had been happy when such menial tasks were passed to servants, but now she wished she were more competent with such handwork.

The afternoon was quite lovely, however, and if a person had to be battling the laundry, Dyea was a very scenic place to do it. There weren't very many businesses, and in spite of the multitudes of people passing through, the area wasn't nearly as lawless as Skagway.

People passing through seemed to be her biggest problem, however. No one stuck around long enough to suggest whether they'd met up with her father or not. They were hurriedly passing from Skagway to the Chilkoot Trail with Dyea as nothing more than a resting-place. Or they were returning dejected and broke from the trail, with no time for the nonsense of talking with Karen about her missing father. She found herself lost in thoughts of what they'd do if she couldn't find him. She worried even more that he might not even be alive. If he was dead, what would she do? There certainly wasn't enough money to return to Seattle. Besides, did she really want to return to Seattle? *I don't know how we'll get through the winter,* she thought. *If we can't live in a proper house, with the necessary articles to protect ourselves and keep warm, we might all die.*

Casting a glance toward the mountains, Karen couldn't help but feel the hypnotic lure of their beauty. It was a kind of madness, someone had said. A kind of sickness that got into a man or woman's blood and refused to be purged. It was as she stood pondering this very issue that Bill Barringer chose to again appear in her life.

"Karen! Karen!" Bill called out as he trudged down the muddy alleyway with two other men.

Karen felt an electrifying tingle go up her spine. Bill was back! That had to be good. He'd been gone for weeks, and the days were getting colder, the threat of snow gradually giving everyone concern for their future. He ambled down the road, however, as if the weather and timing were of no concern.

Karen noted that none of the men seemed in too much of a hurry. The smaller of the two was clearly a native. His shoulder-length black hair stuck out from an exaggerated white felt bowler, while the rest of his costume was a mix of heavy canvas pants, woolen jacket, and handmade knee-high boots. Their companion, a big, broad-shouldered man with dark hair and a thick mustache, appeared similarly dressed, with a rifle and pack slung over his back.

"Bill, have you found my father?" Karen asked, unconcerned with awaiting introductions.

"I haven't found him," Bill admitted, "but both of these men know him and said that up until three weeks ago when they saw him last, he was doing just fine."

Karen drew a deep breath to steady herself. "You actually saw him?" she said, looking to the men collectively.

"Sure did. Brother Pierce was headin' inland last we saw him," the bigger man announced. "Makin' his rounds."

"And he was healthy?" she asked the man.

His dark eyes were fixed on her face as he smiled. "Fit as any man can ever be."

She nodded and allowed herself to relax a bit. "Do you know how I can reach him?"

The smaller man joined in the conversation. "He be back before first snow. He stay here in winter."

"When can we expect first snow?" she asked anxiously.

"Signs don't seem to show it coming for at least a week or two," the big man replied. "Then again, with snow, you can never be sure. A snow could come up tomorrow and seal the pass for a time or just leave a dusting. You can bet he'll pack his way back here unless a blizzard comes. He won't stay in the interior all winter."

"Why not?" Karen asked.

"Brother Pierce has always done business this way," the man replied. "Don't see why he'd change now."

"So you think it might be a week, maybe more, before he heads back here to Dyea?"

"Looks like it. I'd just hold tight."

"Thank you, Mr. . . ."

"Ivankov," he replied. "Adrik Ivankov."

"Adrik is a guide in these parts," Bill explained. "And this is Dyea Joe. I'm afraid we weren't very proper with our introductions."

"That's all right," Karen said, reaching once again for the laundry board. "I'm learning very quickly that time spent in formalities down in the continental states is much better spent elsewhere up here."

Adrik grinned. "Yes, ma'am, now you're learning the Alaskan way."

Karen smiled. "Is that what you call it?" Her mind was still reeling from the news that her father was safe and would return to them in a few short weeks, maybe even days. This thought gave birth to another. "Oh, by the way, has my father a house here in Dyea? I've tried to ask around, but the place is in such a state of confusion. Those who know of my father weren't well enough acquainted to give me much detail."

"He stay with my people," Joe announced. "He no build house."

"Oh," Karen answered, knowing the disappointment she felt was clear in her tone.

"Tent life unbecoming to you?" Adrik asked.

"I just can't imagine living in a tent all winter," Karen replied. "I was kind of hoping to have something more substantial come winter."

"A tent will keep you fine, even at forty below, Miss Pierce. The secret is getting it set up properly. There are a great many ways of keepin' warm up here." He winked.

Karen felt her cheeks grow hot. "I think I'd prefer a house, just the same."

"Looks to me things are being slapped together every day. Why not build yourself a place?" Adrik suggested, as though she had somehow overlooked the possibility.

"We have discussed it," she admitted. Prior to Peter Colton's return from Seattle, they'd been quite low on funds, but Peter had been most generous with his cut to them for their hard work and now they were actually flush again. "I'm afraid," she continued, "I don't know who could do the job. Most of the good contractors are tied up with Skagway and Dyea hotel plans. If not that, then they're busy planning main street shops and such."

"Wouldn't take much to put a place together," Adrik said. "The three of us could do it. And if you womenfolk joined in helping, we could probably have something put up in a day, maybe two."

"You're joking, right?" she said, looking deep into the man's rugged face. She figured him to be somewhere near her own age or older, but the elements had taken their toll on his skin, as had some obvious encounters with danger. From the looks of several small scars on his face and neck, Adrik Ivankov had obviously had his share of run-ins with the wildlife.

"I'm not joking at all," he replied. "If we can lay our hands on the lumber, it won't take any time at all. If we have to fell and prepare logs, then it will take the better part of a week."

Karen's mind began doing mental calculations of what they could accomplish prior to her father's return. Perhaps if she had a house already established for him, he'd feel free to stay with her and the others. That way they could spend all winter discussing plans for spring. On the other hand, if she waited until her father came back, he might have suggestions of his own. She would hate to leave him out of the decision-making process.

"Let me talk to the others," she said, again abandoning the

scrub board. "Why don't you all stay for supper and we can discuss this some more?"

Bill looked to the men, then returned his gaze to Karen. "I'll stay. That way you can fill me in on things that happened while I was gone."

"And you can be with the children," she reminded him.

"I'm afraid Joe and I can't stay. We have business elsewhere. We'll stop by tomorrow morning and see what you've decided," Adrik said.

Karen nodded. "Until tomorrow, then." The big man tipped his battered Stetson while Dyea Joe took his hat off completely and gave her a little bow.

After they'd gone, Karen turned to Bill with a smile. "I can't thank you enough for helping me. I was beginning to worry about you, however. I thought maybe we were going to have to send a search party out for you instead of Father."

Bill looked away as if he'd been caught doing something he shouldn't. "I know it wasn't very thoughtful of me. But by the time I got up Sheep Camp way, there were far too many folks to allow for easy questioning. There were a lot of Tlingit up there, and most of them, even the women and children, were helping to pack the gold rushers up to the summit."

"Sounds like horribly hard work."

"It is," Bill agreed, then looked at her rather sheepishly. "I needed some money myself, so I gave it a try."

"Was it bad? I've heard so many rumors, stories of men who've given up and come back to sell out and go home. Why, we bought up the supplies of at least a half dozen men who were too discouraged to continue."

"There are a lot of them out there. Only the strongest and bravest are going to make it north. That's for sure."

"I read up on this gold rush. The area of Dawson City is

still hundreds of miles away. These people are going to be months, maybe even years on the trail. Do they even realize that? Did you, when you began to head north to search for gold?"

Bill shook his head. "I figured it would be hard, but I didn't know just how hard. Sure enough isn't a place for children."

Karen could see the worried look in his eyes. No doubt his concern for Leah and Jacob weighed heavy on his heart. "No, I don't imagine it is a place for them. You could certainly stay here and earn enough to take you home again."

"We haven't got a home anymore," he said, his voice laced with sorrow. "I was hoping we'd find a home up here."

"But this country is hardly suitable for bringing up a family. You have to consider their needs as well," Karen answered. "What happens when the gold plays out and the crowds leave for the States? Will you just uproot them and follow the masses?"

"I don't know," he replied, looking up to meet her eyes.

Karen had never seen such a lack of hope in a man's face as she had come to see in those lost souls who had given up on their dreams of gold and were headed back to wives and families in homes so far away. But even knowing that look—that despair—she was almost stunned by the depths of desperation and sadness in Bill Barringer's eyes. It was as if a curtain had been lifted on an empty stage. A dark, bleak, desolate stage.

"Bill, I know it isn't my place to speak on such matters, but I feel I must say this," she began. She watched him for any signs of anger or emotion, but there were none. "I'm sorry for the loss you suffered. Your wife was obviously very precious to you—to your whole family. I see the pain in Jacob's eyes, and I've heard Leah speak of things about her mother and then burst into tears. I look at you and I know that you must have loved her a great deal." His eyes sparked with a glint of interest. Karen took the opportunity to drive her point home.

"I cannot imagine that your wife would want you to grieve so deeply for her. She no doubt loved you and your children and she would want you to go forward with life, living each day to the fullest and experiencing great joy, even in her absence. Forgive me for being so bold, but a woman as you have described her to be would never rest knowing you are spending your life—dying. Mourning yourself to death. Leaving your children to fend for themselves in their sorrow."

Bill looked to the ground. "I know, but I have nothing to give them." He looked up, and Karen could see that the emptiness had returned. "I'll think on what you've said, but I need to earn a living and the best place I can do that is packing goods up the trail. I can get the children jobs as well, and then maybe they won't be so lost in thoughts of their ma."

"No!" Karen declared. "They are children and they deserve to be educated and cared for. I will not permit you to drag them off to pack for the miners."

Bill looked at her with some surprise. "You won't permit me?"

Karen drew a deep breath and fought to control her anger. "Bill, just leave them here. They aren't going to do you that much good. You'll earn very little for their work and then just have to turn around and feed and clothe them. Winter is coming up and they'll never make it. Oh, Jacob might be able to withstand the cold, but Leah would probably die of pneumonia. Do you want that on your conscience?"

Bill's expression changed as suddenly as if she'd slapped him across the face. He seemed genuinely overcome by her words and turned away. "They can stay with you, but I have to go. If I can't earn a livin' one way or another, it's not going to much matter whether they have a father or not."

"Bill, that's not true. They love you—love you deeply. I can see that. I've heard Leah talk about it almost daily. She fairly worships the ground you walk on."

"Even so, I'm not doin' right by her or Jacob." He stood with his back to Karen for several minutes before finally looking over his shoulder. "I'll get money to you as I can, but the camps are a good piece up the trail."

"Don't worry about it. Jacob and Leah can do less-strenuous jobs around here and earn their keep that way," Karen replied. "I can also work with them on their schooling. I think both would benefit from it, and that would give them something to do over the cold winter months."

Bill nodded. "I'm obliged. I just wish I could do more."

"Find your will to live," Karen replied softly. "That would be the very best thing you could do for them both."

He shook his head. "I don't know that I can do that. Patience was my life."

"Give it over to God, Bill. He knows your hurt and sorrow. Leah tells me her mother was a strong Christian. That she believed in the power of God to heal and direct. She also said that you used to believe the same. Have you given up on that?"

He shrugged. "I don't know. I guess I've come to realize, as the weeks and days go by, that much of my faith was wrapped up in Patience's faith."

"That can easily happen," Karen said, praying that she wasn't driving her point home too hard. "Sometimes it takes something like this to truly bring a person to God."

"Seems kind of cruel of God to be that way, don't you

think?" he asked, and for the first time Karen denoted some anger in his tone. "Why should it be that one person should have to die in order for another person to get cozy with the Almighty?"

"I've asked myself the same thing," Karen replied. "Every time Easter rolls around, I ask myself that question. Why should Jesus have had to bear my stripes on his back? Why should he have borne my punishment and sorrows?" She softened her voice. "Bill, I don't think God took Patience in some sort of trade-off. Jesus already died for your sins and for your reconciliation to God. Patience had no need to offer that sacrifice a second time. But because we are fragile human beings, we die. She died, not because you were bad or good, but because it was time for her to go home."

Bill dropped his gaze again and nodded. "I know she's in a better place. I'll think on what you've said." He walked away, not even waiting for her to comment.

Karen felt sorry for the man, her heart going out to him in his suffering. He stood on the edge of a towering cliff. One strong breeze could push him over. One simple step back into the arms of the One who loved him could ensure his safety.

"Karen!" Leah called her name, gasping for breath as she ran around from the opposite side of the tent. "Karen, come quick!"

"What is it?" Karen asked. She saw the fear in the child's eyes. "What's wrong?"

"It's . . . it's Jacob!" she panted. "He's been in a fight."

Karen turned back around to see if Bill was still in sight, but he'd disappeared between the rows of tents.

"Please hurry," Leah said, beginning to cry. "He's bleeding."

Karen went quickly with the child, hoping to reach Jacob

before anything worse befell him. They found him slumped over between a couple of the newer buildings. His left eye was already swelling shut and blood trickled from his nose and lip.

"What happened?" she asked, kneeling in the mud beside him.

He looked at her with seeming indifference. "None of your business."

"When there's blood to clean up and you're in my care, it becomes my business. Now tell me what happened."

He shrugged and tried to move away from her. "It's not important. I just got into a fight with some other guys."

"What was the fight about?"

"Nothin'," he answered, struggling to get to his feet.

Karen got to her feet as well, while Leah clung to her brother's arm. "Please let Karen help you. Please!"

Her pleading seemed to affect him, and he leaned back against the wall of one building and eyed Karen as best he could.

"They said my pa was no account. They said he'd deserted us and that he wanted the gold more than he cared about us."

Karen nodded. "That must have hurt you very much, but it's not true. Your father is back, even as we speak. He'll be at supper." At least she hoped he'd still be taking his meal with them.

"He's back?" Jacob said, wiping at the blood on his face. "When'd he get back?"

"He just now stopped by to bring a couple of men who knew about my father," Karen replied. She reached up with a handkerchief and tried to help Jacob tidy himself. "I know he's anxious to be with both of you."

Jacob nodded. "Come on, Leah. Let's go find Pa."

Before Karen could say another word, he had taken hold

of his sister's arm and was pushing her in the direction of the main road. Karen frowned. How would Jacob ever be able to deal with his father's decision to go packing up the Chilkoot Pass? She hadn't the heart to try and explain it to the boy. Hopefully Bill would help him to understand and reinforce that he wasn't leaving them indefinitely.

Karen paused to reconsider the house plans. Perhaps they could all live together. Having Bill around would allow her father to have another male presence, and for those times when her father wanted to minister to the Tlingits, Bill could be the male protection they needed as Dyea grew in size. It was definitely worth considering, but something she would have to take up with Doris and Grace first.

Heading back to the tent, Karen began to pray for guidance. *Show us what we're to do, Lord. Bring my father home safely and help us to know how best to help him. Deal gently with Bill and his children. They are hurting so much, Lord.* She rounded the corner to see Bill embracing his children. Her heart was uplifted by the sight. Surely this was a sign that all would be well for the little family. But in spite of this thought, the sight left her own heart aching.

"Please bring Father home soon," she added with a quick glance upward to the mountains. "I miss him so much. Please bring him back to me."

CHAPTER EIGHTEEN

BY OCTOBER, neither word from Myrtle Hawkins nor the appearance of Wilmont Pierce had arrived in Dyea. Grace felt sorry for her friend and tried to offer what comfort she could, but often her mind was otherwise engaged. Peter Colton kept her thoughts dancing on air most of the time. With each of his trips and comments of pride for her hard work, Grace felt invigorated against the growing cold of the Alaskan autumn.

Now, even as she watched Peter pay the freighters for their final delivery, she felt gooseflesh on her arms. He looked up to catch her watching him and gave her a grin. The action made her knees turn to jelly. In all her twenty years, no one had ever made her feel so light-headed and excited.

He tipped his cap to the men, and then before Grace knew it, he was striding in his self-assured manner right toward her. She drew a deep breath, hoping it might boost her courage.

Why was it whenever she saw Peter, a part of her felt like running away, while the other part felt like running into his arms?

"You grow more lovely with each passing day," he said, stopping to formally lift her hand to his lips.

Grace blushed and looked to the ground. "I see you have brought us an abundance of goods."

"I'd like to think so, but at the rate you sell them, I doubt they'll be abundant for long."

"The stampeders do seem to enjoy the selection," she admitted.

Peter roared with laughter. "They enjoy being waited on by womenfolk. Lovely womenfolk. They come to my store instead of buying in Skagway because you ladies have made a name for yourselves."

"Oh," Grace said, knowing the surprise showed in her voice. "I never really considered it. I just thought that your products were superior."

Peter shook his head. "My father is bringing some of the same goods on behalf of a friend of his who's settled a store in Skagway. You are his biggest competition, and I'm sure if he ever makes his way up here for a personal inspection, he will be green with envy."

"How is it that a man has a store in Skagway but isn't there to run it himself?" Grace questioned.

"How is it that I have a store in Dyea and leave it in your capable hands? People are not always wont to move to a place such as this and set up shop. However, if they have enough money, they can always find a willing soul to help."

Grace smiled and tucked her hands into her deep coat pockets. "I suppose I can understand that. Especially since I'm one of those willing souls."

"So can you slip away for a short walk? I can't stay. I must have my ship ready to leave in a few hours. But I want very much to hear from your own lips as to how things are going."

Grace hid her disappointment at his announcement of a rapid departure. He never stayed long, and she found herself intensely longing for his company when he was away. Was he driven just as mad by the separation as she was? Did these feelings happen to the same degree for both of them? She knew Peter cared, knew he sought her out before he saw anyone else in their party, but he never said anything to indicate or imply more than friendship.

"I can spend a short time away, but just like you, I must return quickly to my work. After all, we've a new delivery to deal with." She smiled rather shyly. "Lead the way."

Peter glanced around. "Things are certainly changing. There are more tents."

"Yes, but not too many buildings. Karen has suggested we build a house before winter, but a friend of Mr. Barringer tells us that tenting through the cold weather is not that difficult. He has offered to help us with whatever we decide."

"A house would be good, but it would leave the store unprotected."

"We've thought of that," Grace replied. "That and many other things." She smiled. "I'm sure God will direct us."

Peter looked away uncomfortably. "You'll find I've brought you all some personal items and some special gifts of appreciation."

Grace looked up to find him watching her. Could he hear her heart pounding? Could he see the way she felt about him in her eyes?

She pushed the thoughts aside. "Gifts?"

He laughed. "Yes. I asked my mother and sister about the things they would most miss if they were taken away from all civilization. They made a list and I went to work selecting a good many of their suggestions."

"Such as?"

"Well, you can see for yourself once I'm gone, but I've brought some teas and woolen cloth, as well as some books for fireside reading."

"Karen will be delighted to hear that. She's been working to help Bill's children to improve their reading. Since they are staying with us, it seems a good way to pass the time after chores."

"The children are staying with you and the Pierce women? What of Miss Pierce's father and Mr. Barringer? Have they deserted you?"

His voice denoted alarm, and Grace quickly worked to sooth his worries. "Not at all. Mr. Barringer, in fact, is the one who found people who knew Karen's father. He is expected back at any moment. Mr. Barringer then took a job with those who are packing supplies over the summit on the Chilkoot Trail. He's trying to earn enough money to get the things he and his children will need so that they can head north as well."

"It was foolish for him to bring those kids up north. They'll never survive."

"Oh, don't say that, Captain Colton. I'm sure God has them here for a reason."

"They are here because their father is a foolish man. I would never so poorly advise my sister or mother on such a matter. Men need to keep their family members in mind before making such harsh decisions. We are to guide and direct, not strike out at whatever appeals to our fancy."

"I'm certain you would no doubt make wiser choices," Grace replied, trying hard to think of another topic of discussion. "So is your sister very young?"

"She is older than you by three years. She's a very beautiful young woman and very proper in her attitudes."

"Is she married?"

Peter shook his head. "No, I've not yet found someone suitable for her."

Grace stopped in her tracks. "You've not found someone? What of her desires? Has she found someone?"

Peter studied Grace closely for a moment. "I forgot that such matters were a delicate topic to you. Forgive me."

"There is nothing to forgive, Captain. I was not offended by your choice of words, but rather the attitude behind them." She could see that he was thoughtfully considering how to reply. Instead of waiting for him, however, Grace continued. "I do not suppose that every woman with an arranged marriage should meet the same fate as mine. However, I do have a strong regard for the American way of finding true love."

"I have nothing against true love, but I only ask Miranda to exercise prudence and not allow her choices to be dictated by emotional heartstrings. She seeks me out on everything, trusting that I can make a better choice for her than she can herself."

"How very sad," Grace said, suddenly seeing Peter in a new light.

"Why do you say that?" he asked. His tone suggested annoyance as well as anger.

"It's just that I believe God has made both male and female to be very intelligent and capable. It would be a tragedy if your sister never felt confident enough to stand up for herself and make a few of her own decisions."

"Why tragic? Women are the weaker vessel. They are to be protected and cared for. Why should that be a tragedy?" He kept his voice very even and calm. Grace couldn't help but wonder if he was worried that she was too weak to hear the full force of his argument.

"I'm only suggesting that your sister would be better served if she were taught how to handle some things for herself. After all, it is nearly 1900 and women are pressing ever closer to having the vote. Times are changing."

"You sound like your mentor," he chided. "I only do what's best for Miranda. My entire family seeks my guidance on a regular basis. They trust me to know the truth of most things, and they need me to give them counsel."

"How very powerful that must make you feel," Grace replied, finding herself growing rather annoyed with Peter's arrogance.

He frowned and narrowed his eyes. "You're suggesting I do good by my family for my own sake?"

"I'm suggesting that God would not have you replace Him in their lives."

Peter stared openly for a moment and looked as if he might reply, but instead he gave Grace a bow and apologized for needing to get back to his ship.

"I'm sorry if I have offended you, Captain."

"Do not trouble yourself with such thoughts. I assure you I am quite capable of hearing your concerns and arguments without buckling under."

He took his leave after escorting Grace back to the tent store. She watched him go with some disappointment. She had offended him with her sudden outspokenness, but she couldn't stand back and allow for his attitude to be viewed as truth and what was right. That attitude, if coupled with a cruel nature, could easily turn Peter Colton into another Martin Paxton. And that would surely break her heart.

"Where's the captain?" Karen questioned as she came out of the tent.

"He's on his way back to his ship. See," Grace pointed, "there he is now."

"I have a list for him," Karen said, holding up her hand. "I suppose I must chase him down to deliver it."

"I suppose so. Just be cautious. He seems to be in a rather troubled mood."

Karen smiled. "And just what could possibly have troubled the dear captain?"

Grace shrugged. "I suppose it was me."

Peter Colton was in no mood for any woman, much less Karen Pierce. Her incessant calling of his name, however, left him little choice but to turn and await her.

"What is it, Miss Pierce?"

"I have a list for you. The supplies and things we need most. The ones we sell the most," she added.

Her blue eyes seemed to twinkle in delight at delaying him, and her long golden red hair caught ever so casually with a ribbon at the nape of her neck blew across her face as the breeze picked up. She easily controlled the hair with one hand, however, as she handed him the list with the other.

Peter stared at her for a moment, almost mesmerized by her hair. Why did a woman her age allow her hair to be down in such a fashion? Didn't she realize the inappropriateness of it? Peter watched, fascinated as the curls wrapped around her fingers.

"Are you quite all right, Captain?"

He snatched the paper from her hand and looked at it momentarily. "I'm very well, thank you." His words were gruffly delivered, but he didn't care. Miss Pierce had been an improper influence in Grace Hawkins' life. It was her fault that Grace would question his actions with his family. Before he knew it, she'd have Grace running about with her hair down as well.

"Do you have questions about any of the items?" Karen questioned.

"No," he replied angrily. "I'm quite capable of reading a list and understanding its meaning."

"Would that men were as easy to understand as lists," Karen replied snidely. "Grace said you were a bit out of sorts, but I couldn't imagine it should make any difference. When aren't you out of sorts?"

"If I am in such a state as you suggest," Peter replied, "it is because of women like yourself."

"Me?" she questioned, raising a hand to point at her throat. "Me? Whatever do I have to do with this?"

"Plenty. You have poisoned the mind of that beautiful young woman with your claptrap about women's rights and personal capabilities. I know she has run away from the authority of her father, and you no doubt had a hand in it."

"I did," Karen replied proudly. "The man her father would have seen her married to beat her. His demeanor was something similar to yours. Women were nothing more than property to him. They were to be silent when told to be silent and useful when told to be useful. You would have liked him, no doubt."

Peter felt his face redden as his hands balled into fists. The list was crumpled in his anger and forgotten as he considered how best to put Karen Pierce in her place.

"Either way," Karen continued, "I know you've hurt my dear friend's feelings. If that is what you consider proper, then

I will continue to encourage Grace against your brand of male civilization."

"It was not my intention to hurt Miss Hawkins, but she made some rather strong statements regarding the way I do business with my own family members."

"Good for her!"

Peter felt his control slip away. Raising his voice, he challenged the woman before her. "I understood you both to be god-fearing women. It was even suggested that you put much of your faith into the teachings of the Bible."

"That's true," Karen replied. "What of it?"

"Is it not a matter of your spiritual teaching that the man is to be the leader of the house?"

"In a manner of speaking, you are correct. The spiritual leadership of the house is indeed the position of the man. He is also to be a civic leader and provider for his family. Oh, and a protector as well."

"Very good. Then I suggest both of you remind yourselves of this when looking to cast disparaging comments on the role I take with my family."

Karen Pierce was undaunted. "It also provides that women are to be the *despot* of the *oikos*. That's Greek, for your information, and a roundabout definition would be 'controlling ruler of all that encompasses her house.' Women are to be the keepers of the home. They are to work with their hands, feed and clothe their families, purchase and plant the lands, and make all other manner of individual choice and decision while their menfolk are off learning God's truth for them in spiritual training and acting as leaders for the community, as well as earning a living to provide those things the woman is incapable of growing or making on her own."

Peter looked at Karen in amazement. She always had an

answer for everything. Now she was even quoting Greek to him.

"Perhaps it is you, Captain Colton, who should take another look at the Word of God."

"I have no time for such things," Peter replied. "I believe the Creator of this world to have endowed human beings with great capacities for learning and knowledge through their daily living. I believe I am quite capable of making sound judgments to guide the steps of my family. I don't need a list of rules and regulations to tell me what is sound."

"Ah," Karen said with a knowing nod. "It isn't Grace who bothers you half so much as what she represents."

"I don't know what you're talking about, Miss Pierce."

"God is what I'm talking about."

He shook his head. "Are you now telling me that Grace is God?"

Karen laughed. "Hardly. I'm saying that Grace's relationship with God is intimidating to you. You aren't half as angry with Grace or with me as you are with the idea that you might need someone bigger than yourself to get through life."

Peter had all he was going to take. Pocketing the mangled list, he tipped his hat. "Good day to you, Miss Pierce. I will endeavor to secure the items you've requested."

"I will pray for your safety and quick return," Karen replied with a smile. "And perhaps I will even pray that God might open your eyes to the possibility of His love and direction."

"Do what you think best, Miss Pierce. So long as you leave me alone and only pester God."

Karen laughed and continued to chuckle even as he turned and walked away from her. How was it that in such a short time he'd left one woman behind with a grievous expression of hurt, and another with a laughter that suggested complete joy? Things were certainly not as they should be. Chaos had crowded in on Peter's very organized life and that was a completely unacceptable condition to be in. He would have to find a way to take charge again—at least so far as his own thoughts were concerned. But while he was confident he could control his own thoughts, he wasn't at all sure about controlling his heart.

CHAPTER NINETEEN

THE HEAVY BROCADE DRAPERIES that lined the floor-to-ceiling windows of Frederick and Myrtle Hawkins' bedroom were pulled shut against the daylight. Myrtle sat silently beside her husband's sickbed. He seldom said more than a few words at a time, but she wanted to be there should he awaken and attempt to explain the dealings they'd endured over the last few months.

Martin Paxton had been as good as his word. He had seized control of the family businesses and stripped them of every hope of earning a living. Myrtle had immediately weaned the house of its staff, retaining only their butler and her personal maid. Together, the three of them worked to prepare meals and see to the household chores, but it was a poor attempt by people who were better suited to their known, traditional ways.

Myrtle failed to understand why her life had so suddenly taken a turn for the worst. Her daughter was now thousands of miles away, and she couldn't even write to Grace and tell her that Frederick had suffered a heart attack. Ever since Paxton had threatened to search their mail, Myrtle had realized the man to be far more powerful than she'd given him credit for. Maybe the suggestion was a bluff—something to spur her into action. But maybe it was the truth. Maybe Paxton had the ability to control every aspect of their lives.

She shook her head and calmed her own raging heart. No, God alone had control. She'd not give Paxton that power. The pastor had said they were under God's grace—that like Job in the Old Testament, the way might not make sense or seem reasonable. But who were they to question God? God had His reasons, and it was Myrtle's job to trust.

But trust came hard as she watched her ailing husband struggle for breath. He was so weary and so very sick. His color was a pasty yellow and he made gurgling sounds when he drew in air. He was dying. The doctor said that couldn't be helped now. The heart had suffered too much damage to sustain life for long. If Frederick remained completely bedfast, he might live as long as another six months, but even at that, the doctor had given her little hope.

"Oh, my darling," she whispered, drawing Frederick's hand to her lips. "We had a good life and now you are being taken away from me. I don't know that I can bear the pain of losing you." She thought of Grace and how hard it would be for her to learn of her father's illness. She would blame herself—just as Myrtle did.

"No," she whispered, "I blame Mr. Paxton more. If I am to blame, it is for somehow failing to obtain the truth of the matter from your own lips, my dearest."

"Mrs. Hawkins," Selma, her maid, called from the doorway. "Mr. Paxton has come again." Myrtle felt her resolve toward Christian charity fade at the announcement. "I told him you were indisposed, but he said he'd heard about Mr. Hawkins and wished to discuss the matter with you."

Myrtle had worked hard to see to it that no news of her husband's illness reached Paxton's ears, but apparently she hadn't worked hard enough. Suddenly she wanted to see him. To tell him what she thought of him.

"Put him in the Oriental parlor and I'll be there shortly," she commanded.

Selma left without another word, and Myrtle kissed her husband's hand once again and gently placed it at his sleeping side. Perhaps it was the effect of the sleeping medication the doctor had given him, perhaps it was a lack of will to live. Either way, Myrtle knew her husband had no concept of her presence.

She prayed on her way down the stairs. Prayed that God would give her strength to deal with Paxton and that He would also show her the truth that had so long eluded her. Something that dwelled within this evil man's heart had taken away the comfort and peace that she had come to rely on. It had also taken her daughter from her and would soon claim her husband's life. And while she could forgive Paxton for rendering them without funds, she could not forgive him for depriving her of Grace and Frederick.

"Mr. Paxton," she declared, pushing back the sliding doors. "I see you have once again come to plague me."

The man, looking far more worn than Myrtle expected, smiled rather coldly. "I feel honored that you have finally decided to share your presence with me."

"Don't," Myrtle said, holding up her hand. "I haven't

come here to make you feel honored in any way. I might as well have called this meeting."

He looked rather surprised. "How so, madam?"

Myrtle took a seat and stared at him hard. "You have done your best to see my family destroyed. I think it's about time you explained yourself."

"I think you already understand perfectly well," he replied.

"No, I don't believe I do." Myrtle folded her hands. "I'm no fool, Mr. Paxton. I've realized from the start that there was more to this than mere gambling debts and a desire to marry into our family associations." She refused to look away from him. She memorized his piercing green eyes and the way his thick black brows narrowed as he considered her statement. She felt that if only there were some way to read his expressions, she might very well figure out the thoughts behind them.

"I want the truth," she stated simply.

"So do I."

"I am not going to tell you where Grace has gone. Do what you will to my husband and myself, but my daughter will not suffer your heavy hand again."

"And what will she suffer when she learns of her father's death?"

"My husband lives."

"But not for long, as I understand it."

Myrtle forced her expression to remain unchanged. He was crafty and wily, and she knew he wanted her to break. She could feel it—could feel him almost willing her to give up. *Oh, God, help me. It's like doing battle with Satan himself.*

"My husband is not the issue, Mr. Paxton. You are. I want to know why you chose our family to destroy. Why you have made it your personal desire to harm us in such a grievous fashion. I don't recall having any knowledge of you in the past. I know of no unsettled scores or business problems that should suggest such treatment."

"Of course you don't," Paxton replied, taking out a cigar.

Before he could pinch off the end, Myrtle shook her head. "I tolerated your ill-mannered behavior once before. I won't tolerate it again. If you wish to have a conversation with me, you will put that away and save it for another time."

He looked at her for a moment, and Myrtle imagined that he was trying to decide whether she'd stand her ground. He was judging her as an opponent.

Myrtle straightened and stiffened her back. She refused to back down and kept her gaze fixed squarely on his face. With a hint of a smile, Paxton tucked the cigar into the inside pocket of his jacket.

"Very well, madam, we shall play it your way for now. You have amused me with your sudden stance."

"I have no desire to amuse you or otherwise entertain you. I mean for this to be the last time you darken the door of our home. I mean for there to be an end once and for all to the destruction you have caused my family. And I mean for it to start now."

"You have no authority to create such an ending. Your husband is the only one who can see this thing through. And believe me when I say, if you knew the truth of the matter, he would no doubt face it completely alone."

"There is nothing you can say or do that will cause me to desert the man I love," Myrtle replied.

"I believe otherwise," Paxton said, this time giving in to a much more evident smile of satisfaction. "You see, this attempt to eradicate the name of Hawkins has not come about as a random act. Your husband greatly wounded my family many years ago. He destroyed those I loved and cared about most. And now, in the telling of it, I will destroy what he cares about most."

"I seriously doubt there is anything you could say or do to cause such a reaction, Mr. Paxton."

"We shall see."

Peter Colton was almost relieved to find his ship delayed in leaving Skagway's harbor. A heavy fog was moving in, making it an easy decision to remain where they were. Besides, his conscience was eating him alive and he knew that if he didn't find a way to apologize to Grace, he'd never be able to sleep through the night. It wasn't that he thought her beliefs to be right, but he hated to leave with hard feelings between them. Perhaps with a little more effort he could help her to see that he had done nothing but benefit his family. That his ability to reason through difficult decisions and issues made him an asset to those who loved and needed him.

After seeing to his ship and men, Peter made his way to the shores of Dyea once again. A cold, heavy rain began to fall before they actually made it to land, and within moments Peter was drenched to the bone. Sloshing through the muddy streets, Peter felt only moderate relief when the tent store came into sight. No doubt there would be little privacy to discuss what was on his mind, but it didn't matter. If need be, he'd wait for a time when he could speak to Grace alone, but either way, he would plead his case once again. Shivering from the cold, icy rain, Peter forced his frozen fingers to work at untying the flap of the tent. It seemed to afford a poor method of security, but within moments he found himself face-to-face with Karen Pierce and a very ominous-looking Winchester rifle.

"Oh, it's you," she said, almost sounding disappointed.

"You were expecting someone else?" he questioned.

"We weren't expecting anyone, hence the reception." She put the rifle aside and reached out to help him with his coat. "You'd better get out of those wet clothes or you'll catch pneumonia. Aunt Doris!" she called.

Doris appeared from behind the canvas partition they'd affixed between the store and living quarters. "Oh my," she said, noting Peter's appearance. "Whatever made you brave this weather, Captain?"

"My departure has been delayed by the storm, and I thought . . . well, that is to say . . . I needed to speak with Grace," he said, ignoring Karen's raised brow.

"Well, perhaps we should get you into something dry first," Doris replied. "There are some of those apronless overalls you brought up to sell to the miners, as well as a few of those chambray shirts. You should just help yourself and let us get you warmed up. Karen, go bring a blanket for the captain."

With a nod, Karen retrieved the Winchester and went into the other section of the tent. Peter, meanwhile, made a forage through the table of goods and found a pair of pants and shirt that would fit him.

"Can't do much about those boots. Boots sell out about as fast as you bring in a load. You can see for yourself the ones you brought us earlier today are already gone." The older woman seemed to size up the situation while Peter glanced at the shelves behind her. "We can set them by the stove and hope they dry out. The way this storm looks," Doris continued, "you might as well just stay the night. Won't be much of a chance for you to get back to your ship without risking great harm."

"That would hardly be fitting," Peter said, surprised to find the very proper spinster suggesting such a thing.

"Pshaw," the woman replied. "There isn't a bed available in town. You might as well take one of your own cots and bed down here. It wouldn't be the first time we had a man under our roof for the night."

"Oh?"

She smiled. "Am I scandalizing you, Captain Colton?"

Peter nodded and grinned. "I believe you are."

"Don't let it bother you. I was just referring to Mr. Barringer and his children. Someone ran off with his tent last week, and we had him here overnight before he headed out once again to help up at the Scales."

"Did he find who had taken his tent?"

"No, but I pity the man when they do. Thieves aren't well received up here. Last week I saw a group of self-appointed officials drive a man out of Dyea with nothing more than the clothes on his back, and all because he attempted to steal a man's rifle."

"Is that why Miss Pierce met me at the door with a loaded Winchester?"

Doris chuckled. "We learned early on how to fend for ourselves, Captain. We don't take chances when we hear someone breaking in to steal your goods."

"Has that happened before?" he questioned.

"Oh, once or twice, but we always get the drop on them."

Peter shook his head. He'd had no idea of what these women were up against. How could he even suggest they continue working in such an arrangement? The dangers might well be too great. On the other hand, he couldn't very well pack everything up and take it back now. The profits had done wonders for his family. He'd been able to pay back many of the debts they owed, and soon they would be back on their feet, maybe even able to completely overhaul their ships.

"Hello," Grace said, emerging from the back of the tent. She held the blanket that Karen had gone to fetch, and Peter couldn't help but wonder if Karen had thrust the duty off on Grace, or if Grace had volunteered.

"Leave the blanket and let the captain change," Doris instructed. "Afterward, you can talk by the fire. This young man is going to be in a bad way if he doesn't get warm soon." Grace nodded and placed the blanket on the back of a nearby chair. Smiling over her shoulder, she and Doris exited the room to give Peter some much-needed privacy.

Peter quickly changed his clothes and used some of the rope he'd crated in earlier in the day to assemble a clothesline to hang his wet things from. With this accomplished, he pulled the blanket around his shoulders and picked up his soggy boots.

Entering the living quarters of the tent, Peter was rather surprised at how cozy they'd made it. A large crate made a decent table, while overhead they'd managed to rig two hooks from which to hang lanterns. In the corner on cots made up with heavy wool blankets, the Barringer children were caught up reading, with Karen sitting between them to help whenever needed. Doris had built up a fire in the stove, and Grace waited with a cup of hot coffee.

"I should get soaked more often," he said, smiling.

"Sit here, Captain," Doris replied, offering a chair by the stove. Without any further comment, she went back to her sewing.

Peter did as he was instructed, positioning the boots close

to the stove. Grace moved forward and took the chair beside him. She extended the cup of coffee almost timidly.

"Are you still mad at me?" she questioned.

Peter shook his head. "I wasn't mad. I was more . . . well . . . frustrated and maybe a bit . . ." He looked around to see if the others were occupied with their own business, then lowered his voice. "I guess I was hurt."

"Because of what I said?"

"You made me out to be some sort of ogre," he said, warming his hands around the tin coffee cup.

"I didn't mean to make you sound that way," Grace replied. She kept her voice low, almost hushed, and Peter found that he had to lean close in order to hear her. "I would like you to better understand what I was trying to say."

"I felt the same way, but you go first and then maybe I can explain."

Grace glanced upward and met his eyes. "I meant no disrespect to you regarding your position with your family. I am certain you are a tremendous help to them in times both good and bad. But people will always fail. We are, after all, human. Our choices are not always the wisest, and often we misunderstand what the most appropriate response should be to any given problem."

"Granted," he said, nodding. "People do fail, but we must listen to the counsel of those who are wiser. Surely even your Bible would support this."

Grace nodded. "The Bible indeed tells us to seek wisdom, but God's wisdom—not people's. God's job is His own."

"Meaning what?"

She blushed and looked away. "Meaning that you should not attempt to take that position in the life of your family. Otherwise, what happens when you fail them?"

"I won't fail them," he replied indignantly.

"Everyone fails," Grace replied without a hint of apology. "God is the only one who never fails. You have put yourself in the position to be a god to your family. You ask them to seek you for their counsel and direction. You would preorder their steps, but God has already seen to that task. I fear your family might suffer far more than they would ever need to suffer if you continue to fight God for first place in their lives."

"This is a ridiculous conversation," he said, taking a long drink of the coffee. How could she say these things? Did she not realize how ludicrous she sounded? He pictured his sister looking up at him with great adoration. Miranda would never say such silly things. Yet there was a peaceful, purposeful manner about Grace. She wasn't ranting and raving at him like a lunatic. She was simply and calmly explaining her beliefs. Her calm only served to unnerve him all the more.

"I don't see this as a ridiculous conversation," Grace finally said. "One of these days, I fear something will happen. Your family will seek you for help—for their salvation—and you will fail them. When that happens, I can't help but wonder what will happen to their vision of God. Or for that matter, their elevated vision of you."

CHAPTER TWENTY

WITH WINTER COMING on in the northern territories, Peter was certain the demand for passage north would slow. He didn't find this to be the case, however. So despite the opportunity to service paying customers in Seattle, Peter made the decision to return to San Francisco. He needed to see his family, especially in light of everything Grace had said. For weeks her statements had lingered in his thoughts, and there was no way to exorcise the torment without spending time with those who loved and understood him.

But now, hours after enjoying a delicious meal prepared by his mother and sister, Peter was rather stunned to hear his father's comments on the past few months. Having suffered a knee injury during one of his trips, Ephraim Colton had turned *Summer Song* over to his first mate and made the decision to spend time at home recuperating.

"Why didn't you tell me about this?" Peter questioned as his father limped across the room to pour himself a glass of brandy.

He raised the bottle toward his son, but Peter only shook his head. "I can't believe you'd keep this from me. You're injured, and *Summer Song* is running without you."

"My men are good men," his father replied. "I trust them to do a proper job. They're running Mr. Paxton's goods and show true enthusiasm for their duties. Oh, we've lost a man here or there to the gold rush—I'd imagine you have as well."

Peter nodded, not wishing to remember that he'd lost an even dozen over the past few months. Replacing the men lasted only as long as it took for the next surge of excitement over gold to build and then some of the men again would go. He'd found that the best replacements were those who had already tried their hand at mining for gold and had come back discouraged and broke.

"I always believed you'd discuss such an important issue with me," Peter replied. "I've contacted you with each of my trips into Seattle and you've never mentioned the need for me to come home."

"Because there was no need," Ephraim assured him. "I'm on the mend and within a short time I'll be back on my feet and firmly planted on *Summer Song*. In fact, I've invited your mother and sister to journey north with me and see the country for themselves."

"What!"

His father threw him a surprised look, one that seemed to border on concern. "Do you perceive a problem?"

Peter shook his head. "No, not necessarily. I mean . . ." He turned away to pace the short distance in front of the fireplace. How could he explain that his father's ability to handle matters in his absence was causing him to feel rather misplaced?

"Wonderful," his father said, not giving Peter a chance to continue. "Your mother is quite excited about the prospects of seeing Alaska, as is Miranda. Both find the idea of an adventure to be something quite appealing."

Peter thought of Grace's words and tried not to feel the sting of their truth in the wake of his father's decisions. His family had once consulted him about everything, and Peter had liked it like that. Perhaps he need only stir the pot with ideas of his own in order to get back some of that control.

"I believe we should build a store for ourselves, Father," he began. Ephraim looked at him quizzically but said nothing. "I know I haven't said much to you on the issue, but I set up business in Dyea with three women to keep the store in my absence. They sell goods out of a large tent, but with winter approaching I know they're concerned about the need for something more structured. I believe we could put a store together and allow them to live in the back portion or even upstairs. They could continue to sell goods and we would net a tidy profit."

"What of Mr. Paxton? He's been most generous and I wouldn't wish to offend him. Especially now."

"I doubt Mr. Paxton would be that affected," Peter replied. "His store is in Skagway and Dyea is several miles away. Both harbors have gold rushers pouring in, and both have the potential for plenty of customers and business." Peter paused, as if suddenly hearing his father's words. "What do you mean, 'Especially now'?"

Ephraim tossed back his brandy and wiped his blond beard. "Well, that's the surprise I've been waiting to tell you about. Mr. Paxton has invested a good deal of money in Colton Shipping. We're to receive a new steamer next spring, and if business continues well we can have that paid off and perhaps even purchase another before summer is out."

"Wait a minute," Peter said, coming to where his father stood. "What are you saying? Have you signed some form of agreement with Martin Paxton?"

"I have."

Peter felt as if he'd been punched in the gut. "What kind of agreement? Why didn't you wait to consult me about this?"

His father eyed him rather intently. "Son, I appreciate the things you've done to keep this business up and running, but Martin Paxton is a longtime friend and astute businessman. I trust his word in matters such as this."

"But I wasn't even consulted." Peter knew he sounded like a whiny child, but in truth, his feelings were hurt. What was it Grace had said about his family replacing him?

"Son, this is still a family business. I didn't mean to leave you out of the discussion, but the matter needed a rapid decision. Mr. Paxton came to me—"

"He was here?"

Ephraim nodded. "He arrived by train nearly a week ago. He left just yesterday. Sudden business, something to do with a search he'd been involved with."

"May I at least read the papers you signed?"

"Of course, my boy." Ephraim moved to the secretary and opened a drawer. "You'll find a most generous offer. Mr. Paxton has done right by this family for years." He held the papers out to his son.

Peter would not find any relief in his father's words until he saw the papers for himself. Taking them up, he immediately began to search for any complications or problems. The investment was most generous, and Paxton himself was taking on the responsibility of securing the new steamer.

"What's this clause?" Peter questioned, coming to a statement regarding grounds for dissolving the agreement. "This makes it sound as if Paxton is a partner rather than a mere investor."

"Well, where the new ship is concerned, he will be a partner. He will be part owner until my debt is repaid. Surely you do not expect the man to put up his hard-earned money without any collateral to support his investment?"

Peter shook his head. "No, but neither did I expect you to take on a new partner without consulting your old partner first."

"Son, you are still in full control of *Merry Maid* and a full partner in Colton Shipping. I would have consulted you had this been an arrangement that would have threatened that partnership. Consider this a separate arrangement. Paxton and I are partnered in this new ship alone."

Peter handed back the papers, feeling completely at a loss. His father had made what appeared to be a very sound business decision without seeking Peter's help.

"You ask them to seek you for their counsel and direction. You would preorder their steps, but God has already seen to that task." Grace's words rang clear in his memory. He could see her sweet face fixed intently on him, her warm brown eyes watching his every expression as if to read his mind. Was this God's preorder for his family? Had God tired of Peter's interference?

Peter shook his head and turned to bid his father goodnight. He didn't believe God worked that way. The God of the universe surely had more on his mind than to worry over whether or not Peter Colton worked overly hard to have a position of importance in the life of his family.

"I'll see you at breakfast, Father," he said, suddenly feeling very tired. "We can discuss the idea of a store in Dyea then, if you feel up to it."

"I shall look forward to it," Ephraim assured his son.

Bill knew that with the months quickly giving way to winter, he'd have no chance of getting to Dawson City before spring. Rumor held that it was far easier to get over the Chilkoot Pass on a stairway of ice and snow, but he wasn't convinced this would be true. He'd been packing supplies for weeks, and with each step up the mountain, he reminded himself that soon he'd be seeing to his own goods and his own way.

He tried not to think about the children. Jacob stared at him with accusing eyes every time he made it back to Dyea, and Leah always fretted over him. The first time he'd gone back to Dyea with his hands all blistered and torn up from the hard labor, Leah had cried and cried. Miss Pierce had dressed his wounds and left him with a new pair of work gloves and an admonition to keep the wounds clean, but even the vibrant young redhead had little comment to make. He didn't know if she understood his plan or just surmised that he was working through his grief. He felt confident that the children didn't realize his plan to leave them in Dyea. The idea both comforted and troubled him. How would they react when they learned he was gone? Hadn't Miss Pierce mentioned Jacob's involvement in a fight based on his supposed desertion of them?

Even now as he made his way back to Dyea, Bill knew he couldn't come clean with the truth. If they knew he'd been working to gain money and supplies to see himself north while they waited in Dyea, Bill wasn't sure he'd be able to leave. He could almost hear Patience's upbraiding for leaving their children in the care of strangers. She would have given him quite the lecture on his flighty behavior and dreamer mentality. She had before.

He loved and adored the woman who had been his wife, but she had never understood his aspirations, his dreams. He had wanted to give her and the children a good life. He had wanted to give them fine china and sterling silver. He had wanted his wife and daughter to know the feel of satin and silk and his son to stand among the privileged gentlemen of society.

Patience had never cared about any of that—even when he'd managed to obtain it for her for a short time. She had had lovely things and beautiful clothes, but she had been just as content when they moved to a house of less fortune and social grace.

Bill looked up to the fading twilight skies. The feel of winter was in the air—a hard bite that bore into him and urged him to be quick with his plan. The less said the better. He would make like this night was no different from any other.

When the tent store came into view, Bill straightened his shoulders and lengthened his steps. He had no idea what would await him, but he wanted to give every impression of confidence.

"Papa!" Leah shouted as Bill approached.

Dressed in a warm woolen coat and mittens and looking years older, Leah discarded the wood she'd been carrying and ran to her father's arms. "Are you back to stay? Some of the folks here said we're due a bad snow."

"Well, the work goes on whether there's snow or not," Bill replied, not willing to give her false hope. He touched her cheek lightly. *My, but you look like your mother,* he thought, and his heart ached all the more for what he planned to do.

Jacob rounded the corner of the tent, his arms loaded with wood. "Pa!" he said in a rather excited tone. "When'd you get back?"

"Just now," Bill replied. "Looks like you two could use some help."

"No, we've got it," Leah said, leaving her father's side to retrieve her own discarded pieces. "You carry things all day. We'll carry this and you come inside and rest. How are you hands?"

"Just fine, princess. I told you once they got used to totin' and fetchin' I'd be just fine."

"I'm sure glad. Karen said they would heal if you took proper care, but without anyone to help you, I wasn't sure you'd be able to do it all alone." Her voice was animated and cheerful, and Bill could have sworn she had a skip to her step.

Following his happy children into the tent, Bill tried not to think of how they would feel when they learned the truth. Somehow he would have to make them understand he was doing this for them.

Liar! his own voice echoed in his mind. He looked guiltily at the sale tables and shelves. *I'm doing this for me, not them. I'm doing this to escape the memories and the pain—leaving them to ease my own suffering!*

"Why, Mr. Barringer," Doris Pierce exclaimed, "we'd just about given you up for lost."

"It's only been three weeks," he replied. "I might not have come back this soon had I not come with word of Mr. Pierce."

"Father!" Karen came into the room just as he mentioned the man's name. "What of my father?"

"Well, he's stuck in one of the villages. Seems there's been some kind of epidemic and they're quarantining the area. Nobody in and nobody out. The Mounties are seeing to it that no one violates this order. They've caught a lot of the Indians trying to sneak out, but so far they've kept them contained."

Karen frowned and her worried expression made Bill uneasy. "Where did you hear this information?" she questioned solemnly.

"Adrik Ivankov."

"Is he here in Dyea?"

Bill shook his head. "I passed him up around Sheep Camp. He'd talked to your father prior to the epidemic hittin' the village. This is the first opportunity I've had to bring you the news."

"Was he all right?"

Bill shrugged. "Apparently so. He had plans to settle here in Dyea, in fact was moving out the next day, but the epidemic hit and Adrik figures he probably stayed to help and then got caught there with the quarantine. Now the heavy snows have come up high, and no one knows how bad this has made the trails."

"I suppose I shall have to learn better patience," Karen replied with a tone of disappointment.

"This is the place for it," Bill agreed, a hollow tone to his words.

Karen had the feeling that Bill Barringer had something on his mind. All evening he sat silently watching his children. Even after supper, when the dishes had been cleared away and the kids had offered to play rounds of checkers with him, Bill had only given it a halfhearted effort.

Perhaps he was worried. Heaven knew she was worried

enough for everyone there. Her father was contained in the middle of an epidemic, and she had no way of knowing if he was safe or in danger.

She tried not to think of her father shivering in the cold of an Alaskan snowstorm. She tried not to think of his dying from measles or whooping cough or whatever the sickness that plagued the village might be. She tried, but unfortunately her imagination ran rampant. Even after the lights had been turned down and they'd settled into their beds for sleep, Karen couldn't stop thinking. Fear crept over her in a sensation of bleak hopelessness that started somewhere deep in her heart and rippled out in destructive waves throughout her body. Try as she might, Karen could not shake the feeling of desperation that consumed her.

Risking the possibility of waking everyone else, Karen slipped from her bed and put a few more pieces of wood in the stove before slipping into the outer room of the tent. Darkness engulfed her, but it was the eerie silence that frightened her. Even the town seemed strangely silent, which for Dyea was a feat all its own.

Karen moved to the tent flap, thinking perhaps she might just slip outside for a moment. She knew it would be freezing, but grabbing up a wool blanket from the shelf, she decided to risk it anyway. Unfastening only one set of flaps, Karen dodged under the remaining closure and stepped into the icy air.

The cold assaulted her nose and lungs in a way that seemed to temporarily ward off her anxiety. The sky was overcast, muting out the light of the moon. Sighing, Karen stood in silence and wondered what the rest of the world was doing. Back in Chicago, Grace's parents were probably safe and warm, sleeping in their fine feather beds under warm blankets of goose down. Winters in Chicago could be horribly cold and damp, and no doubt the servants would keep the fires going all night to make certain no member of the family received a chill.

She wondered only momentarily about Martin Paxton. She could only pray that he'd accepted his defeat and moved on to greener pastures. She hated to think of Grace married to someone so hateful and barbaric.

Peter Colton then came to mind, and she knew there was a very good possibility the man would press his interest in Grace. She wondered if he was right for Grace. He seemed to hold no interest in issues of faith and God. In fact, he seemed downright angry and defiant about anything concerning God. Grace would never allow a man to take her away from her hope in Jesus, of this Karen was certain. No, if Peter Colton wanted Grace for a wife, he'd have to come to salvation first.

Then her mind went to Bill Barringer and his children. She thought again of how odd he'd acted all evening. His expression seemed mournful, almost as if he were experiencing the loss of his wife all over again. Perhaps the children reminded him too much of his wife. Leah said she looked like her mother, that everyone had told her so on many occasions. Maybe Bill found it difficult to be around the child without growing morose. But Leah was such a joy. In spite of her mother's death, she was like a fresh spring bud just waiting to burst to life. She loved to learn, and Karen often found her devouring whatever book she could get her hands on, all for the simple love of knowledge.

Jacob was a bigger worry. He worked all day at various jobs but never seemed satisfied. The wharf business had slowed for a bevy of reasons and with it, Jacob was more often than not sent off in search of another line of employment. He had come home with word that Skagway was actually considering a railroad to the north and that he just might get himself a job laying track if they actually went through with the plans. Karen had thought to condemn the idea but had remained silent. The boy was so clearly troubled and miserable about something. She felt it had to do with his father's leaving and the resentment he felt at being left behind. He resented, too, that the other boys picked on him for it. Most of the boys his own age were laying aside money and provisions to go north, but Jacob was merely trying to survive.

"Oh, God," she whispered, looking into the murky skies, "I want to help them, but I don't know what to do. I want to find Father and help him too, but again, I'm at a loss. I want you to direct my steps, to show me where I might best be used, but am I missing your direction? Have I somehow failed to understand your purpose?"

Down the street she could see some commotion and hear voices raised in revelry. This seemed a good time to slip back inside the tent. She had barely tied the bottom inside flap, however, when she heard voices from just outside the opening.

"Yeah, it's just women in here. Women with plenty of cash and goods. We can get what we need and take what we want, if you get my meaning," the man announced. There was laughter between what sounded like two, maybe three men. The sound left Karen trembling in fear. She felt frozen in place even as she saw the canvas around the inside flap begin to move.

CHAPTER TWENTY-ONE

MYRTLE HAWKINS pulled her coat tight against the brisk November winds. She had cried enough tears to last her a lifetime, and now she was determined that placing her trust in the Lord and seeking His strength would replace her years of greed and self-concerns.

Staring dry-eyed at her husband's mausoleum, she felt her heart break again for the pain and misery he had suffered. Poor man. He had tried so hard to keep from hurting her with the truth. If only he would have shared his misery and mistakes.

I would have forgiven you, my darling, even as I forgive you now.

All that mattered was that Grace remain safe. Martin Paxton had already seized most of their wealth and possessions, at least those he knew of. Myrtle was a smart, resourceful woman, however, and as soon as her world had begun to crumble, she had had the foresight to make provision. Even now her faithful butler was off tending to her business. He would meet her one final time at her hotel, bringing with him all the money he had managed to make by selling her jewelry, silver, and other valuable odds and ends. But it wasn't much, and it certainly wouldn't last long in Chicago.

She looked again to the mausoleum. She had come to bid Frederick good-bye, even though she knew he was no longer bound by the sorrows of this earth. It seemed fitting, however, to come to his tomb for one last moment before leaving the city they had once loved.

Myrtle planned to live in Wyoming for a time with her cousin Zarah Williams. It was here that Myrtle hoped to bring Grace when the time was right. In Wyoming, Myrtle hoped they could patch together the pieces of their shattered lives and learn to be happy again. She prayed it might be so.

Turning from her husband's grave, Myrtle made her way back to the hotel. Her knees ached terribly from the cold, but she refused to give up even the small price of a hired carriage. She would be prudent and frugal, a complete contrast to her old self.

I will make this work for Grace's sake, she told herself. *I will put aside the things of this world and the foolishness of my former self, and I will be a true daughter of God. I will put mankind before property and social settings. I will serve the needs of others instead of myself.*

She chanted this as a mantra, as she had during the days since learning the truth about her husband and Martin Paxton.

"I don't think you want to know the truth, Mrs. Hawkins,"

Paxton had told her quite smugly. *"Truth is not always attractive."*

"No, but it is always liberating," she had replied.

With a shrug, he seemed indifferent. *"Your husband destroyed my life. He dallied with the heart and soul of a woman who never meant more to him than a diversion. He made promises he couldn't hope to keep and used her in such a way that no decent man would have her after he'd finished. That woman was my mother, and your husband put her in her grave—just as I intend to see him in his."*

The news had come as a shock. Myrtle would never have imagined her husband as an unfaithful man. Of course, he was often absent from home, but business took him across the lake on many occasions. Weeks would pass with Frederick working away from home, and Myrtle had always endured them with patience and understanding. Her husband was making them rich. He was giving her all that she had desired and an even higher place in society. How could she fault him for that?

"I know you would probably rather dismiss this as a lie," Paxton had continued, *"but I have letters he gave her, words of love and hope, adoration and commitment. Would you care to see them?"*

Of course she hadn't wanted to see them. She wanted no visible evidence of her husband's adultery. Paxton spoke in detail of events in the life of his mother, including the miscarriage of a child—Frederick Hawkins' child. It was all so awful and complete in detail that Myrtle had no doubt of the truth. Neither did she have to wonder any longer what fueled the rage in Martin Paxton.

Narrowly avoiding an oncoming carriage, Myrtle's thoughts were instantly thrust into the present. Inside the carriage, she recognized the face of a one-time friend. The woman, however, was not wont to recognize Myrtle and quickly looked away.

That's how it had been from the first mention of the Hawkinses' downfall. No one wanted to be associated with a bankrupt man. Proper society would talk about the family in hushed whispers, but they would have no further dealings with them. Not even so much as to acknowledge them when passing on the street.

This is the life I once thought perfect, Myrtle realized. *This is what I aspired to become.* She felt deeply ashamed for her participation in such a world. What a price it had cost her. Her dear husband was dead. Her daughter was a world away. Her servants and friends were scattered like seeds in the wind, and she no longer had a place to call home.

But in her heart, Myrtle held a peace. God had not forsaken her. The trappings of the world had fallen away, but in their place she could see what was real. She could see beyond the trees—the forest she had created for herself.

" 'I see men as trees, walking,' " Myrtle quoted from Mark chapter eight. She remembered the verses clearly because Jesus then touched the man again. The memorized Scripture poured from her mouth. " 'After that he put his hands again upon his eyes, and made him look up: and he was restored, and saw every man clearly.' " Myrtle looked heavenward and smiled. "I am restored in you, O Lord, and in you I see every man clearly."

Martin Paxton joined the captain of *Summer Song* for dinner. Along with his good friend Ephraim Colton, Martin shared the table with Colton's wife, Amelia, and their daughter, Miranda.

The brown-haired beauty sat across from him at the small, yet elegantly set table. She smiled warmly, knowing him to be her father's dear friend, and he easily returned the smile. His attraction to her was something he had not expected; but then, he'd never seen the woman before. She reminded him something of Grace. Her sweetness and naïveté were worn openly as though something to be proud of.

She asked simple questions about a world she'd never seen, and he honored her with patient answers that he would otherwise have never wasted time sharing. *Perhaps,* he thought, *when I truly do take a wife, Miranda Colton would be a pleasing choice.* Of course, that would come much later. Later, after he'd dealt with Grace Hawkins.

Grace was now a personal issue. She had thwarted his plans, defied him to his face, and then without any difficulty whatsoever she had managed to slip from his grasp. He didn't care about Grace Hawkins in any personal way, but the fact that she was an unobtainable part of his previous plans ate at him like a disease. He would find her and he would break her.

"You haven't told us what brings you to Seattle and now here to join us on the trip north to Skagway," Amelia Colton was saying.

Martin smiled, thinking of the most recent message he'd received. "In truth, the trip was most unexpected. My fiancée was taken north with the gold rush madness. I'm hopefully going to make contact with her near Skagway."

"How delightful!" Amelia declared.

"I had no idea you were engaged to be married," Ephraim said, pouring Martin another glass of wine. "Congratulations. Although it's a pity."

"Why do you say that?" Amelia asked her husband.

"He might have considered our Miranda, otherwise,"

Ephraim replied with a wink. Miranda blushed and looked to her plate, while Amelia laughed at the tease.

"She would be a fair prize indeed," Martin offered gallantly. He could see she was clearly embarrassed, and he hoped to win her confidence by changing the subject. He might need Miranda Colton's allegiance at a later date, and he wanted very much for her to consider him a friend. "I am quite pleased with the profits of our business arrangements. I had meant to address the issue earlier."

Ephraim nodded. "The news just gets better with each trip north. My son is quite exuberant about his own venture in Dyea. He hopes to continue in business by building a small general store of his own. I hope you do not consider this as too much of a rivalry."

"Not at all," Martin replied. "As is my understanding of the area, there appears to be room for all."

"Very true. The harbors are poor in Dyea, but that is quickly resolved by building wharfs and docks. As it stands, a ship may drop anchor in deep water and allow barges to take the goods ashore. It's more time-consuming, but for those who prefer to begin their journey from Dyea, it truly becomes more economical."

"And what of Skagway?" Martin asked, already knowing the answer from his own hours of research.

"Skagway is good for shipping. The town is booming, as is Dyea. The passage north from Skagway allows for horses and wagons. At least this is what I'm told. There is some talk of a railroad. I wouldn't count on that, however. The talk can hardly be trusted as more than rumors and innuendoes. I can't imagine trying to cut a path through that wilderness."

"People said the same of our western frontier," Martin replied, knowing well the plans for a railroad north. He even hoped to put himself at the center of such a venture. "Look at us now. Railroads crisscross the country and everyone rides the train."

"Believe me, I know how plentiful those iron beasts have become," Ephraim said. "My business has suffered until now because of it."

"There will always be room for ships and railroads alike. I wouldn't allow it to cause you any more worry. What matters is planning. You have to think toward the future and realize what potential awaits you there. You have to decide what it is you want out of life, then take it."

Ephraim chuckled. "I wish I had more of your enthusiasm. Peter tells me I lack the type of business acumen that would see us as wealthy people, but truly I have no desire to be wealthy."

Martin couldn't imagine any man feeling like this. "What is it you desire?"

"I have all that I could hope for. A loving wife and two wonderful children. I have a home to offer them and the means to earn a living. What more could any man desire?"

Martin knew there was plenty more to be desired, but he said nothing. Smiling, he raised his glass. "To desires that are fulfilled," he toasted.

Later, in the privacy of the best cabin on board *Summer Song*, Martin leisurely enjoyed a cigar and reread a rather unexpected letter from Myrtle Hawkins. The woman had taken his news rather stoically. He had expected tears and sobs at the knowledge of her husband's betrayal, and instead she had remained calm, collected, and even-tempered. People like that unnerved him.

"My mother was your husband's lover," he had told her with great satisfaction. Here at last was the threat that had sent

Frederick Hawkins to his deathbed. Here was revenge for his mother, so painfully wronged.

"She was a beauty, my mother." He had pulled a photograph of her from his pocket and offered it to Myrtle. *"Wouldn't you like to see what took your husband away from you for long weeks and months?"*

She had studied the photograph for a moment before handing it back to Martin. Her color had paled somewhat, but she remained in complete control of her emotions. *"She is a very pretty woman."*

"Was," he corrected. *"She died and your husband killed her."*

That had brought a bit of response from Mrs. Hawkins. Her eyes had grown wide and her brows had raised involuntarily.

"They had a torrid love affair. He cherished her for a time. He gave her everything she needed."

"Are you his son?" she had asked flatly, her expression recovering to one of neutrality.

Paxton had smiled. *"I could lie and say I was, but it really doesn't benefit my case. No. I am not Frederick Hawkins' son."*

Martin drew long and thoughtfully on the cigar. The cherry tip glowed in the dimly lit cabin. Hawkins had died without Martin ever having a chance to gloat over the fact that Myrtle now knew every detail of his wicked past. He would have liked to have seen the pained expression on Hawkins' face when he realized that his beloved wife knew all about his mistress. Better yet, he would have liked to have seen the woman cast the dying man aside. That would have been perfect in his estimation, for it was no less than Hawkins did for Martin's mother. But Myrtle Hawkins had remained at her husband's side—faithful and true to the end.

Perhaps that was why the woman's letter was of such particular distaste to him now. He scanned the pages and found the part that stole his delight.

My husband never knew of your declarations to me. I saw it served no purpose but yours to give him such information, and therefore chose instead to allow the man to go to his grave in peace and comfort. He died believing that I never knew of his shame—that he had preserved his marriage and family.

Martin tensed at the statement. So smug and victorious. Mrs. Hawkins actually believed she had won some small victory. But it was Martin Paxton who had won. The entire world could see it, he told himself. He now held most of Hawkins' holdings and controlled many of his former businesses. He had forced the sale of the house and estates and now held the proceeds of those sales as well. Myrtle Hawkins had won nothing.

He looked again to the letter, frowning at the feminine script.

I pray God deals justly with you, Mr. Paxton. I know of no man who deserves justice more surely than you. You have done what you set out to do, but I will tell you that the outcome is not what you expected. Instead of destroying my family, you have only made it stronger. You have no more power over us, and we will now go forward in a better life.

The only thing in life worth living for is love—something you will probably never understand. Grace understands it, however. And I finally understand it too. You can do nothing more to harm us, Mr. Paxton. It is now your mortal soul for which I fear.

He scowled and tossed the letter to the table beside him.

"You needn't fear for my soul, Mrs. Hawkins, and you needn't be so sure there is nothing more I can do to harm you."

He picked up another piece of paper and read the information aloud.

" 'Grace Hawkins left Seattle for Skagway. There are no records of where she went after arriving, but her name does not appear on the Canadian records showing her to have gone north.' " Paxton smiled and stretched out his legs in front of him.

"Soon, my dear. Soon. We shall have a reckoning, and when we are through, you will be nothing more than a brief entry in my memory. A dalliance—a pleasurable moment—a recompense for my mother."

CHAPTER TWENTY-TWO

PETER ARRIVED IN SKAGWAY a day before the scheduled arrival of his father's ship. Feeling a deep sense of confusion and frustration over his father's recent decision to expand his business relationship with Martin Paxton, Peter found himself in a foul mood. He knew his father respected Paxton as a longtime friend, but the idea that another man, a complete stranger to Peter, could come in and so influence his father bothered Peter more than he liked to admit.

Snow lightly blanketed the ground, making a vast improvement on the appearance of the small boomtown, but even this didn't help to lighten Peter's heart. He felt overwhelmed with concerns he'd never before considered to be of importance. Not only was his father making choices without seeking Peter's advice, but Grace Hawkins had made him reevaluate his entire method of dealing with life and his family.

He had never seen himself ruling over his family in a God-like way, yet given his current feelings, Peter couldn't help but realize Grace had made a good point. This only served to make matters worse, however. Peter had no desire to see himself as the kind of man Grace had described, and yet he had no desire to relinquish the position of respect and authority his family had delegated to him.

I'm a grown man, he reasoned. *Things like this shouldn't be of such concern. Under other circumstances I would have married and perhaps even produced heirs by now.* The thought had crossed his mind on occasion, and now with Grace in his life, it cornered his thoughts on more than fleeting moments. Thoughts of Grace had rapidly infiltrated his daily existence.

But if he married, what would become of his family? His father had little practical sense when it came to business. Never mind that the man had managed his shipping line for longer than Peter had been alive. After all, Colton Shipping had aspired to be nothing more than a local freighting line before Peter became old enough to push for further development. Peter had helped the company expand—to reach its fullest potential. What would happen if he bowed out now?

"Martin Paxton would happen," he muttered. He didn't even know the man, and already he felt a sense of competition with him. All of his life Peter had heard Martin and Martin's mother spoken of in a way that devoted a familylike closeness. Peter's father practically considered Martin's mother to be a sister. He didn't know any real details of their past, only that the family had been friends with his own back East, but apparently Martin Paxton had grown into a man of considerable power and wealth. Perhaps that was what bothered Peter the most. Paxton was successful in Ephraim Colton's eyes, while Peter was merely the son helping to run a business, which up until recently had been failing. Did his father see him as a failure as well?

"But people will always fail. We are, after all, human," Grace had told him.

The words were still ringing in his ears even now, weeks later. Had his family perceived him to have failed? Had he not met their needs somehow? Perhaps he should broach the subject with his father and ask for the truth.

Peter thought about this long and hard as he hopped a ride on a barge up the inlet to Dyea. His anticipation of seeing Grace again was blended with a sorrow that she could not be the woman he desired her to be. Why couldn't she be more like Miranda? *Miranda adores me,* he thought. *Miranda would never question me or consider my counsel to be less than the best. Grace thinks me to be overbearing. She believes me to have placed unfair demands on my family.*

"You have put yourself in the position to be a god to your family. You ask them to seek you for their counsel and direction," Grace had said.

So what's wrong with that? Peter questioned silently. He argued the matter internally, knowing that he needed to be able to share his answer with Grace. But logic would not win out. Instead, he again heard the petite woman's comments.

"I fear your family might suffer far more than they would ever need to suffer if you continue to fight God for first place in their lives."

She's full of religious nonsense, Peter decided. *She's been brought up in such a way that she simply doesn't understand how men must be in charge to see to their family's well-being. I've not chosen to usurp God—on the contrary. God is in His heaven and I am here. It only stands to reason that God would choose certain emissaries to guide the people of this earth.* Surely

Grace had not considered that. He smiled to himself. That had to be the answer. She was a very young woman. Perhaps she was simply ignorant of such matters. After all, her mentor was strong in her beliefs of women's rights, yet Grace's father arranged his daughter's marriage and future. In her simplistic manner, Grace was most likely confused by such contrasts. The thought comforted Peter and gave him new ideas for how to handle future discussions.

A fine, icy rain began to pelt Peter, stinging his face. Grateful for his heavy wool coat, he snugged down his cap and wrapped a woolen scarf around his face. A bitter wind blew from the northern snow-capped mountains. He pitied those who were probably even now trekking their way up and over the extensive passes. And all for the hope of seeing their first hint of gold. All for that elusive rock. Why was it so hard to see that the real gold was here in Dyea or Skagway? A man could get rich with nothing more than a tent and a stack of goods.

Given this scenario, Peter had foreseen great things for Colton Shipping. Had his father not committed to Martin Paxton's plans, Peter would have had them completely out of debt in another month. He'd planned to announce the news to his parents when they'd last been together in San Francisco, but that plan had been thwarted when his father delivered the news of his own venture with Paxton.

Again Peter felt the pinch of his father's decision. What if they no longer needed him? Worse yet, what if Grace was right? What if he had set himself up to be their god? Where did mere mortals go when they were cast from their lofty perches—no longer to serve as elevated deities? The thought haunted him all the way to his destination.

"Well, I must say, you're a welcomed sight for once."

The voice belonged to Karen Pierce, but it was Grace Hawkins who captured Peter's attention as he entered the tent store.

"Good day to you, ladies."

Grace smiled sweetly. "Good day to you, Captain Colton."

Karen pretended to be busy packing blankets into a crate, but Peter could tell she was hardly focused on her work. Both she and Grace wore layers of clothes, along with their coats. Apparently with the traffic that frequented the store, keeping the interior warm was most difficult.

"So I suppose I must ask," Peter said, feeling rather like an animal about to be trapped, "why is it that you welcome my appearance this day?"

Karen didn't even look up from her work. "We need to make a decision now about moving the store. If you aren't planning to do so, you may well have to run it on your own because we're moving."

Peter shook his head and looked to Grace for an explanation. It was then that he noticed Grace was also packing items into a crate. She exchanged a glance with Peter before quickly turning her attention back to her task.

"Well, it is very cold," she suggested. "We manage well enough in the back, but even so, the nights are difficult."

Peter nodded. "But I have a feeling there's something more to this than the weather. In truth, I had planned to move the store with this visit, but I haven't yet chosen a site. There is a gentleman in town who has the ability to build up a place overnight. He charges a considerable sum, but he's quite good and very much in demand."

"We know all about him," Karen replied. "We've been after him for weeks, but he's too busy making outrageous profits to worry over a trio of women who have to live in fear of their lives."

"What is she talking about?" Peter questioned Grace.

"Karen will have to explain," Grace replied. "I only saw the aftermath. She'd already shot the man by the time I came to her side."

"What!" Peter roared the word, not meaning to frighten them. He felt bad when both women jumped at least a foot in the air. His tone brought Leah and Doris running from the back. Doris held a fairly heavy pickax in her hands and looked as though she might even know how to use it.

"It's all right, Aunt Doris," Karen said, turning to comfort the older woman. "Captain Colton is just now learning of our trouble the other night. You and Leah go back where it's warm and we'll continue explaining. If he yells again, just ignore him."

"Oh my," Doris said, not at all interested in heeding her niece. "Has she told you of our peril?"

"Grace said Karen shot a man."

"She did," Leah threw in, "but she didn't kill him. He's been run clean out of town. They put him on the first ship south."

Peter's head was reeling. "Why did you shoot the man?"

Karen finally allowed her gaze to meet his. He noted the stoic manner in which she fixed her expression, but he couldn't ignore the fear in her eyes.

"I shot him because he wouldn't leave and he and his friends were threatening us with bodily harm. I'm sure I needn't go into more detail than that."

Peter felt sickened at the thought of what might have happened. Perhaps he should be grateful that these women were cut from a different cloth. Maybe Karen Pierce's strength and fortitude were a blessing in disguise. "Well, that's it," Peter replied. "You won't go long without a building. I'll see to it immediately. I shouldn't have been so eager to pay old debts. I should have insisted this tent be traded for a building."

"Don't be hard on yourself, Captain," Grace said, coming forward. "We have enough money to put together a payment for a small place, but no one has had the time. Most of the men have gold fever and little time for constructing homes or businesses. It's just as Karen said, we would have to pay double or even triple to have their consideration. We thought to have help from a local guide and a Tlingit Indian man, but they've both disappeared and we've had no word from them in a long while."

"Not since he sent word through Mr. Barringer that my father is delayed in a quarantined village."

Peter nodded. "I'm sorry to hear that. But what of Mr. Barringer? What of his son? They both appear to be strong, healthy men. Could they not lend their hand to constructing a building?"

"Bill Barringer has taken up a job of packing people and their goods up to the summit of Chilkoot Pass. He returns to see us only on occasion," Grace told Peter. "Jacob has been working off and on in a variety of jobs, but he's hardly more than a boy."

"I was capable of running a ship at his age," Peter retorted, having no patience for weak men. "Barringer should never have left you unprotected."

"We weren't unprotected," Karen replied. "The Winchester and I had the matter under control."

"But what might have happened if you'd been asleep?"

"I had tried to go to sleep, but I couldn't," Karen replied.

"Now I believe God was keeping me awake to ensure our safety."

"I don't see God providing a building for you," Peter retorted.

"Well, He did send you," Grace replied, offering him a smile.

Peter couldn't accept that answer as valid. "Think what you will." He looked around the room and shook his head. "I'll send some of my men over to help you box this stuff up. One way or another, we'll move you out. Until then, I'll post guards if need be."

Bill reached up to rub his tired shoulders. Stiff and sore, they served to remind him of the journey ahead, as well as the ones he'd already completed. Packing supplies up the long, difficult Dyea trail was no simple task. Day after day he'd found himself pressed to endure impossible terrain and surly-tempered clients. He'd taken to loading his packs heavier each day and now could handle one hundred pounds, same as most of the Tlingit packers on the route up the Chilkoot Pass. Nevertheless, at the end of the day, he was worn out and ready for nothing more than a hot meal and bed.

Winter had set in, and in some ways this made matters much easier to deal with. Now, instead of struggling to muck through oozing mud paths and climb over boulders and fallen trees, the ground had frozen solid and a coating of packed snow allowed for a more productive means of transporting the goods. Even better, the area between the Scales and the summit had been modified and a stairway of ice had been carved out of the mountainside. The hike was still long and arduous but much easier to master. The packers stood in line for what seemed like miles, rope guide in one hand, walking stick in the other, hunched over under the weight of their belongings.

Coming down was much simpler. Most of the packers took to the side of the carved pathway and slid down the mountain on their backsides. Sometimes they were even lucky enough to sit atop a piece of wood or a shingle for the wild ride down. It sure beat hiking down as they had before the snows were plentiful.

The cold weather actually did more to encourage the stampeders and their packers. A person needed to keep moving in the bitter winds, otherwise they could find themselves quickly freezing to death. Bill and two other men had come across a woman and child only a day earlier, half frozen and starving in a snowbank. Neither were dressed for the climate nor the ordeal of mastering the summit. After seeing them to safety, Bill couldn't help but think of his daughter. He shuddered to think of Leah lying frozen at the side of the road.

The image only increased his resolve to go north on his own. He was ready now. He'd been earning almost forty cents per pound to pack goods and had spent very little until today.

Smiling at the stack of goods he could now call his own, Bill couldn't help but feel a twinge of excitement. Several men had become discouraged with their dreams of gold and had sold out to Bill. As required by the government of Canada, Bill had enough supplies to see him through a year in the wilderness. There was some fifteen hundred pounds of assorted goods, part of which he'd already packed to the summit on behalf of his client. Now the materials awaiting him atop the pass belonged to him. He had the bill of sale and could prove his ownership.

The idea sent a surge of anticipation and excitement coursing through his body. There would still be more than a dozen trips to make up and down the ice stairway, but that was of no real concern. He could do it. He had already come this far and nothing would stop him. Everything was planned. Everything seemed in order.

Bill tried not to think about his intentions to give sole responsibility of his children's well-being to Karen Pierce. With Jacob working and Leah helping at the store, they were no doubt earning their own keep. They couldn't possibly be costing Miss Pierce that much to feed and house. He comforted himself with the reasoning that they were much better off warm and safe in Dyea, no matter who might be helping to care for them.

When I strike it rich, he thought, *then I'll send for them and we'll be a family again. They'll understand that I've done what is right and best.* At least he hoped they would.

He covered the supplies with a tarp and staked it down. His last order of business was to make one final trip down to Dyea. He had to tell Leah and Jacob good-bye, and he had to explain to Karen Pierce what he was doing and why he needed her help. It never really entered his mind until that moment that they might all protest his action and refuse to cooperate. He frowned, trying to imagine what he would do or say should they cause a fuss. Jacob would insist on going north with him, yet there were no supplies for his son. As it was, Bill had teamed up with another group of men and this was allowing for a much easier time. One man had a stove and another the tools. A third man was a walking arsenal, refusing to go north without his beloved ivory-handled pistols, two rifles, and a shotgun. Bill had an entire set of pots, pans, and camp dishes, along with some tools and something more valuable than the others combined—a working knowledge of mining.

No, he'd simply have to explain the situation to Jacob and

insist he remain behind to care for Leah and await the time when Bill could send for them.

"Bill, you heading down to Dyea?" one of the trio he'd partnered with asked.

"Yeah, heading there now."

The man produced a list and a wad of bills. "See what you can get. I've already searched through Sheep Camp and wasn't able to get much of anything."

Bill nodded and pocketed the list with the bills. "My friends run a store in Dyea. I might have better luck. Keep an eye out for my goods, will you?"

The man nodded. "We'll be packing the whole time you're gone, may even get a chance to move some of your stuff up as well."

Bill hadn't considered that his team might be delayed by his brief journey to Dyea. "I could hire a couple of Tlingits to help," he offered.

The man considered the idea for a moment. "I could see to it. You can pack my goods up from Dyea, and I'll see to keeping you caught up with the rest of us."

"Deal," Bill replied, then without wasting any more time on conversation, he picked up the small sack he'd put together for his hike to Dyea. "I'd best get a move on."

The hours of daylight were lessening considerably as the sun altered its course in winter. Bill found the lack of light a minor inconvenience. Having spent most of his adult life in mines of one sort or another, the darkness had never been an impediment to him. Still, the trails were more dangerous at night and he had little desire to be lost to an encounter with wildlife, or worse yet, underhanded humans.

The road back to Dyea was easier in the snow. Hard-crusted paths had been tramped down by hundreds of feet before his, and Bill found it far less complicated than maneuvering through the knee-high mud of late summer and fall. The frozen Taiya River would also afford him an easy path. With exception to those places where fallen trees and logs made artistic combinations with the now frozen water, the river would make a straight run into Dyea and shorten the time Bill would be on the trail. *If I had ice skates, I could make the trip in half the time,* he thought, smiling.

It was nearly dark by the time Bill reached Dyea. He'd already decided he would talk to Karen first. He would just explain the situation as it was and not give her a chance to refuse him. It had to be this way, and the sooner she realized it the better. If he had to, he'd tell her some of the horrors he'd seen along the way. He'd talk about the nearly frozen woman and her child. He'd even talk about the dead—those who had succumbed to the elements or their own weak bodies.

As if by preorder, Bill arrived at the tent store just as Doris and Grace were heading out with Leah.

"Papa!" Leah exclaimed. She hugged him tight and kissed his frozen cheek. "We're just off to do some shopping at Healy and Wilson's store. Do you want to come?"

"You have a store right here," he teased. "Are you deserting the Colton Trading Post?"

Leah laughed. "No. The other store has a new load of goods. They just came in last week. They have bolts of corduroy, and Grace and I are going to make me a new skirt."

Grace smiled up at Bill. She was hardly any taller than his daughter and very nearly the same build. "It's true, Mr. Barringer. Corduroy will make for a very warm skirt, and we must hurry or it will be taken up by the other women. Besides, we want to get back before it's completely dark."

"Then, by all means, don't let me be the reason for the

delay. I'll be here when you get back, princess," he said, patting his daughter's shoulder.

"Are you sure you don't want to come with us?" Leah questioned. "You could hear all the news. There's been talk that gold has been found on the river here in Dyea. You could find out all about it and maybe we'd not have to go so far north to look for gold."

"Gold, here?"

Grace nodded. "That's what's been rumored. There are probably a dozen or more claims already staked. I haven't heard much in the way of success stories and certainly no call of a bonanza strike like they have up in the Yukon. Might just be cheechakos. You know how they can be."

"You've picked up the language pretty well for bein' a cheechako yourself," Bill teased. He liked Grace very much and found her charm and sweetness reminded him of Patience when she had been the same age. The idea of gold in the area intrigued him, and for a moment he thought to abandon his plans. "So who might know more about the Dyea strike?"

Grace grew thoughtful. "I suppose you should talk to the recording office or the assayer. They'd be able to tell you what kind of color they're seeing."

Bill nodded. "I'll do that. You ladies go ahead to your shopping. I need to see Miss Pierce for a moment, and then I'll take you up on your advice and head over to the recording office."

"You won't leave before we get back, will you?" Leah asked hopefully.

"Of course not. I'll stay the night." He said the words as her expression tore at his heart. She trusted him—believed in him. How could he betray her? He watched the trio walk away. They were happy and Leah was healthy and well cared for.

That was far better than anything Bill could give her on the Chilkoot Pass.

"Mr. Barringer, whatever are you doing standing out here in the cold?" Karen Pierce questioned as she stepped outside to throw out a pan of dirty water. "If you're hungry we have a pot of beans on the stove. Leah has just gone off with my aunt and Grace."

"Yes, I saw them," Bill replied. "And I'd be happy to warm up by the stove and eat. Maybe you could share a bit of conversation with me. We should probably discuss the children."

"You're right on that matter. I've had some concerns," Karen admitted. She ushered Bill into the tent and followed him back into their private living quarters. "I've been worried about Jacob."

"Jacob? Why?" Bill questioned. He looked around the room as if the boy might suddenly appear.

"He's gone off to help Captain Colton. We're to move the store into a new building tomorrow."

"A building will be a wonderful change. Where will it be located?"

"Several blocks north on Main Street. I'm sure you'll have no trouble finding us. The captain has arranged a decent-sized building with several big rooms on the back. We'll be living there and you are welcome to come and stay there as you come back and forth."

"Well, that's part of what we need to discuss," Bill began, but Karen quickly continued, giving him little chance to speak.

"Jacob has been very troubled over these passing weeks. He has few friends in this town and his heart seems quite burdened by something. He won't talk on the matter. I've tried working with him on studies, but he holds little interest and while he's good to contribute to our needs by bringing food and sometimes other necessities, he distances himself from all of us, Leah included."

"He's a young man in a house full of women," Bill replied. "I'm sure he's feeling a bit out of sorts."

"It's more than that," Karen admonished. "He's often been in fights."

"It'll do him good to fight for what he believes. That's how it is with men."

Karen shook her head. "He needs a father. As you said, he's surrounded by women. Perhaps he should join you on the trail."

Bill tensed. "I don't think that would be a good idea. The elements are killing people every day. Sometimes from workin' too hard, sometimes the weather. You know there've been floods and mud slides, snow and ice storms. It's a hard life, and I'd rather not see him exposed to it just yet. I'm sure he'll adjust to working here with you in time."

"I disagree. He needs you."

"I think, Miss Pierce, I'm better able to know what my kids need than you are."

Karen lifted her chin, striking a rather defiant pose. "I may not have children of my own, but I know children. I nannied Grace for over ten years. I know when something isn't right and your son is clearly troubled."

Bill knew he would have to explain the situation. "You have to understand that some things have changed. I've been working hard to put together supplies for the journey north, but one man working alone is hardly able to manage very well for himself. The men I'm working with would have little patience for children—that's why I've chosen to keep them here in your care."

"Your son needs you," Karen reiterated. "Who else will show him how to be a man?"

"He already knows how to be a man, Miss Pierce. He's fourteen. He'll be fifteen next month. My father was already dead by the time I'd reached that age and I grew up just fine."

"Fine enough that you give little consideration for the needs of your children. You might as well not even come back for all the good you're doing."

Bill bristled at this. "I'm not going to stand here and argue," he said, forcing his tone to remain calm. He suddenly felt almost panicked by her reaction. He couldn't very well tell her of his plans now. Not when she was being so harsh with him in regard to Jacob and Leah. Turning to leave, he stopped and added, "Jacob will be just fine. He's going to have times when he fights. It's the only way he'll learn."

"Learn what, Mr. Barringer? How to be as coldhearted and unfeeling as you?"

Bill stormed out of the tent, not willing to even answer. He wasn't coldhearted and unfeeling. If anything, his feelings were eating him alive. Karen Pierce didn't know what she was talking about.

Jacob had heard every word spoken between his father and Karen Pierce. He felt horribly guilty for what had transpired between them. After all, they were talking about him. Karen was worried about the fights he'd had—at least the ones she knew about. Trouble was, Jacob found himself so often out of sorts with folks that he was quickly gaining a reputation as being a hoodlum. He felt bad that Karen worried, but he felt worse that his father didn't. How could he just walk away and not care what those fights were about?

Jacob felt tears come to his eyes and angrily wiped them away. He wasn't a baby and he wasn't going to cry. If his own father didn't have time or concern for him, then that was just the way it would be. He wasn't going to shed tears over it, and he sure wasn't going to let anyone know how much it hurt inside.

CHAPTER TWENTY-THREE

A SENSATION OF ANXIETY and anticipation washed over Peter as he made his way up from the Skagway docks. Word had come that *Summer Song* had arrived some hours earlier, as well as news that Martin Paxton had traveled north with the Colton family.

His family was to have rooms in the upstairs quarters of Martin Paxton's mercantile. Being one of the few completed wood-framed buildings, Paxton's store would afford them the best protection from the elements, as well as allow them time to visit with Paxton and make plans for the future.

To say that news of his father's friend coming north was disturbing was an understatement Peter didn't care to explore. He should have been grateful and glad for Paxton's interest in his family, yet he felt like a jealous sibling. For reasons that were beyond his understanding, Martin Paxton's arrival was rapidly diminishing the pride Peter felt in having purchased a building for the Colton Trading Post. He had planned to sit down with his father and explain the situation and the expenditures necessary to secure the store in Dyea. He had hoped to receive his father's blessing and approval for the choices he'd made, and somehow Martin Paxton's presence robbed Peter of the limelight. Peter knew his father would be focused on the old family friend rather than Peter's accomplishments, and it made him feel most uncomfortable.

I have to stop undermining my victories and accomplishments, Peter told himself. *I've worked hard for this, and the likes of Paxton shouldn't be the cause of my defeat.*

Acquiring the building had come at no small sacrifice. He'd had to pay a great deal to purchase the building, and along with this, Peter had to pledge shipments of building supplies that he would turn over at cost to the contractor. With the purchase finalized, Peter had sent half a dozen of his best men to help with the move of the store's goods and had even hired a sign painter to mark the new business properly. He felt good about what he'd accomplished. It had cost him a pretty penny, to be sure, but Grace and her friends, along with the trade goods, would be safe. The expense was worth it. Still, the idea of having to share his news in the presence of a man he had come to feel rather negatively toward left Peter feeling foolish.

Father admires and cares deeply for this man, he reminded himself. *It's hardly fitting that I should despise the man simply for encouraging my father to take proper business risks.* After all, Paxton had the capital to offer along with his advice.

As Peter neared the store he admired an artistically painted red, white, and blue sign announcing *Paxton & Co. Mining Supplies.* An American flag was painted on either side of the name. The sign was new and Peter was notably impressed with the addition. It lent the store a certain flair of wealth and prestige, as well as patriotism. Of course, he wasn't sure that the stampeders would care about the aesthetics, but the tasteful presentation both impressed and discouraged Peter. His own store would be a shoddy example next to Paxton's. *Perhaps I can get my own painter to embellish Colton Trading Post with a bit of flair. I might even bring up several gallons of colorful paint and do the store up proper.* The thought made him feel marginally better.

Peter made his way inside, nodding at the clerk and searching the room for any sign of a familiar face. "I believe Mr. Paxton is arriving today along with my family," he announced.

"Yes, sir. They're all upstairs. You can use the stairs back there." The man pointed to an open door beside a display of sleigh runners and wagon tongues.

Peter nodded and made his way through the well-stocked store. No doubt deliveries from *Summer Song* were quick to be put into order if Mr. Paxton had anything to say about the matter.

Climbing the steep, narrow stairs, Peter wondered what his encounter with Martin Paxton might actually bring to light. The man could be someone Peter might respect and enjoy dealing with. Intelligent men with a mind for business were always of value to Peter's way of thinking.

He opened the door onto the second floor and was greeted by Miranda's laughter and his father's enthusiastic tales of boyhood.

"Peter!" Miranda declared as he stepped into the room. "Oh, do come join us. Father is telling the most delightful story of when he and Mr. Paxton's mother got lost while exploring a cave."

"I'm glad to see you all have arrived safely," Peter said, giving his mother and sister a smile. He turned his attention only briefly to his father before sizing up the middle-aged man at his father's side.

"You must be Martin Paxton," Peter said, not waiting for an introduction.

Paxton smiled and extended his hand. "And you are the man responsible for keeping Colton Shipping in the black. Your father speaks very highly of you."

Peter felt some of his confidence return. He smiled at Paxton, noting a severity in the older man's expression. While he offered a smile and friendly words, the man's eyes seemed to denote a more cautious demeanor.

"And I've heard favorable stories of the Paxtons since I was a small boy," Peter replied, shaking hands.

"We are all very much like family, eh?"

"Indeed we are," Ephraim Colton offered. "Once you have found your bride and are married, we shall endeavor to have you both spend time with us in San Francisco."

Peter was confused by the statement. "Are you looking for someone in particular or simply searching the Alaskan territory for a wife?"

Paxton laughed. "No, I have a particular woman in mind. We were engaged some time ago. She came north with friends and, well, I was to join her here. We'll marry and return to the States before winter disallows for easy passage."

"You shouldn't have any trouble. These harbors are said to remain open year-round. I've not yet experienced the situation firsthand but have heard favorably from other captains."

"That's indeed good news," Paxton replied.

Peter couldn't shake the feeling that Paxton was considering him beyond the mere introduction of a family friend. Paxton's green eyes seemed to take in everything around him all at once, while at the same time be zeroed in on Peter as if awaiting an answer to some unspoken question.

"We told Mr. Paxton you could probably help him in finding his fiancée," Peter's mother began, "but seeing the number of people in Skagway, perhaps it won't be quite that simple."

Peter nodded. "The town is growing daily. I brought a full ship of men and women to the city just ahead of you. All were most anxious to make their fortunes. Nevertheless, Mr. Paxton, if I can be of help in your search—"

"I have hired some men to help in searching through the town," Paxton interrupted. "Although I understand there is another town a few miles away. I believe it's called Dyea."

"Yes," Peter said thoughtfully. "I have friends there who are running a small trading post for me. I would imagine they very well might know your fiancée, especially if she's to be found in Dyea. There aren't a great many women up this way, and ladies of quality seldom pass unnoticed. What's her name?"

"Grace Hawkins," Paxton replied. "She hails from Chicago and is probably traveling with a woman by the name of Pierce. A Miss Karen Pierce."

Jacob knew his father was up to no good when he announced that he would spend a second night with the family. They had just moved into the new building, and his father made the pretense of wanting to be sure that everyone was settled in before heading back up the trail. Something in the situation just didn't seem right with Jacob. He could sense his father's agitation—could feel his discomfort.

"What's wrong with Pa?" Leah asked him in a hushed whisper.

Everyone headed off to their beds with Leah, Jacob, and Bill being relegated to one room while Karen, Grace, and Doris took another. Bill announced that he'd stoke up the fire in the main living area before joining his children for the night. This gave Jacob time to ponder what his father might be up to.

"I don't know what's going on," Jacob admitted to his sister. "But he is acting strange—has been ever since coming back. Maybe he's just worried about the weather."

"Maybe," Leah replied, hurrying to bury herself under the wool blankets on her cot.

Their father entered the room rather expectantly, almost as if he anticipated their questions. When Leah and Jacob only watched him, however, Bill Barringer took the opportunity to question them.

"Have you been minding yourselves for Miss Pierce?"

Leah nodded from her bed. "Yes, Pa. I like Miss Pierce a lot. She's teachin' me the same kinds of things Mama used to show me."

He smiled benevolently on his youngest and turned to Jacob. "And what of you, son?"

Jacob tensed. He knew from having overheard his father's conversation with Karen that he would be wondering about the fights. "I'm doing my best, Pa."

Bill nodded. "Miss Pierce tells me there've been some fights."

Jacob looked to the floor as he moved to sit on the side of his cot. "Yes, sir."

"Well, she doesn't understand how it is with men. Just try

to keep out of trouble. You have a sister who needs you to stay in one piece. Men up here are mighty tight strung. The gold fever is keeping them at odds with everyone, and those that can't put together the wherewithal to get north are going to be particularly surly."

Jacob looked up to meet his father's eyes. "I'm not in any trouble, Pa. The fights are usually because I let my temper get the best of me."

"You know what your ma would say about that?"

Jacob nodded. "She'd tell me to turn the other cheek. To put a guard over my mouth."

"Exactly," Bill replied. "Things will probably seem to get a whole lot worse before they get better." He sat down and began pulling off his boots. "Sometimes folks do things that others have a hard time understanding. Sometimes things don't make much sense and it leaves angry feelings between people who care deeply about one another."

Jacob knew his father was talking about something more than his daily fisticuffs with other local boys.

"Sometimes, without even meaning to hurt their loved ones, people do things that they have to do. Important things that will make it better for everyone in the long run."

"What kind of things, Pa?" Leah asked from her bed.

Bill scratched his beard and pulled off his remaining boot. Jacob could see that his father's hard work had worn holes in the heels and toes of his socks.

"Well, princess, it's like your mama used to say. Sometimes God sends things our way to bless us and sometimes they come to teach us. Some of those teachin' times are hard. They might even cause us pain. Sometimes they take people away from us—people we love and care about."

"Like Mama?" Leah asked.

Jacob wished they'd both just drop the subject. Thinking of his mother only caused him greater grief. Some of his fights had come about because of derogatory statements made about his mother. But more often than not, they referenced his father.

"Look," their father stated, getting to his feet. "I'm going to smoke me a bowl." He picked up his pipe and smiled at them both. "Your ma would be proud of you children. I'm proud too. Just never forget that."

He left them then, closing the door behind them. Jacob reached for the lantern, but before he could turn it down, Leah sat up in bed. Her eyes locked on his.

"He's leavin' us, isn't he?"

Jacob nodded. He felt a lump in his throat that refused to allow him speech. His sister had spoken the truth—an undeniable truth. Their father was leaving them here—leaving them with Miss Pierce and going north.

He blew out the light quickly, not wanting his sister to see his tears. Balling his hands into fists, he punched at the pillow as if to arrange it into proper shape for his comfort. In truth, he was beating out the anger in his soul—an anger that was threatening to eat him alive.

Karen found the coals in the stove were just barely putting off heat by the time she roused herself to prepare breakfast. Adding wood and tenderly nurturing the fire back to life, she grabbed a bucket of water and placed it atop the stove. At least the water hadn't frozen like it had all those nights in the tent. The new building would afford them a much more comfortable existence, and once her father made it back to Dyea, she'd simply convince him to stay on with them.

Finding it still dark outside, Karen lighted a lamp and went to work measuring out oats for their morning cereal. It was as she set the table with bowls and spoons that she noticed the folded piece of paper addressed to her attention.

Puzzled, Karen put down the bowls and reached for the missive. Unfolding it, she found herself completely overwhelmed by the news of Bill's departure.

It might seem unfeeling, she read halfway down the page, *that I should leave my children behind, but you don't know what the trails are like. I've seen people die—kids too. I wouldn't want that for Jacob or Leah. I'll send for them as soon as I can. Please don't be angry and take it out on the kids. I love them, and I know you've come to care for them in your own way. I'll write when I get settled, and I promise to pay you for your trouble.*

He added no personal notes for the children, and Karen couldn't help but wonder if he'd left similar letters for each of them. She glanced around but found nothing. Perhaps if he had, he would have left them in the bedroom he had been sharing with Jacob and Leah. She thought to go searching but decided against it. They would have to know the truth sooner or later. If they said nothing to indicate their father had told them of his departure, Karen would remain silent and save the news for a more private moment.

She quickly refolded the letter and put it in her pocket. A feeling of despair washed over her as the reality of the situation began to sink in. She was now mother to two motherless and fatherless children. Jacob, already angry and unreachable, would not brook this desertion easily. And poor little Leah, who adored her father and mourned her mother, would be devastated. Karen wanted to cry for them both. How could the man have been so heartless?

"I thought I heard you out here. You should have woke

me," Grace said, tying an apron around her waist.

Karen smiled, but her heart wasn't in it. "You look positively domestic, Grace."

Grace smiled. "I actually like the life. I used to feel so completely useless back home. This seems much more fitting. Why should I have servants when I take such joy in doing things for myself? Mother, of course, would be horrified, but I love it all, even the cleaning." She pulled her hair back and tied it with a ribbon before adding, "Wasn't it kind of Mr. Barringer to stay another day in order to see us settled in?"

Karen nodded and turned quickly back to the oatmeal. She had no desire to broach the subject of Bill's departure with Grace. She couldn't even decide how to tell the children, much less announce to Doris and Grace that she was now fully responsible for the care of two children. "I was just setting the table."

"Then I'll finish it," Grace replied as Jacob and Leah emerged from their shared room.

"Where's Pa?" Leah asked, looking around the room.

Karen met her expression, then let her gaze travel to where Jacob stood with a look of stoic indifference on his face. *I can't tell them,* she thought. *I can't hurt them like this. Better to let them think he's simply gone back to work on the trail.*

"He left early," she finally said. At least it wasn't a lie.

Leah's face paled as she turned to Jacob. Karen could see the boy's jaw clench as if in rage. He put his arm around Leah, then met Karen's eyes. Karen trembled without knowing why. They knew. Either Bill had told them of his plans or he had left them similar letters, but either way—they understood what his absence meant.

She pulled the letter from her pocket. "Did your father give you any idea of what is in this letter?"

Leah shook her head. "He didn't say much last night." Her voice sounded frightened and uneasy.

Karen wanted to put her mind at ease but knew the contents of the letter would do nothing of the sort.

"Your father has gone and asked me to take care of you until he's settled," Karen finally stated. She looked to the letter as if to read it, then decided against it. Glancing up, she could see the anger in Jacob's eyes.

"He's gone?" Grace questioned. "Do you mean permanently?"

Karen had expected the question from Leah or Jacob, but not from Grace. She turned to her friend and nodded. "He felt the trail was too dangerous."

Grace nodded, seeming to understand that her reaction would affect the children's reaction. "Well, I suppose that must have been very hard for him," she said softly. "What a difficult choice to make."

Karen gave Grace a smile of gratitude before turning back to the children. "I want you both to know that I won't allow any harm to come to you, if I have any say about it. We can make better plans once my own father returns to Dyea, but for now, just know that you have a home wherever I have a home."

Leah burst into tears and came to wrap her arms around Karen. "What if he doesn't come back?" she cried.

"He'll come back. He promised to in his letter," Karen said, trying to sound reassuring. Her confidence faded, however, as she met Jacob's eyes. They both knew it was a lie. Bill Barringer might never again return. The leaving had been the hard part. Staying away would require little effort.

CHAPTER TWENTY-FOUR

KAREN AND GRACE poured all their energies into making bread for the days to come, while Doris and Leah minded the store. They no longer worried about their safety. Word had traveled fast about Karen's ability with a rifle, and with that reputation, a new respect for the trio of women was born. The rowdies still poured in, demanding and bellowing for their supplies, bemoaning their lack of good fortune, or complaining about some swindle that had left them penniless. But through it all, the customers maintained a kind of silent admiration for the women.

"You ladies are known as the toughest bunch of gals in Alaska," one prospector had told them. *"We drank to your health last night at the Gold Nugget. Then we drank to ours, just in case you took a dislikin' to us."*

Grace had laughed at the sentiment. She still found it hard

to believe that they'd been put in such situations of peril. Her days prior to coming north had never prepared her for the life she was now living, but she couldn't help but enjoy the freedom they now experienced. She thought, in fact, she very well might like to settle permanently in this wild, rugged country.

"So what's so pleasant that I find you grinning from ear to ear?" Karen asked from across the table.

Grace was overjoyed to find she had a few moments of privacy with her dear friend. "I was just thinking about our reputation. I'm sure half the newcomers to the area are too scared to even step foot in the store."

"Yes, but the other half comes out of curiosity and maybe even the desire to consider challenging us," Karen replied. "I don't like having a reputation either way. I'd prefer we be unnoticeable, given the reason we came here in the first place."

"You aren't still worried about Martin Paxton, are you?"

"Aren't you?"

Grace was surprised by Karen's candor and considered the idea for a moment. "Not truly," Grace said as she mixed yet another batch of sourdough. Taking a pinch of the starter, which had come by way of an old Tlingit woman who traded for sugar, Grace worked in the ingredients and waited for Karen to reply. When she said nothing, Grace stopped stirring and looked up. "Are you worried?"

"Some. I guess I've known men similar to Mr. Paxton. They aren't easily swayed and not at all inclined to take defeat—especially from a woman."

"I wouldn't fret over it. We're a long way from Chicago, and Mr. Paxton must have other concerns to busy himself with. Just as we have ours. I was just thinking that I might very well like to settle here. Perhaps I'll stay on, even when Mother assures me that all is well. Maybe I can even convince

Mother to bring Father and come here to join me. Although I suppose there would be little work for Father here, and Mother does love her social events."

Grace paused, noting that Karen was sitting idle, staring off as if lost in a memory. "What's wrong? I don't think you've heard a word I've said."

Karen shook her head. "I'm sorry. What were you saying?"

"Never mind what I was saying. Tell me what has you so worried."

"My mind is just preoccupied. I'm worried about Father, and I'm worried about those children."

"This doesn't sound like the same woman who told me over and over that we had to give our heartaches to God and trust that He would see us through the bad times as well as the good."

"I know God is in the midst of this, but I have a bad feeling about this matter of the Barringer kids. Leah is so heartbroken that her father would leave her behind, and Jacob is angrier than ever. His rage was already getting the best of him—what do I do with him now?"

"Have you tried talking to him?"

Karen picked up a bag of flour and measured some out into a bowl. "I've tried," she said, focusing on her work. "But he wants no part of it. He's almost grown. And with Bill's departure, he certainly isn't open to parental guidance, especially in the form of a substitute mother."

Grace began mixing the bread again and considered the matter carefully. "I would hate to be left behind like that. They must feel completely betrayed."

"And the worst of it is, I can't help them to believe that they haven't been betrayed. I can't offer support for Bill Barringer's actions because I don't believe the man made the right choice. If anything, he should have taken his savings and loaded those kids back on *Merry Maid* and headed for home."

"I agree, but we can't change the circumstances now." Grace set the dough aside to rise and turned to her friend. "And what of your father? How shall we handle this matter?"

Karen put down the mixing bowl and shook her head. "Grace, I'm afraid."

"Why?" Grace could see the anguish in Karen's eyes, but for the life of her she couldn't understand what had given birth to this fear.

"I just have a feeling that things aren't good. I keep imagining that I've come all this way only to lose him."

"He's not lost," Grace said with determination. "He's just stranded for a time. The quarantine will pass and he'll return before the heaviest part of winter sets in. You'll see."

Karen moved to check the loaf of bread already baking in the oven. "I'd like to believe that, but I just feel so . . . so . . ." She looked up as she closed the oven door. "I feel lost."

"But I don't understand why," Grace said, coming to Karen's side. She put her hand on her friend's arm. "Has something happened that I don't know about?"

Karen shook her head. "No. I've had no news, if that's what you mean."

"Come. Sit with me and talk. We've not had a really good talk in so very long."

Karen smiled and followed Grace to the table. "You seem more the mothering figure now than me."

"Then let me bear your burden and help you to release whatever fears you may be holding inside," Grace replied.

Karen folded her hands and looked at them carefully, as if studying them for answers. "I don't know what I'm called to do anymore—what my purpose is. I used to know so clearly, but now I don't."

"What's changed?"

"You have, for one. You're a grown woman," Karen said, looking up. "You don't need a nurse or teacher anymore. You've taken to menial labor like a duck to water—you're better at bread making and sewing canvas than I can ever hope to be." She sighed and continued. "See, as long as you were a child, I knew my purpose. I felt called to be your governess—to stay at your side and see you raised properly. I enjoyed our time together and felt compelled to grow close to you as a friend, as well as a teacher."

"But nothing of that has changed. You are still my dearest friend, and there is still much I have to learn. I'm learning every day."

"Yes, but much of what you are learning now doesn't require my presence. I feel a restlessness in me, Grace. A calling out, if you would. The only problem is, I don't know what I'm being called out to."

"What of the Barringer children? You are taking up with Leah where you left off with me. Then, too, there's Jacob. He needs to be softened and molded into a young man with a heart for God and for good."

Karen seemed to consider Grace's words for a moment. In the silence, Grace could feel her friend's turmoil. It seemed to permeate the air like an odor—not quite unpleasant, but not altogether welcomed.

Karen finally spoke. "I thought maybe God was calling me north to work with my father. I thought perhaps I would teach the Tlingit children."

"And why can't you?"

"I suppose I can, but I don't know that this is the proper

calling either. I have spent a lifetime feeling called to specifics, and now everything seems so questionable. I knew since I was a young girl that I was being called to remain single—to receive an education. Eventually, I felt called to work for you." She looked at Grace and smiled. "Do you remember that at first your mother thought me too young and inexperienced to work as your nanny?"

Grace nodded. "I overheard her tell Father that in spite of your being an educated woman, you knew nothing of life."

"Well, she was partially right, but I knew more of life than she gave me credit for. Anyway, I had no fear of not being hired for the post. I knew God had brought me to you, and I knew it was His will for us to be together. But now I don't know what His will is. I don't know what I'm supposed to do. I can't say whether I'm to remain single or teach or to raise the Barringer children until their father chooses to show up again. I simply feel that the answers are veiled away—hidden from my sight."

"Have you prayed on the matter?"

Karen laughed. "That seems to be all I do accomplish. I pray and pray and pray again. And still I feel no peace in my heart. I feel as though I'm in a constant state of limbo. I can't move forward or backward, nor side to side."

"Perhaps, then, you aren't supposed to move at all. Maybe this is one of those times of resting and waiting. I know it is for me."

"Because of your parents and Paxton?" Karen questioned.

Grace felt overwhelmed with her own feelings and concerns. She had longed to talk to Karen and share her heart, and now her emotions welled up inside her and threatened to spill over. "I think I'm in love."

The words had an obvious effect on Karen. "Peter Colton?" she questioned.

Grace felt her face flush. "I know you disapprove and I know you two grate on each other's nerves, but I find my heart so overwhelmed when he is near. I feel like my stomach is doing flips and my head is soaring high above my body."

"Couldn't we just chalk it off to gold fever or some other type of illness?" Karen questioned. "I mean, does it have to be love? Does it have to be him?"

Grace frowned. "Why do you hate him so?"

"I don't hate him, Grace. I simply see him as the same domineering type of man you've found yourself under all of your life. Your father was like that—Paxton is like that."

"Captain Colton is nothing like Martin Paxton!" Grace declared defensively.

"But I fear he easily could be. He's only a step away from the same kind of insistent cruelty that you witnessed in your former fiancé. I just don't want you to get hurt."

"I'm already hurt," Grace replied, getting up from the table. "I can't love Peter Colton with any real hope of a future. He isn't interested in the things of God and he has no faith in Jesus Christ."

Karen nodded. "That was going to be my next point."

"Don't you think I've already considered all of this? You've told me time and time again how painfully destructive it can be for people to have split philosophies regarding religion. I know that Captain Colton has his own way of doing things and doesn't believe in a need for God, but I can't help that my heart feels as it does."

Grace's heart ached with the truth of her words. She knew deep inside she couldn't let her feelings for Peter take her away from her faith. She couldn't allow him to come between her and God. But she also knew her emotions were set aflutter every time the man walked through the door. She had never hoped to fall in love, not after her horrible encounter with Martin Paxton. She had never believed herself capable of trusting a man after her father's betrayal. But she had been wrong. Her feelings for Peter were very real, and she feared that if she couldn't find a way to control them, they'd also become very evident. After all, Karen had no problem in guessing to whom she'd given her heart.

"I won't do anything foolish if you're worrying over it," Grace said softly. "I'm old enough to know better."

"You may be old enough," Karen said, "but I'm not sure that's the issue. Knowing better is one thing—turning away from a bad situation is entirely different."

"Grace!" Leah called as she opened the door and bound in from the store. "You have a letter."

Grace felt her heart begin to race. "Is it from home? From my mother?"

Leah shrugged and handed her the envelope. "I don't know. Jacob just happened to be up at the post office and found out we had this letter waiting for us there."

Grace took the envelope and nodded. "Yes, that's my mother's script. I'm sure of it." She tore open the envelope and began to read.

Dearest Grace,

Things are quite grim, as we knew they would be, but will work themselves out in time. You must remain in Alaska for a time longer while I work to put things right again. I'll send word when it is safe to write to me, but until then, please send no correspondence. I won't be at the Chicago address anyway, and letters might only fall into the wrong hands.

Yours in love,

Mother

"I can tell by your frown that the news isn't good," Karen said, breaking the silence. "What does she say?"

"It's what she doesn't say that bothers me," Grace replied, handing Karen the letter. "She only says that things are grim. Well, we already knew they were that. She makes no mention of Martin Paxton or of Father. I can only presume the worst. Especially given the news that she won't be remaining in Chicago. Perhaps she has left Father."

Leah patted Grace's arm. "I'm sure your mama will be all right. Your pa too."

Grace smiled, encouraged by the child's words.

"Don't borrow trouble, Grace. You don't know anything of the sort. You can estimate and try to guess all you want, but it won't change matters. We must put it in God's hands and pray for the best. In the meantime, we have to have a positive outlook and believe that everything will come around right. Your mother loves you a great deal, and she would do anything to keep you from harm. It's the heart of every mother—or so I'm told." Karen gave Grace a sad little smile.

Leah surprised them by wrapping her arms around Karen in a possessive manner. "I wish you were my mother," she said without warning.

Karen hugged the child close and kissed the top of her head, all the while looking at Grace. Grace felt her heart breaking for Leah and Karen. They were both without benefit or hope of ever seeing their mothers again, until the time God would join them all together in heaven. At least Grace had her mother. She had to take comfort in that.

We might have wasted a good many years, Grace thought, *but we'll make up for the lost time when this matter is behind us. We will find a way to cross over the years of desert and make for ourselves a place of beauty and hope.*

Part Three

DECEMBER 1897–JANUARY 1898

For God shall bring every work into
judgment, with every secret thing,
whether it be good, or whether it be evil.

ECCLESIASTES 12:14

CHAPTER TWENTY-FIVE

DAYS AFTER BILL BARRINGER LEFT, Jacob disappeared. Karen frantically searched for the boy, seeking out the various places she'd heard him mention and talking to those who knew him. With every denial of the boy's whereabouts, Karen feared that he'd gone north to follow his father. It seemed to be the logical thing for the troubled youth to do.

Oh, God, she prayed as she made her way to the seedier part of town, *protect and keep him. He's just a child—a lost and lonely child. He's suffered so much already, please keep him from harm. Help him to find his hope in you.*

She continued praying, finding strength in the words she shared with her heavenly Father. There was comfort for her in the prayer as well. Karen had long realized the power of prayer and the way it allowed her to feel a connection to heaven and all that God offered. She thought of her father's deep love of

God, his desire to bring the lost souls to the same hope he'd found. Wilmont Pierce didn't care where that desire took him. He didn't mind the cost or the hardship. He simply loved God, and he loved the people God had created.

Karen wanted to love people in the same way, but where her father collectively embraced entire villages, Karen had always felt directed to focus on one or two people at a time. Perhaps it was just a different method of service, she thought, but perhaps it was a self-imposed limitation. She'd always felt divided and too far spread when she'd faced the situation of teaching to a group. Even when she'd worked with the children at church, Karen had found herself wondering if her time was well spent.

Maybe it's an issue of pride, she reasoned. *With one or two people I can easily see the results of my heartfelt work. With a crowd, I'm less certain. There are more possibilities for distraction.* Yes, she decided, it was pride. Pride kept her closed off from the rest of the world and limited her ability to offer herself freely to God.

Karen peered inside one tent saloon after another as she continued her search but found nothing but darkness. The morning hours brought hangovers and misery from nights spent in revelry and drinking. It seemed a shame that such beauty as was found in Dyea could be so marred by such sinful natures. She could only pray that Jacob hadn't fallen victim to such matters.

"Where can he be, Lord?" she whispered softly. She strained her eyes in the direction of the harbor. "He's just a boy."

Picking her way across the rutted frozen mud, Karen felt her efforts were rather futile. Perhaps Jacob would come back when he was good and ready. But then again, perhaps he would never come back. What was Karen to do or say if Jacob never returned? How could she explain it to his father?

Anger coursed throughout her body. Explain? To Bill Barringer? The man had deserted his children, left them to the care of a virtual stranger, and allowed gold fever to drive him away from his true responsibilities. Why, it would serve him right if she simply packed Jacob and Leah up and headed back to Seattle. Perhaps once she found her father she'd do exactly that.

But even as she considered the possibility, Karen knew she couldn't act on her anger. God had a purpose and plan for her life, and even if she was uncertain of the direction at this point, she couldn't make poor choices simply because others had taken that route.

Giving up for the time, Karen made her way back to the Colton Trading Post. She felt overcome with grief and sniffed back tears. What would become of the boy? If she couldn't find him and talk sense into him, what harm might he make for himself?

In a spirit of defeat, Karen paused at the shop door. She peered up Main Street and then down as if perhaps she'd overlooked something. The town was surprisingly peaceful. Perhaps the bitter cold had caused folks to give up the struggle for gold. Or maybe the fact that Christmas was only a few days away had given the townspeople something else to focus on.

"Kind of cold to be out here just gawking around, isn't it?"

Karen was startled by the appearance of Adrik Ivankov. She'd forgotten what a big man he was. Tall and broad at the shoulders, he looked even more massive in his heavy winter coat and fur cap.

"I was looking for someone," Karen replied, trying not to sound shaken. "Seems to be my lot in life."

"Just so long as you aren't planning on shooting anybody," he said, the twinkle in his eye revealing that he knew about her previous exploits.

"I didn't have it planned today," she replied with a smile. "Maybe I can work it in tomorrow."

He laughed with a deep, rich tone that actually seemed to give off warmth. "Given your nature, it wouldn't surprise me." He smiled and his long, ice-crusted mustache raised up at the corners.

His amusement unnerved her momentarily. "Have you had word from my father?" she questioned.

"No, but I wouldn't give it too much thought," Adrik replied. "Your pa isn't used to having to answer to anyone else. He's probably lost all track of time in helping the sick. You can't be takin' offense that he puts the Lord's work ahead of seeing you."

Karen stiffened. "I wouldn't begin to take offense at my father's work. He has a calling. He knows exactly what the Lord has asked of him—what He wants of my father's life. How could I possibly take umbrage over that?"

"How can you worry and fret about it, either?" Adrik questioned. "After all, if the good Lord called him, won't He see to him as well?"

Karen relaxed and nodded. "Of course, you're right. My nature has always taken a tendency of trying to orchestrate the details." She motioned to the store. "Would you like to come in and warm up? I'm sure there's coffee on the stove and you're more than welcome to take breakfast with us."

"Nah, I have to head up to Sheep Camp."

Karen felt a surge of hope. Perhaps Adrik could find Jacob. "Would you consider doing something for me—I mean while you are on your journey north?"

Adrik grinned. "It's hard to turn down a pretty lady. What'd you have in mind?"

Karen felt her cheeks grow hot at the compliment. "Well . . . that is to say . . ." she stammered, trying to regain her composure. "Mr. Barringer has gone north. He's heading to Dawson City, in fact. He's left his children in my charge, but the oldest has disappeared. Jacob is almost fifteen, and he's very angry that his father has left him behind. I fear he's gone off to find him."

Adrik rubbed his chin. "I'll keep my eyes open, but I only saw the boy once and that was from a distance. Bill pointed him out and that was kind of the long and the short of it."

"He's just a couple of inches shorter than me, and his hair is kind of a tawny color and straight. He has blue eyes and," she looked upward as if to draw to mind a clearer picture, "and a sweet boyish face." She gazed back to Adrik and shrugged. "I can't really tell you much more."

"You've just described half the boys on the trail and some of the men," Adrik replied, laughing. "But don't worry. If I see anyone slinking along on their own, I'll check it out."

"Thank you, Mr. Ivankov."

"Call me Adrik."

She'd faced these informalities before, but somehow with Adrik, the notion made her feel uncomfortable. "That wouldn't be very proper. We hardly know each other."

Adrik broke into a roguish grin. "I know plenty about you, Miss Pierce. Your pa has a propensity for talk when the fire is burning down and the stars are high."

Karen felt a trembling run through her body. She looked away quickly. "If you see my father, will you please tell him I'm thinking of him? That I love him," she added, self-conscious of the words.

"Only if you call me Adrik," he replied.

She looked up to find him still grinning. As uncomfortable as he'd just made her, Karen couldn't take offense. "Very well, Adrik."

He nodded approvingly. "I'll do it, and if time permits, I'll get word back to you or make sure that your father sends some word to you."

"Thank you. I know I'll rest better just knowing you've taken the matter in hand."

"Always happy to help a lady," he replied with a wink.

After an absence of three days, Jacob reappeared. It was Christmas Eve and the spirits of the residents of Dyea were running high. He couldn't help but notice the various ways in which people had tried to liven up things for the holidays. Some had cut paper stars and hung them with ribbon from their windows. Some had decorated little trees with silly things like kitchen utensils and yarn. There might be a gold rush on, but the birth of Christ was still very much on the calendar.

Jacob only wished he had a heart for the celebration. After trying without luck to find his father, he'd found himself face-to-face with Adrik Ivankov. The big, burly man assured him that his father would not be easily found and that the trail was too harsh for one as unprepared as Jacob.

The comment had stung his pride, but Jacob's freezing and starving body refused to allow his emotions any leeway. Agreeing to go back to Dyea, Jacob had happily taken a meal with Adrik. Warming up in a small tentside café, Jacob had lamented his ability to only reach Finigan's Point—not but a few miles up the trail.

"You ever consider that God might not have wanted you

coming up this way?" Adrik had asked him. *"Maybe there was a reason for you being in Dyea."*

"I thought I could find my pa and talk him into taking me with him," Jacob had told the big man. He hadn't added that the pain of being left behind was more than he could bear. That he wanted to confront his father—make him answer for his actions—even fight it out. It just hurt so bad.

Coming to the little store on Main and 6th Street, Jacob knew he'd have a lot of explaining to do. He didn't like having to answer for his deeds, but he knew Karen Pierce well enough to know that she'd brook no nonsense regarding his disappearance. With a sigh, he pushed open the door, causing bells to rings from overhead. Someone had nailed sleighbells to the top of the frame and they cheerily announced his arrival.

"Jacob!" Karen exclaimed. She rushed forward and embraced him as though he were her own. "I was so worried. Are you all right?" She held him at arm's length and gave him a cursory examination.

"Let's get you warmed up," she said, pulling him with her to the back of the store. "Are you hungry?"

He nodded but said nothing. Karen guided him to a chair at the table and proceeded to bustle around the kitchen preparing him a meal. Jacob was surprised that she asked no questions about his whereabouts or reasons for leaving. She'd likely already figured them out. Or maybe she didn't care where he'd gone or why. Jacob couldn't help but remember his mother telling him a story about the Prodigal Son in the Bible. The boy came home to a celebration. His father didn't care where he'd been or what he'd done, he only cared that the boy had come home. His mother said that God felt that way about His lost children.

"Where is everybody?" Jacob finally asked.

Karen put a bowl of stew down in front of him. "They've gone to a party, believe it or not." She smiled, but Jacob could see her concern for him in her eyes. "I'll get you some bread and something to drink."

Jacob said a quick prayer, a matter of habit that his mother had instilled in him from his very first memories. He had already started to eat when Karen returned with a huge hunk of bread and a steaming mug of coffee. He eyed the coffee for a moment, then looked up at Karen.

"You said coffee was for the grown-ups."

Karen took the chair opposite him and nodded. "I guess being almost fifteen and living through all that you've endured makes you as close to an adult as you need to be for coffee." She smiled. "With everyone else gone, I was hoping you might talk to me."

Jacob looked at her quietly. She was a pretty woman. He'd noticed that right off. She had curly red hair that she liked to braid down her back. Jacob had watched her braid it once or twice and thought it looked like nothing he'd ever seen. She was a kind woman too. Stern and rather determined to have her own way, but for a grown-up lady, Jacob figured she was decent enough.

He focused on the food for a moment, wolfing down a good portion of the stew and bread, before taking time to comment on her suggestion.

"I didn't mean to worry anybody. I just wanted to find my pa."

"I understand. I'd like to find my father as well."

He looked at her and saw a kind of sadness in her eyes. Yes, she knew what it was like. She'd come to Alaska not for gold, but to find her pa.

He tasted the coffee and frowned. It was bitter and hot and

not at all pleasing. Karen laughed and pushed forward the sugar bowl.

"You might want to sweeten it a bit. I don't have any cream for it, but there's sugar."

He nodded and added a liberal amount of the sweetener before tasting it again. Finding it more palatable, he looked up and nodded again. "It's better now."

They sat in silence for several more minutes before Karen finally just opened up and put her thoughts out for him to consider.

"Jacob, I know you feel miserable. What your father did was wrong. He should never have brought you and Leah north. He should have made a home for you where it was safe and predictable. But he's a good man and he does love you. If he didn't, he wouldn't have cared what you might have had to face on the trail. I don't want you to hate him for leaving. I'd much prefer, in fact, that you try to understand that he did what he thought was for your best."

"He didn't care what I wanted. What Leah wanted." He kept his words flat and without feeling.

Karen seemed to consider the comment. "No, I suppose he didn't. I'm sure if he'd thought overmuch on anything related to feelings, he'd never have been able to go on his way."

"He ain't been the same since Ma died," Jacob said.

"I don't suppose any of you have been."

Jacob met Karen's eyes and saw the deep sympathy she held for him. He warmed to her kindness and found his hard shell of indifference falling away in bits and pieces. It was just too hard to pretend that he didn't feel anything, especially when it came to his mother.

"I miss her." The words were simple, yet heartfelt. Jacob felt his throat grow tight.

"I miss my mother too," Karen replied. "Having her die was probably the hardest thing I've ever had to deal with."

Jacob nodded. *She understands,* he thought. *She knows how much it hurts and how bad I feel.*

"I came north to find my father," Karen continued, "but I also wanted to see my mother's grave. Somehow, I figured seeing where she was buried would help me to better accept that she's really and truly gone."

"How can you accept something so awful?" The words were barely audible.

Karen leaned back rather casually and looked upward, as if the conversation were nothing of any big importance. "It's always hard to accept bad news. I take comfort in the fact that my mother loved God. She had given her heart and life to God's work, and I know I'll see her again someday—in heaven."

"My ma was a Christian too," Jacob whispered. Tears formed in his eyes, and he got up from the table rather abruptly. Karen stood too, looking as though she might try to stop him if he chose to run. Jacob could no longer stand the guilt and pain of his burden. "She put great store in the Bible and getting saved. She wanted that for all of us, but I couldn't give her the peace she wanted."

"What peace, Jacob?" Karen's voice was soft and soothing. She walked to where he stood and looked at him without any hint of condemnation.

"The peace she would have had if I'd gotten saved before she died," he said, his voice breaking.

Karen wrapped him in her arms and pulled him close. In a motherly fashion she stroked his head and let him cry. He felt miserable and stupid for breaking down. What kind of baby would she think him? He pulled away and struggled to regain control. Embarrassed, he turned away.

"Jacob, you don't have be ashamed. You can talk to me, even cry on my shoulder. We all have to shed a few tears now and then."

"Men don't cry," Jacob said, forcing control over his voice.

"Sure they do. I've seen my father weep buckets of tears over lost souls," Karen replied. She went to Jacob and gently touched his arm. "You don't have to be ashamed. I don't think less of you for your tears. Fact is, I'd think less of you if you were without feeling for the things that matter."

"I wanted to please her. I really did. But I just couldn't make a promise to God."

"Why not? Don't you believe that salvation is necessary? Don't you think you sin just like everybody else?"

"Of course I do," he replied rather indignantly. "I'm a terrible sinner."

"Then why not come clean before God?" she asked.

Jacob tensed. "It's not important." He tried to walk away, but Karen held him fast.

"It's only life and death," Karen said. "Why can't you give your heart to Jesus, Jacob?"

Her calm, loving way was his undoing. Jacob's tears returned in a torrent of emotion. "I'd do it in a minute if it would bring her back. I can't bear that I let her down."

"It's my guess that she was only concerned with seeing you again in heaven."

He nodded. "I know. She said that much. But I'm not a good person, Miss Pierce."

Karen smiled. "None of us are. And why don't you call me Karen. It seems to be the way things are done up here, and I might as well give up the nonsense of formalities, especially when much more important things are at stake." She paused and put her hands on his shoulders. "So why is it that you are so far beyond redeeming?"

"I'm just not good. I make a lot of mistakes."

"So?"

His voice rose in agitation. "I know I'll keep making them."

"So?"

Jacob frowned. "Ma said you weren't to make a pledge to God if you didn't intend to keep it. She said it was foolishness, that the Bible said it was better not to make a promise at all than to make one and not see it through."

Karen smiled and nodded. "That's true, but there's also the matter of your heart, Jacob. Would you willingly go into sin? Would you seek it out—desire it for your life?"

"No," he replied, shaking his head.

"See, God knows we're going to make a mess of things now and then," she continued. "We have a sinful nature, and we need the Holy Spirit to help guide us as we go about our way. We need God to strengthen us because we can't do anything on our own."

"But if I give my heart to God and break my promise, won't He hate me—condemn me?"

"God knows your weaknesses, Jacob. He knows exactly where you'll be tempted and where you won't. Besides, the promise is on God's part—not yours. Your part of the promise is to accept His free gift of salvation with a repentant heart. His part of the promise is Jesus."

Jacob had never heard salvation explained in such a manner. He felt a surge of hope. "And even if I mess up, God will still know that I'm trying—that I want to be good and do right?"

Karen smiled, and the look on her face reassured him

more than her words. "He's already seen the future. Remember, Jesus died for you every bit as much as He died for His disciples and friends. He knew you—Jacob Barringer—would need a Savior. He knew all your sins and the things you'd do wrong. He knew the things that would come out of your mouth and the things you'd harbor in your heart. And He still went to the cross because He didn't want to lose you, Jacob. He's just waiting for you to come home—to see how much He loves you."

Jacob's eyes flooded with tears, and he couldn't even see Karen for the blur they created. His heart felt lighter than it had since his mother had first talked to him about salvation.

"Jesus loves you. He loves you and He already knows your heart," Jacob's mother had said not long before her death. *"You can't keep anything from Him."* Her words had been so tender—so gentle. They were given out of love and a desire to show her child the truth.

For some reason the memory eased the aching in Jacob's heart. "I'm just afraid of letting Him down," he finally whispered. "I'm not good at keeping promises."

Karen hugged Jacob tightly. "Maybe not, but He is."

Jacob allowed himself to rest in Karen's arms. She reminded him so much of his mother. Even the way she held him was similar. How he wished he'd allowed his mother to hug him more often. He'd always worried about what his friends might think or say. He'd told his mother he was too big for such silliness.

I'm not too big, Ma, he thought, wishing with all his heart that she might hear and know his love for her. *I'm not too big for you to love.*

He pulled away and looked at Karen quite seriously. "Do

you suppose if I take Jesus as my Lord, that my ma will see and know?"

"The Bible says that all of heaven rejoices when a lost sinner gets saved," Karen replied. "I would imagine she'll be sharing that happiness right along with the rest of heaven."

"Will you tell me what to do—what to say?"

Karen nodded, and holding on to his hand, she knelt on the floor. Looking up at him, she smiled. "I've found that it's best to start from the bottom and work our way up."

CHAPTER TWENTY-SIX

PETER FELT A MOMENTARY REPRIEVE in his worries over Grace when his father announced that Martin Paxton had lost all his hirelings to the gold rush. The man was positively livid and made no secret of that fact when discussing his plans to find Grace. Ephraim had tried to console his friend, reminding him that short of catching a boat south or going north over the passes, there were only a few places Grace would most likely be found. And with winter setting in, only the hardiest souls would even consider heading into the wilderness. Paxton had been unconvinced, however.

Peter still couldn't believe that Martin Paxton was the nightmare Grace had been running from. For all his desire to dislike the man, he was practically a hero to Peter's father. And so far in their business discussions and encounters, Peter had only the highest respect for the man. It all seemed very puzzling.

Knowing that Grace was betrothed to his father's dear friend troubled Peter, leaving little room for any other thought. He'd not even been able to think of leaving Skagway for fear that Paxton would catch wind of Grace's presence in Dyea and then take it upon himself to investigate the matter. Peter felt he couldn't leave without talking with Grace and knowing the truth, and yet the idea of knowing the truth of this situation was almost more troubling.

"Peter, what's wrong with you?" Miranda asked. "It's Christmas and you haven't been yourself all day. Are you ill?"

Peter smiled at his sister. She had dressed in the merriest of holiday colors with a smart-looking green-and-red plaid skirt and a high-collared white blouse. A wide black belt encircled her tiny waist and black patent leather boots peeked out from beneath her hem.

"I don't mean to spoil the festivities," he said as she came to sit beside him. "I suppose my mind is on other things."

She reached out and took his hand. "Such as?"

He looked at her for a moment. *I can trust her more than anyone,* he thought. *I can tell her everything and perhaps even enlist her help.* A plan began to form in the back of his mind.

"Do you remember Mr. Paxton speaking about his fiancée?"

She nodded. "Of course. He's talked about her off and on since boarding *Summer Song.* What of it?"

Peter looked around as if to make certain no one would overhear him. Knowing that Paxton and his parents had gone out to a party where they would meet with potential investors, Peter relaxed a bit. "I know who Mr. Paxton is looking for."

"What do you mean?"

"I know this woman, Grace Hawkins."

"That's wonderful!" Miranda declared. "Mr. Paxton will be so pleased."

"I don't plan to tell him," Peter said flatly. He looked to Miranda to see what her reaction might be. "At least not yet."

"But why not? He's come so far to find her."

"The trouble is," Peter replied, "she doesn't want to be found."

"I don't understand."

"I know," he said, reaching out to pat her hand. "But I want to explain it to you, and then I'd like to have your help."

"You know I'd do anything for you," she said softly.

"I believe Mr. Paxton may not be exactly as he appears. We've so long known him as our father's friend that we've never questioned what he might truly be about. We know nothing of him, except his kindness to Father."

"That's true," Miranda said, nodding.

"I met Miss Hawkins on the trip to Skagway some months ago. She was terribly distressed and told me of her father seeking to force her hand in marriage. She told me the man was a horrible monster who had been violent with her and that she had run away from her father's demands and this man's cruelty."

"Mr. Paxton?" Miranda questioned, eyes wide.

"One and the same," Peter replied. "I realize I know very little of Grace Hawkins. She could have been lying to me, but I fail to see what purpose it would have served. She had no reason to tell me such tales. I merely came upon her feeling frightened and tearful and the story poured out in a most honest manner."

"But if she's not lying, then Mr. Paxton is . . ." Her words faded as she met Peter's eyes. "What are we to do?"

"I've deliberated that for days. I don't wish to anger Paxton or hurt Father by keeping this from them, but I feel I must protect Miss Hawkins. She's younger than you and very quiet and sweet-tempered."

"She sounds very special." She paused, then asked, "Could it be that you've grown an attachment for her?"

Peter smiled. "You are wise beyond your years. I suppose I can confide in you."

"You know I would never breathe a word of it or anything else. You can trust this matter to remain between you and me," Miranda assured him.

"We must seek to better understand Mr. Paxton. Perhaps I've misjudged the situation, and my feelings for Miss Hawkins have caused me to see things as less than clear."

"What can we do?"

"I propose to have you bring up the topic of Miss Hawkins. Perhaps he will discuss his feelings on her and the upcoming marriage. Seek to learn if he truly loves her or if, as Grace says, this was merely a business arrangement."

"Even if it were," Miranda replied, "I would have thought you to support such matters. You've often said that women are poor judges of such things—that our hearts often cloud our thinking and reasoning."

Peter frowned. He had said all of that. He had told her on many occasions that she was far too emotional in her thinking to make a sound, reasonable judgment in matters of matrimony and her future.

"I know what I've said in the past," Peter began, "but I would never subject anyone, man or woman, to a cruel master. Paxton should have nothing to hide in discussing the matter with you. It will appear innocent enough, and there should be no reason to conceal his heart."

"If he will discuss the situation at all," Miranda replied.

"I've no reason to believe he wouldn't. In a quiet, non-threatening setting such as this, Mr. Paxton would have little to concern himself over. He will simply see you as curious—perhaps even caring. When Mother and Father return, I shall take them aside for a private chat. Perhaps then you could have Mr. Paxton's attention." Just then they heard a commotion coming from the stairs. "They're back. Just try to think of any way in which you can get him to talk about Grace and how he truly feels about their union," Peter said, getting up rather abruptly.

Miranda nodded. "I'll do what I can."

Peter met his parents as they topped the landing, with Martin Paxton right behind them. "I wonder if I might steal my parents away from you for a moment," he said, smiling at Paxton.

Cold green eyes met his gaze as Paxton nodded. "By all means. After all, it is Christmas and we've hardly made merry together. Perhaps you had something in mind for a celebration?"

Peter shook his head. "I hadn't given it serious thought, but perhaps as we discuss other matters, we can consider that as well." He looked to Miranda and smiled. "We'll just be a minute, and then maybe we can all go out for a celebration dinner. That is, unless everyone has closed shop for the day."

Peter's parents looked at each other and then to Peter. "Would you mind accompanying me back downstairs?" he asked them.

"Of course not, but what's this about?" Ephraim questioned.

"We can discuss it in private," Peter replied, casting one

quick glance over his shoulder at Miranda. "It won't take long."

Miranda studied the handsome man as he crossed the room and poured himself a generous glass of whiskey. Paxton held up the bottle, almost as an afterthought.

"Would you care for some?"

"No, thank you. I don't imbibe in spirits."

He nodded, then replaced the stopper in the bottle. "So what do you think of the frozen north? Are you ready for the warmth of your home?"

"San Francisco is a lovely place to live," she replied, trying desperately to think of how she might turn the subject to Paxton's fiancée. "Perhaps you might consider living there after you marry. My father would be pleased to have you so near."

Paxton shook his head. "I'd say there's little chance of that."

"Oh. I . . . uh . . . suppose your fiancée wouldn't care for the climate?" Miranda asked hesitantly.

"I have no idea. I do, however, have a home in Erie," Paxton replied. He took a seat opposite her and cocked his head to one side. "Why is it that a woman as lovely as yourself has not already taken a husband?"

Miranda felt her entire body grow warm. She was certain to be blushing and looked quickly at her hands. "I suppose because the proper mate has not yet come along. Peter and my father are very good to look out for me. They've not yet approved of a suitor."

"Spoken like a proper young woman of breeding," Paxton replied. "There are far too few of your kind."

"How so?"

"Women today are not at all inclined to do as they are told. Most want to marry for love—if they marry at all. This push for women's rights has become a most annoying affair. They don't seem to be able to make up their minds even among themselves. They want equal rights with men—the vote, positions in the government—including a woman president. As if that would ever be possible."

"I have never desired such things," Miranda admitted. "But I do desire love. Would you not desire love as well?" Miranda questioned, daring to raise her face to his.

He eyed her intently, almost hungrily. She felt unnerved by his sudden interest. "Desire and love," he said softly, "are often absent in a marriage. However, were you to be a part of the union, I've no doubt both would play an important role."

She felt her breath quicken. My, but he was charming. His soft, smooth voice caused her skin to prickle. "How fortunate you are," she began uneasily, "to have found those things for yourself. I'm sure your Miss Hawkins is a most honored woman."

"She is a spoiled brat," he said, tossing back the drink and breaking the spell. "Ours is an arranged marriage. Nothing more."

"You don't love her?"

He laughed and got up to pour himself another glass. "As I said, she is a spoiled child. It is hard to love someone so willful and misguided. She has no idea of how to be pleasing or properly behaved. But I'll see that taken in hand."

Miranda felt her heart racing again, but this time it was for an entirely different reason. Paxton's cruel edge seemed quite apparent as he picked up his glass and stared at her from across the room.

"Marriage is all about business, Miss Colton. I would,

however, dare to say that marriage to one such as yourself might well be the exception. Business and love could no doubt be had in one union."

"Pity you are already engaged," Peter said, coming through the door.

Miranda felt a wave of relief at the sight of such support.

Paxton laughed. "Nothing lasts forever."

"Do you really believe that marriage is nothing more than business? I mean, of course, on the whole."

Paxton shrugged and reclaimed his chair. "I believe simpleminded ninnies marry on a daily basis because they cannot control their emotions or bodily urges. I believe sound-minded people consider a broader base. They look to the future and how they might benefit financially and physically by joining their lot with that of another person. It's no different than what you observe in monarchies, where brides are chosen for reasons of making treaties and pacts with other countries."

Peter look rather ashen-faced, and Miranda couldn't help but wonder if he agreed with Paxton. After all, she'd heard some of the same philosophy from her older brother on more than one occasion. In fact, Martin Paxton's views were essentially similar. Only coming from Peter they had never seemed cruel.

She looked at her brother intently, and when he turned his head to meet her gaze, Miranda felt an awakening in her soul. Perhaps a spirit of familiarity was all that separated Peter from Martin Paxton. Perhaps a kinder upbringing would have made Paxton more like her brother. The contrasts and similarities were startling.

"But it is all of little concern," Paxton replied, nursing his drink rather thoughtfully. "I cannot have a wedding without a bride. Miss Hawkins has been remiss in explaining her whereabouts, but I've hired a new group of men. Men to whom I am paying such an outrageous amount, they wouldn't dare desert me for the Yukon."

Miranda saw the flash of panic in her brother's eyes and hoped he would conceal it before turning back to face Paxton. She needn't have worried, however. Appearing as unconcerned with the matter as if Paxton had been discussing the price of fish, Peter merely shrugged.

"The lure of gold makes men do strange things."

Paxton laughed. "The lure of many things can drive a man to do what he might never have considered before. Even murder seems quite reasonable when one's own life or livelihood is threatened."

Miranda felt her blood run cold. What was he implying? Could he possibly mean to murder Miss Hawkins? Was that why he had followed her here to the Yukon? Was that why he spoke of nothing lasting forever? She shivered, feeling his gaze upon her. What if her father had chosen him for her? Might she have done the same thing that Grace Hawkins did?

CHAPTER TWENTY-SEVEN

PETER PACED UP AND DOWN the street in front of the Colton Trading Post. The trip from Skagway to Dyea had seemed neverending. He thought only of Grace and the need to protect her, but upon arrival found her to be gone from the store. In fact, the place was locked up tight and there was no sign of the women or even the Barringer children. He rationalized that with it being Christmas evening they might have gone to a party or even to church. He shivered against the cold and wondered silently what he should do. It seemed silly that the store was his own property and yet he had no key with which to let himself in from the elements.

He heard laughter and singing coming from down the street. Perhaps he would find Grace there. He made his way in long, rhythmic strides, forcing his mind to not deliberate unnecessarily on the situation at hand. He was determined that Paxton's plans could not be allowed. Peter didn't know how he would yet stop the man, but he couldn't see such a loveless arrangement for Grace. Not when he desired to offer her so much.

He peered inside a tent marked *Coffee and Donuts* and searched the crowd for any sign of the women. It seemed the entire town was caught up in something. Laughter poured from the tent as the group broke into a hearty chorus of "Deck the Halls." A woman dressed in a flashy shade of gold and orange plopped herself down on the lap of a miner and began to play with his beard, while another woman, much younger than the first, watched Peter from several feet away. Her eyes gave a pleading, almost desperate look as she smiled and curved her shoulders forward to give herself a bit of cleavage. It was definitely not the kind of place Grace would visit.

Backing out of the tent, Peter looked frantically up and down the street. The light was fading fast and with a heavy overcast threatening snow, it would be pitch black before another half hour passed. Where could Grace be? Had Paxton's men somehow found her?

Don't let your imagination get carried away, he chided. *Grace is fine. She's no doubt with Miss Pierce and her aunt. Paxton has no way of knowing that she's here.* But even as he gave birth to this thought, another more imposing one filled his mind. Ever since Karen Pierce's shooting incident, the women had gained a bit of a reputation. Perhaps Paxton had caught wind of this. Even so, Peter reasoned, the reputations and descriptions were nothing like the real women. It was even said that their numbers were ten or more, not merely three. One rumor said they were a tribe of natives who had banded together to fight off the imposition of the gold rusher. Another bit of gossip suggested that while beautiful, they were really servants of the devil and any man who looked into their eyes would lose their soul. It might have been comical if Peter hadn't felt so weighed down with worry for Grace's safety.

He walked back to the store contemplating what he should do. He had just decided to check the windows in case any were unlocked, when he heard the unmistakable sound of Leah Barringer's animated chatter.

"I love singing songs about Jesus' birth," she was saying.

Peter watched and waited as they rounded the corner of the building before hurrying forward to greet them. "Merry Christmas!" he declared.

"Oh, Captain Colton," Doris replied, "a most merry Christmas to you."

Karen and Leah were arm in arm, with Jacob walking in close step behind them. Grace walked alongside Jacob and smiled up warmly.

"We're just returning from church. Pity you could not have come earlier, then you might have joined us," Grace said.

Peter nodded but had no desire to explain that while he was happy to make merry on the holiday, religious nonsense had never really accompanied the celebration. His family recognized the birth of Christ, knew the stories of Bethlehem and the wise men, but other than counting these as stories from long ago, they'd never given them much thought.

"You will stay for supper—perhaps even the night, won't you?" Doris questioned as Karen unlocked the front door of the store.

Peter wondered if his absence back in Skagway would be questioned. "I will stay for supper, but perhaps it would be less than appropriate for me to stay the night."

"Nonsense. As we've said before, there's plenty of room and it is your property," Doris replied. "Leah can sleep with us, and you and Jacob can share the other room. There's no room for the same proprieties up here as we clung to in Chicago. Why, we had one woman come into the store the other day telling us how she was saved from death on the trail when two complete strangers put her in a bedroll between them. Scandalous stuff for our civilized world, but not for the likes of Alaska."

Peter considered the idea for a moment, then allowed his eyes to travel the length of Grace's hourglass figure as she took off her coat. She wore a trim little gown of blue wool and black braid trim. A delicate white lace collar edged the high neck of the bodice, and blue ribbons were woven throughout her brown hair. She caught his expression and blushed. No doubt she could read his desire merely by looking into his eyes.

"Be that as it may, I'll just stay for supper," Peter said uncomfortably.

They spent a leisurely time over a most unusual Christmas dinner. Smoked salmon trimmed with a berry sauce made up the main course. Peter marveled at the flavor and complimented the women for their efforts. His favorite had been a concoction of rice and beans flavored with spices that nipped at his tongue. It wasn't at all an expected cuisine for the far north.

"I learned to make that dish in Louisiana," Doris told him as he ate a second portion. "The recipe was given to me by a Cajun woman who taught me a thing or two about cooking, while I taught her to read."

"It's marvelous," he replied. "Such a welcome change from pork and beans or dried cabbage soup."

"Even the eggs are dry up here," Leah replied. "I'd never seen dried eggs before coming up here."

Jacob nodded. "Guess we've seen a lot of things up here we've never seen elsewhere. Never had to worry with Indians in Colorado. They'd all been moved out by the time we got there."

"You don't have to worry about them at all," Karen replied. "The natives here are friendly and helpful."

"But they do look kind of mean," Leah threw in.

"You shouldn't judge people by their looks. A person can look harmless and beautiful and be deadly. Just as a person can appear unseemly and be good. Anyway, the Russians were dealing with the Tlingit for a long while before Americans started coming up here. Many of them can speak Russian and English. It's amazing, especially when you consider that most people consider the natives to be ignorant heathens. My father and mother often wrote of their generosity. A good many were even receptive to the Bible being preached. The Russians made many converts, and now the American missionaries are doing likewise."

Peter said nothing. He concentrated on the food and tried to figure out how he was going to convince Grace to come back to San Francisco with him. He'd already decided it would be to her benefit if she left the area altogether. He thought he might convince Miranda to join him and act as chaperone for Grace. He didn't want anyone getting the wrong idea, and Miranda's presence would surely put an end to any gossip.

Of course, if Martin Paxton caught wind of it, the matter might not weigh well for Peter's father. That troubled Peter only momentarily, however. Paxton would have no way of knowing of Grace's departure. *Not if they did it right. Let the man search for her and believe her to have gone farther north. Let him assume she had tired of the cold as winter came on the area and had left for warmer climates.* He didn't care what Paxton thought. He only knew a fierce desire to protect Grace at all costs.

"Captain, would you care for dessert?" Grace asked him softly. She smiled warmly and extended him a piece of cake.

"This is indeed a party," he declared, eyeing the treat with great interest. He hadn't had a decent piece of cake in a long while.

"Well, it is Jesus' birthday," Leah offered.

Again Peter said nothing. He wasn't inclined to wax theological with a child, and no one else appeared concerned with the matter. He returned his thoughts to Grace and how Paxton had talked so harshly about marriage.

Peter watched her from the corner of his eye. She was so graceful and even-mannered. Even when Jacob dropped his cake, making a big mess on the floor, Grace only laughed it off and handed him another piece.

"Why don't you and Leah take your cake over by the stove," Grace suggested as she knelt to clean up the cake. "You can play checkers while you eat and give us a little time to talk to Captain Colton about his departure."

"Talk business on Christmas Day?" Doris questioned.

Grace laughed. Her brown eyes seemed to twinkle. "No, Aunt Doris, I wouldn't consider it. I merely thought to find out when the captain intends to return to Seattle. I had hoped to send a Christmas letter to my mother. I'm hoping she'll be back home in Chicago by now. I know she told me not to write to her just yet, but I figured that if we pass the letter through Karen's sister and tell nothing of our whereabouts, then even if someone should intercept the letter, it won't give away our location."

Peter nearly choked on his cake. He coughed for a moment, gratefully accepting a glass of water from Grace.

"Are you quite all right, Captain?" she asked softly. Her hand touched his as she took back the glass.

"I'm fine," he replied. He cleared his throat. "I would like an opportunity to talk with you alone. Perhaps later." Grace nodded, and Peter turned his attention back to the other ladies. "The youngsters have certainly thrived under your care and attention. They look healthy and well-adjusted to the harsh conditions here."

Karen nodded. "We've had our moments." She lowered her voice. "It hasn't been easy, especially with their father leaving them."

"Leaving them?" Peter questioned. "You mean while he works?"

Karen sighed and shook her head. "No, he's gone north. Gold fever got the best of him and once he collected enough to put himself in good standing with the officials at the border, he took his leave."

"And deserted them?" Peter asked, looking past Karen to where Jacob laughed at his sister's antics as she set up the checkerboard.

"Mr. Barringer stated in his letter that he intends to come back for them," Grace offered, pouring Peter a cup of coffee. "But we wonder if that will truly happen. The children have been very upset."

"Yes, but I think making peace with God has helped Jacob to make peace with his father's actions," Karen said, stacking several of the dishes to make more room on the table.

Peter thought of the things Grace had said to him in the past. Such talk of God and of making peace with Him and celebrating His birth were fairly foreign to Peter. He'd gone to church long ago as a child, but for as long as he'd been able to work aboard a ship, he'd been away from religious gatherings.

Without thinking, Peter asked, "What did he do to make peace with God?"

Karen smiled. "What does anyone do to make peace with the Almighty? He accepted that he was a lost soul without Jesus and repented of his sins."

"And that made him feel better?" Peter questioned. "Seeing how bad a person he was in the eyes of God gave way to making peace in his soul?"

"But of course it did," Grace said, sitting down beside Peter. "Has no one ever shared with you the forgiveness and love of God, Captain?"

"I know God to be judge over all," Peter admitted. "I believe Him to have set things in motion, perhaps even nudged them in a particular direction, but I don't concern myself with the extremes of such things as love and joy. Emotions seldom result in reasonable decisions." Even as he said the words he thought of his own emotional heart. He thought of the way Grace made his blood run hot and his heart pound with a maddening beat. Just sitting near her made him both uneasy and elated. Then his mind went back to the conversation he'd overheard between his sister and Paxton. A sinking feeling washed over him. *I sound just like that man.*

"What of truth, Captain?"

"Please," he said, looking to each woman. "We needn't argue."

"Who's arguing?" Karen questioned. "Does talk of God and spiritual matters make you so uneasy that you instantly give it over to argument?"

Peter pushed back from the table and shook his head. "No. It's not that. I merely meant to say that it seems a very weighty subject for such a festive occasion."

"But Jesus Christ is the reason for this festive holiday," Karen countered. "I wouldn't think it a bit out of place to discuss the need and purpose of God's direction in our lives."

Peter reminded himself that his real need was to discuss Grace's circumstances and Martin Paxton's arrival in Skagway. Not feeling he could wait any longer, he said, "I really should be heading back. Supper was very good. If you ladies give up the mercantile business, you could easily open a restaurant." He stood, hoping that Grace would take the opportunity to speak with him alone.

"I'll walk you out, Captain," she said, smiling shyly.

"Don't forget your coat, Grace," Doris called.

Grace looked up at Peter and smiled. "I won't forget."

Peter lost himself in warm chocolate brown eyes. Indeed, she would need no coat if only he had the right to hold her in his arms.

They made their way outside and Peter was relieved to find the wind had died down. The cold was more bearable and the night skies overhead were clearing out to allow just a bit of moonlight. Perhaps it wouldn't snow, after all.

"What did you wish to tell me, Captain?"

Peter fought the urge to pull her into his arms. "Something's come up. I felt it was important to come see you myself."

Grace smiled. "I'm glad you did."

He sensed her approval and pleasure in his singling her out for a private moment. She showed no sign of fearing his company. She certainly bore no hint of the terror she'd felt for Paxton. He could still remember the look in her eyes as she conveyed her feelings toward the man who was to be her husband.

"Will you be leaving tomorrow?" Grace asked.

Peter nodded. "That's part of what I wanted to talk to you about." Just being this near to Grace caused him to consider running away with her. He could imagine them making their way under cover of darkness. He could see himself fighting Paxton to the death for her honor.

No longer thinking of the information he needed to relay, Peter pulled Grace into his arms. She didn't resist, and in feeling her yield to his touch, Peter tilted her head to meet his ardent kiss. He touched her lips gently at first, then more insistently. He held her tightly and although he felt her momentarily melt against him, he could also sense her tensing—pushing away.

He knew he had to let her go, but it was the last thing he desired to do. Loosening his hold, he allowed Grace to slip from his arms.

"Captain Colton! That's quite uncalled for!" She raised her hand as if to slap him, then halted in midair. Her expression softened as she lowered her arm. "The holiday spirit has made you forget yourself. I shall not be cross about it—however, you must promise to never take such liberties again!"

She left him standing in the street without any hope of explanation. Peter felt the urge to go after her but held himself in check. He had frightened her. He had treated her no better than Paxton had. Growling in disgust, Peter pulled down his cap and headed out in search of a place to spend the night. He had no desire to return to Skagway, and fear for Grace told him he'd be better off to stay close by.

"I'll tell her the truth tomorrow," he promised himself. "I'll tell her I know all about Martin Paxton and that he has come to take her back."

CHAPTER TWENTY-EIGHT

GRACE SCARCELY SLEPT a wink all night. Touching her lips, she kept remembering what it felt like to be kissed by Peter Colton. Her heart pounded at the memory of the experience. She had lost all reasoning in that fleeting moment—that moment when she'd known without any further doubt that she belonged to this man, heart and soul.

How was it that two men could be so different? Peter's kiss had filled her with wonder and anticipation. It was the complete opposite of the horrible treatment she'd received from Martin Paxton.

Comparing the two men made her remember the past and in the darkness of the night, she worried terribly about her mother and father. What if Paxton hadn't left them alone as they had hoped he might after Grace's departure? What if he were punishing them for Grace's actions?

She knew things couldn't be right because of her mother's last letter. The tone had been so bleak, but worse yet were the things her mother hadn't said. Reading between the lines, it was easy to see that their problems were far from over. Grace realized that as much as she loved this wild land, she wanted to go home. She wanted to see for herself that her family was safe—that Paxton hadn't hurt them in her absence. Yet she knew she'd come this far and must stay in order to see it through; otherwise everything they'd done would be for naught.

There was also another matter. Peter Colton had created a complication she'd not planned on. She hugged her arms to her body and remembered his embrace—so strong and warm. She thought of the look in his eyes, the desire and passion that she recognized when he'd touched her. She felt the same desire. Had he known?

Grace was embarrassed for how she'd reacted to his kiss. *I should never have been so harsh, especially when I wanted the kiss as much as he did.* She rolled uncomfortably to her side. The cot was a most unbearable companion and did little to afford her any real consolation.

By the time she fell asleep it was quite late. Her dreams were haunted with visions of Paxton and Peter Colton. Always she was caught between the two men and always Paxton's cruelty won over.

She awoke in a cold sweat. A dim light shown under the closed door and glancing at the empty cots, Grace realized both Doris and Karen were already up and about their business. She yawned and stretched. Her muscles ached terribly.

"Oh, I'm already old at twenty." A thought came to mind. "I'm soon to be twenty-one."

Sitting up, Grace remembered her birthday was in a few

short days. She hadn't even considered this matter since coming north. On the thirty-first she would be twenty-one. Her father could no longer assert his authority in a legal manner, and therefore Paxton would no longer be a threat. The thought gave her a moment of excitement. Perhaps she could go home.

Thinking of home, however, caused her to wonder what she would find there. Had her parents been forced to sell off all of their possessions? Had they been forced to sell the house itself? She'd not considered this before. Perhaps that was why her mother had told her not to write to the Chicago address. Perhaps Paxton now owned the house and her parents were left to find a new place to live.

"Perhaps I could go to Seattle and stay with Karen's sister until I locate Mother and Father," she said softly. Even if they'd lost the house, they could start again. They were a family, after all. Perhaps she could even convince them to come north. Martin Paxton would never think to look for any of them in Alaska.

Besides, once she was twenty-one, Paxton would have no reasonable hold on her. The fact that she might have once married the man simply to keep her father in good standing was no longer a worry to her. If Paxton had carried his threats through as her mother had implied, there was probably nothing to worry about anymore. Everything he could have done to hurt them, he would have already done.

The idea gave her a new energy. Perhaps she could talk to Peter about allowing her passage to Seattle. Her cheeks heated up at the thought of Peter.

I love him, she thought. *I love him so much that I could have forgotten myself when he kissed me. Oh, God,* she prayed, *what shall I do? He's not a man who seeks after you.* She knew well enough from years of hearing Karen speak on the delicate matter of marriage that the best ones were made of like-minded people. She and Peter were not like-minded. At least not in spiritual matters.

The idea of losing Peter before she really even had him caused a dull ache in her heart. *But I love him, Lord. I love him so and can't imagine my life without him.* The strength of her emotions was a surprise, even to Grace. *I live for his return each time he goes away. How can I leave Alaska and venture away never again to see him?*

But what if he changed? She considered the idea for a moment. Surely she could help him to see the truth. Perhaps that's why they'd been allowed to come together. Karen always said that nothing happened by chance. Everything is carefully ordered by God. *That would have to include my falling in love with Peter.* She smiled and felt a warmth of hope, whispering, "I could lead him to God. I could help him to see the truth, and then we wouldn't be unequal in our thinking."

"Oh, good, you're up," Karen announced as she opened the door and spied Grace. "I thought perhaps you were sick, then I thought I heard voices."

"I was just talking to myself," Grace said, smiling. "I'm sorry to have left the morning chores to you."

"It's of no matter. Look, Peter has come back and said it's imperative that we join him for a discussion. He says it's quite serious and that he should have told us about it last night, but he didn't have a chance."

Grace felt her heart begin to race. "I'll get properly dressed and be out in a moment."

She hurried to pull on her brown corduroy skirt and yellow blouse. The lower neckline of the blouse was better suited to summer, so Grace drew a woolen shawl around her shoulders and fastened it together with a topaz brooch her mother had given her.

The children were just sitting down to breakfast when Grace emerged from the bedroom. She finished tying a brown ribbon to the bottom of her single braid and looked up to catch Peter watching her. She could feel the heat of his stare. *Goodness,* she thought, *he doesn't even make a pretense of looking away.* She looked to Karen and forced a smile of ease, even though her hands were shaking.

"Captain Colton suggests we talk in the other room," Karen explained, heading toward the door to the store.

Peter stood just to one side of the portal and nodded. "The privacy is necessary," he assured.

Grace nodded, having no idea why he should appear so serious. He had mentioned needing to talk to them of his departure. Surely that couldn't be such a grave matter.

She followed Karen into the front area of the store, stepping out from behind the counter in order to distance herself from Peter. It was of no use, however. He simply followed to where she stood and fixed his stare on her face.

"This news will come as a surprise," he said, pausing to wait for Doris to join them. The older woman closed the door to the living quarters and positioned herself beside Karen.

"What is this about, Captain Colton?" Doris questioned.

Grace looked at Karen, who remained somber-faced. She merely shrugged as if to say she was as confused as Grace about the urgency of the situation.

The sleigh bells over the front door jingled as two broad-shouldered men entered one after the other.

"I'm sorry, but we've not yet opened for business," Karen told them.

The first man held the door while his companion moved

to one side to admit yet a third man. Grace felt the blood drain from her head as she met the smug expression of Martin Paxton.

"Good morning, my dear," he said, not even having the decency to call her Miss Hawkins. "It would seem you're a bit remiss in remembering dates of importance. I've come to remind you that you missed our wedding day. It was good of Captain Colton to find you so that we might correct the matter."

Grace looked to Peter who was already shaking his head. "No, Grace," he whispered.

"You?" she could barely speak. He knew how terrified she was of this man. How could Peter have brought him to her doorstep?

"Grace, don't listen to him," Peter begged. "Listen to me. . . ."

But hearing him was impossible as the room went black and she fainted dead away.

Peter caught Grace as her knees gave way. Pulling her into his arms, he easily lifted her and held her tight.

"How could you?" Karen declared, accusing Peter.

"I didn't," he growled out. "This is what I came to tell you."

"Of course," she said snidely. "How dim-witted do you suppose us to be?"

"I suppose you all to be very dim-witted," Paxton declared, pulling off gray gloves. "Did you truly think to defy me? I've met over lunch with men more powerful than you could ever imagine, only to drive them to their knees before supper. Surely you didn't believe yourself a match for me."

He sneered at Karen as he sized her up. Doris stepped

closer in an attempt to offer Karen protection. As if the women no longer concerned him, Paxton turned to Peter. "Your father will be proud of you, Captain. We were just discussing you over breakfast and I told him I could see that you were a man of action."

"Not any action that will lend itself to you marrying Miss Hawkins," Peter replied. "I came here to warn her, not to serve your purposes."

"Do say! With the interest you took in my plans for marriage, I would have thought you to feel otherwise. Well, it really doesn't matter, does it?" Paxton replied.

"I believe it does. Miss Hawkins told me of your cruelty to her. I could scarcely believe it when I learned you were the same man my father so highly esteemed. Nevertheless, as I listened to you discuss the matter of marriage with my sister, I realized that Grace had to be telling the truth about you."

"Grace, is it? I suppose you've taken quite a fancy to my bride." He raised his brow and slapped his gloves into his hat and handed it to the man on his left. "I do hope you haven't ruined her for me."

"Why you—" Peter started to charge forward, but with Grace in his arms, it would have been impossible to fight. The two men on either side of Paxton closed ranks at the perceived threat.

Karen rushed forward to take hold of Grace. "Give her to me," she told Peter. "You've done this to her. You've ruined her life by bringing this monster here."

Peter turned to Karen. "No. I didn't. I came to warn her. I came to take her away."

"That won't be necessary. I have plans for her." All eyes turned to Paxton as he added, "Long-overdue plans."

"I won't allow it," Peter replied. Grace stirred in his arms, moaning softly as she struggled to regain consciousness.

"You have no choice," Paxton stated without emotion. He pulled a folded paper from his pocket. "Grace is my ward. She is not yet twenty-one, and you'll find here that I have guardianship of her and her father's blessing for marriage."

Grace rallied about this time and looked up at Peter with a hazy expression that suggested she'd forgotten the circumstance that had put her in his arms.

"What? Why are you . . ." She looked over her shoulder at Karen and then seemed to remember all at once.

"Put me down," she said, barely whispering.

Peter did as she said but held on to her arm. "Are you certain you can stand?"

She looked at him, as though uncertain whose side he was on. "Did you bring him here?"

"No. I promise you, I didn't. He's a friend of my father's and arrived in Skagway on *Summer Song*. I found out he was the man you had run away from when he told us of how he'd come to find his fiancée."

Paxton interrupted. "This is all rather boring to me. I have other things to see to."

"Then why don't you leave," Karen more demanded than questioned.

"Yes, go," Doris added.

"I have come for my bride. She is my legal charge."

"I'll be twenty-one in five days," she said, looking up to meet Paxton's eyes.

"That might be. However, you'll be my wife before the day is out," he replied.

"Never!" Grace declared with surprising strength. "I will not marry you. You have no say over me now."

"I have every say. Your father gave me the legal guardianship of you before he died."

Grace blanched and leaned heavily into Peter's side as though she might faint again. "My father . . . is dead?"

Paxton cocked his head to one side and appeared thoughtful. "Oh, that's right. You probably hadn't heard. Since you ran away and left your family, you weren't there when he grew ill."

"What of my mother? Have you killed her too?"

"Tsk, tsk," he replied, smiling. "I've killed no one—yet. Although watching the way in which Captain Colton handles you makes me wonder if there might not be a reason to consider such things."

"Your papers and pretense of law won't wash up here, Paxton. Grace is not obligated to you in any way."

"Even if those papers are real," Karen added, "which I highly suspect they are not."

"Well, it really doesn't matter what you think, Miss Pierce. I've no doubt you've played an ample role in depriving me of my wife. But that is about to end. Mr. Roberts and Mr. Tavis here are going to watch over my little bride while I go finish up the arrangements for our marriage. The wedding is to take place at two o'clock in Skagway." He turned to first one man and then the other. "See that she is there well in advance." They nodded.

"I won't allow this mockery to take place," Peter declared. Grace was clinging to him like a drowning woman and he felt empowered by her action. No matter what she thought of him, she clearly felt safer with him than with Paxton.

"You had better reconsider your part in this, Captain. I have a new agreement with your father that extends to most all of his holdings. Holdings that I believe you have some part in. Should you insist on interfering in a matter that is clearly none of your concern, I will be forced to deal rather harshly with you."

"I know all about your new dealings," Peter countered. "I saw the contracts prior to leaving San Francisco."

Paxton smiled. "I said that I have a new agreement."

Peter tightened his grip on Grace. What had his father done now? He forced his voice to remain even. "What of your lifelong friendship with my father? What of the fact that he was the only friend your mother had when everyone else deserted her?" Paxton appeared most uncomfortable at this and it fueled Peter's anger. "That's right, Father told us many stories about her and about you."

"Then he no doubt told you of Mr. Hawkins' adulterous affair with my mother. The years of suffering and anguish he left her in once he threw her away like so much used trash."

Grace began to sob softly and Peter wrapped his arm around her shoulder and drew her close.

"Get out of here," Karen said, moving forward. Neither Paxton nor his bodyguards moved a muscle. She raised her hand as if to strike Paxton, but he grabbed her wrist in such a lightning-quick move that even Peter was surprised.

"You might do well to ask your little Grace what happens when women slap me."

"I don't have to ask. I saw what you did to her. I dressed her wounds in the aftermath."

He chuckled as though Karen had brought to mind a pleasant memory. Releasing her, he pushed her away and refolded the paper in his hand. He tucked it carefully inside his coat pocket, then motioned to the man who held his hat. Taking his gloves, Paxton pulled them on in a methodic, slow manner as he addressed them collectively.

"You are all welcome to witness our marriage, but I will not allow for any nonsense. The law is clearly on my side." He looked up at Peter and added, "And if you don't wish to see Colton Shipping lost to your family, I would suggest you cooperate and mind your own business. After all, that is what this is all about. Business. Grace Hawkins is my business . . . mine alone."

CHAPTER TWENTY-NINE

THE WORLD SEEMED TO SPIN around Grace as Peter led her back to the privacy of her living quarters. Jacob and Leah had come to stand in the doorway and had apparently overheard the entire conversation.

"That man isn't going to take Grace away, is he?" Leah questioned.

"Not if I can help it," Peter replied.

"I'll help you too," Jacob stated, sounding years beyond his age.

Grace felt a heaviness in her heart as she took a seat at the table. "I can't allow any of you to get involved. I don't want you getting hurt, and I know this man well enough to know that he would do anything to have his way."

Karen joined her and patted her hand. "Don't fret, Grace. This battle isn't over. We'll find a way to defeat Paxton."

Grace shook her head. Why couldn't they understand? She sighed. "He has already ruined my family and killed my father. Oh, my poor mother. How she must grieve." Tears came unbidden. "She adored my father. They were always very close. At least until this. If what Mr. Paxton said is true, and if he shared the news of my father's indiscretion with my mother, then I'm certain her heart is broken."

"Grace, none of this is your fault. You couldn't marry that man under any circumstance. He wants only to cause pain and suffering. What do you suppose he had planned by marrying you?" Karen questioned. "You are nothing more than an extension of his revenge."

"It doesn't matter. If I'd remained in Chicago and married him last summer, my father might still be alive." She looked up to see her dear friends gathered around the table—watching her as if they were servants awaiting instruction.

"You've all been so good to help me, but the time has come for me to face facts. I have no choice."

"That's not true," Peter said. "You have many choices."

"You don't understand. He'll destroy you too," Grace replied, her once brave tone dissolving into complete resignation. "You heard what he said. He has some sort of agreement with your father. If you interfere, he'll destroy you and your family. I can't live with that on my shoulders."

"I don't care what Paxton threatens. I only care that you are safe. It won't be your responsibility—it will be mine."

Grace looked deep into Peter's eyes. How she loved this man. God help her, but she loved him more with every word that came from his mouth.

"So what are we to do?" Karen questioned.

"I have a plan," Peter replied, "but it will require all of you helping. With Paxton's bodyguards standing by to deliver

Grace to Paxton for the wedding, we're going to have to act fast."

"No! I won't let you do this. You'll only be hurt!" Grace declared, getting to her feet. "I have no choice. I will marry Mr. Paxton."

"No," Peter said, coming to stand beside her. "You can't marry Paxton if you're already married to me."

"What a perfect solution," Doris said innocently before anyone could comment. "You two have been sweet on each other since our first meeting. This would solve the matter once and for all."

Grace kept her gaze fixed on Peter, her voice low and intent. "You can't do that. Paxton will destroy your family. I won't be responsible for that."

"That's exactly what I told you," Peter said, taking hold of her hand. "You won't be responsible. I can handle the likes of Paxton. You leave him to me. The real problem is going to be getting you out of here. Paxton is waiting for a bride."

Doris chuckled. "Too bad we don't have my young actress friends."

Karen smiled and then laughed. "But perhaps we have someone just as helpful."

She pulled Leah with her and positioned the girl alongside Grace. "With a heavy veil, Leah could easily pass for Grace."

"It's true," Doris replied, nodding. "They are very nearly the same height. We have that heavy lace tablecloth I brought with us from Chicago. I could fashion it into a veil for Leah to wear. No one would be the wiser."

"Unless they insist on checking her out," Peter replied. "Of course, if we delay things until the last minute, perhaps they would be less likely to worry about it. They'd see a bride and figure Grace to be cooperating."

"But that still doesn't explain how we can get you and Grace to a preacher and then safely out of Paxton's hands," Karen said, looking to Peter for an answer.

Grace felt helpless to comment. They seemed to have taken the matter entirely out of her hands. A million thoughts danced in her head. Peter was offering to marry her. He had proposed to make her his bride and to take her away from Paxton, even if it caused his own ventures to be threatened. Surely he loved her!

But what of their differing views on God? She didn't wish to go against the Bible, what she knew God intended for her. Yet what else could she do? Surely God understood her dilemma.

"We could disguise Grace," Peter finally said. "If we're disguising Leah, why not disguise Grace as well?"

"But if we make Grace over to be Leah, the men will see her and easily recognize that we've switched them around."

"True," Peter agreed. "However, if we dress Grace as Jacob, smear a bit of dirt on her face and tuck her hair up under a cap such as Jacob has taken to wearing, they just might not give it much consideration. I could make like Jacob was joining me on the ship for our departure. Once they figure out what has happened, I'll already be steaming toward Seattle."

"What a splendid idea!" Karen declared. "I believe it will work. Now what of arranging your marriage?" She paced a bit. "I just wish my father were here. He could marry you in a minute."

Doris smiled. "I'll go run for the pastor. I'll tell those ninnies outside that Grace is in need of godly counsel. We can bring Pastor Clark here, have him marry Grace and Peter, then leave with us as the wedding party heads to Skagway. With so many people to keep track of, Paxton's hoodlums are certain to be confused."

"Of course!" Karen exclaimed excitedly. "Their focus will be on our poor, veiled Leah." She turned to the child. "Do you suppose you could do this?"

Leah laughed. "I think it sounds like great fun! An adventure!"

Karen nodded. "Do you suppose you could cry or at least sound like you were crying? Nothing is more certain to irritate a man than a woman's tears. If you were wailing and crying, they might hold themselves at a distance, leaving me to tend to you."

Leah instantly began to sob and wail as though her heart were breaking.

"That's very good," Doris said, nodding enthusiastically. "You are a natural actress."

Leah halted her sobs and smiled. "I'm glad to help Grace. I'm just sorry she has to go away."

"I'll bring her back when it's safe," Peter stated. "She can visit you from time to time when I make trips to deliver goods."

Grace couldn't believe what she was hearing. They were planning out her wedding, and Peter talked like they were already well on their way to a life of normalcy and pleasure. Was this an indication of God's blessing?

"All we need is five days," Grace reminded the group. She wanted very much to know that Peter was marrying her because he loved her and not because of a misplaced sense of duty. "You really don't need to give up your life, Captain." She walked away, and Peter looked to each of them. "I appreciate what you're planning on my behalf, but I can't put your lives in danger."

"Would you all give me a moment alone with Grace?" Peter asked.

Everyone nodded and Doris even decided that she would go for the preacher, just in case the plans came together. One by one, they filed into the store while Peter closed the door behind them.

"Grace, I want you to listen to me. This is a reasonable way to take care of the matter. Your friends want to keep you safe—so do I."

Grace looked to the floor, suddenly unable to meet his gaze. "I won't be safe until Paxton is either satisfied or dead."

"Would you rather I kill the man instead of marry you?"

Her head snapped up in alarm. "I should say not! I don't desire that you suffer yourself in any manner. I cannot abide that you would sacrifice either way on my account."

He came forward and took her hands in his own. The warmth of his touch reminded her of the night before.

"Grace, marriage to you would not be a sacrifice. Surely you know how I feel."

"We hardly know each other and you've not cared at all for my opinions on your family and of God and spiritual matters."

"Grace, please listen to me. I love you."

Her heart raced and her breath caught in the back of her throat. He loved her! Oh, how she cherished the words. The nagging thought of his lack of love for God was quickly pushed aside. Surely once they were married, he would see how important God was to her and give his life over as well.

"I thought you were just doing this—"

He pulled her into his arms. "I love you and I want you to marry me, Grace."

He lowered his face to hers but didn't kiss her. The inches

between them were maddening to Grace. She longed for the feel of his lips against her own. She felt her arms involuntarily embrace him, pulling him closer and closer.

"Oh, I love you, Peter." Her voice came in a breathless whisper.

"Then don't be afraid. You are always saying that we must trust God. Why not trust Him now?"

His words brought a wave of reassurance. Grace nodded. "I do trust Him."

Peter smiled. "Then trust me as well."

Karen opened the door of the store to find the two burly henchmen waiting patiently outside.

"You ready to leave?" one man questioned.

"No, in fact, I was looking for my aunt. She went to bring our pastor. Grace is very close to him, and we thought perhaps he could offer her some comfort and prayer."

The man scoffed. "Praying won't help now."

Karen smiled sweetly. "I think otherwise."

Just then Doris and the preacher rounded the corner. The man had a look of sheer terror on his face. Karen felt sorry for him. He was very young and new to the ministry and no doubt this matter did not bode well with his sense of heavenly peace and order.

"Pastor Clark, we're so glad you could come," Karen said, extending her hand. "Grace will find great comfort in your presence."

The man nodded. "I will do what I can." His Adam's apple bounced up and down as he replied. Karen would have laughed at the funny, frightened man had she not had her own fears to contend with.

"You'll find Grace preparing for her wedding," Karen said, looking to the two ruffians at her side. "We're to head over to Skagway as soon as she's prepared."

"Yeah, hurry it up, preacher," the man at Karen's left said with a low, growling tone. He reminded Karen of a bulldog, complete with lower teeth that seemed to protrude just a bit up and over the top set.

Leaving the guard behind, Karen was about to follow the preacher and her aunt inside when she heard her name being called.

"Miss Pierce!"

She looked down the street to find Adrik Ivankov bounding toward her. She smiled, but the look on his face did not suggest the action well-served.

"Sorry to bother you like this," he said.

"Is something wrong?" she asked. "Have you seen my father?"

Adrik stopped long enough to take inventory of the men standing outside Colton Trading Post. "These guys giving you trouble?"

Karen smiled. "No, they're just annoyed that the store is closed for business. Why don't you step inside, Mr. Ivankov . . . I mean, Adrik."

He looked at the men for a moment. "Why don't you fellas head over to Healy and Wilson's. They're open."

"Just mind your own business, stranger."

Adrik squared his shoulders and narrowed his eyes. He was about to say something, when Karen took hold of his arm and pulled him forward. "Come, Adrik. I want to hear the news."

They stepped onto the creaky wooden floor of the store, and Karen quickly closed the door behind them. Leaning against the frame as if to keep the two men from entering, she turned to Adrik. "So what of my father? Have you news?"

Adrik looked around the empty store as if to check for anyone else. "I'm sorry, but the news isn't good."

Karen put her hand to her mouth. She didn't even realize she was holding her breath until her ribs began to ache from the tension. Adrik seemed willing to wait for her prompting, but Karen didn't know if she could ask the question that so desperately needed asking.

Letting out her breath, she looked at the floor and tried to gather her courage. "Is he . . . dead?"

"I don't know. A man brought me word that he was gravely ill. There's been a round of measles and dysentery and many in the village have died. I'm guessing that your father has fallen ill with one or the other. He may already be gone, but I felt it important to return from the Scales and let you know."

Karen didn't know what to say. It was possible that her father might still be alive, but the situation didn't look at all promising. "What should I do?" She looked to Adrik, realizing she'd vocalized the question.

Adrik's rugged features softened, his square jaw seeming to relax as he spoke. "You can't do much. You can't get to him, and most likely he'd be gone by now if he's going to die."

"But he's alone," she said, biting her lower lip to keep from crying.

"No, he's not alone. You know better than that," Adrik said, his voice low and husky. "I've never seen a man or woman who was closer to God than your pa. One thing's for certain, he ain't alone."

Karen nodded. "I know you're right. Oh, this is so hard.

To have come all this way. Others came for gold and I came for him."

"Treasures come in all forms," Adrik replied.

She looked up to meet his sympathetic gaze. He seemed so concerned for her well-being. He looked at her as if he were preparing to jump into action. Almost as if he expected her to fall to pieces any minute, only to be responsible for putting her back together.

"Please don't say anything to my friends. We're in the middle of a rather delicate situation, and I wouldn't want them to fret over me."

"Does this have something to do with the men outside?"

She nodded. "But honestly, it's under control and you don't need to worry. Will you be around town until evening?"

"What'd you have in mind?"

There was no hint of teasing in his tone and for this Karen was grateful. "I'd like to discuss this further, perhaps even decide what I should do. I'd like your advice, but I can't discuss it now."

"Then I'll come back. Say, around eight?"

"That'd be fine."

Adrik nodded. "I'll return then."

Karen waited until he'd gone to make her way back to the others. She wouldn't say a word, not even to Doris. After all, if her father was dead, there wasn't anything anyone else could do.

She opened the back door and gasped in surprise as she observed Peter and a rather boyish-looking Grace embrace and kiss. Leah, dressed in Grace's cream-colored day dress, wore a heavy veil that covered her from head to foot.

"We tried to wait the ceremony for you but figured we should get first things done first," Doris told her.

"I'm glad you went ahead. Congratulations, Captain and Mrs. Colton," she said, grinning. "I guess we're well on our way to seeing this thing through to completion."

Peter nodded. "I think we'd better give some serious thought to getting on our way. Those two thugs aren't going to wait patiently for much longer."

"You're right about that," Karen replied, forcing a smile. "They were just making a fuss about all the time we're taking."

"We're ready," Leah said from behind the veil. "Jacob's even hiding."

Karen looked around the room. "Where is he?"

"He's in my steamer trunk," Doris replied. "If those men come to search out the place and see if anyone else is here, they'll only find the silence as their companion."

Karen took up her coat. "Then we'd best get a move on. Leah, you might want to start your crying. Oh, and, Aunt Doris, please bring Grace's coat for Leah. It's bitterly cold outside." Doris nodded and helped Leah into the heavy coat, while Grace shrugged into a brand-new coat they'd taken from Peter's newest shipment.

"Are we ready?" Karen questioned, looking to the conspirators.

"We're ready," Peter said, helping Grace with a pack. He took up a heavier one for himself but didn't bother to put it on.

The entourage reminded Karen of a strange, out-of-place funeral procession. Walking with a slowness that denoted sorrow and loss, the group refused to be hurried by the angry guards.

"We'll be all night at this rate," the taller of the two men grumbled.

Peter waited until Pastor Clark took his leave from the

group to begin complaining about the entire matter. "Grace, I'm sorry about all this. I wish I could have helped you escape Paxton."

Karen took up the cause. "Oh, be quiet. If you weren't such a coward you would go with us and see her protected."

Leah wailed loudly and the two bodyguards exchanged a scowl of displeasure. "Does she have to carry on like that?" the bulldog man asked.

"She's hardly going into this willingly," Karen replied. "You men think you can push us around, make us do your bidding, and then you fail to understand when we dare to be less than pleased with the affair." The men muttered but said nothing more.

The party boarded an awaiting boat and set out on the short trip to Skagway. With every stroke of the oars, Karen prayed their ruse might work.

Leah continued to sob, only softer now, and from time to time Doris would lean over and gently pat the girl's arm for comfort. Other than this, the group remained silent.

Once they'd arrived, however, Peter no longer held his silence. Making a great show of his disgust, he made his move.

"I'm leaving," Peter announced. "I can't bear to watch this mockery of marriage. My condolences to the couple." He pulled the bulky pack onto his shoulders. "Jacob and I will write. And we'll come check in on you with the next load of goods."

"I'm sure you've done all the harm you can, Captain," Karen replied. "Why don't you just leave us be?"

"I'm going, Miss Pierce." He turned to Grace. "Come on, boy. Pick up your feet, no sense in us staying here any longer."

"That's right. Leave us to fend for ourselves in our darkest hour," Karen replied, trying to keep up the farce. She tried not to think about her father's health or Grace's trembling figure dressed in Jacob's clothing. She tried not to imagine the fears that were running rampant in Grace's mind because her own were so close to being unleashed it was sure to be her undoing.

Tears came to her eyes. Real tears of sorrow. She hated seeing Grace go but knew she had to let her. And she hated thinking of her father dying all alone in the frozen wilderness.

"He's not alone." Adrik's voice rang out in her memory.

He's not alone. I'm not alone, Karen thought. Glancing upward, she whispered a prayer. "Oh, God, please help us now. I know deception is a sinful thing, but this is for Grace's good." Leah alternated sobbing with a mournful, howling kind of cry. The noise was almost haunting—like something very primitive. Karen thought it would have been very easy to imitate the sound based on her own misery.

The bodyguards paid little attention as Peter and Grace hurried off toward the harbor.

"Get moving. We're already running late," the bulldog man ordered.

Leah clung to Karen's arm, crying for all she was worth as Karen gave the impression of attempting to urge her along. She had to give Peter enough time to get safely away with Grace. And somehow, she would have to keep Paxton from learning it was Leah under the veil until the last possible moment.

CHAPTER THIRTY

MARTIN PAXTON PACED the confines of his second-floor apartment. He'd not been available when Ephraim Colton and his family had departed for San Francisco aboard *Summer Song*, but he gave it little consideration. It was better that he now had the place to himself. With his wedding about to take place, he would appreciate the privacy afforded him in their absence.

Smiling to himself, he took time out to light a cigar. The tip burned bright as he drew a long breath. The plan had taken far more time and effort than he'd originally hoped, but nevertheless, his revenge was about to be made complete. Grace would be his to do with as he pleased, and then he would discard her. Of course, there was some disappointment in the fact that Frederick Hawkins wouldn't be alive to see it. How he hated that man. Hated him so completely that the power of that emotion had killed Hawkins as sure as a bullet. Paxton rather liked the idea that his merciless drive had taken the life of his enemy.

And just as his hatred had consumed Frederick Hawkins, Paxton's lust and greed would destroy Grace. Everything precious and important to Hawkins would be destroyed and utterly wasted. This was a day of celebration, Martin decided. He sucked on the cigar as he poured himself a shot of whiskey.

Holding the glass aloft, he pulled the cigar from his mouth. "To revenge both bitter and sweet!" He tossed back the drink and turned at the sound of people on the stairs. His day was about to be made complete.

Karen Pierce was the first to pass through the doorway. She stared at Paxton with an air of haughtiness that suggested she would somehow manage to win the day after all. Her eyes narrowed as they shared a wordless exchange.

Next came the veiled figure of Grace. She sobbed softly and moved slowly. Paxton smiled and leaned over to his desk to put out his cigar. "Ah, the happy bride."

Doris Pierce came behind Grace, and the two henchmen he'd hired followed wearing a sober look of disgust.

"Mr. Tavis," Paxton began, "the preacher is cooling his heels in the storeroom below." The man needed no further instruction. He turned heel and stomped back down the stairs to fetch the preacher.

"I'm sure it's a waste of time to ask you to reconsider this," Karen stated.

"You're right. It is a waste of my time." Paxton considered the attractive redhead and smiled. His private thoughts were loosed on images of an intimate nature, but he said nothing more. First he'd deal with Grace. Then he could worry about

Miss Pierce. After all, she'd helped Grace to escape to Alaska. She deserved to be punished.

The women heard the heavy steps of two men on the stairs and turned back toward the door. Paxton found the panic in their eyes a strong stimulant. He felt the blood course through his veins in anticipation. He felt empowered by their fear.

Mr. Tavis appeared first and then a pudgy man who looked to be in his late fifties. The man panted breathlessly as he bounded into the room with Bible in hand.

"I believe, Miss Hawkins, it would be appropriate for you to come to my side," Paxton stated firmly.

Karen gripped the arm of her friend and shook her head. "I cannot let this happen. To move forward with this wedding would be wrong. Grace doesn't love you. She'll never love you. Doesn't that mean anything to you?"

Paxton shook his head. "Not a thing."

"She hates you. She'll never make you happy."

"I'm unconcerned with such notions," Paxton replied coolly.

Karen turned to the preacher. "You're a man of God. You must help us here. This woman has no desire to marry this man. You must intercede on her behalf."

The man turned to Paxton, eyes widening in apparent concern.

Paxton held up his hand. "This marriage will take place. I have come thousands of miles, and I am not leaving without my bride. Whether Miss Hawkins loves me or is happy about this arrangement is of no concern to me. I have her father's legal permission to marry her. She has not yet reached her majority and therefore must heed her father's direction."

"You're a man without feeling, Mr. Paxton," Doris said, shaking her head in a disapproving manner. "Shame on you for forcing yourself upon this child."

Paxton grinned. "I'm certain she can come to enjoy our arrangement."

He crossed the room in a rather casual manner and took hold of Grace's arm. "We need to stop wasting the preacher's time," he said, pulling Grace forward.

Karen refused to let go. She followed them the few steps to the preacher and threw Paxton a murderous glance. She glanced over her shoulder as if contemplating their escape. The action made Paxton laugh.

"You'd never make it, so don't even think of causing such a scene."

The preacher quickly opened his Bible, clearly uncomfortable with the situation. "Dearly beloved," he began.

"We need no formalities here," Paxton interjected. "Just get on with it."

The preacher nodded. "Does anyone know a reason why these two can't be wed?"

"I do."

Paxton looked to Karen, not the least bit surprised that she'd made one last attempt to halt the ceremony.

"She doesn't want to marry him. That should be reason enough," she pleaded.

"We've already covered this," Paxton replied in a heavy tone of annoyance. "Let's get on with this."

"We haven't covered anything. You've dictated terms to us."

Paxton's patience had reached an end. "I am the girl's guardian. She is not yet twenty-one and therefore under my authority."

"You are correct in saying she's not yet twenty-one," Karen answered. "She's only twelve. What preacher in his right mind would marry a twelve-year-old to any man? Besides, you aren't her guardian. I am."

She's gone mad, Paxton thought. The matter has rendered her absolutely daft. Stepping away from Grace momentarily, Paxton went to Karen.

"You would do well to stop this nonsense. This wedding will take place with or without you. I'll have my men remove you, if necessary."

Karen stood her ground. "I'm quite serious," she told the pastor. "This girl is only twelve and Mr. Paxton doesn't even know her."

At this, Paxton had had enough. He yanked off the heavy veil and tossed it to the ground. "I know this woman very well," he declared. He looked to Grace, but instead of seeing his terrified fiancée, he found instead a child.

"Who are you?" he asked.

"I thought you knew her very well," Karen said smugly. The look on her face was one of pure satisfaction.

"Where is Miss Hawkins?"

"Miss Hawkins is now Mrs. Colton." Karen drew Leah close before pushing the child in the direction of Doris. With no one between them, she raised her chin defiantly. "Grace married Peter Colton a few hours ago. She is safely in his care at this time."

Paxton felt his satisfaction fade. He looked to his men. "Where is Colton?"

"He headed off for his ship," the bulldog man replied. "But he weren't in the company of no woman. He just had a young boy with him."

"Fools!" Paxton declared. "That was her!"

Karen laughed. "My, my, but you are a smart man. But not smart enough." She turned to leave. "Sorry, preacher, but there won't be a wedding today."

"You'll pay for this, Miss Pierce. I swear, you'll all pay. Colton included!"

"You don't worry me, Mr. Paxton," Karen said, putting her arm around her aunt. "With God on my side, there is nothing you can do to harm me."

"You've already seen what I'm capable of accomplishing," Paxton replied dryly. "If I were you, I'd question the loyalty of your God."

"No need," Karen said, smiling with joy. "I just witnessed it this day."

It felt good to leave Paxton in stunned anger. Karen nearly jumped down the steps two at a time. She supposed it wasn't a very positive Christian attitude to display, but in light of the events, she felt it a definite win of good over evil.

"Let's hurry and get back to the store and to Jacob," she said, encouraging her aunt and Leah. "Let's hire a wagon to drive us. It's too cold to walk." She shivered and pulled her scarf around her face. The wind was no doubt responsible for her trembling. Surely it wasn't her fear that Paxton might actually cause them harm.

I won't give in to such thoughts, she reasoned. *God is more than able to deliver us from the hands of someone like Martin Paxton. Of course, Frederick Hawkins had lost everything in the battle—even his life. Poor Grace. How hard to learn of her father's death in such a brutal manner.*

This gave Karen thoughts of her own father. Had he already died? Did he lay delirious in some makeshift bed? Was there a doctor nearby to help ease his suffering? Tears came to her eyes and quickly froze against her lashes. *I can't think such despairing things. I must have hope.*

They arranged passage with a man who managed to squeeze them in between crates of dried foods and canned milk. He had a commission to haul goods up to Sheep Camp, and Dyea was one of his stops along the way.

Karen offered the man money, but he waved her off. "It's too cold to be out here walkin', ma'am," he said, barely taking time to raise his head to speak. He quickly tucked his face back into the folds of his coat.

"Perhaps you would care to come inside our store to warm up once we reach Dyea," Karen suggested.

The man nodded and gave a muffled reply. "That'd be good, ma'am."

Karen felt the barter was satisfactory and settled back against one of the crates. She tried not to think of what the hours to come might mean for either her or Grace. She wanted only to focus on the direction in which she should go. She thought of Adrik Ivankov. If he wouldn't help her, she didn't know what she'd do.

After seeing that the driver had warmed up with nearly half a pot of coffee and several sandwiches, Karen bid the man farewell and checked the clock. It was nearly time for Adrik to come. She quickly made another pot of coffee and then decided to tell Doris the truth.

"Mr. Ivankov caught up with me just before we left the store earlier today," she began. "He had bad news, I'm afraid."

"Wilmont?" Doris asked. Her stern expression softened. "Is it Wilmont?"

"I'm afraid so," Karen replied. "He's not at all well. In fact, he may have already succumbed to an outbreak of measles and dysentery that has devastated the village."

"Oh dear. Oh my." She sat down hard on the nearest chair, and Karen began to fear for Doris's health as she clutched her hand to her heart. "I was afraid this might be the case. I've felt nothing but uneasiness for days."

"Perhaps God was helping you to prepare for the worst," Karen said, taking a chair opposite her aunt. She was grateful that Jacob and Leah were out collecting wood for the fire. "I suppose we have to face the fact that he might not make it. Mr. Ivankov said it was very bad."

Doris nodded and twisted her hands together. "This country has killed them both. I suppose it will kill me as well."

"No!" Karen exclaimed, reaching out to still her aunt's hands. "Don't even say such a thing. We must trust that God has a plan in all of this. No matter what, we mustn't lose hope."

"I know you're right, but my heart is heavy," Doris replied. "I think I'll take to my bed early. You don't mind, do you?"

Karen shook her head and thought how pale her aunt suddenly looked. She wasn't aging well in this harsh environment. Perhaps it was time to consider sending her back to Seattle.

"You have a rest. Mr. Ivankov should be here any minute and we shall decide what's to be done."

Doris got up from the table slowly. Squaring her shoulders, she drew a deep, ragged breath. "We can at least comfort ourselves in our deeds today. We saved Grace from a horrible fate."

Karen considered the reality of the situation for the first time. They'd married Grace off to Peter Colton without even allowing her much say in the matter. Karen began to feel hesitant, knowing that Peter didn't know God in a personal way. All the time Grace had spent under her care, Karen had tried to stress that an unequally yoked marriage could only spell heartache.

"I hope we did a good thing," she finally replied. "It seemed like the only option at the time."

Doris nodded. "I'm certain it was."

Karen then heard the deep baritone voice of Adrik Ivankov as well as Leah's laughter. Adrik must have spotted the children as they worked over the woodpile.

"You rest now, Aunt Doris. I must see to Mr. Ivankov." She turned to head over to the door, just as an empty-armed Leah waltzed through.

"Mr. Ivankov is carrying my wood," she volunteered as Karen looked to the motley crew.

Adrik smiled and nodded down at the wood. "Where do you want it?"

"We have a woodbox beside the stove. That would work just fine," Karen answered. "Would you like some coffee? I just put a fresh pot on to boil."

"Sounds good," Adrik said, hardly seeming inhibited by the mass of logs in his arms.

He deposited the wood, and Jacob, who'd just entered the room with an abbreviated version of Adrik's pile, grunted a greeting. "It's cold out there. I figured we'd better have extra."

Karen smiled at the boy. He was becoming more and more likeable. He still had his moments of rebellion, but now he seemed far freer to communicate when things were going wrong. She prayed that in time his heart would heal and the pain over his mother's death and father's desertion would subside.

"I need to speak with Mr. Ivankov in private," Karen told Jacob and Leah. "Would you mind going to your room for a time?"

Both kids grew wide-eyed. "You aren't leaving us, are you?" Leah questioned.

Karen heard the fear in the girl's voice. "Oh, Leah, I don't plan to. Something has happened, however. My father is very sick. Mr. Ivankov was given word of this by one of the Tlingit."

"I'm sorry, Karen," Leah said somberly. She came to stand by Karen and squeezed her hand.

"Come on, Leah," Jacob motioned. His eyes met Karen's for a brief moment, and in his expression Karen found a world of compassion. *He understands,* she thought. *He knows exactly how it feels to be separated from those you love.*

She waited until the children had closed the bedroom door before turning back to Adrik. Smiling rather timidly, Karen looked to the floor. "So now what do we do?"

CHAPTER THIRTY-ONE

"HOW WE DECIDE to help your father depends mainly on what you want to do," Adrik stated.

"Well, take off your coat and hat, have some coffee, and we'll go from there," Karen replied, picking up a heavy white mug. "I find that I can think best when all the other amenities are taken care of."

Adrik took off his heavy coat to reveal a well-worn flannel shirt. Red flannel underwear peeked out from the top of the outer shirt, which Adrik had carelessly left unbuttoned. He seemed to realize this, along with the haphazard way his shirt had come untucked in the front, and casually put himself in order before sitting down to the table.

Karen smiled as she poured the coffee. She liked this big man. Maybe because he was a good friend of her father's. Maybe it was just because of his open personality. He made no pretenses, yet didn't mind seeing to proprieties.

"I would very much like to see my father," Karen said, handing Adrik the coffee. "I don't know if that's possible, but I would like it nevertheless." She took the seat opposite him and folded her hands. Looking into his dark brown eyes, she questioned, "Is it possible?"

Adrik tasted the coffee, then nodded. "Anything is possible. With God, all things are possible. The question here should be, is it more beneficial than harmful. The answer to that is no."

"Why do you say that?"

Adrik scratched his dark beard and shrugged. "Because it's dangerous, even deadly. The passes are snowpacked, the storms descend on the interior without warning, and the temperature is steadily dropping well below zero. You aren't accustomed to such things—not that you couldn't get accustomed," he added quickly. "It's just not the wise thing to go trudging off just now."

"The miners are doing it. Folks are still heading north over the pass," Karen protested.

"Yes, but they're holding up when they reach the lakes. Oh, some are still working to get north. Some are trying to pack out across the frozen lakes, but many of those folks are going to die. This gold has done nothing but corrupt men's thinking. Women's too. And in the process of turning their own lives upside down, they're workin' pretty steadily to destroy everybody else's."

"I'm sure it's hard on the tribes in the area."

"You don't know the half of it. The Tlingit owned the trails up north until the white man came along. For a while they even charged those passin' over their trails. They'd charge for the trail, charge to guide them, charge to sell them goods.

They made a steady income from the whites. Better still, they made a steady income from the Sticks—the Yukon First Nations people who live in the interior. The Tlingits kept the First Nations people from coming down to the coast to trade. They insisted on being their sole source of goods. Even earlier in this century, when the Russians came with all kinds of goods to trade for furs, the Tlingits ran the show."

"But not now?"

Adrik shook his head. "They're inundated with gold rush maniacs. They're sufferin', that's to be sure."

Karen felt almost intrusive for having come to Dyea. She wanted to understand the people her father so loved, but even more, she longed to know whether God would have her stay in this land and help her father with his ministry. She had never considered that he might die before God gave her a clear sign. A horrible thought crept in. What if her father's death was her sign?

Adrik seemed to understand her mood. "Look, I didn't mean to get you sidetracked. The truth is, I couldn't look your pa in the eye if I was the one who ended up riskin' your life. But I can make you a deal."

Karen couldn't imagine what he might have to suggest. "What?"

"I'll go myself. If he's dead, I'll see to it that he's properly tended to and I'll bring his things back to you."

Karen sat quietly for a moment, then realized it was probably all she could ask for. She wanted to offer Adrik some kind of compensation for his suggestion, but she didn't want to insult the man. Honesty seemed the best choice she could make. "Mr. . . . Adrik, I don't want to insult you by making the wrong suggestion, but I would like to see you properly compensated for such a thing."

He grinned. "Well, truth be told, I would be making the trip anyway. At least I was planning on heading up near to where your pa was last situated. I don't mind making the extra leg of the journey." He sobered. "Your pa was good to me when he came up here. Good to my folks and people."

"You were already living here?"

"To be sure. Well, actually we were up and down the coast. My grandfather was Russian. He married a Tlingit woman. They met in the years after the wars between the Tlingits and Russians. They lived in Sitka and that was where my father, and later I, was born."

The man's dark hair and tanned skin revealed his heritage. Karen wondered why she hadn't thought of this possibility before now. "So you're part Tlingit," Karen said, nodding. "No wonder you care so much about their plight."

"I'm not the only one. Your father felt a calling to save their souls, but he was far less intruding than other missionaries in the area. Some came in whoopin' and hollerin', using the Bible like the natives should already know what it was all about. Others came in more conservatively but still sought to change the people. They were excited to show the Indian a new way of doin' things. Excited to show them modern conveniences, new foods, new ways of carin' for themselves. They put the Tlingit children in schools and forced them to give up their native tongue, made them dress like Americans, and cut their hair. This was just as bad. The Tlingit are very proud people."

Karen nodded, for she had dealt with some of the women from the Dyea village. She knew them to be proud, almost arrogant in their trading. Yet they were also very efficient and trustworthy.

"It must be hard on them, having the land so overrun with outsiders."

"Indeed it is," Adrik replied. "But we can't very well stop the flow. We can't even slow it down until the gold itself plays out."

Karen sighed. "Sometimes I wish that I'd never come." Her voice sounded distant—almost distracted. She felt her guard slipping away. She trembled at the thought of revealing her heart to this big bear of a man. Catching him watching her with great interest, Karen smiled. "Well, wishing it doesn't make it so, as my mother used to say."

Adrik laughed. "I can remember her saying those very words."

"You knew her?"

"Don't sound so surprised. I've known your folks since they came up this way."

Karen shook her head. "I had no idea. How wonderful! Maybe you could tell me where she's buried. I had wanted to see her grave but didn't know if anyone would know its whereabouts."

"It's right here in Dyea," Adrik said. He drank down the coffee and got to his feet. "Put on your warm things. Bundle up good. I'll take you to her grave."

Karen didn't say another word. She hurried to take up her coat and hat, then quickly checked in on the children.

"Mr. Ivankov is going to show me where my mother is buried," she told Jacob and Leah. "I'll be back soon." The kids gave her somber nods.

Adrik took up a lighted lantern and motioned toward the door. Karen drew a deep breath and followed. She tied her bonnet snugly, then fished her heavy wool mittens from the pocket of her coat. She felt silly, almost childish, at the feeling of hesitation that crept over her. Seeing the grave would make her mother's death a very visual reality. Could she handle the pain? What if she broke down and cried? Would she offend Adrik?

They didn't have far to walk. The cemetery was positioned on the northwest edge of town. Karen had known of its whereabouts, but she'd never thought to check it out. *Funny,* she thought. *It was right here all along.*

The sounds of the waterfront and gambling houses faded as they hurried in the crisp winter air. The town had probably tripled in size just since Karen's arrival, but the bitterness of the cold made everyone take to indoor activities. She suddenly felt very swallowed up by the looming mountain ranges and the passing shadows. Shivering, she tried to keep her mind on the big man at her side. He would never allow for anything bad to happen to her. She felt safe in his presence.

That's the way I'm to feel at all times with God, she thought. How silly I am to doubt God's company and care, when this man whom I hardly know has my utmost faith simply for being a friend to my father.

"Here we are," Adrik said, holding the lantern aloft.

Karen braced herself and followed the muted light to a single headstone. The simple white wooden marker bore only her mother's name and the year of her birth and death.

Kneeling down, Karen touched the marker, then looked up to Adrik. "Were you with her when she died?"

He squatted down and shook his head. "No, but I wasn't far away. Word came to me that she was sick. I was on my way to see if I could be of any help when she passed on."

"And my father?" Karen questioned. "How did he . . . manage?"

"He took it better than most men might have. He knew

she was out of her suffering. The pneumonia had left her in great pain and unable to breathe without fierce spells of coughing. She was just plain worn out, he told me. We prayed together and then arranged to bury her here."

Karen nodded and fought back tears. She could allow herself a good cry later. In fact, she could mourn her mother's passing and Grace's departure all in one very long fit. The idea made her smile.

"I see that," Adrik said with amusement in his tone.

Karen got to her feet, almost embarrassed. "My mother wouldn't want me to be sad."

"No, indeed," he said, getting to his feet. "Come on. We'd better get back. Now that you know it's here, you can come see the grave in the daytime."

They walked side by side for several feet before Karen paused. She could see the stars overhead and the moonlight reflecting off the snow-covered mountainside. People were driving themselves to madness to cross those mountains. They were looking to the mountains for their salvation.

"I will lift up mine eyes unto the hills, from whence cometh my help." The psalmist seemed to have written her heart's cry in this passage. *"My help cometh from the Lord, which made heaven and earth."*

Gold wouldn't comfort her in the loss of her loved ones, but God would. She felt her spirit take rest and smiled. Looking up at Adrik, she nodded. "It is well with my soul. Should my father have joined my mother, I will yet praise God."

He smiled. "You've found a treasure that many never find. Your pa would be proud."

Grace found herself nearly as restless in Peter's cabin as she had been that first night aboard *Merry Maid* so many months ago. She was married! The very thought was only now beginning to sink in. Now, after washing up and clothing herself in her own feminine gown, now after realizing that this was to be her wedding night, Grace wondered if she'd done the right thing.

Everyone had said it was her only way out. No one seemed at all concerned that she was running away yet again. No one—not even Karen—had made mention that Peter had no interest in the same spiritual matters that were most vital to Grace.

Grace herself quickly cast those doubts aside. At least she tried to. God could work miracles. She had to trust that He would bring Peter to an understanding of the Gospel message—that His love would be revealed, drawing Peter to Him.

Grace clung to this hope. It had to be true; otherwise God would surely have given her another way out of the situation. Peter was there, convenient to her need and to the matter at hand. It had to have been orchestrated by God.

Wasn't it?

No matter her determination to see this as a positive thing, Grace couldn't help but be nagged by those haunting little doubts. Peter was unsaved. Not only that, he held an almost irreverent opinion of God. Peter was also domineering when it came to dealing with his own family. Would he be any less with Grace?

"We hardly know each other," Grace whispered. She nervously picked up her hairbrush and began working with a fury to comb through her long brown hair. "What have I done?"

Her trembling made it difficult to handle the brush. The future before her felt overwhelming. Were it just the thoughts of her wedding night and what was to be expected of her there, she might have called it "marital jitters." But this was so much more.

Martin Paxton would be livid when he learned of her deception. If Karen told him of the marriage, then Peter's own family and their business would be at risk as well. If Paxton learned of her whereabouts, he just might come searching after her—he might not even mind that she and Peter were legally married.

Her heart ached for the counsel of her dear friend, or even her mother. *Oh, Mother, I wish we would have been closer. I wish you would have understood my need for you sooner. How you must grieve without Father.*

Tears sprung unbidden to her eyes, and it was in this state that Peter came to the room. He saw her face and the tears and seemed at once to worry that he was somehow to blame.

"Did I do something wrong? Are you upset with me?"

Grace shook her head and put the hairbrush aside. "I'm sorry. I suppose I'm just a bit overcome with all of this. I couldn't help but think of my mother and father. Oh, Captain . . ." She looked down to the floor. "Peter," she corrected herself. "I can't help but worry about what Mr. Paxton is going to do when he learns of this."

"He's no doubt become completely aware. He has no power to hurt you anymore."

"That's not true," Grace replied. "And you know it."

Peter came to her and gently touched her wet cheeks. "I can take care of us, Grace. Have some faith in me. I know what I'm doing."

Her conscience was pricked again. "What if we've done the wrong thing?" She started to mention the issue of faith, but Peter interjected before she could explain.

"We love each other and this can only be the right thing.

Two people who care about each other as much as we do should be together. You needn't worry about Martin Paxton. I won't let him bring harm to you."

"And if he destroys your business? What then?"

"He won't. He and father are too close. He only spoke out of anger. You'll see. By your own admission you scarcely knew the man."

"Yes, but in the short time I knew him, just look what he accomplished."

Peter shook his head and pulled Grace tenderly into his arms. "There's only room here for you and me. Mr. Paxton will have to wait."

Grace gave in to the passion of his kiss. When he lifted her in his arms and carried her to his berth, she put aside her concerns and instead lost herself in the magic of their first night as man and wife. Surely God would make everything right.

Shortly before the dawn, Grace awoke to find Peter gone. Her body chilled at the absence of his warmth, she wrapped a heavy wool blanket around her flannel nightgown and snuggled against Peter's pillow. The scent of her husband warmed her more than the blanket. She was married. Truly married. The thought both delighted and terrified her.

Sometime in the night, as they'd lain together, whispering and dreaming of the future, Peter had promised her a wedding band.

"I feel bad that you had to supply your own wedding ring," he'd commented. During the ceremony, Grace had slipped off a ring she'd been given for her sixteenth birthday and handed it to Peter. He'd lovingly put the ring on her left hand but later

confessed to hating the fact that he'd nothing of his own to share with her.

As she'd faded into sleep, he'd told her to dream of him and the ring that he'd buy her. He promised her the most elaborate ring her heart might desire. But even now, wide awake with the memory, Grace knew her only dream was for a small gold band. A simple, understated pledge.

The idea of gold made her smile. They had traded in furs and gold at the Colton Trading Post. There had been enough gold passing back and forth across their counter that Grace could have had an unending number of rings made. *So many dreams of gold,* she thought. *So many hopes pinned on a yellow substance that could neither think nor feel.*

Oh, God, she prayed, pulling the covers ever tighter, *keep my eyes on you. Let me only desire you. Let me serve you faithfully, no matter the price. And let Peter know you.*

She thought of her husband and hugged his pillow tight. "I love him so much, Lord. The wonder of his love is more than I ever expected." She remembered his loving touch . . . the way he drew his hands through her hair . . . his lips on hers.

With these thoughts, sleep was impossible. Grace rose and quickly dressed and made her way to the deck in hopes of finding Peter. *I just need to see him,* she thought. *I just need to make certain this isn't a dream.*

The wind whipped mercilessly at her heavy wool skirts, but the glow of light just now touching the outline of the mountains drew Grace's attention. The sky suddenly seemed to glow, and gradually the heavy blue-black of night was pulsating with a magenta and lavender. Grace stood transfixed at the deck rail. The sun rose in a promise of hope for the new day. The light offered a blessing in colors too wonderful for human hands to have painted.

Looking skyward, Grace thought of the psalms. " 'Unto thee lift I up mine eyes, O thou that dwellest in the heavens.' "

"Have you taken to talking to yourself, Grace?"

She turned sharply to find Peter watching her curiously. "I was just inspired by the beauty of this sunrise."

He smiled and moved to stand beside her. Opening his arms to her, he wrapped her snug against his woolen coat. "I was feeling the same, only my inspiration comes from you. You're quite lovely, Mrs. Colton."

Grace would not allow him to make her the focus of the morning. "God did a wondrous thing out there. The colors and the mountains—the skies and the way the night is turning to day. I couldn't help but praise Him for what He has done. I praise God even more that I can appreciate such divine architecture."

Peter didn't seem inclined to contradict her feelings, and Grace took that as a positive sign that things would fall into place as they were meant to be. She turned in his arms and leaned back against his chest. She didn't want to miss seeing a single thing. It was as if she had been given new sight.

Slowly the ship sliced through the icy cold waters of the passage. *Merry Maid* was taking them south to freedom and a new home in a land Grace had never seen. Her heart held great hope for what could be, and God held her heart. It was enough, Grace thought and smiled in the strength of this love. It was enough.

Escape with Janette Oke and T. Davis Bunn's

SONG OF ACADIA

With more than 20 million books sold between them, Janette Oke and T. Davis Bunn are two of the most beloved writers of Christian fiction. SONG OF ACADIA is their first historical series written together and represents a powerful combination of their storytelling strengths.

A Chance Encounter Will Forever Change Their Lives

At the beginning of *The Meeting Place*, two young women, their lives shadowed by nations in conflict, begin a friendship that will propel them on a journey from which they can never turn back....

Worlds Apart

The year was 1753, and the lines of separation were firmly drawn. The French had named the region Acadia, their "beloved home." When the British came soon after, they battled with the French on the new continent as they had in Europe for centuries.

The settlers of Acadia were either French or English, and though their villages might be but a stone's throw apart, most could go an entire lifetime without speaking to someone from the other side.

And then came the chance encounter of Catherine Price and Louise Belleveau in a meadow of wild flowers.... From this unexpected friendship, Oke and Bunn spin a tale of devotion, loss, renewal, and bonds stronger than blood and faith stronger than tragedy.

BETHANY HOUSE